TUCKER'S INN

Janet Tanner

severn
House

This first world edition published in Great Britain 2003 by
SEVERN HOUSE PUBLISHERS LTD of
9–15 High Street, Sutton, Surrey SM1 1DF.
This first world edition published in the USA 2004 by
SEVERN HOUSE PUBLISHERS INC of
595 Madison Avenue, New York, N.Y. 10022.

British Library Cataloguing in Publication Data

Tanner, Janet
    Tucker's Inn
    1.   Orphans - Fiction
    2.   Love stories
    I.   Title
    823.9'14 [F]

    ISBN 0-7278-6022-4

Typeset by Hewer Text Ltd.,
Edinburgh, Scotland.
Printed and bound in Great Britain by
MPG Books Ltd., Bodmin, Cornwall.

Paris – 1794

*T*he tumbril jolted over the cobbles, each creak of its wheels taking those packed shoulder-to-shoulder within it closer to their deaths. For the most part they stood proudly, striving not to shiver, though the biting wind cut cruelly through the thin lawn of their bloused shirtsleeves, their fierce determination not to give the baying crowds who lined the route the satisfaction of seeing the fear that churned within them a final act of defiance in their earthly lives. One woman wept, her arms wrapped around her body, which was clothed in the remnants of what had once been an extravagant court gown, but her sobs were drowned by the jeers of the jubilant mob and the funereal beat of the drums. They would die as they had lived, these high-born men and women, generations of breeding called upon now as the cart, pulled by a single black horse, bore them to the guillotine.

The man stood unobserved towards the back of the crowd. Like them, he wore peasant garb, and it suited his tall, broad frame as well as the silks and buckskin that were his more usual attire. His head was bare, he wore neither hat nor wig, and the wind teased dark curly strands from his pigtail and blew them about his face. Had any of the mob spoken to him, he could have replied to them fluently in their mother tongue, for he spoke French as well as he spoke his native English.

But no one spoke to him. They were too fired up with the spirit of revolution, too drunk on the evil tide of exhilaration that fed each day on the spectacle of aristocratic heads rolling and the gutters running with blood.

1

As the tumbril passed by, his features set solid as granite, his sharp eyes scanning the faces of the damned. God be praised, she was not among them. He might yet be in time to save her. But first he must discover her whereabouts. To do so would be as difficult and dangerous almost as spiriting her out from under the noses of the Revolutionaries.

He turned away, merging with the crowds. He was appalled by their bloodlust, for although he understood something of the years of repression that had spawned it, the Terror could not be excused. The innocent should not be condemned to die terrible deaths alongside the guilty, and he was proud and glad he had been able to help some of them escape to England.

But until he found those for whom he searched he could not take the slightest satisfaction in his achievements. They were at risk because of him and he would do whatever he had to in order to save them. Almost certainly that would mean saving the neck of a man he would gladly have seen go to the guillotine; it could well cost him his own life too. And he would give it, gladly, if that was what it took.

To live with the guilt of having done nothing was more than he could bear. It would be a life not worth the living.

One

T he sky was weeping and I wept with it.
I scarcely saw the incessant drops that showered down
between the bare branches of the churchyard trees; my mourning veil was thick, and in any case, my eyes were too full of
tears. I did not feel the chill wind that drove the rain in
shimmying gusts; I had been icy cold now for what seemed
like for ever, a cold that shivered constantly over my skin and
settled as a dull ache deep in my bones. I certainly did not notice
the heavy, leaden grey sky, for it was merely a mirror image of
the dark numbing fog that surrounded me and addled my brain
like the after effects of a dose of laudanum.

And yet, at the same time, I was heart-wrenchingly aware of
the newly dug grave that scarred the sodden green grass. It
gaped before me as my father's coffin was lowered into it, deep,
dark, menacing. Every creak of the straps that supported the
coffin was like the mewling cry of an infant, scraping on my raw
nerves.

'Ashes to ashes, dust to dust . . .'

The minister was speaking too fast, anxious, no doubt, to get
his duty over and done with. My father had never been a
regular worshipper at his church; burying him was a necessary
and rather tedious duty, and the sooner it was over and done
with, the sooner Reverend Collins would be able to get home to
his fireside and a glass of warming brandy.

But my father would not be going home. My dear, sweet
father, who had raised me alone since the death of my mother
when I was just five years old, would remain here, in the rain
and the cold and the dark.

3

A fresh flood of tears coursed down my cheeks, the only touch of warmth on that biting February day. And the question that tormented me echoed again in the black fog that filled my heart, my mind, my very soul.

Why?

Why should such a terrible fate have befallen my beloved father? I would still have wept, of course I would, if he had been old and sick. But death would at least have come as a kindness to him, and perhaps even as a sort of relief to me, tempering my grief, whispering to me that his suffering was at an end. But my father had not been old and sick. Though no longer a young man, he had still had his health and strength, still enjoyed life as he always had. Why, on the very evening that he had met with his terrible end, he had been working as usual in the bar of the coaching inn that had always been my home, and which I had helped him to run from the moment I was old enough to chop vegetables for a stew pan, launder fresh sheets for the beds, and carry a jug of ale to the dining tables for the refreshment of the weary travellers who were our guests. When I had retired to my bed he had still been there, yarning with a little group of passengers who had come in on the Bristol to Plymouth coach, and a couple of locals who had ridden over from the nearby village to enjoy an evening's conviviality.

'I'm very tired, Father,' I had said. 'The warming pans are in our visitors' beds, and yours too, so if there's nothing else . . .'

He had smiled at me, eyes twinkling above cheeks that, to be truthful, had become a little rouged over the years from making free with the good ale he sold, and bushy whiskers that had once been jet black, but were now speckled with grey.

'Be off with you, m'dear.' There was affection beneath the gruffness of his tone. And to his companions he added: 'She was up with the lark this morning, and will be again tomorrow. I work her hard, you know, so the likes of you can enjoy a bit of comfort.'

'And much appreciated she is, too,' one of the men said, with the sidelong glance I had grown accustomed to over the years, and learned to ignore.

'She's a good lass, our Flora,' my father said, winking at me. 'I couldn't manage without her, and that's for sure.'

Colour tinged my cheeks. 'Goodnight, Father.'

'Sleep well, Miss.'

I little knew it was the last time he would ever bid me goodnight.

I fell asleep, as I had known I would, the moment my head touched the pillow, for I was indeed very tired, and I had no presentiment of the horror the night would bring. But some time later I was awakened by the sound of hammering on the heavy inn door.

For a moment I lay staring wide-eyed into the darkness, thinking I must have been dreaming. Then it came again, loud and insistent, and I heard boards creak on the landing as my father passed my door on his way downstairs. Still I felt no real sense of alarm. This was, after all, a coaching inn, and our guests did not always arrive at sociable hours, especially in the dark days since the Terror had taken France in its grip. My father was sympathetic towards the beleaguered aristocracy, and sometimes those brave men who had spirited away fugitives from their horrible fate on the guillotine would bring them to our door to rest before they continued their flight to friends and relatives in Bristol, or London, or wherever. Invariably they arrived at unearthly hours, for the boats which brought them across the channel did so under cover of darkness, and by the time they had disembarked and made their way inland most God-fearing folk were sound asleep in their beds.

Who was behind the rescues I did not know, and I was not sure my father knew either. I had asked once, and he had merely shaken his head.

'Ask no questions, Flora, that's the best way. We give shelter for a few hours to poor souls who have lost everything – their homes, their possessions, their loved ones. That's all we need to know.'

'But who brings them, Father?' I had persisted. 'Could it be the Brotherhood of the Lynx, do you think?'

The Brotherhood of the Lynx was the name adopted by a

group of brave men whose sole purpose was to sneak into France and smuggle out aristocrats who would otherwise have met their end at the sharp blade of the guillotine, and their leader – whose identity was known to no one – was The Lynx himself. It was, to my mind, a most appropriate name, for they moved with all the speed, stealth and daring of a big cat, and I have to say that I was enthralled by the romance of it all, perhaps more than I should have been. The very idea that these celebrated, yet anonymous, heroes might have set foot in Tucker's Grave Inn excited me, the thought that I might have unwittingly spoken to one, thinking he was just another traveller, teased my imagination. Half England was consumed with curiosity as to their identity, in awe of their daring, and many a young woman's heart beat faster at the mere mention of The Lynx's name. Why should I be any different? I was twenty-three years old, with a head full of dreams and a life too full of mundane tasks to be able to spare time to make any of them a reality. Who could blame me for asking about the mysterious men who brought French fugitives to our door and disappeared again like shadows into the night?

But I could get nowhere. If he had the slightest inkling as to their identity, my father was not going to share it with me. And now he never would.

That fateful night, however, I did not think our visitors were fugitive French nobles, for when I slipped out of my bed and went to the window, curious as ever, there was no coach drawn up in the courtyard as there usually was when our elusive guests came, but when I opened the casement wide and leaned out I could see two horses tied up at the hitching rail, pawing restlessly.

The first twinge of alarm ran through my veins. Was something wrong? Had something terrible happened in the village? The frenzied knocking echoed in my head; I had to know.

I grabbed my wrap, which lay across the chair beside my bed, pulling it on, and thrust my feet into my slippers. My heart beating very fast from the suddenness of my awakening and from the chill of foreboding that was assailing me, I hurried along the landing.

The doors to the chambers where our guests were sleeping were all closed; if they too had been awakened by the thunderous knocking it seemed they had sensibly decided it was no business of theirs. As I reached the head of the stairs the moon must have emerged from behind the curtain of cloud, for suddenly they were illuminated dimly with flickering, fitful light. Glad of it, for I had not stopped to light a candle, I started down.

I could hear voices now, but before I could make out anything that was being said, a tread creaked loudly beneath my feet and the voices stopped abruptly. I hesitated, guilty suddenly as a child caught in the act of trying to listen to a conversation he is not meant to hear. Then I heard the rough, low growl of a voice I did not know, saying something I could not make out, and the door at the foot of the stairs opened, framing my nightshirt-clad father against flickering candlelight.

'Is that you, Flora?' He sounded angry; now I think it was anxiety for my safety that made his voice sharp.

'Father, what is happening?' I asked.

'Nothing to concern you, Miss. Go back to bed.'

'But Father . . .'

'Don't argue with me. Just do as I say. Go on now.'

I could not remember when my father had last spoken to me so. Every instinct was warning me something was very wrong. I was not in the habit of disobeying him, but I disobeyed him now.

'Not until I know what's happening,' I said defiantly. 'And please don't talk to me as if I were a child. I'm twenty-three years old.'

'But not too big to be put across my knee! And if you don't go back to your room this minute and shut the door behind you, that's exactly what I'll do. This is men's business, Flora. Do you understand?'

There was nothing more I could do. Desperate as I was to know who had come calling in the middle of the night and what they wanted, it seemed I would get no answer. And I had no hope of catching a glimpse of them either. My father's big, nightshirted frame was blocking the doorway and I guessed that even had it not been, the men who had hammered for his attention were keeping well out of my line of vision.

'Go on, off with you,' my father ordered.

They were the last words he would ever speak to me.

I turned and went back up the stairs like a whipped dog with its tail between its legs. I couldn't understand why my father should speak to me so, and my anxiety was sharper than ever; more than anxiety, I was frightened, without really knowing why.

I went back to my room as I had been told, but I did not shut the door. I wanted to hear when my father came back to bed. I slid under the covers still wearing my wrap, for I was shivering and the sheets had grown cold whilst I was out of them.

I lay wide-eyed, straining my ears though I knew I had no hope of hearing what was going on. But I might hear the slam of the great oak door, and the clatter of hooves on the cobbles when they left. Certainly I would hear the creak of the boards when my father came back upstairs.

What I heard was the sharp crack of a gunshot.

Instantly I was bolt upright, my whole body frozen by shock and a rush of white-hot terror. Time stood still, silence reigned, except for the echoes of that shot, seeming to reverberate from the floor and walls of my room, though I expect they were only in my head.

And then came the other sounds, the ones for which I had been waiting. The slam of the door, a single shout: 'Giddup!', the clatter of hooves.

I moved then, leaping out of bed and running to the window. Two horses were galloping out of the courtyard, their riders bent low across their necks.

'Father!' I cried.

This time I did not wait to put on my slippers; my bare feet and trembling legs sped me along the landing. This time, too, the door to one of the guest rooms opened a crack and the figure of a man, clad in nightshirt and cap, appeared, bleary, alarmed.

'What . . . ?'

I ignored him, running down the stairs. The door at the foot was closed; I turned the handle and threw it open. Then I stopped short, my hands flying to my mouth to stop my gasp of utter horror.

My father lay in the centre of the room. He had dragged over a chair with him as he fell; the back of it was across his chest, the legs pointing away from him. Blood spread scarlet across his nightshirt and pooled on the flagged floor.

'Father!' I sobbed again, and ran towards him, throwing the overturned chair aside and falling to my knees beside him.

My father's lips moved, but no word came, only a gurgling sound and a bubble of blood. His eyes were open, but I don't think he saw me. He seemed to be gazing past me, his expression more surprised than agonized. Then the breath rattled in his throat, his whole body jerked once, convulsively, and his eyes glazed.

'Oh Father, Father, what have they done to you?' I sobbed distractedly, but I knew already I would get no answer, now or ever again.

My dear, sweet, beloved father was dead.

I remember very little of what remained of that terrible night. It is mostly a nightmarish blur, with certain images standing out as contrastingly clear vignettes, moments caught in time, little beacons to light the trail of events.

The driver of the Bristol to Plymouth coach, who was overnighting with us, was very good to me, I know. He drew me gently away from my father's body, soothing my hysterical protests and leading me to the snug, where he urged me down on to the settle, found a cloak to wrap around my shivering frame, and put a glass of brandy between my trembling hands. Then he got dressed and set out to ride to the village for the constable, leaving me in the care of one of his passengers, the same one who had emerged from his room as I passed. He was, I remember, a flabby-faced merchant who was so clearly shocked by events he was in truth no use at all, and the rancid smell of the nervous sweat that poured from his body made my already churning stomach turn so violently I thought I was going to vomit.

I set down the brandy glass and pushed myself to my feet.

'I have to go to my father.'

'My dear – no!' His soft hands plucked at my arm.

I shook him off, turning my head away from that nauseating smell.

'I have to! He needs me!'

Even as I said it, I knew it was not true. My father would not need me ever again. But I needed him. And I could not bear to think of him lying there alone in the bar in a pool of his own blood.

I stumbled back along the passage, holding the cloak tight about me. My teeth were chattering, my breath coming in short sobbing gasps. The coach passenger, to my immense relief, did not come with me. The spectacle of my father sprawled on the floor was more than he could stand, I suppose, and who could blame him? It was not a pretty sight. Even I squeezed my eyes tight shut for a moment as I re-entered the bar, summoning up the courage to face what I felt I must.

I did not kneel beside him again; there was no point. Instead I made for a chair, skirting the pool of blood. It was then that I noticed my father's blunderbuss lying on the floor beneath the rack on which he kept it, and realized what must have happened.

There had been an argument of some kind, my father had gone to get his gun to threaten his visitors into leaving, and seeing what he intended, one of them had drawn his own gun and shot him. The blunderbuss had fallen useless from his hands and he had staggered back across the bar, mortally wounded.

Who were these men who had come in the dead of night, and what had brought them here? What had they quarrelled with my father about, and why had it come to this? I did not know, and could not speculate. I knew only that my beloved father was dead, and even that was too much, as yet, for my befuddled brain to take in.

My trembling legs refused to support me for another moment, I flopped heavily into the chair and remained there, my arms folded round myself, my gaze fixed on the body of my father. I was still there when the coachman returned with the constable and the doctor.

A doctor! As if there was anything *he* could do! The sight of him, carrying his medical bag, was enough to bring me to hysterical laughter. But perhaps the coachman had brought him, not for my father, but for me, for he attempted to persuade me to take a dose of laudanum and go to bed.

I refused. Nothing could take away my pain, only dull it for a little while, and I did not want to sleep. I somehow needed to be aware – as aware as I could be – of what was going on. To lose myself in a fog of drugs would, it seemed to me, be a final betrayal of my father. And I might somehow be able to help piece together the evidence that would pinpoint his killers and bring them to justice.

Nothing I could tell the constable was of any use, of course. I had not seen the men, nor even heard them clearly. Their horses had been – well, just two horses. I couldn't even be sure what colour they were, for in the fitful moonlight they had simply been dark shapes.

The constable was unable to find the smallest clue; the identity of my father's murderers seemed likely to remain an unsolved mystery.

And so, as I watched his coffin lowered into the ground, the question still haunted me.

Why?

As the first clods of earth thudded on to the oak lid, the tears ran once again unchecked down my cheeks and I reached out and dropped the small bunch of snowdrops I had gathered this morning to fall amongst them.

'Goodnight, Father,' I whispered, and, echoing the words he had spoken to me each night since I was a little girl: 'Sleep well.'

Then I turned, head bent against the driving wind and rain, and began to walk away from the grave.

* * *

A touch on my arm arrested me. I stopped and looked up to see the tall figure of a man beside me.

For a moment I could not think who he was. Certainly I had not noticed him at the grave side, but then, in my grief I had not looked at any of the mourners who had gathered to pay their last respects. Their faces were nothing but a blur to me.

I stared, puzzled, into the strong dark face beneath the black beaver hat, and the man smiled faintly.

'Louis Fletcher. I don't suppose you recognize me.'

Then, of course, I knew. Louis Fletcher, a second cousin of my father.

My first reaction was surprise that he had travelled the fifteen or more miles from their home for the funeral. We had never had much contact with the Fletchers – 'the rich relations', my father had laughingly called them, for that is what they were.

'They don't want to lower themselves associating with the likes of us,' he had used to say, good-naturedly enough – but then, that was my father all over, and I could not help but suspect there was some kind of feud, or difference, at least, between the two branches of the family, for it seemed strange they should live within such easy distance and yet see so little of one another.

Peter Fletcher, my father's cousin, was a well-to-do merchant, though what he dealt in I was never entirely sure – and as such was certainly much higher in the social scale than my father, a humble innkeeper. And since jealousy was not in my father's nature, I could only think that it was Peter who kept his distance from my father rather than the other way around. Certainly their way of life was very different to ours.

Once, when I was very small, and being taken to visit relatives of my mother's in Cockington, my father had stopped the carriage and pointed across the valley to a grand house set in its own grounds and overlooking the River Dart.

'See there, Flora? See that fine place? Who do you think lives there?'

I remember staring in awe at the balustrades and parapets; to me it looked like nothing so much as a fairy-tale palace.

12

'A princess!' I said.

My father smiled. 'Try again.'

I screwed up my small face, thinking hard. 'A prince?'

He laughed aloud this time. 'No, Miss, you're wrong there, though it's an easy mistake to make. No, it's your very own cousin twice removed.'

'My cousin!' I could scarcely believe it; he was teasing me, I thought. 'But I don't have a cousin!'

'Twice removed, like I said. He's my cousin, my mother's brother's son, and that makes him your cousin too. Now, what do you think of that?'

I didn't know what to think. I was overwhelmed, as well as still being confused.

'Are we going to visit him?' I asked at last.

'Oh no, we can't go calling on folk like that without an invitation,' my father said, jovially enough. 'You'll have to make do with the fisherman's cottage down Cockington, and your Granny Livesay, I'm afraid.'

'I don't mind,' I said loyally. I loved Granny Livesay and the dear little cottage with the doorway so low that Father had to bend his head and hunch his shoulders to go in, and the tiny garden at the rear full of hollyhocks and sweet briar roses and a blackberry bush that I could feast on when the fruit was ripe, as I hoped it would be today.

But as we drove away I cast a longing glance towards the great house on the hillside overlooking the River Dart just the same. It looked so impossibly romantic, and I couldn't help wishing that perhaps one day we *would* go to visit Father's cousin who lived in a house fit for a fairy-tale prince.

We never did. Once, some time later, a portly man in fashionable attire and wearing a tricorne hat and woolly hedgehog wig had called at the inn on his way to Devonport, he said, and I learned that this was Cousin Peter. He had with him two boys, his sons, Louis and Gavin, but they were much older than me, almost grown up really, and so they had no time for a little girl like me, and I was too shy to make any overtures of my own.

The younger boy, Gavin, did ask me if it was true that there were secret passages beneath the inn, running from the cellars to the crypt of the old ruined monastery down the road, and when I told him eagerly that there were, and that they had once been used by priests escaping from the soldiers who had come to sack the monastery, the two boys had become very excited and asked if they might explore them. Their father soon put a damper on that idea, however, saying he had no intention of turning up in Devonport with the pair of them looking like chimney sweeps, and after that I don't think either of them spoke more than a dozen words to me, though the family stayed long enough to take refreshment with us.

'Proper little gentlemen, aren't they?' my father remarked after they had left. 'I suppose that's what comes of being sent away to school.'

'Sent away to school?' I was puzzled. For me, school meant the gathering of pupils of all ages at the home of Dame Hibbert in the village, and not all the children I knew kept regular attendance there, even.

'Boarding school,' my father explained. 'It's where the gentry go to learn their lessons – and how to behave themselves in polite company,' he added darkly.

'Boarding school? You mean they have to stay there all night?' I asked, amazed.

'All night, and weekends too,' my father said.

'Oh!' I said. 'I shouldn't like that! Not to be able to come home . . . !'

'And you're not likely to have to,' my father said. 'Girls don't go to boarding school.'

'Then I am very glad I'm not a boy!' I said, feeling some sympathy for my distant cousins.

My father laughed. 'You wouldn't go to boarding school even if you were,' he told me. 'I couldn't afford the fees.'

'But Cousin Peter can?'

'Certainly he can! And he wants his sons to know all it will take for them to succeed him in his business, I expect,' my father said.

And that was that. I don't recall ever having met Cousin Peter, or Louis, or Gavin again, though when Cousin Peter died I did hear that the boys had indeed taken on the running of the family business.

Yet now here was Louis, attending my father's funeral.

I looked more closely at him, trying to see the young man who had once come to the inn with his brother, and begged to be allowed to explore the underground passages, but I could not. Hardly surprising, since it must have been at least fifteen years ago, and probably more. The smooth boyish face I remembered had developed the planes and angles of manhood, and a faint shadow of shaven beard darkened a strong jawline. Louis seemed taller than I remembered him, too, and perhaps he was, for boys often continue to put on the inches long after girls have ceased to grow, I believe, and though he was still quite slim, his shoulders were powerful and his chest broad beneath his heavy dark woollen redingote.

He had, I thought, all the stature of a man who had not only inherited wealth, but added to it by his own efforts, for there was nothing of the fop about him, rather he exuded a slightly disconcerting presence.

Somehow I gained control of myself and found the power of speech.

'It is very kind of you to have come,' I said. 'My father would have been touched.'

Louis inclined his head slightly. 'We were sorry indeed to hear he had met with such an untimely and violent end.'

The tears constricted my throat once more; I did not feel capable of continuing a conversation.

'Thank you again,' I murmured thickly, and made to turn away, but Louis' voice arrested me.

'Flora – we need to talk.'

I turned back, puzzled.

'Are you going direct back to the inn?' he asked.

'Yes, but . . . I'm not holding a wake,' I said. 'I'm afraid I couldn't face that.'

'All the better,' he said. 'We can have our discussion in private.'

And still I did not understand. All I could think was that I wanted to get home and be alone with my grief.

'You must forgive me if I seem inhospitable,' I said, 'but I have just lost my father in the most distressing circumstances and I don't feel up to entertaining.'

The dark eyes narrowed beneath the brim of the beaver hat.

'Flora, this is not a social call. Surely you must realize that?'

His tone was hard, his expression serious. The first glimmer of comprehension pierced my bewilderment – and with it a feeling of panic. I stared at him, wanting desperately to turn and run, anything to avoid hearing what I knew in a blinding flash he was going to say.

'Surely you know, Flora, that I am your father's closest male relative, and as such the beneficiary of his estate? Tucker's Grave Inn belongs to me now. I thought you would be aware of that.'

Two

For a moment I thought I would faint. The blood drummed in my ears so loudly it drowned out the patter of the rain and the roar of the wind; the mist thickened before my eyes and the world seemed to be going away from me.

If I had thought about it, of course, I did know. I was a woman, and under the cruel laws of the land, women could not inherit. But I had not thought. My mind had been too numbed, I had lived through these last days in a daze of shock and grief, barely able to think about the immediate tasks that had to be carried out, certainly giving no thought whatever to the future.

This new blow stunned me. I reeled beneath it.

Louis must have noticed me sway, for his hand went beneath my elbow, steadying me.

George Doughty, the blacksmith from the village, must have noticed too. George and his wife Alice had been very kind to me during these last dreadful days, and they had brought me to the funeral in their trap. Whilst I had been talking to Louis they had maintained a respectful distance, presumably not wishing to intrude; now they were at my side, fussing anxiously.

'Flora, it's time we got you home,' George said to me. And to Louis: 'This has been a terrible ordeal for her, more than flesh and blood can stand. If you'll excuse us . . .'

Louis made no move to relinquish his hold on my arm.

'I am family,' he said in a tone that made Alice take a step backward. 'I am sure you mean well, but I will see Flora safely back to the inn.'

George was made of sterner stuff. 'And we are friends. It's

17

folk who love her the maid needs at a time like this.' His ruddy face was indignant on my behalf.

I felt a rush of gratitude towards him. But I knew there was nothing he could do to help me. Little as I wanted this interview, now or ever, it could not be avoided. Better to get it over with and learn the worst. At least then I would know exactly where I stood.

'It is quite all right, George,' I said, straightening myself and trying to shrug off the unwelcome grip of Louis' hand on my elbow. 'This gentleman is indeed my father's cousin, and we have some business to attend to.'

Perhaps George understood the import of what I had said, for he looked very sad suddenly. 'Well, if you are sure, m'dear . . .'

I nodded, my head jerking like a stringed marionette.

'I am sure. And thank you for all your kindness.'

'You know where we are if you need us, Flora. Any time of the day or night, remember.' He glowered at Louis, seemingly unimpressed by the fact that Louis was a gentleman whilst he was only a humble blacksmith. 'Don't you go upsetting her, mind, or you'll have me to answer to.'

Louis ignored him. 'Shall we go, Flora?'

I nodded again. Then, with my head erect, I started across the wet grass to the path and thence to the road and the waiting carriage.

It was a far grander carriage than the one in which I had travelled to the burial, drawn by a fine matching pair. But I was far less comfortable in it. I was very aware of Louis sitting beside me, and though there was plenty of room for us to sit side by side without touching, I moved as far as I could into the corner so there was no risk of the slightest contact.

Louis Fletcher might be my cousin, but I did not know him from Adam, and besides, he felt like an enemy, and a very disturbing one at that, the man who was cruel enough to intrude upon my grief and tell me he was now the owner of the only home I had ever known.

If I had not been so numb I would have hated him, this arrogant stranger in his heavy dark redingote and leather boots; as it was I felt nothing but abject misery.

'I'm sorry if this has come as a shock to you,' he said as the coachman shook the reins and the carriage rolled off along the lane between the bare and dripping hedges.

The regret in his tone, which I assumed to be false, struck a discord on my shattered nerves.

'Why did you have to come today?' I demanded. 'Why couldn't you at least let me bury my father in peace?'

Heavy brows drew together. 'I thought it best that the matter should be settled as soon as possible,' he said.

'Settled?' I echoed sharply. 'What do you mean, settled?'

He glanced at me. 'Don't you think it would be better if we waited until we are at the inn before we have this conversation?' he said, and it was not a request, but an order, a decision made.

'I have to say I wish we did not have to have it at all!' I returned defiantly.

He smiled faintly. 'I am sure you do. However, unfortunate as the circumstances might be, there is no changing them. And at least I've come myself. I could have had my lawyer sort things out with your father's representative – always assuming he has one. But I have little time for the members of the legal profession. There are occasions, of course, when employing them is unavoidable, but more often than not they charge exorbitant fees for what one can handle far better oneself.'

I tightened my lips. So, for all his obvious wealth, Louis Fletcher was a skinflint. But I was glad, all the same, that he had not asked for a meeting with my father's solicitor. It would have been highly embarrassing to have to admit that I had not the slightest idea whether he had one or not. On balance, I doubted it. Our simple way of life had never, to my knowledge, given cause to need legal representation.

Nothing more was said until the coachman pulled into the courtyard, Louis opened the door without waiting for it to be done for him, got out and handed me down. Then he stood for a moment looking speculatively at the old grey-stone building.

'Yes, it is as I remember it,' he said. 'We came here once, my brother and I, with our father. You may have forgotten.'

'No,' I said. 'I remember it well. Your brother asked if it were true there were underground passages and when I told him there were he wanted to explore them.'

'Yes, that would be Gavin,' Louis said, as if he himself had forgotten the details of the incident. 'Always the adventurer. He hasn't changed, I'm afraid. He may be older, but he's no wiser.'

Well at least he is not here gloating over my misfortune, I thought bitterly, but I merely enquired: 'Where is he today?'

'In France. On business. It often takes him there.'

'But not you?' I asked.

'Occasionally.' His tone was short. 'Shall we go inside out of the rain? I assume the door is locked.'

'Oh no.' I turned the heavy iron handle and pushed the door open. 'We seldom lock the doors in daytime.'

I stepped inside and Louis followed me.

'A casual attitude,' he remarked. 'Especially given what befell your father.'

Colour tinged my cheeks. 'That was different! They came at night, when the door was bolted, and it didn't stop them, anyway! But in the hours of light . . . people round here trust one another. And we've very little worth stealing – except the ale of course.' A small hysterical laugh gurgled in my throat suddenly as an incongruous picture rose in my mind's eye of some intruder, helplessly drunk, on the bar floor.

Louis eyed me narrowly.

'I fail to see that it is a laughing matter. A coaching inn is very vulnerable. Highwaymen, footpads – they must all use this road.'

'Well if they do I don't know of them,' I said tartly, annoyed that he seemed to be criticizing our ways. 'It's more than thirty years since the last highwayman was hung around here. Won't you take off your redingote? You are dripping water all over the floor.'

'And so, my dear Flora, are you.'

It was true. Small puddles were forming at both our feet, and our footprints were wet on the freshly washed flagstones. Just this morning I had scrubbed them to give myself something to do. Now they would have to be done again.

We hung up our outerwear and Louis placed his beaver hat and malacca cane on the scrubbed wood table next to my mourning bonnet.

'Can I get you something to drink?' I asked, mindful of my manners and, truth to tell, in need of something myself. 'Tea, perhaps?'

'No, but I'll take a brandy.'

His forwardness astounded me; then I remembered. The brandy, like the inn itself, belonged to him now. In a flush of resentment I poured a sherry for myself, drank it in one quick gulp, and refilled the glass.

I saw Louis' eyebrows rise, but he said nothing, swirling his brandy around the glass and sniffing at it before he drank.

In all likelihood he thought I was a tippler, I thought, brought up in an inn and with a taste for liquor. Well, let him think what he liked. I didn't care.

'So you did not see who it was that attacked your father?' he said, returning to the subject of intruders.

I shook my head, cradling the sherry glass between hands that were suddenly trembling again.

'No. I did come downstairs to see who had called so late at night, but they were in the bar and Father would not let me in. He ordered me to go back to my room and I did as he told me,' I said. 'If only I'd known! I would never have left him!'

'Then you might have been murdered too,' Louis said harshly.

'No! Maybe I could have prevented it! I think they shot him because he was going for his gun. If I'd been there . . .'

'They were clearly desperate men, prepared to stop at nothing,' Louis said. 'And have you no idea what it was they wanted? Did you hear nothing of what was said?'

'Nothing.' I had turned away so that he would not see the distress in my face, which I could do nothing to hide, but I could feel his eyes boring into the back of my neck. 'I am totally at a loss to know what it was all about. The only thing I am certain of is that there were two of them. I saw their horses tethered in the courtyard and I saw them ride away. That's all.'

'Then it seems unlikely they will ever be apprehended,' he said. And then, almost as an afterthought: 'Unless they try the same thing elsewhere, of course.'

'Do you think they might?' I asked.

'I rather doubt it. It seems to me their quarrel, whatever it was, was with your father.' His face was still dark, but it seemed to me he had relaxed a little. I, however, was far from relaxed.

'I never knew my father to quarrel with anyone!' I said, rushing to his defence. 'He was not the quarrelsome sort, but the most equable man I have ever met. Everyone liked him!'

'But someone murdered him, nevertheless,' Louis pointed out.

A mist rose before my eyes; once again I seemed to see my dear father lying here on the flagged floor in a pool of his own life's blood. My knees went weak; the faintness assailed me again. I should not, I thought, have downed the sherry so quickly.

'Shall we sit down?' I said.

If I didn't sit, and soon, I thought I would fall, but I did not want to place myself at a disadvantage by sitting whilst he stood.

He glanced at the upright wooden chairs. 'Is there nowhere more comfortable?'

'The parlour . . .' But I wasn't sure my legs would carry me that far.

'Shall we go through then?'

Somehow I regained control of my senses. I didn't want this man in our parlour, it was a little private sanctuary, and I felt his presence would taint it somehow. But it was no longer *our* parlour, I reminded myself, it was his. I had no right to refuse him entry, and in any case I would be glad to be out of this bar where my father had breathed his last and his spectre still seemed to lie on the flagged floor.

The parlour, off the rear of the bar, was the smallest room in the inn, stuffed with too much furniture and too many memories. But there was a log fire burning in the grate that George Doughty had stoked up for me before we left for the funeral. I crossed to it now and took the poker to stir it back to life.

'Let me.' Louis took the poker from my hands and turned over the logs. 'You are cold, Flora. Come and warm yourself before we continue our conversation.'

They were the first kind words he had spoken to me, but far from comforting me, they only caused the tears to ache in my throat once more.

'No, just say what you have to say and get it over with,' I said. 'Then maybe you'll have the good grace to leave me in peace.'

He laid the poker down and turned to me. Firelight flickered over the hard angles of his face.

'Flora, I do not think you fully understand the situation.'

'Oh, I think I do!' I retorted. 'You are now the owner of my home. But I don't suppose you propose to live in it, since you have a fine home of your own.'

'No, I don't suppose I do.' His lip curled slightly. 'I don't think a country inn would suit me too well. But you must see – you can't remain here either.'

The world reeled about me. 'What do you mean – I can't stay here? It's my home! I have nowhere else to go! You wouldn't turn me out, surely?'

He straightened. 'It would be highly irresponsible of me to leave you here all alone, especially given what has happened. In any case, you could not possibly continue to run the inn on your own, so you would have no income on which to live.'

My future, and what plans I must make for it, had, I must admit, crossed my mind more than once these last days. But I had not been able to gather my thoughts sufficiently to formulate any clear solution. I had procrastinated, deciding to leave the decision making until I was less shocked, better able to take an overall perspective.

Now, however, the half-formed ideas came tumbling out.

'I can hire in help!' I said fiercely. 'I'm sure there are

responsible men in the village who would be willing to work for me. I would need a cellar man, of course, to carry out the heavy tasks, and someone to help serve food and ale when we are busy. And perhaps it would make sense for me to employ a woman to do the cooking and the washing, so that I can be left free to do the ordering and the accounts and all the other things Father used to do to keep the inn running smoothly.'

'Good gracious!' Louis said. 'You have this all worked out, don't you?'

'No,' I admitted. 'No, I don't. I haven't felt like making detailed plans. But I could do it! I know I could! I've grown up in this trade, after all. There's nothing I don't know about Tucker's Grave and its custom.'

'I am not so sure that is true,' Louis said. He said it quietly, so that it was almost an aside, yet there was a ring of steel in it. If it had not been such an outrageous idea, given that he was a stranger here, who had only once before set foot in the place, and that when he was no more than fifteen or sixteen years old, I might almost have thought he knew something that I did not.

As it was, the remark twanged on my taut nerves and I responded angrily.

'I assure you, Mr Fletcher, I helped my father with every aspect of running a coaching inn! And what I'm not familiar with I can quickly learn.'

He regarded me levelly. 'Please call me Louis. I am, after all, your cousin, if a few times removed.'

'Oh indeed! A cousin who wishes to turn me out of my own home, if I am not much mistaken!' I was trembling now, from head to foot.

'I wouldn't see you put out on the streets, Flora,' Louis said mildly. 'But surely you must realize such an idea is neither practical nor proper. There are women who run such establishments, I grant you. But – how old are you? Eighteen? Nineteen?'

'I am twenty-three,' I said with hauteur. 'I shall very soon be twenty-four.'

Those full lips curved a little. 'You don't look it. In any case, the women I spoke of are all a great deal older. They are either worldly wise widows or women who are no better than they should be. All of them have far more experience of life than you – and I mean that in a far wider sense than merely knowing how to draw a pot of ale or make up a bed or cook a joint of meat. How would you cope with trouble if it arose? Full-grown men in their cups? A fight, maybe? The advances that might be made towards you?'

'Our visitors always treat me with respect!' I flared.

'When your father was here to keep them in their place, maybe. I think you might find things a little different if you lived here alone. No!' He raised a hand to silence my ready protest. 'I'm sorry, Flora, but this matter is not for discussion. I would be failing in my duty as your closest living relative if I allowed you to remain here under such an arrangement.'

'So what is going to happen to Tucker's Grave?' Tears were stinging my eyes; for the moment the fate of the inn that had been my home for the whole of my life, and which I still felt foolishly was my heritage, seemed of far more importance than what was going to happen to me.

'I'm not sure yet,' Louis said carelessly. 'I may put in a landlord to run it, or I may sell it. I haven't yet decided. The one thing I am decided upon is that you cannot remain here alone. I think you should get some things together and come home with me.'

I stared at him. 'Home?'

'Belvedere House. Yes.'

Belvedere House. The mansion in its own grounds that as a child my father had shown me across the valley, the house I had thought must be home to a prince or princess.

My mouth had gone dry.

'You are proposing to take me to Belvedere House?'

He shrugged, a little impatiently. 'Where else? As I say, I wouldn't turn you out on to the streets. And you have no other relatives, have you?'

'No, but . . .'

'Then the least I can do is offer you a home. You'll have your own rooms – there's no shortage of space. And I'm sure we can find ways for you to occupy your time. The skills you have learned here won't be required, of course. I have a staff of servants to take care of such things. But perhaps you can learn new ones. Secretarial skills, for instance. I could do with some clerical assistance in regard to the business – Bevan, my secretary, is old now, and often sick at this time of year. He'd be glad, I think, to be given the chance of retirement. I am sure you would be able to take on some of his duties, considering you thought yourself capable of handling the business affairs here,' he added drily.

I was still too dumbfounded to reply, and he went on: 'Then there's my daughter. She is thirteen years old now, and could do with some young female company.'

The suggestion that he was bracketing me in a similar age group to his thirteen-year-old daughter outraged me.

'And what does your wife think of this idea?' I asked coldly.

His lips tightened, dark eyes hooded.

'I do not have a wife.'

'Oh!' I was startled. 'I thought . . . if you have a daughter . . .'

He ignored my underlying question. Clearly, for the moment, he had no intention of satisfying my curiosity as to what had become of his wife.

'We are a small household,' he said. 'Apart from myself and Antoinette, there is just my brother, Gavin. You remember Gavin?'

'Yes.' The boy with the devil-may-care eyes who had been so eager to explore our underground passages.

'Gavin has never married,' Louis went on. 'He's too much of a rake, I'm afraid, to want to settle down. He has a house at Dartmouth, which is convenient since much of our business is conducted through the port there, and he travels a good deal. But from time to time, when we have things to discuss, he takes a meal with us and makes use of the old Lodge at Belvedere.'

There was a certain censure in his tone; he did not, I thought, totally approve of his brother. Oh well, that was not so unusual. Siblings were very often two sides of a coin and did not get along too well. Certainly, if Gavin was a rake, as Louis had said, he must be very different to this rather severe man. But he was, most likely, a great deal more fun!

The thought dragged me back to my present situation. How could such a word as 'fun' even cross my mind with my father just laid to rest and my world crumbling about me?

'It is very kind of you to offer me a home,' I said stiffly, 'and even employment of sorts. But I have to say the very idea of moving away from the area where I was born and brought up is a daunting one. I've just lost my father, and it seems I am about to lose the only home I have ever known. I don't want to lose all my friends as well. I really would prefer to stay within reach of them.'

Louis looked at me closely with something resembling a scowl, though why he should scowl at me declining his offer, I could not understand. Perhaps putting a roof over my head salved what conscience he had; perhaps he saw me as a cheap option for replacing his aging secretary – for hadn't I already marked him down as a penny-pincher? I did not know, and did not, in truth, care much. All I know was that I did not want to be uprooted from everything that was familiar and dear to me and transported to that grand but lonely-looking house over-looking the River Dart.

'Are you saying, then, that someone in the village will take you in?' Louis asked harshly, and immediately I realized that I could not, with any certainty, say that.

George and Alice would offer me shelter without hesitation, I felt sure. But their little house was scarcely big enough for them, let alone me as well. And it was the same with everyone else I knew and counted as my friends. They weren't well off, any of them, and they had their own lives to lead, their own families to think of. I couldn't impose on any of them.

'I don't know . . .' I faltered.

'Well?' Louis persisted. 'This must be settled at once. I have to tell you, Flora, I am not prepared to go back to Belvedere and leave you here alone for even a single night. Quite simply, it is not safe for you. Either I see you settled with a decent family in the village, or you return with me. Which is it to be?'

I bit my lip. Little as I liked the idea of going with him, I could not see that I had any choice in the matter. I lifted my chin.

'Very well,' I said stiffly. 'Since you have made it clear I am not to be allowed to remain in my own home, then I will come with you. But just until I can find some way of supporting myself. I don't want to be dependent on your charity, Mr Fletcher, and neither will I be for a moment longer than is absolutely necessary.'

His breath came out on a long sigh; once again, it seemed, he relaxed a little.

'Good. Go then and get your things together. Make sure you have everything you need, for I don't know when I will be able to bring you back for anything you might have forgotten. And whilst I am waiting, I think I shall have another glass of that excellent cognac.'

I went to my room. Little had I thought when I left it that morning that I should not be sleeping in it tonight or perhaps ever again.

I dragged out the old travelling chest that had stood unused beneath the window for as long as I could remember, for my father and I never went anywhere for more than a single night.

I did not own many gowns, but I packed the ones I did have carefully and slowly, making the task last as long as I could, putting off the moment when I must leave Tucker's Grave for good. I folded my freshly laundered underwear into neat piles and rolled the things I had not got around to washing in the last terrible days inside a lawn petticoat. I collected my toiletries and a few knick-knacks and put them in the trunk too, together with the few pieces of jewellery I owned, apart from the pearl collar my father had given me for my eighteenth birthday, which I intended to put in my reticule. The collar meant a great deal to me and I did not want it out of my sight. The locket containing a small miniature of my mother and a lock of her hair I fastened around my neck and pushed out of sight beneath

28

the high neck of my mourning gown, and all the while my heart was heavy as lead.

I wished with all my heart that I had a miniature of my father, too, to place in the locket, but I did not. Father would have scoffed at the idea of having his portrait painted; he would have regarded it as a vanity, something that only ladies and high-born gentlemen did, not rough and ready innkeepers such as he.

Was there nothing I could take to remind me of him? Not that I would need reminding, but I did so want a keepsake.

I went to his room and collected his mother-of-pearl-backed hairbrushes and his snuff box, his one concession to accoutrements he considered to be the prerogative of the gentry. Into the chest they went, concealed in the folds of my gowns. With all my heart I hoped that we would not be held up by one of the highwaymen or footpads of whom Louis had spoken. If I was robbed of these small treasures, which were now the whole world to me, I didn't think I could bear it.

I could delay no longer. Already the grey afternoon was deepening towards dusk, and I knew that Louis must be anxious to be on his way.

I went down the stairs, my legs as heavy as my heart. Louis was standing before the fire, which was now burning low, the tails of his redingote lifted so that he could feel the warmth on his legs. In the dim room he made a forbidding figure, tall, broad and dark. So dark. My heart lurched with trepidation.

'I'm ready,' I said.

'Good. I'll have Thompson bring your things down. It's taken you long enough.'

'You did tell me to be sure to pack everything I needed,' I said with asperity.

'Quite right.'

He called Thompson in and gave the coachman a hand down the stairs with the heavy chest. When it was stowed in the carriage he came back to the bar, where I was fastening my still-damp cloak around my shoulders.

'We'll lock the door this time,' he said. 'You do have a key, I presume?'

I fetched it and handed it to him. He took one last look around, ensuring the fire was safely damped down and the windows secured. Then he went to the door.

'Time to go, Flora.'

A lump rose in my throat, tears misted my eyes. I crossed the threshold quickly, not wanting to prolong the agony, and stood biting my lip and staring through a damp haze at the familiar scene.

The door thudded shut, I heard the heavy key turn in the lock. Louis put a hand beneath my elbow to guide me towards the carriage, and as he did so, slipped the keys of Tucker's Grave into the pocket of his redingote.

It was that simple act that truly brought home to me the reality of what was happening.

The keys that had been my father's, the keys to my home, were now lying in the pocket of another man, another master.

Nothing, I thought, would ever hurt me more.

Three

D arkness had fallen by the time we had travelled the fifteen or so miles to Belvedere and I was denied any glimpse of the house until we arrived at the impressive front door.

I had been aware that we had turned into a long straight drive that ran first under a canopy of bare dripping trees, and then through open land which was, Louis told me, a deer park, but of course I saw no deer. They, sensible creatures, were taking shelter from the inclement night, and even had they not been, it would have been too dark for me to pick them out. The courtyard we drew into was broad and ran the length of the house, with a structure of some kind that I thought might be a fountain in its centre.

But it was the house itself which I found myself staring at, my first view of it since I had looked across the valley as a child and seen a palace fit for a fairy-tale prince.

Close to, it was vast, uniform in design, with tall narrow windows and a roof topped with parapets. Much of it was in darkness, but at some of the windows lamps burned, small welcoming pools of light.

I did not feel, however, that they were welcoming me. I felt as lost and bereft as if I were a traveller staring at an alien landscape. I wanted nothing more than to go home to my familiar little room at Tucker's Grave. That I could not was a physical ache within me, just another layer of pain.

The coachman came around and opened the carriage door; Louis climbed down first, then turned and handed me down, and I was glad this time of the strength of his arm. The jolting and swaying of the coach had made me feel a little queasy and I had taken nothing to eat all day, which was perhaps in the circumstances rather fortunate.

Someone must have been at one of the windows and seen the carriage on the drive, for as we approached the front door it was opened by an elderly man who I assumed was one of the servants Louis had mentioned. This was confirmed when he said: 'Good evening, sir. Mr Gavin saw you were home and rang for me to open the door for you. It's a filthy night.'

Through his hand on my elbow I felt Louis stiffen.

'Mr Gavin is home?' He sounded surprised.

'Yes, indeed he is, sir. Home safe and sound, praise the Lord.'

'He has only been on a business trip, Walter, not off to fight in some bloody battle,' Louis said impatiently.

'Well, yes, I know, sir, but these are dangerous times . . .' The old man turned to me, not seeming in the least surprised to see me standing there.

'And this must be the young lady. There's a room ready for her as you instructed, and Cook has catered for an extra mouth at dinner tonight.'

So, I thought, Louis had planned to bring me back with him even before he set out for my father's funeral. Well, I suppose that was to be expected. He had had a few days in which to decide to take his rightful inheritance of Tucker's Grave Inn and remove me from the premises. I was still puzzled by his decision, however, and the firm stance he was taking. It seemed to me that bringing me to Belvedere would cause him far more inconvenience than leaving me at the inn until he decided what to do with it, and considering I was a stranger to him, despite our kinship, I was surprised he felt it necessary to take on responsibility for my welfare. There was nothing about Louis Fletcher that struck me as charitable. Rather, he was a cold hard businessman concerned only with his latest acquisition.

I found myself wondering whether Gavin was as unapproachable as his brother. Certainly on that long-ago visit he had seemed the merrier of the two, with his ardent desire to explore the secret passages beneath the inn. Well, I would soon find out, it seemed.

As the servant, Walter, took my cloak, I looked around. The entrance hall was large and square, bigger than our little parlour at the inn, with four or five doors opening off it, and a broad staircase with carved newel posts led up to the upper storey of the house. A long case clock ticked somnolently, an ornate mirror hung above a small half-moon-shaped table upon which stood a bowl of pot-pourri. I caught a glimpse of myself in the mirror and was shocked by the paleness of my face. In my mourning black, with that white face, I might have been a ghost, had it not been for the bright gold of my hair.

'Shall we go through?' Louis suggested.

He pushed open a door on the left of the hall and I stepped into a room so elegant I was quite taken by surprise. The colour scheme was a deep rose pink, carried through the velvet upholstery of the chairs and chaise and the floor-length drapes which had been drawn against the wild night outside. The myriad light from a chandelier glinted on gilt and glass and highly polished wood, my feet sunk into a deep, richly patterned rug which covered most of the floor. However grand the house, however much it had resembled a fairy-tale castle, I had not expected this, for the rather feminine opulence was totally at variance with my impression of Louis as a very masculine man, with no time for fripperies.

Then I reminded myself – this house had been his father's before it was his, and I seemed to remember my father saying that his cousin Peter had married a French wife. The decor here must have been her choice, and however little it was to his taste, Louis had never bothered to change it for a cosier, more English look. He was, in all likelihood, so used to it that he barely noticed it any more. And given his parsimonious nature, he would no doubt resent spending money on refurbishment in any case, I thought, a little censoriously.

Again to my surprise, the room was empty. I had expected to find Gavin here – and perhaps Antoinette, Louis' daughter, too. But as I turned to say as much to Louis, the figure of a man appeared in the doorway.

'Well, well, Louis! And what have you been up to whilst I have been away?'

At first glance there was no mistaking that they were brothers. They were of similar height, though Gavin was, if anything, the taller by an inch or two, and similar build, slim of hip yet muscular, with broad, powerful shoulders. Their colouring was similar too – dark, curling hair no longer hidden by the powdered wigs that had been so fashionable just a few short years ago, clearly defined features, olive skin, dark eyes.

But with the purely physical, the likeness ended. The set of their faces, their entire demeanour, made them different as chalk and cheese. Gavin's generous mouth was not set in a hard line like his brother's; by comparison it looked almost soft in its readiness to smile. And the devilish light was still there in his eyes – the light of a young man looking for adventure. I could see in an instant that Gavin was possessed of all the easy charm that Louis lacked, and I felt a huge rush of relief that I was not to spend my first evening here alone with the dour man who had unilaterally assumed responsibility for me.

'I didn't expect you back for another week or so,' Louis said. There was a coldness in his tone that hinted he was less than pleased to find his brother at home.

'The business was concluded more speedily than I expected,' Gavin said. 'That happens sometimes, as well you know.'

'Just so long as it was also concluded satisfactorily,' Louis said without so much as the hint of a smile.

'Naturally. But you haven't answered my question, brother. What have you been up to in my absence that I find such a beautiful young lady at your side?'

His eyes were on me, appraising, appreciative, I might almost have thought. I flushed. I know I flushed, for there was more warmth in my cheeks than there had been for almost a week now. I felt it spread down my neck and chest beneath my gown. Surely he did not think that Louis and I . . . ?

'This is our cousin, Flora,' Louis said. 'Well, the daughter of our father's cousin, at any rate. You remember Tucker's Grave Inn? We went there once with Father when we were boys.'

'Yes, of course I remember!' Gavin's eyes were still on me. 'But you can't be the little girl, surely . . . ?'

'It was nigh on twenty years ago, Gavin,' Louis said drily. 'Little girls grow up.'

'And what a good thing they do!' Gavin smiled. 'Yes, I suppose I can see it now. Who could forget that wonderful golden hair!'

You had, clearly, I thought wryly. And given the scant notice either boy had taken of me, that was scarcely surprising.

'But why is she here?' he asked now.

'A great deal has happened in your absence,' Louis said shortly. 'Flora has suffered a sad bereavement. Her father has been interred this very afternoon.' He turned to me. 'Perhaps you would like a little time alone, Flora. Walter said your room was ready for you, did he not? I expect you'd like to see it, and have the chance to freshen up before dinner.'

Without waiting for my reply, he reached for the bell pull; I heard it tinkle somewhere deep in the house, and a few moments later a maid appeared.

'Would you show Miss Flora to her room please, Polly?' he said briskly.

'Yes, sir. Of course, sir.' She was a rather plain girl with a snub nose and mouse-coloured hair that looked, I thought, none too clean. She was eyeing me up slyly but her eyes held none of the appreciation I had seen in Gavin's. Rather, I think, she was taking in the quality of my attire and finding it wanting. Well, that was hardly surprising. Any guests here would be ladies of fashion, I felt sure, and just one of their gowns would, in all likelihood, be worth more than my entire wardrobe.

Well, I couldn't be bothered about that. I had far too much on my mind to care about the disdain of a servant.

'Walter will ring the gong when dinner is served,' Louis said. I nodded. 'You're very kind.'

But glad as I was to have the opportunity to be alone for a little while, I couldn't help feeling that it was something other than consideration that had prompted Louis to offer me the refuge of the room that was to be mine for the duration of my stay here.

He wanted me out of the way, I suspected. He wanted to talk to his brother alone, perhaps about me, and his plans for Tucker's Grave.

Once more I was struck by the feeling that something was not quite right here. Once more I felt there was more to Louis' motives than met the eye. But beyond material gain, I could not imagine what it could be.

I followed the maid out of the room and up the stairs.

The room Polly showed me into was, I discovered, almost as richly furnished as the parlour had been, and in much the same colour scheme. Louis' and Gavin's mother had been, I decided, very fond of pink.

Unless of course it had not been their mother who had chosen the decor, but Louis' wife. In spite of his bald statement: 'I have no wife', he must have been married at some time, since he had a daughter. What had become of her? I wondered. Presumably she was dead, but the cold tone in which he had spoken of her seemed to suggest that all had not been well between them.

Well, no doubt I would learn the facts in time, and for the moment I had far too much on my mind to concern myself with something that was none of my business. Louis' wife, whoever she had been, and whatever had happened to her, was not here now, and therefore of little importance to my situation.

My trunk had been brought up and stacked on a low stool beside the window. I opened it and began unpacking, searching firstly amongst the folds of the petticoats for the small precious mementoes I had brought with me. Father's mother-of-pearl-backed brushes went on to the cherry-wood dressing table, a little china rabbit I had owned since I was a child I put on top of the chest of drawers, midway between the candlesticks and dainty powder pots that already adorned it. The other things I placed in one of the drawers and covered them with a pile of clean linen.

The wardrobe was huge, far more space than I needed to hang my few good gowns. As I was shaking one out, concerned that it should not retain the creases of packing, there was a tap on the door and Polly came in carrying a jug of hot water.

'The master thought you'd like to freshen up,' she said, setting it down on the washing stand.

'Thank you. Where will I find a towel?'

'In the cupboard under the washing stand.' But she made no attempt to get one out for me. Not that I especially wanted her to – I was not used to being waited on – but I was a little disconcerted by the deliberate lack of respect.

'Will there be anything else?' Polly asked, making the customary question sound somehow impertinent.

'No, thank you.'

She left, closing the door after her, and I returned to the task I had set myself of hanging my gowns, such as they were, in the great wardrobe.

When the trunk was empty, I suddenly realized the box containing my pearl choker was missing. My heart sank as I realized I must have left it on the dressing table in my own room at Tucker's Grave Inn. Oh, it would be safe enough, I supposed, but it was very precious to me; I wanted it with me. Such a small thing, but to me at that moment it seemed like a mountain, and it shattered the last of my fragile control. My lip quivered, and no matter that I tried desperately to stop them, the tears came again, coursing down my cheeks.

I sank down on to the pink counterpane, buried my face in my hands, and wept uncontrollably. I had lost my father and my home, I was grieving and alone in a strange and hostile environment, and I had left behind the gift my father had given me on my eighteenth birthday. I had always thought of myself as strong and resilient but I did not feel strong or resilient now. I felt bereft, lost, and afraid.

The tears fell and went on falling, the rain beat scudding tattoos against the windowpanes, and the water Polly had brought for me went cool in the jug.

I do not think I could have stopped those tears for a king's ransom.

* * *

By the time the gong sounded, echoing through the great house, I had composed myself, washed my face and hands in the now tepid water, and tidied my hair.

Taking a deep breath, I opened my door and went along the landing to the staircase. I wished I could have excused myself from dinner; though I had eaten nothing all day I was past hunger and I knew it would be a struggle to force so much as a morsel of food down my dry and aching throat. But it was expected of me, and in any case, I could not avoid Louis and Gavin for ever.

Another door off the great hall was open; the clanking of chafing dishes being set on the sideboard and the sound of the men's voices floated out. This must be the dining room, I thought, and they had already repaired there. I ran my hands quickly over the thick upsweep of my hair, though I had only just tidied it, and went in.

Louis and Gavin were indeed there, and the atmosphere in the room was tense. They had been arguing about something, I knew it instinctively, and the heightened colour in Gavin's cheeks and the tightness of Louis' lips confirmed it. I only hoped it was some business matter that was the cause of their falling out and not the fact that Louis had brought me here without any reference to his brother, and certainly Gavin made every effort to make me feel welcome.

'Flora! Are you feeling a little better now?'

'I'm well enough, thank you,' I said.

'Are you sure that's the truth? Come and sit down.' He pulled out an ornately carved high-backed chair. 'You'll be beside me, and I shall make certain I take good care of you.'

Louis moved impatiently, his face dark, and the anomaly struck me; it was almost as if their roles had been reversed, as if it were Gavin who had imposed me upon Louis instead of the other way around.

'You must be very upset,' Gavin said solicitously.

'These past days have not been the easiest I have lived through,' I agreed.

'Indeed not. It was you who found your father dying, Louis tells me.'

I nodded, my throat closing. I really did not want to talk about it.

'And you have no idea who could have been responsible for such a terrible thing?'

'No, I simply can't imagine.' I forced a small shaky laugh. 'Certainly we have nothing worth stealing. We have always lived very simply.'

'Perhaps it was *you* they wished to steal away,' Gavin suggested. 'You are a very beautiful young lady, Flora. Is there a lover you have spurned, perhaps?'

I stiffened. 'Certainly not!'

'Gavin, I don't think . . .' Louis interrupted, but Gavin ignored him.

'You must have suitors, surely?'

'No,' I said sharply. 'I've never had time for such things.'

It was not quite the truth, but I was not about to discuss my personal affairs with a stranger. There had been a young man, Ralph Tooze, from the village, who could have been said to be courting me. I had known him since we were children, and we had been the best of friends until he began to seek a change in our relationship and even hinted at marriage.

I was fond of Ralph, but he was more like a brother to me than a lover; I felt no spark of attraction, quite the opposite. The more his ardour grew, the less I wanted to spend time with him, and when he tried to kiss me I hated it. I had no wish to swap my busy, fulfilled life at the inn for the role of wife and mother to Ralph's children, and I told him so in no uncertain terms. So I suppose it could be said I had spurned him.

But the suggestion that he might have been behind my father's murder was so ludicrous I knew it could not possibly be true. Ralph was a simple country lad, hurt by my rejection, yes, but certainly incapable of violence to further his designs on me.

There had of course been a number of customers or guests who had made advances towards me, too. But I had handled each and every one of them with the tact that is an innkeeper's daughter's stock in trade unless she wishes to get a bad name for herself. Apart from one, whose face I had resorted to slapping, and who had been thrown out bodily by my father when he heard the commotion and came to investigate. But that had been more than two years ago now. The culprit had never returned, and the thought that he might have done so with murder on his mind that terrible night was almost as unlikely as the suggestion that Ralph might be responsible.

No, whoever had quarrelled with and killed my father and for whatever reason, I was certain it had nothing to do with me.

'I never saw the men who came to the inn that night,' I said tautly. 'All I know is that they destroyed my world.'

Quite unexpectedly, Gavin reached out and squeezed my hand.

'We'll try to make you smile again, Flora,' he said softly, and I was moved again almost to tears by the small gesture of kindness. As I struggled to overcome them, I was almost unaware of Louis, standing stony-faced, until he moved impatiently.

'Where is Antoinette? Did she not hear the gong?'

Another maid was in the room, a small, dark-haired girl who looked not much older than Louis' daughter herself.

'Clara, will you please go and see what is keeping her?' Louis ordered. 'Be sure to tell her to come at once.'

The girl scuttled off.

'I would prefer it if you did not discuss Flora's loss and the manner of it in front of the servants,' he said tetchily to Gavin.

Gavin frowned. 'But they hear everything!'

'And talk about it amongst themselves. A murder is always the subject of much speculation. Flora's grief is her own private affair.'

I bowed my head in bewilderment. Perhaps I was misjudging Louis. Perhaps he was as concerned for me in his own way as Gavin, and simply had a rather strange way of showing it. And then again, perhaps he did not want my father's murder discussed for some other reason of his own, though I could not for the life of me guess what that might be.

A rustle of silk in the doorway; I was aware that someone else had entered the room.

I turned and saw a slender young girl standing there. She wore a simple gown of apple green, which fell straight from a high waistline to her feet, and boasted tiny puff sleeves. Even I, country bumpkin that I was, recognized it as the very latest fashion. Rich coppery hair fell loose to her shoulders, framing a face that was undeniably pretty, though there was a foxy look to her slanting green eyes, and there was certainly nothing very pretty about her expression. Her lips were buttoned as tightly as her father's into a small hard line and she looked at once both sullen and defiant.

'I see you have deigned to join us, Miss,' Louis said tartly. 'Did you not hear the gong?'

She returned his stare evenly. 'I was busy.'

'Busy? Busy doing what? Trying to make yourself look too old for your years again, I suppose. I will not have it, Antoinette. And I certainly will not have you keeping us all waiting for dinner. Do you understand?'

'Yes, Father.' But the defiance and resentment were still there in her eyes.

'It is especially ill-mannered of you since we have a guest,' he went on. 'This is Flora, a distant cousin of ours.'

'I know who she is,' Antoinette retorted. 'You told me this morning you would be bringing her home with you.' She turned to me, tilting her head to one side and regarding me with those foxy eyes.

'Do you always wear black, Flora, or is it mourning for your father? You shouldn't wear it, or not for any longer than you have to, especially with your colouring. It does drain you so.'

I thought Louis would explode. He took a step towards her, his face dark, fists clenching.

'You will apologize for that, Antoinette. It is an unpardonable thing to say!'

'I only spoke the truth! Black is very draining. I would never wear it.'

'Apologize this instant!'

For a moment they faced one another, father and daughter,

eyes locked in a silent battle of wills that I imagined had been fought many times before and would be fought many times again. Then she lifted her narrow shoulders in a slight shrug and turned to me.

'I'm sorry if I offended you, Flora. I'm afraid I'm given to speaking my mind.'

'You are given to rudeness! And rudeness is something I will not stand for!' Louis stormed.

Gavin took a step forward. 'Let's not embarrass Flora any more. Antoinette has apologized as you asked her; let's forget it now and eat. I, for one, am starving!'

For a long moment Louis ignored him, still glaring balefully at his daughter. Then his breath came out on a long sigh.

'Very well. But we shall talk about your behaviour again, Antoinette.'

He took his place at the head of the long table; as Antoinette moved to his right, I saw Gavin give her a surreptitious but unmistakable wink, and she responded with a twitch of that tight little mouth before sitting down, eyes demurely lowered.

Once again discomfort fluttered within me.

Bad enough that I was a stranger here, a bereaved, wretched stranger, but there were all manner of undercurrents to contend with too. I didn't care that Antoinette had insulted me, I knew she had spoken nothing but the truth. After all, hadn't I caught a glimpse of myself in the mirror earlier and thought I looked like a ghost?

No, I didn't care what she had said, but I could not help wishing she was a more likeable girl. But then again, I must not judge her too readily. She was at that difficult age that lies between childhood and womanhood and she had no mother to guide her. I knew only too well, from my own experience, just how that felt. My father had been kind and wise, but there had been times all the same when I had desperately longed for female guidance. Louis seemed cold, remote and censorious, and I could not imagine he made much effort to see things from Antoinette's point of view. Perhaps, I thought, when we got to know each other better, I could be a friend to her.

Dinner was served – watercress soup, followed by some sort of game pie, and somehow I forced some down.

No further mention was made of my loss or even my enforced situation here, and I imagined they were avoiding the subject for fear of upsetting me further. They did not even talk of business; that, I assumed, had formed part of the discussion the brothers had had when I had been despatched to my room. To be honest, I cannot clearly recollect anything that *was* said – I was, for the most part, lost once more in the fog that had suffocated me now for days.

Then, quite suddenly, I became aware that Gavin was addressing me.

'It must have quite a history, Tucker's Grave Inn.'

'Yes,' I said. 'I suppose it has.'

'Unlike our home.' He smiled. 'Father had this place built when his business became successful. We are only the second generation to live in it. But that old inn . . . it must have a few stories to tell.'

'It's a very odd name for an inn,' Antoinette said, her foxy eyes brightening as she saw her chance to make a few more jibes at my expense. 'I wouldn't want to sleep in a place that was called a *grave*.'

'It is named for a highwayman who was hanged at the crossroads close by,' I explained. 'Before that, I believe it was known as the Bell, but since everyone began referring to the crossroads as Tucker's Grave, the inn became known as Tucker's Grave too.'

Antoinette affected a theatrical shiver. 'A highwayman was actually hanged there! How gruesome!'

Not so gruesome as finding your own father dying in a pool of blood, I thought. But I did not want to go down that road.

'Did they leave him on the gibbet until he rotted away?' Antoinette persisted.

'Antoinette!' Louis reprimanded.

She ignored him. 'Did they?'

'I really couldn't say,' I said. 'It all happened a long time before I was born. All I know is that when he was cut down he was buried right there at the crossroads because they would not allow his body back into the village, and certainly not to be interred in consecrated ground.'

'Does his ghost haunt the spot?' Antoinette had changed suddenly from a precocious young woman to a curious child.

'If so, I have never seen him,' I said.

'And presumably if there were ghosts at the inn, they were more likely to have been the ghosts of persecuted monks,' Gavin put in.

Antoinette's eyes went round. 'Persecuted monks? What persecuted monks?'

'Wasn't the inn linked by underground passages with a monastery?' Gavin said. 'I seem to remember . . . ?'

So, after all these years, he still remembered the fascination of a fourteen-year-old boy with the mysterious links to an age of persecution.

'The monastery half a mile away, yes,' I said. 'I sometimes think the passages were first tunnelled out so that the brothers could sneak into the inn and enjoy a drink at times when the Abbot forbade it. But certainly they were used during the times of persecution, and some escaped into them when the monastery was sacked and burned.'

'And some did not, or so I have heard,' Gavin said. 'Were not some entombed by the soldiers?'

I was surprised he knew so much of the history of Tucker's Grave. That long-ago boyhood visit must have made quite an impression on him, and he had asked questions about the place that fascinated him so.

Before I could answer, Louis intervened.

'I don't think Flora wants to discuss such morbid matters, tonight of all nights,' he said.

'I don't mind,' I said. It was true; I did not mind. In a strange sort of way it made me feel closer to my home, talking about all the legends that were so familiar to me they were like a second skin. 'According to local lore, some of the monks were indeed trapped. The soldiers came to the inn and sealed off the escape route by barring the trap door into the cellar of the inn, and of course their retreat was cut off too, for the monastery was burning.'

'So they died like rats.' Gavin was enjoying himself.

'I really don't know,' I said. 'It may be just a tale. These stories are so embroidered over the years as they are passed down, no one can be sure where the truth lies.'

'Well I certainly wouldn't care to live in a place with such a history!' Antoinette said. 'Didn't the very thought of it make your flesh creep when darkness fell?'

'No,' I replied truthfully. 'Why should it? I was born and brought up there, after all, and I certainly never had any bad feelings about it. It was my home!'

'And now it belongs to Papa . . .'

'That will do, Antoinette!' Louis said sharply.

He looked at me, and for the first time I saw what I thought was genuine regret in his eyes.

'I expect, Flora, that you are very tired. If you want to leave us now and go to your room, we shall quite understand.'

I nodded, touching my napkin to my lips and pushing back my chair.

'I would be grateful.'

'We'll talk more about the future in the morning,' Louis said. 'Try to get some sleep now.'

For some reason the consideration in his voice made my cheeks burn. For a moment I was totally flustered. Coming on top of all my other tumultuous emotions, it was simply too much for me.

With another hasty nod I turned and gratefully escaped from the dining room.

Four

Those first days at Belvedere House passed in much the same blur as the ones that followed my father's death. For the most part I was left to my own devices, for Louis told me I should have the chance to grieve, and also to settle in, before he began introducing me to the secretarial duties he had planned for me.

He also told me that he had arranged for Tucker's Grave Inn to be boarded up for the time being and that he had sent men to do the job first thing in the morning following the day I had left.

I suppose he told me this thinking it would set my mind at rest to know the place would be secure against vandals who might break down the door or force the windows when they found they were denied access to their ale, and vagabonds who might break in to steal whatever they could lay their hands on, but to be truthful I found the very thought of boards at the windows and bars at the doors an upsetting one.

'What will happen to the travellers?' I asked. 'How will they manage with nowhere to change their horses and rest overnight or find refreshment?'

'There are other inns on the road,' Louis replied airily. 'They will have to make use of them.'

'But if they fall into the habit of going elsewhere, they may never come back,' I protested feebly. 'It could mean the end of Tucker's Grave.'

Louis shrugged; I could see it did not concern him in the slightest, and why should it? He did not need the income. But it hurt me to think that my old home should deteriorate to an unloved, dilapidated ruin.

Something else was concerning me too. Supposing the Brotherhood of the Lynx should come in the middle of the night with noble French fugitives? It could be disastrous for them to find the place all locked up, for there might not be another safe house within many miles. I had been proud of the part we had played in helping the beleaguered nobles who had escaped the guillotine by the skin of their teeth and the bravery of the Brotherhood; now I was anxious on their behalf.

But of course I made no mention of this concern to Louis. These were dangerous times, and there were things one did not talk about even to close acquaintances, let alone near strangers.

'At least I suppose my pearl collar will be safe then,' I said, grasping at the one positive result from Louis' action.

'Your pearl collar?'

'Yes. It's very precious to me. Father gave it to me for my eighteenth birthday, and I intended to bring it with me. Unfortunately, in my haste, I left it on the dressing table in my room,' I said. 'I wish with all my heart I hadn't come without it. I know I can't wear it at the moment, whilst I am in mourning, but forgetting it makes me feel as if I had betrayed Father in some way – as if I didn't care . . .'

'That's foolish talk, Flora,' Louis said. 'It is quite understandable that you should have overlooked something, leaving as we did. You must try to put it out of your mind.'

I turned away, the ready tears pricking my eyes. The last thing I wanted was for him to see them.

For one who had his own apartments in the old lodge, Gavin seemed to spend a good deal of time in the great house, but I could not help but be glad of it. He was, without doubt, a good deal more approachable than his brother.

The business their father had begun, and which they now ran together, was, I learned, the importing of wine and the exporting of woollen cloth and minerals from Dartmoor, and many of the transactions conducted were in France. It crossed my mind to wonder if all the trading was strictly legal, for Dartmouth had something of a reputation as a so-called 'free port'. Its situation beside deep water and within the shelter of the winding River Dart made it a busy landing stage, whilst the sparsely populated countryside which surrounded it on three sides meant there was little defence against the smugglers who made use of the caves and sandy coves along the coast. Additionally, it did seem to me that someone who could so coldly take possession of my home, though it was lawfully his, would have few scruples about making money by whatever means came to hand and was the most profitable. But I could not be overly concerned about the legitimacy or otherwise of the family business, or the source of the wealth that had built Belvedere House. I had too many other things on my mind, and it really was no business of mine.

Antoinette's continued antagonism, however, did concern me. It seemed she was determined to resent me, making barbed remarks when the opportunity arose and merely glowering at me with those foxy eyes when it did not. My only consolation was that she seemed equally antagonistic towards her father and I guessed that she was at an age where she hated the whole world if it failed to fall in with her whims. And I still pitied her, too, trapped here in this great house with no friends of her own age or sex.

One morning when Louis had repaired to his study and we were left alone at the breakfast table, she rose suddenly and announced she was going riding. It was a wretched day; the rain had stopped at last, but a thick blanket of fog hung over the countryside. From the window of the morning room it was impossible to see more than a few feet and I could guess that up on the moors it would be even worse.

'Is that wise?' I asked before I could stop myself.

Immediately she turned on me. 'What do you mean?'

'You can scarcely see your hand in front of your face,' I said. 'You could gallop into a ditch and never see it.'

'I know every inch of the land around here,' she said haughtily. 'And Perdita does too. She'd never be so foolish as to gallop into a ditch.'

'Nevertheless,' I said, 'I really think you should speak to your father before you go out riding on such a morning. He may not share your confidence.'

Her lips tightened; her eyes blazed.

'I do as I like!' she said scornfully. 'And I certainly won't be dictated to by someone like you!'

I felt my hackles rising.

'And what do you mean, Antoinette, by *someone like me*?'

She tossed her head. 'Why, a poor innkeeper's daughter living here on my father's charity.'

She had gone too far and I think she knew it, but she held my gaze defiantly all the same.

'Antoinette,' I said fiercely, 'I know you don't like my being here, but I would remind you it is not of my choosing. Your father insisted on bringing me here – against my will, I may say. The moment I can see my way to making other arrangements, I shall do so, and you will not have to put up with me any longer. Until then I am afraid we shall just have to get along as best we can.'

'If you say so.' She turned, flouncing towards the door, then stopping abruptly and turning back to me. 'Why did he bring you here?' she asked unexpectedly.

'I don't know.'

I had asked myself the same question over and over. It wasn't that he had wanted to put a tenant innkeeper into Tucker's Grave immediately; he had boarded the place up. And I couldn't see why he should be sufficiently concerned about my welfare, moral or otherwise, to impose me upon his household. I was nothing to him, nothing at all. Even the vague dark remarks about my safety were unconvincing. My father's murderers had come to the inn to see him and he had invited them in. The subsequent quarrel that had resulted in his death had been between them; I could not see the men, whoever they were, coming back to harm me. Though I had to admit what I found most disturbing – the thing I could not forget nor explain – was that he *had* invited them in.

I had tried to tell myself he had thought they wanted a bed for the night, yet I still felt instinctively it was more than that.

He had not wanted me to know what was passing between them – he had sent me back upstairs. He had not asked me to raise the alarm, or sought help from the burly coachman sleeping upstairs. And the conclusion I could not escape, however reluctant I was to admit it, was that he had known his killers.

Yet none of this was good reason for Louis to have boarded up the inn and brought me here.

'I don't know, Antoinette,' I said. 'I have to admit I am as much in the dark as you are.'

'Well,' Antoinette flashed, 'it wouldn't have happened if my mother was still alive, that I do know.'

My curiosity stirred, I admit it.

'Your mother is dead, then?' I asked before I could stop myself.

'Well of course!' Her tone was biting sarcasm. 'Where did you think she was?'

'I don't know that either,' I admitted. 'Has she been dead very long?'

'Oh yes,' she said airily. 'I killed her, I think.'

'You mean she died giving birth to you?'

'No. She died of a fever. But I gave it to her.'

'Ah!'

'She was very beautiful.' For the first time I saw some animation in Antoinette's delicate face. 'She had chestnut hair and green eyes, and every man she ever met fell madly in love with her. She was French, you know.'

'Oh!' I said, surprised. 'I thought that was your grandmother.'

'My grandmother was French too. Her father was a merchant who traded with my grandfather. But Mama – Mama was high-born. An aristocrat. Oh yes, I have French blood on both sides, from my father and my mother. That's why I am called Antoinette. That's French, too.'

'I know that much,' I said, smiling. I was anxious to keep this conversation going, both because it was the first real communication I had shared with Antoinette, and because I was curious, more curious than I had any right to be. 'Your father must miss her very much.'

She tossed her head. 'Oh, I don't think so. Papa is interested in nothing but business and making money.'

'I'm sure that's not so!' I felt bound to protest, though from what I had seen I could not help feeling it was not too far from the truth.

'And when I am bad, he says I am too much like my mother,' Antoinette went on.

'He says that? To you?' I was shocked.

'Not to me. I've heard him say it to Uncle Gavin. But he wouldn't say that if he had loved her, would he? Not when he thinks I've been bad.'

'I'm sure he doesn't mean it in the way you think,' I said feebly. 'I expect he simply means that she was high-spirited and perhaps a little wilful.'

She shrugged. 'I don't care, anyway. I'm *glad* I'm like her. Anyway, I'm going for my ride now, and please don't try to stop me.'

'Antoinette . . .'

'I know,' she said impatiently. 'Papa told me he thought you would be company for me, and I expect he said much the same to you. But I don't need your company, and I certainly don't need you mollycoddling me.'

I sighed. For a few minutes I had thought I was actually getting through to Antoinette in some way. Now, once again, she had become the sullen, defiant child I had seen on the first night I had come here.

'Well, take care anyway,' I said.

She shot me a disdainful look and left the room. A little while later I saw her galloping off down the drive on Perdita, her sleek bay, and once more I was alone with my memories and my thoughts.

I had been at Belvedere House for almost two weeks and I did not like the enforced inactivity. I was used, after all, to being kept busy from dawn till dusk and falling exhausted into my bed at night. Now I had nothing to occupy my days and far too much time and opportunity for brooding.

One morning I woke to see that at last the rain had stopped and the fog lifted. The view from my window was breathtaking – a wintry blue sky stretching towards some admittedly threatening clouds on the far horizon and pale sun shining on the acres of deer park that fronted the house. Somehow the improvement in the weather fired a sense of resolve in me. If this was to be my life for the time being, then I must make some attempt to live it, or fade into the sort of weak, useless woman I had always despised.

When I went down to breakfast I found Louis already there, tucking into a hearty plate of bacon and kidneys, and as soon as I had fetched myself some food from the chafing dishes lined up on the sideboard, I broached the subject uppermost in my mind.

'You said you would like me to do some secretarial work for you in order to earn my keep,' I said. 'Well, I am ready to begin.'

Louis looked up at me, eyeing me closely. 'Are you sure?'

'Yes,' I said firmly. 'Quite sure.'

'Very well. Come to my office when you have finished your breakfast and we'll make a start. I think I can spare the time to show you the books before I have to go out.'

I felt a little flush colouring my cheeks. Stupidly, it had not occurred to me that to begin with I would be more of a hindrance than a help.

If I had imagined, though, that I would be working alone with Louis, I was mistaken. When I presented myself at the door of his office, half an hour or so later, I saw that an elderly man was already there, engaged in writing in a ledger with a spidery hand.

'I don't think you have met Mr Bevan,' Louis said. 'He hasn't been well enough to come in for the past couple of weeks – the ill weather we have been having makes his chest bad. As luck would have it, he has chosen this very day to return to work, though I'm not altogether certain he is well enough.'

As if in confirmation of his opinion, the old man began hawking noisily, but when the coughing fit subsided I fancied I saw in his faded eyes the same resentment I had encountered over and over again since coming to Belvedere House. No one wanted me here, least of all this faithful old servant, who no doubt saw himself being edged out of the position that was his whole life.

'It seems that after having had to fend for myself for too long, I now have an abundance of assistance,' Louis went on easily. 'But at least it means I can leave it to Bevan to familiarize you with our methods of working. As I think I mentioned earlier, I have to go out and make some calls, and since Bevan is here, I can leave without delay.'

For no reason I could explain, I was aware of a stab of sharp disappointment.

'I'll leave Flora in your capable hands, then,' Louis said, and strode out, leaving us alone.

'I don't know what it is he wants me to show you,' the old man grumbled, hawking again.

'Just how things are done, so that I can be of some use if I'm needed,' I said, drawing on all the reserves of tact that I had perfected through years of dealing with awkward guests and customers. 'If you should be taken poorly again you wouldn't have to be worried about the work piling up here if I could deal with some of it for you.'

'Hmm.' He squinted up at me. 'You won't be here for that long, will you?'

'I . . . I don't know,' I said, startled by his remark.

A small ironic smile twisted his shrunken lips. 'No, I don't think you'll be here long. Miss Antoinette will see to that.'

'What do you mean?' I asked.

'She can be difficult, Miss Antoinette. When she was younger she had governesses. They never lasted more than a few weeks or months.' He shook his head, reminiscing. 'She's her mother's daughter, and no mistake.'

His words were almost an echo of what Antoinette herself had said, the curious, rather dark reference to Louis' dead wife, whom he had dismissed on the first day I met him with the cold phrase: 'I have no wife', and whom he seemed reluctant to so much as mention, except, perhaps, when he was ruing Antoinette's taking after her. And it occurred to me quite suddenly that this man must know all about the mysterious, nameless woman who had once been mistress of Belvedere.

'You remember Antoinette's mother, then?' I said, unable to contain my curiosity a moment longer.

'Oh aye, I remember her all right. Lisette wasn't a woman to forget.'

'It must have been a terrible thing when she died,' I prompted.

His rheumy eyes narrowed, he looked at me, looked away, and was silent.

'She caught the fever and succumbed to it, Antoinette said,' I persisted.

'Oh did she now? Well, if that's what you've been told, it's not for me to contradict, is it?'

My curiosity was well and truly roused now.

'You mean she did *not* die of the fever?'

Bevan shook his head. 'Oh no, I won't be drawn into gossip, Miss. I haven't kept my position here all these years by gossiping. If you want to know about Miss Lisette, then you must ask Mr Louis. He's the only one in any case that knows the whole truth of the matter, and what he doesn't discuss with the likes of us, I doubt he'll discuss with you. Now, shall I be showing you some of what we do here, or shall Mr Louis come back and find everything just as he left it?'

'Yes, of course, I'm eager to learn,' I said, and tried to put the disturbing conversation concerning Louis' wife out of my head.

Certainly I needed all my wits about me to take in the proliferation of facts regarding the business with which Bevan attempted to acquaint me, and all at once.

He showed me the ledgers in which transactions were recorded, and fat files of correspondence with other merchants. He showed me addresses of contacts and carriers, and details of huge shipments of woollen cloth bound for the continent, and cargoes of wines and spirits, perfumes and silks coming in. If I had entertained any doubts about the legitimacy of some of the trading, they were quickly put aside, for it seemed to me everything was meticulously recorded, enough to satisfy the most industrious customs officer.

'Mr Louis is very particular,' he said when I commented on the complexity of it all. 'He likes everything kept proper. Perhaps it would be best now if you were to just sit quietly and watch while I make up these books. I'll tell you what I'm doing as I go along.'

A very good idea! I thought. My head was spinning. How had I for one moment imagined I would be capable of stepping in and working at something so complicated, and of which I had no knowledge at all?

Once during the morning I heard horse's hooves on the drive and thought perhaps Louis had finished his business and was home sooner than he had thought to be, but when the study door opened it was Gavin who put his head round.

'Flora!' he said, surprised, when he saw me there, inky-fingered, and with strands of hair coming loose because I had been scratching my head as I concentrated. 'What are you doing?'

Bevan answered for me. 'I'm teaching her the business, Mr Gavin, as Mr Louis has asked me to.'

'Good heavens!' Gavin looked amazed. 'And how are you finding it, Flora?'

'Complicated,' I admitted. 'But I'll get there in the end.'

'Clever as well as beautiful, eh?' His wicked eyes teased me. 'When my brother said he could make use of you as a secretary, I thought he meant nothing more taxing than dictating a few letters. Well, good luck to you! I wouldn't like to have to contend with the paperwork the business generates.'

Gavin, I could not help feeling, would in all likelihood prefer not to have to work at all, though the frequent trips he made abroad, ostensibly to strike new deals, were possibly to his liking. They were, I guessed, the sum total of his involvement, and even they had to be duplicated by Louis more often than not, judging by tidbits of conversation I had overheard.

Gavin's lack of commitment and inability to pull off profitable deals very likely lay behind Louis' impatience with him, in my opinion. I had not been in the house for almost two weeks without realizing that. But his fecklessness was all part of his charm.

'Louis not here?' Gavin asked now.

'Gone into Dartmouth on business, and even farther afield, if I'm not mistaken,' Bevan said.

'Oh well, I'm glad he's keeping busy to make us a crust,' Gavin remarked lightly, underlining my thoughts. Then he turned to me, his eyes challenging. 'You don't want to spend a lovely morning like this cooped up with a lot of dusty ledgers, Flora!'

'The ledgers are not dusty!' Bevan protested, as if such a suggestion was personally offensive to him. 'They are well looked after, Mr Gavin.'

'Oh, you know what I mean!'

'Indeed I do know. But these ledgers, Mr Gavin, are what keeps you in comfort,' Bevan scolded.

Gavin ignored him, giving me the full benefit of his most charming smile.

'Can't I persuade you to come for a little stroll in the sunshine?' he wheedled. 'Tomorrow it will no doubt be raining again, and it's wise to take advantage of what opportunities come one's way in this life. In any case,' he added, 'I should very much like the chance to get to know you better. I've never yet been able to talk to you without Louis or Antoinette being there, and there is so much I would like to know about you, Flora.'

He spoke almost as if we were alone, quite ignoring Bevan, and though I must admit to being just a little flattered, I felt quite discomfited by his all-too-obvious approach. Bevan, too, must have been put out, for he began a coughing turn, as if to remind Gavin of his presence.

I mustered what I could of my dignity.

'I don't think it would be right for me to walk alone with you,' I said.

Far from being abashed, Gavin looked amused, and those tantalizing eyes held mine.

'Even though you spend a great deal of time alone with my brother?'

My metal was up, and my colour with it.

'That is simply not true!' I said furiously. 'Louis and I are never alone! Apart from the carriage drive when he brought me here, I have never been in his company with no one else around. And I don't care at all for what you are implying!'

He laughed out loud then, a shout of delight.

'Ah, Flora, I see you are a young lady of spirit! I apologize for my crass remark. I did not mean to imply that anything improper was occurring between you and my brother. Perish the thought! No, I'm simply jealous of him having your company here, whilst I am banished to the lodge like the black sheep Louis seems to think me.'

'I accept your apology,' I said, somewhat mollified. 'But as for being banished – I can scarcely believe that. If you spend time in your own apartments in the lodge, surely that is because it suits you to have your privacy?'

'Oh, my privacy is certainly important to me.' Gavin chuckled, rather wickedly. 'But believe you me, it's banishment all right. Louis wouldn't have me within a hundred miles of him if it weren't necessary for the smooth running of the business and the fact that he promised my late mother on her death bed that he would allow me to remain in the lodge.

'But we don't want to talk about Louis, do we? Come now, have I persuaded you to take that stroll with me?'

A little smile touched my lips.

'I'm afraid not. Not today, at any rate. I've far too much to learn here, and I don't want Louis to come home and find me shirking.'

Gavin smiled back. 'No, that would never do! Well, perhaps another day, Flora, when you are less busy – and less worried about proprieties.'

'Perhaps.'

'I shall look forward to it,' he said. 'No, I'll leave you to get on with this very pressing lesson, and wait for my brother in the parlour.'

'You're likely to have a long wait,' Bevan said warningly.

'Oh, that's all right. My time is my own today.' He went out, closing the door behind him, and his footsteps echoed on the marble floor of the hallway as he crossed to the parlour.

He was going to help himself to some of his brother's good cognac, I rather thought. Waiting for Louis was just an excuse!

'You were very wise, Miss Flora,' Bevan said, looking up from the ledger.

'Wise?'

'To refuse to be seduced by Mr Gavin.'

'I am sure he was not trying to *seduce* me,' I protested, though I rather thought the opposite was true. 'And I'm very sorry if his teasing caused you discomfort.'

'Oh, I'm well used to Mr Gavin's ways, don't you worry. But like I say, you'd do well to give him a wide berth – and Mr Louis, too, if it comes to that.'

For some reason my heart had begun to hammer very fast.

'Louis?' I echoed. 'But Louis isn't in the least like . . .'

'They both spell trouble where the ladies are concerned,' Bevan said darkly. 'They set one another off, and always have. Steer well clear of both of them, that's my advice to you. And now . . .' He pulled the chair out for me to sit beside him again. 'I've said a good deal too much this morning, Miss Flora. I'm just a garrulous old fool.'

And I knew I would get nothing further from him by way of explanation.

We worked on, and only one small thing that I found vaguely disconcerting occurred.

Bevan asked me to file away a pile of documents. Some went into labelled boxes on a shelf, but I could not find homes for all of them, and attempted to open a bureau where I imagined more were stored. The door refused to budge when I pulled on the handle, and I exclaimed aloud in surprise.

'Oh, it's locked!'

Bevan was on his feet in an instant, with surprising speed, in fact, given his precarious state of health.

'Not that one, Miss Flora. That's for private matters only. What is it you can't find now? Let me see . . .'

I suppose there was really nothing strange about a locked bureau for private papers; I might have thought nothing of it had it not been for Bevan's obvious agitation, which somehow went beyond a normal reaction. I was not, after all, about to force the lock and pry – or at least, not until Bevan aroused my suspicions by the violence of his response! As it was, I couldn't help thinking that the secretary was very well aware of what was in the locked bureau, and edgy about it. Could it be I had been correct in my earlier suspicions, and there were less than legitimate transactions being recorded in this office?

Shortly before one o'clock Louis returned. He came into the office, and as always his presence, brooding and forceful, seemed to fill the room.

'How have you been getting along?' he enquired.

Bevan ignored the question.

'There are some letters here, Mr Louis, that require your signature.'

'I'll deal with them later,' Louis said. 'First, I am in need of some refreshment, and I would think it is time that you and Flora took a rest, too.'

'I'd prefer to finish what I'm at first,' Bevan said primly. 'I'm a little behind, what with having to explain everything to Miss Flora.'

'As you wish. But I would like Miss Flora to come with me.'

Puzzled, I rose. There was something purposeful in the way he said it.

I followed him across the hall and into the parlour. There was no sign of Gavin; if he had been there drinking Louis' cognac, he had clearly grown tired of waiting and gone elsewhere.

'Flora, I have something for you,' Louis said without preamble.

From the pocket of his redingote he took a small casket that I recognized immediately.

'My pearl collar!' I exclaimed. 'But . . .'

'I know how upset you were at leaving it behind,' Louis said.

'My travels took me not far from Tucker's Grave, so I thought I would get it for you.'

'You've been to Tucker's Grave! But I thought it was all locked up . . .'

'I do have a key, remember,' he said.

'Yes, but . . .' The thought of Louis, free to come and go in my home when I was not, was somehow disturbing.

I put the thought aside. It was kind of him to have remembered my distress at leaving my pearl collar behind, and to have put himself out to collect it.

Unless, of course, he had some other reason entirely for wanting to go to Tucker's Grave . . .

No, I wouldn't think it. I would accept it as a gesture of friendship, the first real kindness he had shown to me.

'Thank you,' I said.

I opened the box, feasting my eyes on the creamy pearls that I had feared I might never see again, running my fingers over them and feeling them warm to my touch.

I remembered my eighteenth birthday when my father had given them to me, fastening them around my neck, which had felt so bare since this was the first day I had put up my hair; remembered too the love and pride in his dear eyes.

'They are so beautiful, Father!' I had said, and I had seen him swallow at a lump which suddenly constricted his throat.

'No, *you* are beautiful, Flora. The pearls just complement your beauty. And they always will, throughout the years. Take care of them, and they'll grace your neck for a lifetime.'

'Oh Father . . .' A lifetime had seemed to me then to stretch away into eternity. For both of us. Now, my father's life was ended, but his gift to me, at least, was safely in my possession once more, thanks to Louis' unexpected thoughtfulness.

I looked up, my eyes brimming with tears, and surprised an expression on his face that I had never thought to see.

He was looking at me with something that could only be described as tenderness. The hard lines of his face had softened, his eyes held a thoughtful smile.

And in that moment something equally strange happened to

me. My stomach tipped, tiny shivers of warmth ran through me and prickled on my skin. Never in my life before had I experienced such a sensation; it was disturbing, and yet at the same time extraordinarily pleasant.

Disconcerted, I lowered my eyes.

'Thank you,' I said again, and to my own ears my voice sounded breathless and a little shaky. 'I'll put them away at once for safe keeping.'

And on legs that felt curiously unsteady, I fled the room.

Five

I met Gavin on the staircase, almost colliding with him in my haste.

'Why all this haste?' he asked, steadying me with a hand on my shoulder.

'Oh, it's my pearl collar!' I replied, the words tumbling out. 'I left it behind when I left the inn and Louis has kindly collected it for me. I am taking it to my room.'

'Louis has been to Tucker's Grave?' Gavin sounded startled, but at the time I thought nothing of it. I was too full of confusion.

'So it seems,' I said.

'He's a dark horse, my brother.' Gavin was making no attempt to move aside and let me pass. 'Well, since you are so clearly delighted to have your pearl collar in your possession again, why don't you wear it?'

'Oh, I can't! I'm in mourning . . .'

'The neck of your gown is so high you could wear it beneath and no one would know,' he suggested.

His hand moved a little up my shoulder and towards my throat. Flustered as I already was by the look I had surprised on Louis' face and my own unexpected response to it, I recoiled instinctively. His touch, though light, was a little too intimate for comfort.

'I . . . I think I'd rather . . .'

'The hell with propriety, Flora!' He laughed softly, and it occurred to me that he was talking about something more than the wearing of a pearl collar when I should not be. 'Live a little dangerously! Do what you want to do, not what others decree you should! That's the maxim I live by, for life is too short to do otherwise.'

A door opened into the hall beneath us; I looked down and saw the maid, Clara, carrying a plate of cold meats into the dining room.

'Clara will help you to put it on!' Gavin said. 'By God, you should have a maid to help you dress. It's every lady's right. I shall speak to my brother about it.'

'I have no need of a lady's maid!' I protested, but Gavin took no notice.

'Clara!' he called. The girl re-emerged, looking up at us questioningly, and Gavin turned me with that hand that still lay upon my shoulder and urged me back down the stairs. 'Go with Miss Flora into the morning room and help her with her pearls.'

It seemed easier to fall in with his instruction than to argue, and in any case I had to admit the idea of wearing my precious pearl collar, albeit secretly, was a comforting one. Perhaps such adornment was not the done thing at a time of loss, but how could it possibly be wrong when it only served to make me feel closer to my dear dead father? I went with Clara to the morning room and when the door was closed behind us, I stood passively whilst she unhooked the high neck of my gown, fastened the collar around my throat, and rehooked my gown.

'It doesn't show, does it?' I asked anxiously.

'Not a bit. You'd never know it was there, honest, Miss Flora.' Her earnest little face wore a sympathetic and almost conspiratorial expression, and I warmed towards her. Perhaps having a lady's maid would not be so bad if it also meant I found a friend.

As we emerged from the morning room I heard the sound of raised voices – Louis and Gavin arguing again.

'You seem to be spending more and more time here in the house these last few weeks.' Louis' tone was strident; it carried clearly into the hall.

'Because I've had business here.' Gavin sounded a trifle defensive.

'Are you sure that is the real reason? I'm not so sure. And I don't like it, Gavin. You know that after what happened I said I would not have you under my roof.'

'For the love of Christ, Louis, that was almost ten years ago . . .'

'And as fresh in my mind as if it were yesterday. I could have turned you out to fend for yourself, but I did not. I bought the house in Falmouth to give you somewhere to live – a generous gesture, I think, in the circumstances – and when necessary for the sake of the business I allow you to use the Lodge. Now, however, it seems you are trying to worm your way back into the house.'

'It is my family home,' Gavin said.

'Perhaps. But I would remind you it belongs to me. And I don't want you here. Do you understand?'

'I understand very well,' Gavin said. You are a hard and unforgiving man, Louis.'

'Some things, Gavin, are unforgivable. I very much hope you will continue to abide by my wishes, or you will find I can be harder yet.'

Gavin muttered something too low for me to hear, the door flew open wide, and he came storming out. His eyes narrowed when he saw me standing there, rooted to the spot like a rabbit caught in the bright light of a poacher's flare, but he said nothing to me. He simply grabbed up his redingote and strode to the door, shrugging into it as he went.

And still I could not move. Louis would emerge at any moment and know, too, that I had overheard the quarrel, but I simply did not know which was worse – to remain where I was or to be caught fleeing like some peeping Tom.

What did it mean? Clearly the antagonism I had noticed between Louis and Gavin was indeed very real and not in my imagination, clearly it was rooted in something that had occurred long before I came to Belvedere. But equally I could not help feeling that I had somehow unwittingly caused this most recent fracas.

You seem to be spending more and more time here these last few weeks . . .

These last few weeks. Since I had been here? Certainly Gavin had been paying me a great deal of attention. Certainly he had just all but accosted me on the stairs. Was that the reason Louis had lost control of his temper? Did he think there was something between Gavin and me? But what connection did our exchange have with whatever had occurred in the past, whatever it was they had fallen out over?

Hot colour burned in my cheeks. I had done nothing to encourage Gavin's attentions, yet I felt as guilty as if I had done just that, and strangely anxious to assure Louis it was not so.

'Has Uncle Gavin gone?' Antoinette's voice, coming from the staircase, sounded surprised and regretful.

'Yes,' I said. 'I think he has.'

'Oh – and I wanted to talk to him about Perdita!' Antoinette was pouting. 'Why did he have to go?'

Louis emerged from the parlour. He had clearly heard every word she had said.

'Your Uncle Gavin does not live here,' he said sourly. 'I'm afraid you will have to make do with Flora and me. Now, shall we eat? I've a busy afternoon ahead of me.'

He spoke with impatience. There was no sign now of the tenderness I had glimpsed earlier. The man who stomped ahead of us into the dining room was the same overbearing, driven one who had insisted I come to Belvedere, yet still there was the same strange fluttering in my heart as I looked at his straight, retreating back. For only a moment I had glimpsed a different side of him and it had called up a totally unexpected response in me, a response I must have already been feeling for him, deep inside, without realizing it.

Yet he was the man who had treated me so callously, so cruelly, with my father scarcely cold in his grave, the man who had robbed me of my home, the man who could refer to his dead wife with no emotion whatever, only icy dismissal. Why, there was even some mystery about her death, if Bevan was to be believed.

I must be going mad, I thought, to have feelings for such a

man. And I must take care to control them, or it did not bode well for the future.

After a somewhat strained meal, we went our separate ways, Louis riding off once more, Antoinette to her rooms, and I to the study, where the industrious Bevan was still poring over a ledger. I spent another hour or so familiarizing myself with the books until Bevan put down his pen and got rather stiffly to his feet.

'That's enough for one day, I think. I'm away home now. I'll be back in the morning, God willing.'

He put on his redingote, preparing to depart, and I could not see that I could do much more here without his assistance. I toyed with the idea of seeking out Antoinette, and perhaps suggesting a game of cards, for I thought she must be very lonely, but in the end, uncertain of the reception I would get, I decided against it. Perhaps it was best to leave her to make the first move. She had, after all, made it abundantly clear she did not want my company, and I felt too raw and vulnerable to risk another rebuff. Instead, I would go for a little walk and explore the grounds, I decided. Though cold, it was a pleasant enough afternoon, with the sun still shining palely. Those clouds I had seen this morning on the horizon seemed to have moved away and I felt I could do with a breath of fresh air.

The great house was very silent, very still. Only the clatter of pans coming from the kitchen, where, no doubt, Cook and the kitchen maids were preparing dinner, told me that I was not quite alone. I put on my cloak, then decided I would be wise to wear my gloves too if I did not want my fingers to freeze. I went up to my room to fetch them, opened the drawer where I had stowed them, and hesitated.

My things were not as I had left them. I had piled my garments neatly; now they were a little askew. Puzzled, scarcely able yet to believe that I was not mistaken, I opened another drawer, and another. Just like the glove drawer, the others looked as if they had been disturbed, so much so that the knick-knacks I had hidden beneath my petticoats were now poking out.

I frowned, no longer able to escape the conclusion that someone had been going through my things. And my father's snuff box and brushes had been moved too, I was certain of it.

Could it have been one of the maids? I wondered. But somehow I did not think so. The maids had been into my room every day since I had been here, tidying the bed (which I still made myself every morning, though I knew they expected me to leave it for them to do), dusting, sweeping, taking out the slops, but I had never noticed that my personal possessions had been interfered with in any way. The maids would, in any case, know that they would risk dismissal if they were found prying.

No, it was not a maid who had rifled through my belongings, I was almost certain of it. The most likely culprit, in my opinion, was Antoinette. It would be very like her to nose around when she thought I was safely out of the way, working with Bevan in the study. The thought made me angry. Bad enough to be forced to live in this strange, ill-tempered household, without having my privacy invaded in this way.

Well, she wouldn't get away with it. I'd have it out with her, and if she knew she had been found out, perhaps she would refrain from poking about in my room again.

I went in search of her. I had not yet been to her suite of rooms, but I knew which ones they were. Without stopping to take off my cloak, I marched along the passage and knocked on the double doors at the end.

There was no response. I knocked again, then turned the handle and looked in. The door opened into a small drawing room which had once, I thought, been her mother's private domain, for it was decorated in the pink which she appeared to have favoured. If anything, the decor was even more outrageously feminine than the other rooms, but Antoinette had made her mark on it too, with a row of dolls, long since abandoned, sitting lined up on the window seat. A bag of silks lay open on the small occasional table, a tapestry frame beside it. But of Antoinette there was no sign.

Beyond the drawing room was the bedchamber.

'Antoinette!' I called sharply. 'Are you there?'

She did not reply. And yet some sixth sense told me she was there.

'Antoinette!' I called again.

And this time I heard movement within the room, a scuffling sound. Then the window banged and a blast of cold air ruffled the open drapes at the dividing door.

I was across the drawing room in a flash, pushing aside that billowing drape, then stopping short in astonishment. Antoinette was there all right, standing in the centre of the room like a startled fawn. But someone was climbing out of the window! I just caught sight of a dark head before it disappeared from my view.

'What on earth . . . ?'

I started towards the window; Antoinette stood transfixed still. Just as I reached the window there was a tearing sound and a cry, followed almost immediately by a sickening thud. My heart leaped into my throat. I leaned out of the open window and saw a boy lying in a heap on the gravel walk beneath.

'Dear God . . . !'

As I stared down in horror, the boy picked himself up, gave a quick frightened glance up at the window, then began to run away with a limping gait. I just had time to take in ragged brown breeches and coat and a black and white mongrel at his heels before he disappeared around the corner of the house.

My first immediate reaction was relief that he was not badly hurt; great heavens, if he had fallen far he could have broken a leg or even his neck, and it would have been my fault! But close on the heels of relief came a wash of horror.

Antoinette had been entertaining a boy in her bedroom! And a pretty rascal at that, from the look of him. I swung round on her, noticing her flushed face and tumbled hair, seeing her hastily pulling the neckline of her gown back into place.

'Antoinette!' I challenged her. 'What has been going on here?'

'Nothing.' But her eyes were avoiding mine.

'Who was that boy?' I demanded. She was silent, and I asked again: 'Come now, who was it? And what was he doing here?'

She tossed her head, guilty but defiant.

'It was only John.'

'And who is John?'

'The gamekeeper's lad. He's my friend. We've been friends for as long as I can remember.'

'Indeed! And does your father know of this friendship?' I asked sharply.

She shrugged. 'My father isn't interested in what I do, or hadn't you noticed?'

'I am sure he would be very interested indeed to know you are entertaining this boy in your room!' I flashed. 'How could you think of such a thing, Antoinette?'

She bristled. 'I have to have friends! In the summer we meet outside, but when it's cold and wet . . . Sometimes we meet in the stables, but it's much more comfortable here.'

'So this is not the first time he has been to your room?'

'No.' She was defiant now, pleased with herself almost, as if my shock and outrage provided an additional thrill. 'He comes and goes by the creeper that grows up to the window.'

'Well I don't think he'll be doing it again,' I said.

She frowned. 'John does as he pleases. There's no one to tell him what he can and cannot do.'

'I think you will find you are wrong there, Antoinette. And in any case, much of the creeper was pulled away when he fell. It's going to be a long while before it's strong enough to take his weight again. Unless, of course, he is foolish enough to risk life and limb.'

She was silent, and I went on: 'How could you even think of entertaining a boy in your room? You must know it's wrong – and dreadfully foolish. Why, anything could happen . . .'

I broke off, colour creeping into my cheeks as I looked at her rumpled appearance, and remembered the protective way she had drawn the neck of her gown together as I entered the room. Antoinette might only be thirteen years old, but already she had the body of a woman, and there was a knowingness about her that far exceeded her tender years.

'You do know what I am referring to, don't you, Antoinette?'

'My reputation, I suppose,' she said airily. 'Well, that's of no interest to me whatsoever.'

'It will be,' I said, 'when you come to look for a husband and find no respectable man will give you a second glance.'

'Oh, I haven't the slightest intention of marrying, ever,' Antoinette declared. 'Why would I want to be someone's wife, and no better than his property? I'd much rather be just me, living here as Mistress of Belvedere.'

This was not the time, I thought, to point out to her that such a state of affairs could not be, that she was a girl, and when the time came the estate would pass into the hands of the closest male relative, whoever that might be, just as Tucker's Grave had passed to Louis. It was not for me to disillusion her, and in any case it had no bearing on what was concerning me – her present dangerous behaviour.

'It is not just your reputation that is at stake here, Antoinette,' I said. 'A boy in your bedroom may well lead to certain liberties, and those liberties to a most unwelcome outcome. I know you don't have a mother, and perhaps no one has explained this to you. But . . .'

'Oh, don't lecture me!' Antoinette snapped. 'Of course I know all about *that*. I've been brought up on a country estate, remember, surrounded by animals – and having no mother meant there was no one to make me turn away when they were breeding. In any case . . .' Those foxy eyes narrowed. 'What makes you think that I would find the result of my fun *unwelcome*? At least if I had a baby of my own I wouldn't be so lonely. At least I'd have someone to love!'

'Antoinette!' I was aghast. 'That is a dreadful thing to say! I'm lost for words!'

She smiled triumphantly. 'I've shocked you. Well, I don't care. It's no more than the truth. John is the only friend I have in the whole wide world.'

'I could be your friend!' I ventured, desperately sorry, suddenly, for the lonely little girl isolated here in her fairy-tale mansion.

'You?' she returned scornfully. 'What fun would you be? No

more than the governesses I used to have, or the stupid stuffy daughters of Papa's friends, whom he invites to stay sometimes as company for me. John and I have fun together!'

'Antoinette,' I said despairingly. 'You cannot have fun, as you call it, romping in your bedroom with the game-keeper's boy!'

'Oh, I don't just mean that! John knows everything – all the best places to go and the best things to do! He taught me to tickle a trout when I was just seven years old, and spin pebbles across the river, and make a swing in the trees. Every year he takes me to see the pheasant chicks when they are hatched, and . . .'

Her eyes were bright now, she might have been a child again, enthused with all the wonders of the natural world which might, without the friendship of this boy, have been denied her. But she was no longer a child and the scene I had surprised in her room had been, I feared, far from innocent.

I could see, however, that I was getting nowhere with my arguments, and really it was not my place to deal with this. Little as I liked the idea of it, Louis would have to be told. Really I could not imagine how he had allowed such an unsuitable friendship to develop in the first place!

'You realize I shall have to speak to your father about this,' I said.

She pursed her lips, tears shone suddenly in those foxy green eyes. For a moment I thought she would beg me to keep my silence, then she tossed her head as if she knew her pleas would fall on deaf ears. 'Oh, do what you like.'

I turned to go; as I reached the doorway, her voice stopped me. 'Why did you come to my room anyway?'

In all that had happened I had quite forgotten what it was that had brought me here. A little nosey-poking around amongst my belongings was trivial by comparison with what had been going on this afternoon in Antoinette's room! But since she had asked, I would tell her.

'I came to say that I know you have been meddling with my things,' I said. 'And to ask that you do not do so again.'

71

Her eyes widened. 'I haven't touched your things!'

'Please don't lie, Antoinette, on top of everything else,' I said tersely. 'I could tell at once they had been disturbed, for they were not replaced at all the way I had left them. I don't own a great deal, but what I do have is mine and I would appreciate you respecting my privacy.'

'I didn't touch your things!' Antoinette reiterated fiercely. 'It's all in your imagination, I expect. But if it's not – if someone really has been poking about amongst your possessions, I can assure you it was not me!'

She spoke with such forcefulness I was quite taken aback. But I did not want to have further argument with her now.

'Whatever you say, Antoinette,' I said wearily. 'All I hope is that whoever it was was satisfied with what they saw and will refrain from doing it again.'

Then, weary suddenly, I turned and hurried from the room.

I heard Louis return at about five thirty. Nervous but determined, I went downstairs and tapped on the drawing-room door.

Louis was standing before the fire, redingote tails raised to warm his legs at the blaze, just as he had that first day at the inn. He looked tired but undeniably handsome. My heart contracted a little – with anxiety for what I had to do – or something else . . . ?

'Flora?' He looked surprised to see me.

'I must speak with you,' I said.

His lips curved slightly upwards. 'About something serious, it would appear from your demeanour. If it's the argument you overheard this morning between Gavin and myself, I have to tell you that you were not the cause of it, whatever you may think. The differences between Gavin and myself far predate your coming here. Though it is true I do not trust him within a mile of any beautiful young lady.'

The colour rushed to my cheeks. So he *had* thought . . . And he had called me beautiful!

Somehow I composed myself. 'No, it's about Antoinette. But it is serious, I'm afraid.'

Louis sighed. 'I might have known it! Has she been rude to you again?'

'Far more serious than that. Quite a delicate matter in fact.' I hesitated. 'Did you know of Antoinette's friendship with a gamekeeper's boy by the name of John?'

Louis' face darkened. 'Is that still continuing? I have forbidden her to have anything to do with that young scoundrel. From the time they were children she has sneaked off to spend time with him. He's not suitable company for her, and leads her into all kinds of mischief.'

'Worse than mischief this time, I'm afraid to say.' I hesitated, steeling myself, then went on: 'This afternoon I found them together in her room. From what she said I don't think it's the first time. He comes and goes, it seems, by way of the creeper that climbs up around her window. When they realized they were about to be discovered, he made a hasty exit and fell, but apart from a twisted ankle, I don't think he did himself any serious injury. Certainly the last I saw of him he was running away.'

'He'll have a good deal worse than a twisted ankle by the time I've finished with him!' Louis said furiously. 'I've done my best for that family, giving John a job as soon as he was old enough to set a trap so that his mother would have some money coming in – she's a widow who lives in a cottage in the woods, and he's her only son. But enough is enough. If this is the way he abuses my patronage, I'll dismiss him tomorrow. As for Antoinette . . . I shall deal with her right away.'

My heart was in my mouth. I had had no choice, I knew, but to tell Louis of what was going on. But the consequences did not bear thinking about. A poor widow woman losing her only source of income was a very serious matter. She and the boy could starve because of me . . .

No, not because of me! I reminded myself. Because of his own actions. And in any case, it might not come to that. When he cooled down, Louis might decide to give the lad another chance on the understanding that he kept away from Antoinette.

My heart went out to her. What she had done was wrong, but she was very lonely.

'Don't be too hard on her,' I begged. 'I think she is desperate for company.'

'Of the wrong sort!' Louis retorted. 'I have done my best for her and she will have none of it. She treated her governesses with such disrespect they all left in no time, and the girls of her own age that I have brought here in the hope she may make friends, she has treated even more disgracefully. She put a toad in the bed of one of them, and frightened the poor girl out of her wits. She spilled ink all down the gown of another when they sat down together to write letters, and claimed it was an accident. She has made no attempt whatever to make friends of her own age and sex when the opportunity has been there for her – quite the opposite. She is determined to antagonize them.'

I bit my lip. Antoinette herself had admitted as much.

'And yet she seeks the company of this boy.' Louis was beside himself. 'Bad enough when she escaped to run wild with him like some peasant, but if she is now sneaking him into her room . . .' He broke off, looking at me with a hint of awkwardness. 'He wasn't . . .? They weren't . . . ?' Clearly, consideration for my feelings was preventing him from putting into words the question that was most worrying him.

'No,' I said, deciding to give Antoinette the benefit of the doubt. 'I saw nothing improper. But I do think you would be wise to make certain such a thing does not occur again. She may only be thirteen years old, but she seems, frankly, rather grown-up for her age in some ways, though in others she's still just a child. I do think that she might allow liberties, perhaps as some sort of rebellion, if the opportunity arose . . .'

For a moment Louis stood stock still, as if he had been turned to stone, and I wondered if I had gone too far in mentioning such a thing, though I had felt I had to. His face was like thunder, yet not simply anger but something like anguish. Then he turned away from me, bringing his fist down so hard on to the mantelshelf that all the china ornaments shook and the clock chimes reverberated with a shrill tinkling.

'So soon!' He was speaking softly, more to himself than to me. 'I knew it would happen one day. She's her mother's daughter, all right, in every way. But she's too young yet, too young! Oh, dear God, is it to begin all over again?'

His head bowed, his shoulders bent, Louis looked like a man reliving some private agony, and my heart went out to him. For although I did not know then what it was – did not know any of it beyond a few hints that were but a tiny part of the whole terrible story – I was sure of one thing.

If Louis sometimes appeared hard and unfeeling, if he sometimes looked as black as a thundercloud, it was because he had good cause.

And because he still lived in his own private hell.

Lisette

Louis had known, if truth be told, from the first moment he set eyes upon her, that Lisette du Bois could mean nothing but trouble and heartache for any man. At fifteen years old she was already too beautiful for her own good – and for that of any red-blooded male who came within the orbit of her bright star. She was tall, slender, with tumbling red-gold hair, slanting green eyes and the fine features of the noble family into which she had been born. But there was a knowingness in those eyes, a sensuality about her full lips, and a provocativeness, barely concealed behind an ostensibly demure manner, that was far beyond her years.

Louis saw it, and did not care. He was only eighteen years old himself, and so smitten by her that he could not think beyond the passion she aroused in him, the thundering of his blood in his veins, the ache of longing in his loins. He had never before seen anyone quite like her – the young women he had known paled into insignificance when compared with her – childish, prim, simpering, unexciting.

Sometimes, years later, when his ardour had cooled enough to allow him to think logically of that first meeting, he wondered if it had been engineered by his father with the express purpose of establishing an alliance with the French nobility, an entrée into the society which, for all his wealth and the success of his business enterprises, still eluded him. Peter Fletcher had always been an ambitious man – ambitious for himself and ambitious for his sons, so much so that he had cut himself off from the rest of his family, whom he considered bourgeois. He had married a French wife himself, but Jeanne, Louis' mother, was from the same social stratum as Peter himself, the daughter of a self-made merchant.

Lisette, on the other hand, was pure-born aristocracy, with links stretching unbroken to the court of King Louis XVI. Her family had estates in Normandy and a mansion on the Rue des Archives in Paris; in those years before the downtrodden masses rose in revolution they had power and riches almost beyond imagination.

It was at the chateau in Normandy that he first set eyes on her. His father had taken him to France to acquaint him with some of his business contacts there and he had found himself invited to a masked ball. It was not Louis' idea of entertainment; he preferred hunting or hawking by day and roistering by night in the little leisure time his father afforded him, and he had agreed to go with bad grace. He had felt ill-tempered as he changed into the finery he hated and was sullen on the drive to the chateau. As he entered the great hall, lit with chandeliers and decorated with banks of fresh flowers, he believed that all his worst fears had been realized, for all the revellers were a great deal older than him, the kind of fops and mincing ladies he most despised.

And then he saw her. She was coming down the great sweeping staircase on the arm of a slightly built man in a powdered wig, whom he took to be her father, but later discovered was, in fact, her uncle. She was a striking figure in a gown of buttermilk satin. The fichu dipped daringly low to expose the swell of small firm breasts, the skirt flowed full and graceful from a tiny waist. Her arms beneath the frothy sleeve frills looked small enough to be circled by a man's hand, her glorious hair tumbled about her bare shoulders and put every extravagantly adorned wig in the room to shame.

But it was her eyes that drew him most of all, those foxy green eyes that sparkled through the slits of her feathered mask. Louis stared, his heart beating a tattoo in his throat. At his side,

Peter smiled with smug satisfaction; this was working out exactly as he had planned. But Louis was totally unaware of it, even when his father murmured: 'Quite a beauty, my son, don't you agree?'

'Who is she?' Louis did not look at his father as he spoke. He could not tear his eyes away from the girl.

And Peter replied: 'Why, that is Lisette du Bois. I think, don't you, that we should arrange an introduction?'

Louis could only nod in silent, stunned agreement.

He danced with no one else the entire evening, and followed her with his eyes when she was whisked away to meet other guests. He drank champagne with her, mesmerized by those green eyes above the rim of her glass, enchanted by her giggle as the bubbles tickled her nose.

'This is the first time I have been allowed to attend a real grown-up ball,' she confided, and he was charmed by the glimpse of an unsophisticated child beneath the alluring woman.

The evening passed in a whirl for him; he was drunk on champagne – and lust. He wanted this girl more than he had wanted anything in his life, but she was a butterfly beyond his reach.

His last glimpse of her was on the arm of the same man who had escorted her down the sweeping staircase as they bid goodnight to their guests; when his turn had come she had kissed him demurely on both cheeks, but those mesmerizing eyes had tantalized him with an unspoken promise before she dipped her head coyly, as befitted a young lady of gentle breeding.

Louis did not notice the proprietorial sidelong looks of the man beside her, he did not notice the way his slender white fingers lay almost caressingly on her bare arm. Why should he? His gaze was for Lisette, and Lisette alone.

And he had no notion of what would take place when the musicians had finally packed away their strings and the last carriage had rolled away. Indeed, it would be many years before he learned the truth of the life Lisette led behind the elegant facade of the Chateau du Bois.

She had left her Uncle Armand drinking a last glass of champagne in the flower-decked bower off the great ballroom and climbed the staircase to the balcony that overlooked it. Her feet were sore from all the dancing and her ankles ached, for the heels on her new brocade shoes were higher than she had ever worn before. But she did not feel in the least tired, only exhilarated.

As she had confided to Louis, this had been the first grown-up ball she had attended – in the past she had been allowed only to peep at the grand proceedings, sitting out of sight on the floor of this very balcony and watching round-eyed through the balustrades – and she had enjoyed every moment of it. Wearing her new gown, basking in the appreciative glances, sipping champagne, dancing until she thought her feet would drop off, flirting outrageously from behind her feathered mask . . . and the young Englishman, Louis Fletcher.

Most of all, Louis Fletcher.

He was so handsome, so virile, so unlike any other man she knew. The English, of course, were noted for being roughnecks, a little uncouth even, compared to her refined, mannered, compatriots. She had heard they liked nothing better than to fight, be it a duel or a brawl, and certainly Louis had that hard edge of raw masculinity. It excited her and called to the wild fire in her blood that no amount of tutoring in the art of being a lady had been able to tame.

And he liked her too, she was certain of it. Something had sparked unspoken between them each time their eyes met, and excitement had shivered deliciously in the deepest parts of her. It shivered again now, just thinking of him, making her squirm with pleasure.

Lost in her dream world, she did not notice Uncle Armand approaching up the great staircase, and she jumped at his touch on her arm.

'Lisette . . .'

She spun round to see him standing beside her, a little too close for comfort. He was smiling at her, his lips curving downwards as they always did, so that his smile was not truly a smile but a smirk, and there was the lascivious look in his hooded eyes that she had learned to hate – and fear.

'So – how did you enjoy your first ball, ma chère?' he asked. His tone was silky.

'It was wonderful.' But the familiar feeling of being trapped like a rabbit in a snare was beginning in her gut, spoiling her pleasure.

'And it's not over yet.' His fingers began to stroke the soft skin on her forearm. Panic twisted within her once more.

'I am tired, Uncle.' She tried to move away, but his fingers tightened, restraining her.

'No, you are not, ma chère. You are wide awake and brim full of joie de vivre.'

'I *am* tired!' There was no coquetry in her eyes now, only pleading. 'I am going to bed.'

'Without showing me how grateful you are that I have allowed you such a memorable evening? Come, petite!' His arm went about her waist. 'I have had to watch you all night dancing with other men, smiling at them. You know how that made me feel? That boy, for instance. You liked him, did you not?'

'Yes, but . . .' She knew that to admit it would inflame him further, but she could not lie.

'He's just a boy!' The silky voice was low and scornful. 'He can never do for you what I do! What we share is special, is it not? All the more so because it is our secret.' He bent closer, whispering in her ear. 'You are my special girl, and I am your special uncle. Isn't that so?'

His hot breath against her bare throat made her flinch inwardly, but she no longer tried to pull away. It would be useless, just as it always had been.

'Yes,' she whispered back.

He took her hand, guiding it to the hard, swollen member which strained beneath the silk of his breeches.

'He does not have this for you, chérie. Because he does not love you as I do. Come now, no more talk of being tired. You shall sleep afterwards in my bed, between my silk sheets. And I will be there beside you, protecting you. Isn't that what has always made you happy, ever since you were a little girl?'

Her lip trembled; she caught it between her teeth, but she did not draw her hand away. Instead, she did what he had taught her over the long years since her parents had died and she had become his ward. Even before that, it had begun, when he had come to visit. One of her earliest memories was of him drawing her on to his knee, touching her intimately beneath her little gown, and encouraging her to touch him. And when she had come to the Chateau du Bois he had begun to go much, much further.

She had not liked it then and she did not like it now. But for all that, she associated it with security, and, because he had so often told her so, with love. And perversely, in view of the distaste she felt, she enjoyed the feeling of power that came after it was over. She had not felt that as a child, she had merely felt guilty and unhappy, but she felt it now. She could abstract herself from the disgusting touch of his milk-white hands, abstract herself from the acts he asked her to perform, look down as if she were floating on the ornately carved ceiling and see that this man who ruled her life was actually putty in her hands, made weak and helpless by his desire for her.

And tonight . . . tonight would not be so bad. She could close her eyes tonight and pretend she was lying, not with her uncle, but with Louis Fletcher.

'Come, my sweet Lisette.' Lust rasped in the silky-soft voice, and the hand about her waist slipped down to the firm swell of her buttocks.

He guided her up the stairs and along the vaulted corridor to the luxurious master suite he occupied.

The door shut after them.

It was almost a year before Louis saw Lisette again, and he had, truth to tell, almost forgotten her.

In the early days when he and his father had first returned to England, he had thought of her constantly, his blood stirring, his mind awhirl with the new sensations she had aroused in him. It was as if she had taken over his mind and his body, he dreamed of her at night, found her constantly in his thoughts by day, yearned with a fierce sharp intensity to see her again. The fascination she had excited in him would not be dimmed no matter what he did. When he hawked, he imagined her there beside him, watching in awe as his birds soared and struck. When he drank with his friends he saw her small nose wrinkling as the champagne bubbles tickled it. He heard her laugh in the wind, smelled the faint rose scent of her perfume on every summer breeze.

But as the weeks became months she began to recede. He thought of her less often, taking out the memory of her to savour rather than being obsessed by it, and by the time winter came he scarcely thought of her at all.

When, the following spring, his father told him that they had been invited to stay at the Chateau du Bois he was almost regretful, for that night seemed to him now a distant dream which would turn to dust if returned to reality. She would be less beautiful than he remembered, perhaps she would have a lover. Certainly he would be tongue-tied and foolish when faced with the girl who had so obsessed him.

'I think I would prefer not to go,' he said to Peter, and his father frowned.

'What's the matter with you? It's a great honour. Why don't you want to go?'

Louis avoided his father's eyes.

'It's not to my taste, the kind of life they lead. While the poor are starving, they spend a king's ransom on amusing themselves and living off the fat of the land.'

'That's no business of ours,' Peter said harshly. 'It's not for us to question their ways. And there may be great advantage in it for us.'

'I fail to see what,' Louis argued. 'It's not as if they are merchants we can strike deals with. They think themselves above that kind of thing.'

Peter snorted impatiently. He had no intention of spelling out to Louis the advantage he had in mind, and no intention of arguing further, either.

'I have already accepted the invitation,' he said tersely. 'We leave in a month's time.'

Louis tried one last tack.

'Why don't you take Gavin in my place? He'd enjoy it, I have no doubt.'

'I am sure he would,' Peter agreed, his mouth tightening. Already Gavin was showing signs of preferring to waste his time in the pursuit of pleasure instead of knuckling down to work in the way Peter would have wished. 'But Gavin is still too young to be an ambassador and I have no intention of indulging his liking for the easy life. It is you who has been invited, Louis, and it is you who will accompany me. Now, the matter is closed.'

And so it was that a reluctant and somewhat apprehensive Louis accompanied his father to France, and to the Chateau du Bois.

The moment he set eyes on Lisette, however, all the tumultuous feelings he had experienced the previous year came flooding back.

If anything, she was more beautiful than he remembered her, but of course, she was almost a year older, he reminded himself. Her little breasts had filled out to an enticing swell, her tumbling hair was now pinned up, revealing a slender neck which was somehow the more vulnerable for being exposed. Her lashes were darker than he remembered, her eyes just as green, just as tantalizing, her lips fuller and redder, though he could see no evidence of paint upon them.

But although she still laughed and teased, there was an edge that had not been there before, as if she were hiding some secret unhappiness. The child playing at being grown-up had gone, the woman who had taken her place had about her an air of mystery that not even the feathered mask had been able to confer upon her. Louis looked at her and forgot that he had not wanted to come here. He was unaware of anyone else in the room, tolerant suddenly of the foppish men and haughty women, even the Marquis du Bois, Lisette's uncle, though the man inspired in him a feeling of dislike. And he scarcely noticed the young girl, a new addition to the household, a slight, dark child of eleven or twelve who was introduced as another niece, come to live at the chateau. Once again, he had eyes only for Lisette.

As for her feelings for him, he simply could not be sure. Sometimes those eyes met his and challenged so that his heart beat a tattoo and breath constricted in his throat. Sometimes she seemed to ignore him so deliberately he was plunged into the depths of despair. She flirted most outrageously, he noticed, when her uncle was present, as if the game she played was more for her own amusement than for his benefit. And he was tossed about on a sea of emotion more wild than any storm the English Channel had thrown at the schooner on the voyages he had made across it.

On the fourth day they went riding together. Lisette, he discovered, was an expert horsewoman with a skill and daring that matched his own. As they galloped and raced, taking low hedges and ditches as though they were flying, all her artifice seemed to fall away as she laughed with exhilaration and kicked at her horse's flanks, urging the fleet little mare to an even faster pace. Once, her hat blew off, bowling ahead of the horses on a stiff breeze. Louis caught up with it, scooped it up on his riding crop and turned to watch as she caught up with him. Her cheeks were flushed, her eyes bright as emerald chips, her hair, no longer held in place by her cap, coming loose from its pins and blowing in long red-gold curls about her face.

'Your cap, ma'mselle.' He held it out to her but she made no effort to take it.

'You keep it for me. If I put it back on it will only blow off again.'

The velvet was smooth to his touch and warm from the heat of her head. He was only too glad to hold it, for the reins pressed the material against his palm so that he had an illusion of intimacy with its owner.

'Let's walk awhile,' she said. 'I want to talk to you. We've never really talked, have we? Though, truth to tell, I haven't much breath left. You will have to be the one to do the talking.'

Panic assailed him; he could not think of a single thing to say.

She laughed, low in her throat.

'Come on now, don't be shy. And you cannot pretend your silence is because your French is not good enough. You speak it every bit as well as I do.'

'Because my mother is French,' he said. 'My brother and I were both raised to use one language as fluently as the other. It satisfied both my mother's pride in her native country and my father's ambition for us to be able to hold our own with the French merchants and not be cheated through a lack of understanding.'

'Ah!' she said. 'Now tell me, is England as rough as they say it is? I've never been there, and I want to know all about it.'

'I think you should visit then,' Louis said, bold suddenly. 'I shall ask my father to invite you.'

Her eyes met his, teasing, challenging.

'I would much rather, Louis, that the invitation came from you.'

The horses were walking shoulder to shoulder; she was close, so close to him, and yet so far away.

'Of course it comes from me,' he said. 'I would like nothing better than to show you England, Lisette.'

And so much more besides, he added silently.

They had reached the edge of a small copse, bordered by a stream. The horses slowed to a halt, looking longingly at the cool clear water that ran there. Louis dismounted in a quick fluid movement; Lisette followed suit.

'The horses are thirsty, and so am I.'

She twisted the reins loosely around an overhanging branch, went upstream of the horses and dropped on to her knees on the lush grass. As she scooped water into her cupped hands and drank, Louis knelt beside her, doing the same. The water was icy cold and tasted sweeter than any wine. He savoured it, and as his parched throat grew cooler, the blood in his veins ran more hotly.

He looked at her, kneeling there, the water sparkling in droplets on her flushed face, and the longing for her grew stronger than his fear of rejection.

'Here . . . let me . . .' He drew a kerchief from his pocket and reached out to dab the droplets from her cheeks. Her face was tilted towards him, her lips full and pursed, just right for the kissing. He framed her chin with his hands, holding it steady, met that tantalizing gaze with his own. Their faces were now just inches apart; desire twisted deep within him.

'Lisette . . . I want you so.' His voice was rough. But she did not try to turn away.

'I know,' she whispered.

His body ached for her, the blood thundered in his ears with the gentle song of the stream as it gurgled over the pebbles and washed against the low banks.

Slowly, as if in a dream, he drew her towards him until their mouths hovered and touched. And the spell was broken and there was nothing left but urgency and overwhelming need. Her mouth tasted sweet like the spring water, her lips were soft beneath his, then moving with the same hungry need, parting, pressing, sucking. His tongue went between them, hers moved against it in a response he had not dared to expect.

'Oh Lisette, Lisette . . .'

Their bodies were now as close as their faces; pleasure sparked like lightning before a storm as they fell back together into the moist grass, intent only on satisfying the crying need that overwhelmed them.

He scrabbled up her skirts and petticoats; her thighs, long, slender, soft, parted to his touch. She writhed beneath him like a small frantic animal, rearing her hips to his. With a groan he freed himself of his breeches, burying his throbbing hardness in the soft place where his fingers had touched, and quite suddenly he felt her stiffen beneath him, pushing him away.

'No! No!'

It was too late; he could not stop now. He drove into her;

with a few frantic strokes it was over. For a moment the intensity of it blinded and deafened him; he lay upon her heavy, spent, unmoving. Then the enormity of what he had done began to impinge upon his consciousness, a thin disturbing trickle that quickly gathered into a flood.

He rolled away from her and sat up. She lay still on the grass, her face wet now, not with spring water, but with tears. The neck of her gown gaped, her skirts, still bunched about her hips, revealed thighs that glistened with his seed. He reached over to pull them down.

'Lisette, I am so sorry! What can I say?'

She stared up at the sky, her lower lip caught between her teeth, and still the tears escaped the corners of her eyes and trickled down her cheeks.

The guilt was a knife thrust in his heart.

'I've hurt you and dishonoured you. What sort of a wretch am I to treat you so?'

She shook her head slowly. 'Don't blame yourself, Louis. It was not your fault.'

'Of course it was!' he grated angrily. 'You told me no, and still I . . .'

'No!' She moved at last, sitting up and laying a hand on his arm. 'No – you did what any man would do. The fault is mine, all mine. There are things about me that you do not know . . .'

For some reason her willingness to accept her share of the blame angered him. She was a sixteen-year-old innocent. He was a man of nineteen and old enough to know better. Yet he had taken advantage of her as if she were some tavern wench or woman of ill repute. The responsibility for what had occurred was his and his alone.

'There is no excuse for me!' he said angrily. 'I've wanted you, yes, I admit it, from the first moment I set eyes on you. But I should have been able to control my urges. This is not the way it should be, taking you like a dog takes a bitch on heat. Faith, if your uncle knew what I have done . . .'

She turned her head away; he did not see the look in her eyes at the mention of her uncle.

'How can you ever forgive me?' he asked, and it was a cry of anguish.

High in the trees a wood pigeon fluttered, the beating of its wings loud in the stillness of the afternoon; the horses shifted their feet and flicked their ears against a swarm of midges.

'Why did you do it?' Lisette asked softly.

Louis threw back his head and groaned.

'Oh Lisette! Because I wanted you, of course. You are the loveliest, most desirable woman I have ever known.'

'And for no other reason?' Her voice was soft, urgent, full of pleading.

'What other reason could there be?'

And then, quite suddenly, he knew what she was asking him. She was offering him an excuse – a reason for his unpardonable behaviour. He took it.

'Because I love you,' he said.

He had never spoken those words to anyone before, nor thought he could. *I love you* was a baring of the soul he had thought beyond him. 'Love' was not a word in his vocabulary, it was a word for women and fops. Even obsessed with her as he had been, *love* had not entered his head. Now, as he said it, to please her and to assuage his guilt, he realized with a sense of shock that it was the truth.

He loved her. Loved her with a fierce, bright, all-consuming love he had never felt for anyone before, and doubtless never would again. And it was so much more than the physical need that had recently consumed him. It was delight in her presence, desolation when she was out of his sight. It was a desire to cherish and protect her, make her happy, keep her safe. And he had betrayed all that with his impetuosity, his disastrous loss of self-control. He bowed his head, his shoulders bent beneath the weight of regret and guilt and self-disgust.

Lisette touched his cheek, her fingers tracing the line of his jawbone. Startled, he looked up. She was gazing at him intently.

There were no longer tears in her eyes, and her mouth had curved into a small satisfied smile.

'You love me?' she asked softly.

'God help me, I do. And now, fool that I am, I have ruined everything.'

She leaned over, touching her lips to the line her finger had traced.

'No,' she whispered, her breath warm against his skin. 'I am the one who spoiled it. I am a very foolish little girl.'

The tenor of her voice was almost childish, lending emphasis to her strange choice of words, but Louis did not notice. He was aware only of the first stirring of hope – and renewed desire. She twined her arms round his neck, pressing her face against his, looking at him coquettishly from the corner of her slanting eyes. She moved on to his lap, rucking up her skirts once more as she did so, moving sensuously against him as, against his will, he grew and hardened once more. She nibbled his lips, her teeth sharp as a puppy's, and tangled her fingers in his hair.

'Shall we begin again?' she whispered.

Louis was powerless to resist.

She came to his bed that night, creeping down the corridor when the house was silent and sleeping. Though he was lying awake, his head too full of all that had occurred that day to even drowse, he heard nothing but the click of the door latch, startlingly loud in the stillness, and then the shift of the mattress as she pulled aside the covers and slipped into the great feather bed beside him.

'Lisette?' he murmured, startled, as she curled her warm body around his. 'What . . . ?'

She put her fingers to his lips. 'Hush! Do you want to waken the whole house?'

'You should not have come to my room!' he whispered. 'If your uncle should find you here . . .'

'He won't. He has other things on his mind.' There was bitterness in her tone, but it did not occur to him to wonder what she meant by it. He could think only of lithe arms twisting round his body, long slender legs tangling with his, a mane of soft scented hair spreading across his bare shoulder and tickling his nose. Her shift was finest lawn; when he touched her breasts the buds of her nipples rose erect against it, as clearly defined as if she had been naked.

She straddled him, moving with a sensuous grace that surprised him, then sliding down and taking him into her mouth. He did not stop to wonder where she had learned such tricks, he was too intoxicated to think for even a moment that her behaviour was more that of a practised courtesan than a sixteen-year-old girl who had, presumably, been a virgin until he had deflowered her today. She was simply Lisette, provocative, enchanting, from a different world and a different culture, elusive as an exotic butterfly, sensuous as a kitten.

When it was over she nuzzled into his neck, one leg lying carelessly across his.

'You never did tell me about England.'

'No, but I promised to show it to you.'

'When?'

'As soon as you want. I'll speak to my father about it, and . . .'

'I don't know if Uncle Armand would allow it,' she said. 'He might not think it proper for a young lady to travel alone.'

Louis almost laughed aloud. Here she was in bed with him, doing things he had scarcely dreamed of, and she talked of what might be considered improper!

'I think it might be permissible, though, if I was going to be your wife,' she said, and he was quite oblivious to the calculation in her tone.

'My wife?' he repeated, startled.

'Mm. I think, Louis, that you should ask me to marry you. Especially now . . .' She trailed a fingernail across his stomach.

His heart was pounding against his ribs. This was all happening too fast. It felt unreal. And yet . . .

There was nothing, Louis knew, that he wanted more. He could not bear the thought of leaving Lisette in France; if the only way to keep her with him was to marry her, so be it.

'Will you marry me, Lisette?' he asked.

She pressed her lips to his throat, purring like a little cat. 'Oh Louis, yes!'

ii

He expected opposition, encountered none. His father beamed with pleasure; it was, after all, what he had hoped for from the outset. Armand du Bois gave his blessing readily. Jeanne Fletcher shed tears of joy when her son returned home with the news that she was to have not only a daughter-in-law but a compatriot in her household. The only sour note was injected by Gavin.

'You are a fool, Louis,' he said bluntly.

'That is a harsh judgement, since you have not even set eyes on Lisette,' Louis responded.

'What she looks like has nothing to do with it. There's not a woman in the whole of Christendom that would talk me into marriage. Where's the sense in being shackled to just one, who will doubtless turn into a shrew, when there's a whole garden of rosebuds for the picking?'

'Because she is the only one I want,' Louis said.

Gavin laughed. 'For now, maybe. You'll change your tune before long, just mark my words. And you'll live to regret wedding her in such haste. Like I said, brother, you're a fool – and it's this Lisette who's made you one.'

Louis turned away. He did not want to quarrel with his brother, though that was all too easy. They were chalk and cheese – he had no time for Gavin's feckless ways, and Gavin was scornful of his industry. As small boys they had fought on countless occasions, rolling over and over in the dirt until their clothes were muddied and torn and their bodies battered and bruised. Now it was verbal conflict only, but no less virulent for that. And he did not want his happiness marred by Gavin's spiteful interference.

He had thought the marriage would take place in France, but

since Lisette had no mother or close female relative to help her with the preparations, it was decided that it would instead be at Belvedere.

Lisette arrived, accompanied by a lady's maid, and Jeanne took her under her wing, arranging for the finest seamstress in Plymouth to come down with patterns and fabric samples for the wedding dress, and planning what would be the grandest reception ever held in the district.

Louis had looked forward eagerly to her arrival; every day without her had seemed like a lifetime. But their reunion was not quite what he had hoped for. There was a distance about her, a remoteness, that disappointed him when he greeted her, and as the days went by, caused him a certain uneasiness.

Perhaps, he thought, the journey had upset her. Certainly she had admitted to being dreadfully seasick on the crossing. But the maladie de mer usually passed quickly once the rocking of the boat ceased. Perhaps she was homesick, then. But she had been so eager to come to England, and for good, and had not voiced a single regret for leaving France. In fact, it had almost been as if she had wished to escape . . .

The thought, when it came to him, was a most unwelcome one. Could it be that Lisette had some other motive than love in wishing to be wed to him – boredom with her life at the chateau, perhaps, so that marriage and England had seemed an adventure to her, a means of escape? Did she now look back with longing to the chateau which had felt like a prison when she had lived there, and see only a haven she had lost for ever?

Louis decided he must ask her. Though the thought that she might have changed her mind was an unbearable one, he could not force her to go through with this if she was now unhappy about it. He loved her too much.

Since her arrival they had been alone together very little, for it seemed that Jeanne had appointed herself chaperone as well as marriage arranger, and in some respects Louis was glad of it. He had made up his mind there must be no more love-making until they were man and wife, but he was not sure whether he could trust himself to keep his vow when simply looking at Lisette aroused his body and inflamed his senses. But he had to speak with her in private, and soon, for the arrangements were rolling along apace and dragging bride and groom along in their wake.

His chance came one afternoon when his father and Gavin were both out on business and his mother entertaining visitors in her drawing room. When they had first arrived, Lisette had gone to the drawing room so that Jeanne could make the introductions, but a little while later she must have made her excuses, for looking out of the window he saw her in the rose garden, alone.

He put aside the books he had been working on and went outside. It was a beautiful June afternoon, the warm sun drawing heady perfume from the heavy blooms that covered the rose bushes, but Louis scarcely noticed. He saw only Lisette, sitting forlornly on the small rustic bench in the arbour. She glanced up as he approached, and his heart sank as he saw that her eyes were bright with tears.

'Chérie?' he said huskily. 'Is something wrong?'

'Louis!' She looked away for a moment, blinking hard, and when she turned her face towards him once more she was smiling, a brittle, forced smile. 'What could be wrong?'

'I don't know,' he said, 'but something is.'

She laughed shortly. 'Just because I don't care to sit in the parlour drinking tea with your Mama's tedious friends . . .'

'No,' he said. 'It's more than that, and it's not just this afternoon. You are unhappy about something, Lisette. Is it that you have decided you don't want to marry me after all?'

There. It was said.

For a moment she sat motionless, her green eyes very far away. He waited, heart in mouth. Then: 'Whatever makes you say such a thing, Louis?'

'Because . . . you are different. And I can't help wondering if perhaps you have had a change of heart.

'Have you?' she asked, her eyes very sharp suddenly.

'No, of course not! I want nothing more than that you should be my wife! But . . .'

She drew a deep breath. 'And that is what I want too. Only

does it have to be such a grand affair? Why can't we just run off somewhere and be wed in secret?'

The great rush of relief he felt to know she was not going to jilt him was quickly followed by confusion.

'But I thought every girl dreamed of being a bride.'

'Of being stared at like a heifer going to market, you mean! And I can't bear all these fittings, and discussions about arrangements. Oh, couldn't we go to the priest, just you and me, and . . . ?'

'Oh Lisette!' There was nothing that would suit him better but his father and mother – his mother, especially – would never forgive them, he knew, if they were cheated out of this great occasion. 'I really think we are going to have to do things properly, for others, if not for ourselves.'

'Oh!' She pursed her lips. 'Well, I knew you'd say that.'

'It's not what I'd choose either,' he tried to console her. She ignored him.

'There's another thing, too. I don't like the way your brother looks at me.'

'Gavin? Oh, take no notice of Gavin! He doesn't agree with me being wed . . .' He broke off, realizing from the look on her face that he had misunderstood her meaning. 'He's jealous, I expect,' he added lamely. 'Gavin has an eye for the fair sex. And you are a very beautiful girl. You must be quite used to men admiring you.'

'That doesn't mean I have to like it,' she said, and again he was puzzled. Lisette seemed to blossom when she attracted admiring looks; he had rather thought she enjoyed the attention she attracted, and maybe a little more than she should.

'He looks at my maid, too,' she went on, 'and it will go further than looking soon, if I'm not much mistaken.'

'That wouldn't surprise me,' Louis conceded. 'Mariette wouldn't be the first servant to take Gavin's eye. But if it's upsetting you, I'll speak to him about it. Not that I think he'll take much notice of me. Gavin does as he pleases, I am afraid, and he certainly has no great respect for me.'

'Well, I hope he doesn't ruin her, that's all. I should hate to be without Mariette.' She was silent for a moment, then she sighed, reached out and took his hand. 'Oh, I suppose I shall just have to endure this grand wedding,' she said resignedly. 'At least then *I* shall be respectable, shall I not?'

Was that it, then? She thought that *he* had ruined *her*, and she had no choice but to marry him?

'You are not with child, are you?' He could scarcely bring himself to ask it, but he knew he must.

She laughed suddenly, becoming once again the enchanting girl he had fallen in love with.

'Of course not! Oh Louis, I tell myself every day how lucky I am that you love me and I am to be your wife. No one ever cared for me as you do. They want me, yes, as Gavin does, but they are not kind to me. They don't love me as you do.'

She pulled him down on to the bower seat, twining her arms about him.

'You won't discard me when you grow tired of me, will you? Please promise me you won't do that!'

'Never.' He held her, kissed her, keeping a tight rein on his mounting desire to do more, far more.

She was an enigma. An entrancing puzzle, with moods like quicksilver, and really he did not know her at all. But she did not want to renege on her promise. In a few weeks' time she would be his wife. Nothing else really mattered at all.

They were married in the Catholic church in Dartmouth, the same church where Jeanne went every Sunday and Holy Day for Mass.

Armand du Bois travelled from France to give Lisette away, and with him came the young girl who now lived at the chateau. She was to be Lisette's only attendant, clad in a gown of blue watered silk that had been made for her in France especially for the occasion, since she could not attend for fittings in England. Lisette was cool with her, considering they were cousins, Louis thought, but then, truth to tell, Lisette was cool with all members of her own sex, and men, too, unless it pleased her to be otherwise. But he was not going to dwell on that today.

Lisette looked utterly beautiful – a vision in pewter-grey watered silk. She had decided to forego the more traditional white because she thought it would not go so well with her colouring – or that, at least, was what she said. Louis had paused to wonder if the reason might be because she felt she would be betraying the symbolism – white was for a virgin, and she and he both knew that was something she was not. But whatever her reasons, the choice was stunning, enhancing the whiteness of her skin, complementing the red-gold of her hair. The design, too, was voluptuous – the silk moved sensuously with every movement of her body, and the matt surface of the silk caught the light of the church candles, giving sudden unexpected depths and highlights.

And Lisette was radiant too, sparkling, and if there was a brittleness to that sparkle, it was still bright as the hoar frost on a sharp winter morning. She made her vows in a firm, clear voice that could be heard in every corner of the church, her green eyes never leaving Louis for a moment.

When they emerged from the church to a shower of rose petals and congratulations, his heart was soaring, the pride swelling within him. Lisette was his wife now. He was the luckiest man alive. And he would make her happy. Whatever demons within her were the cause of her troubled moods, he would exorcise them with his love. All their lives lay before them. On his wedding day, at least, Louis had no presentiment of the torments to come.

They had been married just a few short weeks when Lisette told him she was expecting a child. Louis was both surprised and delighted.

'Are you sure?'

She nodded. 'Yes. Yes, Louis, I am sure. But oh . . .' Her small face was serious, there was no joy in her eyes. He was consumed with concern for her.

'Don't be afraid, chérie. You'll have the best doctor in Devon to attend you, I'll make sure of that.'

Her chin came up proudly. 'Oh, I'm not afraid!'

'Of course you are. It's only natural.'

'I am not afraid!' she returned fiercely.

He frowned. 'What is it then?'

She bunched her fists in the folds of her gown; tears sparkled on her dark lashes.

'I don't want to have a baby! Not yet! I'll grow fat and ugly and you won't want me any more.'

He put his arms around her. 'That is nonsense, chérie! I'd never think you ugly, especially when you are carrying our child. And I certainly won't stop wanting you.'

She bit her lip. 'Not even if . . .'

'What?'

She pulled away, turning her back on him. 'Nothing. I don't want this child, Louis. Don't you know anyone who can help me?'

'Help you? What do you mean, Lisette?'

'There must be an old woman in the village who knows about these things. Someone who could rid me of it, and no one ever know.'

He was appalled. 'Faith, you can't mean it! You cannot seriously wish to rid yourself of our child!'

She spun round to face him once more. 'I am perfectly serious! I can't go through with it! It will spoil everything!'

For the first time in his life, Louis felt a surge of anger towards her.

'You don't know what you are saying!' he ground out.

'And you don't know what it will mean!'

'I know very well. You would have an innocent baby – our baby – torn from your womb – murdered – at God knows what risk to yourself, just because you don't want to be fat for a few months? I can't believe you can even think of such a thing, let alone suggest it!'

The tears spilled over and ran down her cheeks. For once, he was unmoved by them.

'Truly, Lisette, I am shocked.'

'But Louis . . .'

'No!' He raised his hand, clenched it to a fist, and slapped it against his thigh. 'I won't hear another word. This is a terrible thing you are suggesting. Don't even think of trying to do away with the child. If you do, I swear I will never forgive you.'

Her shoulders bowed, her chin dropped to her chest, her hands clasped one another for comfort in the folds of her skirt. She looked, he thought, more forlorn than he had ever seen her.

'You are a Catholic, Lisette,' he said more gently. 'You must know human life is sacred.'

'And this is a sin.' She spoke so softly, her voice muffled in the flounce of her gown, that he could scarcely make out her words.

'What are you talking about?' he asked, bewildered. 'How can a child born of our love be a sin? Oh, perhaps we were wrong not to wait until we had the blessing of the Church before we demonstrated our love for one another, but it happens all the time, and no priest would condemn us for it, I'm sure, now that we have regularized our union before God. Go to confession, if you must, and I am confident the priest will tell you the same.'

Still she made no move and he drew her into his arms.

'The babe was not conceived before our marriage in any case, was it, or you would have known before now. So please, stop torturing yourself like this! Think of the happiness a little one will bring! A boy for me to teach to hawk and shoot, or a girl as demure yet full of mischief as you – and perhaps with curls like yours too! I swear, Lisette, when you hold our baby in your arms you will forget every one of these foolish doubts and thank God for such a blessing, for there is not a woman alive who could fail to love the child she must nourish and protect and give life to.'

'I won't,' Lisette muttered mulishly. 'I suppose I shall have it if I must. But I tell you, Louis, I don't want it. Now or ever.'

For all that he had warned her against it, Louis was very afraid Lisette might do something to try and rid herself of the unwelcome new life that was growing within her. But if she did, her efforts met with no success. Soon her breasts were fuller, and her belly more rounded, and it was clear for all to see that she was with child.

There were no more outbursts over her condition, but there was no joy either. Lisette seemed to have resigned herself to the fact that she was to be a mother, whether she liked it or not, but she could not bring herself to see it as a happy event, and the continuation of her black mood worried Louis and spoiled his own pleasure in the prospect of becoming a father.

'Does this happen sometimes?' he asked his own mother one day when Lisette's mood seemed blacker than ever. 'Can a woman really have no feelings for the child she is carrying?'

'Well of course!' Jeanne reassured him. 'It's common, I'm sure, amongst girls who fear they have been ruined, though I've not often seen it, I must admit, in a happily married woman. But Lisette is very young. She does not feel ready to leave her carefree youth behind, I expect. And she has been very unwell, has she not? It's not a pleasant thing to feel nauseous all the time. Very lowering for the spirits.'

'That's true enough,' Louis agreed.

Certainly Lisette seemed very unwell. She was pale as a ghost, her face seeming to grow thinner as her body swelled. But the malaise seemed to be worsening as the weeks went by rather than passing, as it usually did after a while.

'Don't worry, my son,' Jeanne said. 'I am sure when she holds her baby in her arms she will feel more love than she ever knew herself capable of.'

With all his heart Louis hoped she was right, but he was not so sure. Jeanne had not been party to Lisette's despair on the day she had told him she was with child; Jeanne had not witnessed her weeping in her sleep. Louis was very much afraid that Lisette's opposition to becoming a mother was rooted in something far deeper.

With some four weeks to go until her due date, Lisette went into labour. Louis was filled with alarm when he found her in her drawing room groaning and doubled over with pain.

'But it's not time yet!' he protested weakly.

As the spasm passed Lisette straightened, though her hands still clutched her stomach where the pain had seemed ready to tear her apart. 'Time or not, it's coming, Louis!'

'But . . . it shouldn't be! Go to bed, Lisette, lie down, and maybe all will be well.'

'Oh, don't be a fool!' she spat at him. 'And don't think you can make it go away just standing there and looking, either! You had better go for the midwife, and fast . . .'

She broke off, gasping, as another pain knifed through her, and Louis experienced a gush of panic.

'All right, all right . . . I'll ride for the midwife. I'll get my mother too . . .'

With one last frightened look at the small agonized face he loved so much, he ran from the room, fearful the baby was about to make its appearance into the world before his very eyes.

He need not have been in such haste. When he returned with the midwife – who was none too pleased to have been dragged so unexpectedly and so unceremoniously from preparing her family's dinner – she took one look at Lisette and announced that it would be hours yet, and she could have eaten, as well as finished cooking, her bit of beef before she was needed.

'You cannot leave her now!' Louis protested, appalled.

'I suppose I might as well stay now, as I'm here,' Mistress Cope replied sourly. 'But there'll be extra on my bill for a spoiled dinner.'

'Money is the least of my worries,' Louis snapped. 'Just take care of my wife, if you please!'

Mistress Cope was proved correct in her assessment. It was almost twenty-four hours later, and she had partaken of two good meals and even dozed a little in the chair beside Lisette's bed, before she emerged with the news.

'You've a fine strapping daughter.'

Louis, who had been pacing the floor, agonized by the screams and cries that had echoed through the house for hours, gripped her by the arm.

'Lisette is well?'

'Well enough to make enough noise to waken the dead,' Mistress Cope said scathingly. 'I've never known a Devon girl to make such a fuss.'

'And the baby?' He was still anxious, considering that his child had been born a month before her time.

'Strapping, like I said. She doesn't look like a poorly eight-month babe to me.' Mistress Cope was rolling down her sleeves to cover her brawny forearms. 'You'd better go in and see your wife and daughter.'

Lisette was lying back, exhausted, against the pillows, the baby in a tiny crib which Mistress Cope had placed at the side of the bed.

'Chérie!' Louis crossed the floor in a few hasty strides, wanting only to take Lisette in his arms, but afraid to touch her in case he hurt her. 'Oh chérie, are you . . . ? Was it . . . ?'

'It was terrible,' Lisette murmured weakly. 'Oh Louis, I don't want to have to go through that ever again!'

'It's over now,' he soothed. 'And we have a little daughter.'

For the first time he looked into the crib, at the small, angry red face and the downy head dented all around the temples as if a tourniquet had been applied to the soft baby skin. Wonder filled him, that this child could be his – his and Lisette's, the living proof of their love.

'She's perfect,' he said softly.

Lisette was silent.

'Don't you want to hold her?' he asked.

She shook her head, still silent.

'Come,' he murmured. 'She looks to be in need of her mother.'

'Oh, that's what that grizzly old midwife said!' Lisette snapped. 'I don't want to hold her. Leave me alone, can't you? I'm tired and sore and I want to rest.'

Louis' heart sank, his relief and joy overshadowed as if a black cloud had crept across the sun.

'Rest then,' he said gently.

She closed her eyes. A single tear escaped and rolled down her cheek. He wiped it away tenderly.

'You are exhausted, chérie. You'll feel differently tomorrow.'

She said nothing, but in her silence he sensed the stubbornness which he now knew was an intrinsic part of her make-up.

He bent and kissed her forehead, still damp with perspiration and the cool water with which the midwife had sponged her.

'I love you, Lisette.' The words came easily to him now. 'I love you and I always will, no matter what. Never forget that.'

She opened her eyes, looking up at him, reached out and took his hand, her fingers curling around his with the same fierce grip that a drowning man might use to clutch at a piece of drift-wood. The expression on her face bewildered him, so many emotions seemed to be mingling there, flickering across her lovely delicate features. But the look in her eyes might almost have been one of utter despair.

'I am so sorry, Louis,' she whispered.

'For what?' he asked gently.

'For being what I am.'

'Lisette, you are talking nonsense,' he chided. 'Sleep now. We'll talk when you are rested.'

'Will you stay with me?' she asked.

'Of course I will.'

The baby began to wail, a thin soft mewling; Lisette seemed oblivious to it. Mistress Cope came bustling in, and he spoke to her over his shoulder.

'Can you take the baby out so as not to disturb Madame? She needs to rest.'

The woman sniffed disapprovingly but she did as Louis asked.

Dusk was falling, muzzing the room with soft greyness. Lisette slept, and still Louis sat there, holding her hand in his and praying that tomorrow, when she was refreshed, Lisette would see things differently. And fearing, with an awful sense of foreboding, that she would not.

Louis was right to be afraid. The morning, grey, overcast, and thick with a mist off the river, did nothing to bring with it a change in Lisette's attitude. She did not want her baby. She did not want to hold it. She certainly did not want to feed it. The baby cried pitifully, and Lisette turned her face to the pillow and covered her ears.

'Make it stop! I can't stand that awful wailing! Make it stop, or I swear I'll go mad!'

'She's hungry, poor little mite!' Rose, the maid who had been engaged for nursery duties, protested. 'Put her to the breast, Madame, and she'll be satisfied and fall asleep.'

'I won't! I don't care if she starves! I won't do it!'

Jeanne was sent for; she spoke to Lisette for a long while in French, first cajoling, then becoming angry, but all her entreaties fell on deaf ears. Lisette was becoming so distressed, in fact, that her face flushed unhealthily whilst her body tremored, and Jeanne began to fear she would succumb to the fever that could follow childbirth and even claim the life of a new mother.

'We'll have to find a wet nurse then,' she said at last, conceding defeat. 'Is that what you want?'

And: 'Do what you like. I don't care!' Lisette cried.

When she emerged from the bedchamber, Jeanne rounded on Louis.

'Didn't you have any inkling of the way she felt?' she demanded. 'I know it's not a nice thing to discuss, but if I had been warned she had this aversion to feeding the child herself I could at least have made arrangements. As it is, we shall have to send into town, with everyone knowing our business, and hope some woman can be found who is willing and able to do what Lisette should be doing herself. I don't know what we'll do if no one is forthcoming. We can try cow's milk, I suppose, or flour and water, but babies don't thrive on it – in fact, many die. I've told her that, and it seems she doesn't care.'

'Shall I speak to her?' Louis suggested, and Jeanne shook her head.

'Better not. She's in no fit state. If the fever takes hold she could die, and then where would we be? No, the best thing you can do is saddle a horse, ride into town, and seek out a wet nurse. But it doesn't bode well, Louis. I don't like the attitude Lisette is taking one bit. It's not natural for a mother to be so indifferent to her own newborn child.'

'She's weak and ill. She'll come around when she's stronger,

103

I'm sure,' Louis said, making excuses for Lisette though he did not believe them himself.

'When the milk comes in and she's throbbing and uncomfortable, you mean,' Jeanne said grimly. 'Well, I suppose we must hope for the best. But I've never seen anything like it in my life.'

Beside himself with anxiety both for Lisette and his baby, Louis rode into Dartmouth, where, fortunately, he was able to secure the services of a wet nurse. She was not what Louis would have chosen in a woman to suckle his child, a big, raw-boned woman with a large family of her own, and who smelled disgustingly of fish, but at least she had plenty of milk, and when the little one had fed greedily, she fell asleep and the terrible insistent mewling ceased.

The days went by and as the danger of fever passed Lisette grew stronger. But still she showed no sign of changing her hard-hearted attitude towards her child.

'We have to name her,' Louis said, sitting on the edge of the bed and holding Lisette's hand. 'We can't call her "the babe" for ever.'

Lisette shrugged and looked away, uninterested. 'Call her what you like.'

'A French name I think, don't you?' he wheedled, desperate to elicit some response. 'After all, you are French, and so is Mama, and I have a French name myself. There must be something you like. Thérèse, perhaps? Or Jeanne, after my mother?'

For just a moment, something stirred in those hard green eyes.

'Antoinette,' she said.

'Antoinette? You like that name?'

'Yes. Yes, I do.'

A frisson of hope flickered within him.

'Antoinette.' He looked at the baby, sleeping rosy and replete in the crib beside the bed. 'Yes, I think that suits her very well.'

'Yes,' Lisette said. 'I think it does.'

It was the only contribution she was prepared to make.

iii

Louis passed through stages in his feelings concerning Lisette's continuing lack of interest in Antoinette in much the same way as a grief-stricken man passes through the stages of mourning. Desolation gave way to anger and was eventually succeeded by resignation overlaid with an ever-present feeling of sadness.

The child was well cared for; she had a nurse who adored her and a grandmother who gave her the loving her own mother withheld – Jeanne's maternal instincts had all been reawakened by the helplessness and innocence of the newest addition to the household. It was Jeanne who reported Antoinette's first smile to Louis, and her first tooth; it was Jeanne who was there in the nursery when the little girl took her first unsteady step from the arms of her nurse and fell triumphantly into Jeanne's own waiting arms. When she was sick, with a croupy cough or suffering from one of the earaches that plagued her, Jeanne sat up, taking turns with Rose, the nursemaid, cradling her gently on her lap so as to ensure the tarred rope which was placed around her neck to help her breathing did not chafe her tender skin, holding the hot flannels against her throbbing ear to ease the pain. When she was well, she played with her in the garden or the nursery, allowing her to do all manner of things she would never have allowed Louis or Gavin to do when they were small. And when high spirits gave way to tantrums and finally tears, she would take Antoinette in her arms, rocking her and murmuring words of comfort.

Louis himself spent as much time as business allowed with Antoinette, taking her riding, propped in front of him on the saddle, just as soon as her little legs were long enough to afford her some sort of balance. Jeanne disapproved of this, saying it was no way to raise a little girl to be a lady, but Louis was determined she should grow up easy with the horses he loved, and he enjoyed Antoinette's unfailing excitement when he proposed a ride, and her breathless laughter when they cantered or galloped.

Even Gavin took pleasure in Antoinette as she grew from a

sturdy toddler into a long-limbed child with the sparkle of mischief in eyes which were every bit as green as her mother's. He played with her and spoiled her and often slyly slipped her the sweetmeats that were supposed to be strictly rationed, since both Rose and Jeanne were of the opinion that too many were not good for her.

No, Antoinette did not lack love and attention. What she did lack was a mother's special care, for Lisette remained totally indifferent towards her. It was, Louis thought, almost as if the child did not exist. Lisette arranged her life to suit herself, quite content to leave Antoinette's care to others, and when their paths crossed she behaved as if Antoinette was someone else's child, not hers at all. She was no longer openly antagonistic towards her, but neither did she show the slightest interest. The continuing indifference still had the power to hurt Louis, but as time went by he accepted the sad truth that Lisette had no inclination towards being a mother.

But still he loved her, and with the same intensity as when he had first set eyes upon her. Though she could infuriate him and bring him to the edge of despair, yet still she held him in her spell. Those teasing eyes could still make his heartbeat quicken, her touch turn anger to desire. Her mercurial changes of mood left him confused, her black depressions and flashes of temper could turn, almost in a moment, to brittle gaiety, and her passion, when roused, was as unfettered as it had ever been. On occasion he wished he had never met, let alone married, her, yet he could not envision life without her. He loved her, and that, he sometimes thought, was the cross he had to bear.

Besides her continuing lack of interest in Antoinette, there was one other aspect of Lisette's behaviour which caused him some concern – her habit of flirting outrageously with other men, and Gavin in particular. But Louis told himself that she was a beautiful woman who enjoyed the power she was able to wield. There was no harm in it, he told himself; in the last resort he was her husband, and whilst the men she had teased and titillated were left with their inflamed desires unsatisfied, it was to his bed she came. But he wished, all the same, that she would desist, whilst knowing instinctively that to raise the matter with her would only serve to make things worse. To forbid Lisette to do something was to incite her to open rebellion; even drawing her attention to a fault was enough to make her the more determined to exhibit it. So he said nothing, and accepted that her ability to behave outrageously was part of her charm, one of the things that kept his own interest as sharply alive as it had ever been.

One evening, however, his patience was tried beyond endurance. It had begun as a cosy family soirée. Antoinette was in the nursery and fast asleep, and when they had dined, Jeanne suggested a little musical diversion. She was accomplished on the harpsichord, and both Louis and Gavin had fine baritone voices, whilst Lisette, too, loved to sing. After half an hour or so of the old favourites, Lisette stood up, smoothing her skirts.

'Gavin and I have a party piece we would like to perform for you.' She was bubbling, her old, vivacious self.

'And what might that be?' Peter asked. Like all men, he was enchanted by Lisette.

She twinkled back at him. 'Don't ask so many questions! It's a surprise. But we have been practising, Gavin, have we not?'

'Not quite enough yet.' Gavin rose too. 'We need a few more minutes alone before we are ready to face an audience. If you'll excuse us . . .'

Louis frowned. He did not like the easy familiarity which existed between his wife and his brother, but to object would be to mar the pleasant mood of the evening.

Lisette and Gavin left the room, Jeanne continued to play, and the minutes ticked by whilst Louis felt tension building within him like a coiled spring. At last he rose impatiently.

'We've waited long enough. They can do their turn whether they are ready or not. We're only family, after all, not a paying audience.'

He strode out of the room. Of Lisette and Gavin there was no sign. He could hear no voices practising a song either. Then, through the half-open morning room door he saw them. They were facing one another and holding hands, Lisette laughing up at Gavin, he, his eyes narrowed in his handsome face, gazing down at her. Louis halted, turned momentarily to stare, and saw Gavin pull her into his arms, twisting her round so that his body was pressed against her back and his face buried in her neck. And she, little minx, was wriggling sensuously and smiling.

Louis moved then, throwing open the door.

'Great heavens, what is happening here?'

Gavin, looking guilty and startled as well he might, let his arms fall to his sides and stepped away from Lisette, but unabashed she met Louis' eyes defiantly.

'We are practising, of course. What do you think?'

'Practising for what?' Louis ground out. 'Practising to deceive me?'

'Oh, don't be so silly!' She tossed her head. 'Our dance, of course.'

'A strange dance,' Louis stormed. 'Not one I have ever seen in any ballroom.'

'Of course not! It's a *stage* dance – Pierrot and Pierrette. It's for your entertainment.'

'And you think I should be entertained by seeing my wife in another man's arms? My own brother, no less? You think Mama and Papa would be entertained by such a spectacle? They would be outraged, and so am I!'

'Oh Louis, you can be so stuffy!' she said, haughty now, and trying to wrong-foot him.

Louis' mouth set in a hard line. 'That is as may be, but I won't have it. Lisette, do you understand? Now, get back to the parlour. I'll speak to you later.'

'Our dance . . . !'

'Did I not make myself clear? There will be no dance.'

Her small face set furiously; she saw that for once there was no arguing with Louis. She flounced past him, refusing to look at him, and Louis turned to his brother, raising his hand furiously.

'Try something like that again, Gavin, and you'll be sorry.'

Gavin raised an eyebrow; suddenly he no longer looked abashed, but smug.

All his life he had felt resentment for his brother. Louis was the elder son, leading the way, finding favour with his parents for his industry. When Louis had been given his first pony, bought especially for him at the horse fair, Gavin had had to make do with pretending the quietest old nag in the stable was really his; until he grew as tall as Louis he had been forced to wear his hand-me-downs, for although the Fletchers could well have afforded new clothes for him, Jeanne was possessed of a thrifty streak and saw no point in spending money when Louis' almost unworn garments hung in the wardrobe. But what irked him most of all was knowing that his home and everything in it would one day go to Louis. He would have no right to any of it, with the exception of the small bequests his father and mother might make. All the while, as he fooled and idled and played the careless young rake, the jealousy and resentment at the injustice of it simmered within him, spawning a dislike for his brother that sometimes came close to hatred.

Now, quite suddenly, he saw a way to even the score in one respect at least. Louis, the invincible heir to Belvedere, had an Achilles heel, and that Achilles heel was Lisette. His smile grew broader.

'Lisette was right, Louis,' he sneered. 'You are stuffy, though if it were left to me, I'd choose a stronger term. And with a wife as pretty and as wilful as yours, I'd be wary, if I were you, or you might find she prefers the company of a man not afraid to live life to the full and enjoy every minute of it.'

Still smirking, he passed Louis and followed Lisette back to the drawing room.

Louis stood for a moment, still angry at what he had seen, yet aware that to say more than he already had would be to make himself ridiculous. For all he knew the manoeuvre could have been a part of some sensuous dance Lisette had concocted, and as basically harmless as her constant flirting. It was not beyond the bounds of possibility, it would even be in character that she should delight in shocking him, his mother and father with it, and Gavin might well have been a willing accomplice, for he too had an exhibitionist streak.

It was going too far, of course, a good deal too far for Louis' liking, but all the old arguments for holding his tongue still held. He had made his feelings on the matter clear, to say more would likely only be to inflame the situation. Better, perhaps, now to let it be.

He did not think, for all her flirtatiousness, that Lisette would cuckold him. Their love-making was still more than satisfactory. And even if it were not, he did not think she would risk everything by going further than the kind of tempting game-playing he had witnessed, especially with her own husband's brother.

In this, as in so much else besides, Louis was wrong.

In the summer that Antoinette was three years old, tragedy visited the Fletcher family. Peter had been to London on business and for once neither Louis nor Gavin had gone with him. Travelling back, after dark, for he was anxious to finalize the deal, his carriage was held up by a highwayman.

It was not in Peter's nature to hand over his valuables without putting up a fight. Shots were fired, the frightened horses bolted and the coachman was unable to control them. The carriage overturned, throwing the coachman clear. He escaped with a broken arm and a broken head. But Peter, trapped in the wreckage, was so badly injured that by the time help arrived, it was too late. Peter was dead.

In the house of mourning Louis took control as he had always known one day he must, though he had not expected the responsibility to fall upon his shoulders so soon. Though grieving for the father he had loved, and shocked by the manner of his death, he slipped seamlessly into his new role as master of the house and head of the business empire.

The demands it made on him, however, were onerous. Complete control was very different to assisting; two men were now doing what three had done before, and Gavin showed no signs of mending his idle ways and shouldering his fair share of the burden.

Why should he? he asked himself, the jealousy and resentment burning more brightly than ever when the will was read and he saw everything pass into Louis' hands. He had the estate, he had the business, he had the power. Well, let him have the worry of it too. But he kept his true feelings as well hidden as ever, concealing them behind the easy charm that came so easily to him, and his reputation as a hellraiser.

Louis had less time for family life and less time for Lisette. And, engrossed in business, he did not notice that she was, once again, spending more and more time with Gavin.

In the early spring of the year following Peter's death, Louis was to make a business trip to France. He took his leave of his family and rode into Dartmouth, where he expected his schooner, the *Demoiselle*, to be ready for him to embark. But problems had arisen. The *Demoiselle* had just endured a stormy crossing which had caused damage to the main mast. Repairs had to be made before she sailed, Louis was told, and it would be at least twenty-four hours and possibly more before she was ready.

There was little point in Louis wasting a day or more in Dartmouth with nothing better to do than kick his heels, and he decided he would go home to Belvedere, where there was plenty of work to do, and return the following day.

It was early afternoon as he rode back up the drive and encountered his mother, Antoinette, and Rose, her nursemaid, driving in the open-topped carriage in the opposite direction. All were well wrapped up against the cold, and Antoinette's small face was already rosy and her eyes sparkling at the prospect of the outing.

'What's this?' he asked, smiling, as he drew alongside. 'Are you all deserting Belvedere the moment my back is turned?'

'Certainly not!' Jeanne returned. 'But we were in need of some fresh air, and though the wind is cold, the sun is bright enough. And Antoinette wanted to go for a drive, didn't you, chérie?'

'Yes – yes – I did! Will you come with us, Papa?'

'No, I'm afraid I cannot.' Louis explained why he was not halfway across the Channel, and added: 'I've books to do here, and letters to write, so I thought it best to make use of the time by coming home to deal with them.'

Jeanne nodded. 'I'm sure Bevan will be pleased to see you, at any rate. When I last saw him he was disappearing into the office with the look of a man who has the cares of the world on his shoulders.'

Louis' eyes narrowed. 'Is Gavin being of no help to him, then?'

Jeanne smiled faintly. 'You know Gavin as well as I do, Louis.'

'Indeed I do,' Louis said, tight-lipped. 'He's certainly been of little help to me these last months, so I dare say I cannot expect him to be any different when it comes to Bevan.'

Jeanne smoothed the wrap that lay over her knees and those of Antoinette. Her eyes were sad.

'Don't quarrel with him, please, Louis. He is your brother whatever his faults. And I am sure when he's a little more mature he will be better able to assist you.'

'He is *able* to assist me now,' Louis snapped. 'He just doesn't choose to, that's all.' Then, seeing Jeanne's distressed expression, he relented. 'Go and enjoy your drive, Mama, and don't worry about me and Gavin.'

The gig moved off. Louis turned to watch them go, then walked his horse to the stables and entered the house by the rear door.

In the kitchen, Cook and two maidservants were busy preparing vegetables for the evening meal, chattering as they did so. Otherwise the house was silent. As he divested himself of his redingote Louis glanced at the closed door to the office, where he knew Bevan would be hard at work, and wondered where he would be without the knowledgeable and industrious secretary. He was about to go in and announce his return when a sound from the parlour attracted his attention – a soft, muffled gasp. He froze, listening, and it came again. Suspicion flared. He moved soundlessly across the hall, threw the door open, and froze again at the sight which met his eyes.

Lisette, her skirts rumpled up to her waist, lay on the floor. On top of her, naked from the waist down, Gavin thrashed and flailed between her bare legs. She must have been alerted by the click of the door handle, for her eyes, wide and guilty, met his directly over Gavin's shoulder.

For a brief moment Louis stood as if turned to stone, then, in two strides, he crossed the floor to the hearthrug where they lay, grabbing his brother by the shoulder and hauling him to his feet.

Gavin's expression was as startled as Lisette's had been, his mouth falling open, his jaw slack. Louis' fist cracked into it with all the force he could muster and Gavin reeled back, colliding with a small French chair, overturning it and crashing to the floor. Blood spurted from his lip where his own teeth had bitten into it and from a cut that was opening at the corner of his mouth. Louis went after him, intending to drag him to his feet so that he could strike him again, but Lisette, who had scrambled up, rushed at him, grabbing his arm.

'Louis – no! Louis – stop it!'

He shook her off, not even bothering to glance at her. 'Get to your room, Madame!'

'But Louis . . .'

He swung round, more fury in his face than she had ever thought to see, or believed him capable of. It burned in his eyes and on his cheeks, his mouth was twisted into a snarl.

'Do as I say, or you'll be sorry!'

Gavin had taken the opportunity of the diversion to put the spindle-legged table between Louis and himself. As Louis advanced on him once more he raised a hand to fend him off.

'Louis, for the love of God . . . !'

Louis brushed the table aside as if it were a matchwood toy and grabbed his brother by the throat, dragging him towards him so that their faces were only inches apart.

'Fornicating bastard! So help me, I'll kill you . . . !' Without releasing the vice-like grip on Gavin's throat, he drove him back across the room until his back encountered the wall and his head cracked sickeningly against it with the force of Louis' furious thrust. 'Take my wife, would you . . . ?'

His grip tightened still more; Gavin, eyes bulging, fought for breath.

'Louis – you'll throttle him! Stop – stop . . . !'

Lisette, who had retreated to the doorway, rushed once again to intervene, tugging frantically at Louis' shirt. For timeless moments Louis maintained the pressure, teeth bared, beside himself with rage. Then, quite suddenly, he released Gavin, whirling furiously on Lisette.

'Didn't I tell you to get to your room?'

'Louis . . .' She was shaking now from head to foot.

'You are every bit as bad as him,' he ground out. 'Worse! Get out now – go on – before I kill you too!'

The look in his eyes struck terror to Lisette's heart. This was a Louis she had never seen before, a man so beside himself with fury he was capable of doing as he threatened. She backed away and fled, frightened suddenly for her own life.

Gavin slumped against the wall gasping and clutching his throat. Louis turned back to him, his lip curling with distaste at the pathetic sight of his half-clad body.

'And you . . . you get out, too! Out of my sight. Out of my house!'

Gavin tried to speak; only a croak came from his bruised throat.

'Go on – get out! And don't come back, or I swear . . . !' The fury erupted in Louis once more. Another moment and he would most certainly throttle the life from his treacherous brother. Clenching his fists tight to his sides, he turned on his heel and marched from the room and from the house.

He rode, as he always did when anger consumed him or when the weight of the burdens upon his shoulders became too much to bear. He took his horse to open ground and kicked him to a gallop so wild that he could think of nothing but the ground that rushed up at him beneath the thundering hooves. The cold wind cooled his burning face, and with it his temper. When at last he reined in, a great wave of outrage and despair washed over him and he felt sick to his stomach.

He could still scarcely believe the scene that had met his eyes – his wife coupling with his own brother. It was insupportable; the betrayal was more than flesh and blood could stand. He tried to blot it out of his mind and still it rose before his eyes, burned for ever on his retinas, an abomination he would neither forget nor forgive to the end of his days.

He was shaken, too, by how close he had come to killing his brother. Faith, but he had wanted to, and he could have done it, too, if Lisette had not distracted him. He almost wished he had, for perhaps vengeance would have done something to expurgate the betrayal, ease the terrible pain that was now tearing him apart. But even as he thought it he knew it was an illusion. Nothing could do that, certainly not the murder of his own flesh and blood. He turned cold inwardly as he imagined his mother's distress and the guilt he would bear, for all his outrage and need for revenge. Gavin's death at his hands was not the answer.

But he could no longer live under the same roof as a brother who could cuckold him. Gavin was not the only guilty party, he knew. Lisette, he could well believe, had tempted Gavin beyond endurance. But Gavin should have been honourable enough, loyal enough, to resist.

The loathing burned within him again. His brother had betrayed him and everything he held dear. He would never have the opportunity, if Louis could help it, to do so again.

As for Lisette . . . at that moment, Louis had no wish to look on her ever again, but there was no avoiding his responsibility. Reluctantly he turned his horse and started for home.

The carriage was in the stable yard; Jeanne and Antoinette had returned, then, from their drive.

Louis found them in the parlour, Jeanne sitting with Antoinette curled against her whilst she read from a storybook. She looked up and smiled at him as he entered the room, then the smile froze on her lips when she saw the thunderous expression on his face and his hair wild from the ride.

'Gavin is not here, I trust,' he said harshly.

'Gavin?' Jeanne repeated, puzzled. 'He is in his room, I think.'

'The devil he is!' Louis turned away, intent on establishing his brother's whereabouts.

'What's wrong, Louis?' Jeanne asked sharply. 'Have you two been quarrelling again?'

'A little more than that, Mama.'

'Oh!' Jeanne sighed in exasperation. 'I saw that he had hurt his mouth. He said he had fallen. It was you, wasn't it? You did that to him.'

'With cause, Mama,' Louis said bitterly. 'He's lucky to escape so lightly. I was hoping he would have had the good sense to be gone by the time I returned. I want him out of this house. I have told him so, and I meant what I said. I won't have him under my roof tonight, or any other night.'

'What are you saying?' Jeanne was shocked. She was used to her sons and their differences, but clearly this was far more serious than their usual disagreements. 'You can't turn your brother out! This is his home!'

'No longer,' Louis said coldly.

'But what has happened, Louis, to bring it to this?'

Louis looked at Antoinette, squashed still against her Grandmama's skirts. She had caught the fact that something very serious was occurring though she did not fully understand; her lip was held tight between her teeth, and her eyes, wide and alarmed, were on her father.

This was not something that should be discussed in front of her, he knew.

'Where is Rose?' he asked.

'In the nursery, preparing the child's tea . . . Louis, what . . . ?'

'Antoinette, go to the nursery,' he said. 'Not to your mother's room, and not to Uncle Gavin's, but to the nursery. Do you understand?' His tone was kindly but firm, a tone Antoinette, for all the wilfulness she sometimes displayed, knew better than to disobey.

116

She wriggled down from the chaise.

'Go along now,' he said.

'So, Louis,' Jeanne said when Antoinette had left. 'What is it that is so serious it cannot be discussed in front of the child?'

'Mama . . .' He hesitated, ashamed suddenly, as if the whole outrageous incident had been his fault. 'Mama, I hardly know how to tell you this. It's not a pretty story.'

'We don't have to distress Mama with the details of our quarrel, surely, Louis?'

Louis swung round at the sound of his brother's voice, his anger rising again in a hot flood tide.

Gavin stood in the doorway. His lip had swollen now, and the hoarseness was still there in his voice, but the tone he employed was silky smooth as ever, and he was even attempting a parody of his usual charming smile.

'I thought I told you to get out of my house!' Louis grated.

'Oh Louis . . . I thought you would have thought better by now of your rash threat. You can't really mean to turn me out!' He looked towards his mother, enlisting her support, and confident, too, that Louis would not repeat his attack in Jeanne's presence.

'I most certainly do mean it!' Louis said harshly. 'After what happened here today I cannot believe you can seriously think for one moment that things can continue as before.'

'Is someone going to enlighten me as to what is going on?' Jeanne asked.

'It was nothing, Mama . . .' Gavin began.

'Nothing!' Louis interrupted furiously. 'You take my wife in my house and call it nothing! Sweet Jesus, Gavin, your sheer effrontery takes my breath away! Why, I don't believe you are even sorry for your dastardly betrayal!'

'Perhaps,' Gavin said before he could stop himself, 'you should spend a little less time on trying to emulate Papa's business acumen and a little more on keeping your wife satisfied. Then she would not need to look elsewhere for her pleasures.'

'Why, you . . . !' Louis moved furiously towards Gavin, on the point of striking him again.

'Louis – Gavin – stop this at once!' Jeanne's tone was the same one that had disciplined them as unruly boys. 'Neither of you might be willing to tell me what has happened here, but I'd be an innocent fool not to be able to guess. How could you cuckold your own brother, Gavin? I know you are wild – you always have been. But this . . .'

'Mama . . .'

She silenced him with an imperious gesture and turned to Louis.

'As for you, Louis, you should know that brawling like a common roughneck will solve nothing.'

'Brawling, Mama? I'd like to kill him! And he'd do well to get out of my house as I told him to before I do!'

'I think, Gavin, you would be wise to do as Louis says,' Jeanne said.

'But Mama . . .'

'I can well understand that Louis does not want you here – why, at this very moment, I don't know that I want you here myself! The situation would be intolerable! I suggest you go to an inn for tonight at least until we can arrive at some acceptable solution to the problem you have created by your own unpardonable behaviour. Go now, and pack some things together, and let us try, all of us, to bring a little decorum to this disgraceful situation!'

'Oh, if that's the way you want it,' Gavin said impatiently. 'I see I am cast as the villain of the piece, as usual.'

'I am afraid, Gavin, on this occasion, it is no more than you deserve,' Jeanne said fiercely. 'And I fail to see how you can continue to justify yourself. As it is, there is nothing to be gained by discussing this further, except to say how shocked and disappointed I am. I had hoped that losing your father so tragically would be a reason for you to act more responsibly. Unfortunately it seems my optimism was quite misplaced.'

A haunted look crossed Gavin's face suddenly. 'Perhaps, Mama, I know that whatever I may do I shall never hold a candle to Louis in your eyes, just as I never did in Papa's. All right, I'll go. But do not be surprised if I never come back.' As the door closed after him Jeanne sank back on to the chaise, head bowed, fingertips pressed to her brow.

'Oh Mama,' Louis said helplessly. 'I am so sorry you should be distressed so.'

'It's not your fault, Louis.' She looked up at him. 'But neither do I think it is entirely Gavin's.'

'Lisette encouraged him, you mean? I dare say, but . . .'

'Well, yes, that too, I suppose. Yes, almost certainly. But that was not what I was thinking of. Gavin is jealous of you, Louis. He always has been, since he was a small boy. I've seen it and tried to compensate him in small ways, but it does no good. Nothing can change the order of things – you are the elder son, and inherit everything. He has always felt worthless by comparison, even believing, foolishly, that your father and I valued you more. His behaviour, over all the years, is a sort of rebellion, I believe, and this is just another way for him to put himself on an equal footing with you.'

'Cuckolding me, you mean. I am sorry, Mama, I am afraid I cannot see it as charitably as you seem to.'

'Oh Louis, I do not for one moment condone what he has done . . .'

'Good,' Louis said harshly. 'For I am afraid, Mama, that I shall never be able to forgive him.'

Neither, did he think, would he ever be able to forgive Lisette. That night, unable to bear the thought of sharing a bed with her, he had a couch made up in his dressing room and lay on it, sleepless, while the creeper, blown by the wind, slapped mournfully against the window and the scene played and replayed itself before his wakeful eyes.

A small sound – the creak of a floorboard – impinged on his consciousness. He stiffened, aware suddenly of the scent of Lisette's rosewater in his nostrils. She crossed the floor almost soundlessly, her hair fanned across his face, her lips were on his throat. He twisted his head away as if she were a vampire preparing to suck his life's blood.

'Louis . . .' She was pushing aside the covers, caressing him with the practised ease of a courtesan, soft, gentle, pliant. Briefly the familiar need for her flared in him, then died, as once again he was tormented by the knowledge that she had used those same wiles on Gavin.

'Go back to your bed, Lisette!' he grated.

'Don't send me away, Louis, please! It's you I want! Always you . . .'

The angry words of accusation rose to Louis' lips – that she had not wanted him when she had lain this afternoon with Gavin. She had betrayed him, hurt and humiliated him, and the very thought of touching her was repulsive to him. But there had been enough recriminations today, he was weary of them, and wanted only to be alone to lick his wounds. Impatiently he jerked the covers over his body, pushing her aside and turning his back on her.

'Leave me be, Madame. This time your wiles won't work, for I no longer want you.'

For long tense moments she knelt there, her fingers hovering over his shoulder as she debated whether or not she should touch him again, tears starting to her eyes and running down her cheeks. Louis sensed her continued presence and ignored it, hardening his heart against her.

He had no way of knowing how real was her regret, how deep her despair that she could seemingly never control the need for reassurance that she was desired – loved!

And he had no way of knowing either that his display of anger this afternoon had made her burn with desire for him. Of late she had grown used to a sober Louis, with no time for pleasure, no energy for, or interest in, anything but work. 'Stuffy', she had called him once, and it seemed an apt description, whereas Gavin had flattered and flirted, seeming to match her wildness and mischief with his own. But today . . .

Today, she had seen a new Louis, and what she had seen excited her. This was a man who could crush and master her, and perhaps, in so doing, exorcise the demons that tormented her.

At last, defeated, Lisette crept from the dressing room back to her own bed. For a little while she sobbed loudly, hoping that he might hear her and yet come to comfort her and make up their differences. When he did not, the emptiness of rejection ached within her, as it had ached once before, with another man, and Lisette made a vow.

Somehow she would regain Louis' love. She would be in his arms again.

She little knew that the first was beyond her grasp, lost for ever by her own foolish faithlessness, and the second, when it eventually came, would be far from the passionate idyll she imagined.

iv

In spite of all that had happened, the state of high tension and open warfare within the family could not continue for ever. As the weeks passed, life returned to some semblance of normality. But it was a thin veneer only, covering the bubbling cauldron of suppressed passions.

Louis, unmoved from his edict that Gavin should no longer live under his roof, but, out of deference to his mother, unwilling to see his brother on the streets, purchased a house in Dartmouth for Gavin to occupy. It proved a sensible plan, for it meant that Gavin could be on hand to oversee the movement of goods within the port and be readily available to deal with the captains of their schooners, and it provided an explanation to the outside world as to why Gavin had left the family home.

Though he was at first bitterly resentful that Louis had the power to exile him, Gavin soon found the new arrangement suited him rather well. He liked the freedom having his own house afforded him, liked being able to entertain and roister without his mother and elder brother to answer to, and actually discovered a new incentive to work harder than before.

With peace now reigning once again between England and France, traffic between the two countries became easier and Gavin often made the trip across the Channel, making new contacts and forming fresh liaisons. His easy charm was a formidable asset in this respect, and for the first time the two brothers began to use the differences between them to the advantage of the business – whilst Louis was able to give the rock-solid stability that was so important in bolstering the confidence of associates, Gavin had the ability to reel them in with a smile, a joke and a shared brandy.

On one trip to France, Gavin secured an introduction to the Marquis de St Valla, and the two immediately struck up a firm friendship. Both were young, wild and handsome, both had an eye for – and a way with – the ladies. And when the Marquis came to England and was invited to stay with Gavin at his house in Dartmouth, more than one young lady turned a hopeful eye in his direction, just as they did at Gavin – much to the dismay of their mothers, who were hoping for more suitable matches.

Though he no longer lived at Belvedere, Gavin still visited, since their business partnership meant the brothers were still in regular contact. And it was there that the Marquis and Lisette first met.

Lisette was desperately unhappy. In spite of all her efforts, it seemed she was unable to win back Louis' love, which she now craved so desperately. With every rejection she only wanted him the more until her desire for him obsessed her, but there was no way, it seemed, that she could break through the cold barrier he had erected between them.

She was lonely, too, for she had never been close to Jeanne, and since her indiscretion the relationship had deteriorated still further, for Jeanne was unable to forgive her for her betrayal of Louis and the upheaval in their lives which had ensued. In her desperation, Lisette had even tried to form some kind of relationship with Antoinette, who was growing into a rather precocious little girl, but it was too late. Antoinette's love was for her father, her grandmother and her nurse; it was to them she turned, never to the mother who had shunned her. So when the handsome, charming Marquis came into her life, Lisette clutched at his company as a drowning man clutches at a plank of driftwood.

He was a compatriot, who not only spoke to her in her native tongue, but also knew many of her relatives and friends from the old days. He fed her tidbits of gossip about them and their doings, which she gobbled up eagerly, and told stories about them which amused and diverted her. He was also a charming and handsome man who took no trouble to hide the fact that he found her desirable. Lisette, who had begun to doubt her powers of seduction, basked in his attention, in the compliments he paid her and the looks he gave her.

She did not want him. She wanted no one now but Louis, but she still found his admiration for her persuasive and as her confidence returned, a dangerous idea came into her head. If Louis were to see that other men were still attracted to her, then perhaps his feelings for her would be stirred and reignited. It was, after all, when she had been the centre of men's attention that he had first been attracted to her; perhaps it was her pliant attitude and constant efforts to please him that kept him cold towards her. If he thought she no longer cared, perhaps he would look at her through different eyes, the eyes that had seen a butterfly fluttering outside his reach, and fallen in love with it. He needed to be shown, Lisette thought, that there were others who thought her desirable even if he did not, and that she would not always wait for him like some lovesick puppy.

And it did not occur to her to realize that it was the faithlessness that had caused him to cool towards her in the first place. Somehow, that truth had become distorted in her mind with the passing of time. She had been schooled from too early an age to believe it was her favours which secured for her everything she wanted, not the withholding of them. And if Louis failed to respond to her directly, then perhaps a little nudge towards jealousy would elicit the required response.

Lisette began her dangerous game, flirting with the Marquis directly under Louis' nose. It excited her and made her feel empowered again. Intoxicated as she was by the sensations that had lain dormant for too long, she forgot the very real threats

Louis had made, forgot everything but her intention to remind him that she was a very desirable woman.

Lisette failed to realize she was not the mistress of her own fate, as she believed, but the author of it.

'I wish to speak to you, Madame.'

She was brushing her hair, sitting before the mirror in her dressing room. Louis' tone was cold as ice; she raised her glance to catch sight of his reflection and saw that his eyes, too, were cold and his face set in hard lines.

Desire twisted within her. This was the Louis who excited her almost beyond endurance. But she was determined not to let him see it. She matched the coolness of her tone to his. 'For what reason?'

'I think you know very well. You are returning to your old ways, Lisette.'

'What are you talking about?' She raised her brush for another stroke through the thick fall of her red-gold hair and the wrap she was wearing fell a little further open at the neck, revealing the creamy swell of her firm breasts. She did nothing to pull it together; the image reflected in the mirror was exactly the one she wanted to present – careless grace, demure temptation.

'I am talking about your shameless behaviour with the Marquis de St Valla. I thought I made it clear to you, I won't tolerate you making a fool of me.'

Her green eyes opened wide. 'I've done nothing!'

'Don't play the innocent with me!' he ground out. 'You cannot help but act the seductress, it seems. You are a wanton woman, Lisette.'

'Louis . . .' She rose, and took a step towards him, ensuring the neckline of her wrap fell even further open as she did so. 'Why are you always so cross with me? Don't be cross, please . . .'

'Cross with you?' He laughed harshly. '*Cross* is a very little word to describe my feelings towards a wife who cuckolded me with my own brother. And in the name of decency, cover yourself. If you think you can seduce *me* with a display of your body, you are much mistaken. Once, maybe. But not now. I know you too well.'

He turned on his heel, and despair and an overwhelming sense of rejection made Lisette reckless.

'So you walk away from me!' she cried. 'Is it any wonder I look to other men for my pleasures when you treat me so?'

His hand was on the door to his own dressing room, gripping it so hard the fingers turned white.

'Don't make excuses for yourself, Lisette. We had a normal married life until you betrayed me with my brother. But it was not enough for you. You had to have more. Now, I am going to bed before I lose what little control remains over my temper, and I do something I shall regret.'

'Oh!' she cried. 'And what might that be? I don't believe you are enough of a man to carry out any of your threats. And I don't believe you're capable of satisfying me either . . .'

She broke off as he whirled round, crossed the floor in three quick strides, and grabbed her by the wrists.

'What did you say?' His voice was a low snarl of rage.

Lisette felt a moment's sharp fear, and with it a twist of something like triumphant excitement.

Then: 'If you want a man, Madame, by God you shall have one!' he grated.

One hand went beneath her knees, the other around her shoulders, and he lifted her as if she were a child, carrying her across the room and flinging her down roughly on to the bed. She gasped with shock at the violence of it, gasped again as he tore her wrap open.

He was towering over her, holding her down and at the same time undressing himself, and as his weight came down on her she knew that this was not what she wanted at all. The triumphant excitement had all gone, swamped by fear.

'Louis – stop – stop!' She beat at him with her hands, panic making her voice shrill. He took no notice. With one hand he forced her flailing legs apart, then drove into her. She cried out as white-hot pain knifed through her again and again with the furious thrusts of his body and he covered her mouth roughly with his hand, cutting off breath as well as her cries. The final thrust seemed to tear her apart, the whole of her body was nothing but pain – her tortured lungs, the hand biting into her cheek, the screaming agony of torn tissue in the core of her. And, worst of all, the memories the pain had awakened. Lying helpless, terrified and suffering, Lisette became once again the child she had once been, drowning in the blackness that had swamped her then, and swamped her now.

It was over in minutes – minutes which seemed to her to last a lifetime. As Louis released her she drew in precious air on a series of great sobbing gasps and curled in on herself as if afraid he might take her again. He rolled away from her, getting up and reaching for his breeches, discarded on the floor beside the bed, without a word.

'You beast!' she whispered, the tears starting in her eyes.

'I thought that was what you wanted.' His voice was rough now, more from shame than anger.

'How could you?' she sobbed. 'You are no better than him!'

Louis tensed, half-in and half-out of his breeches.

'No better than who?' She was silent and he turned, gripping her by the shoulders. 'No better than who, Lisette? He didn't take you by force, did he? Gavin? Sweet Jesus, I'll kill him! I should have killed him . . .'

'No,' she sobbed, frightened now by what she had started. 'Not Gavin. No!'

'Then who?' His fingers bit into her shoulders. Still she could not answer, and he shook her as a dog shakes a rabbit. 'Who, Lisette? Who else have you been with and I know nothing of it?'

'It wasn't my fault!' she sobbed.

'It's always your fault!' he ground out. 'You play at driving men to distraction. You are no better than a common whore.'

Suddenly, for all that she was still afraid, Lisette was angry too, so angry that she forgot her fear. How dare he treat her so! How dare he say such things! And when she had kept her terrible secret all these years for his sake, too!

'I am not a common whore!' she cried. 'I am not of peasant

stock like you! I have noble blood, and don't dare to forget it. But if you want the truth, Louis, then you shall have it. Have you never wondered why I want nothing to do with Antoinette?'

Louis' blood ran cold suddenly. 'Don't bring my daughter into this.'

'*Your* daughter?' She laughed shortly. 'Antoinette is not *your* daughter. I was already with child when I married you. And every time I look at her, I am reminded of it.'

His mouth had gone slack, his eyes narrowed with shock.

'You foisted another man's child on me?'

'Foisted? No! You took her willingly – just as you took me. Oh Louis, it was so easy to make you love me then, when I was young and fresh . . .' Tears filled her eyes once more; she blinked them away. 'Now, just like him, you no longer want me. *He* found someone younger and fresher, and so will you. Men! I despise them!'

Louis' fingers bit into her shoulders once more.

'Who are you talking about? Who was your lover? Who is . . . ?'

Antoinette's father, he had been about to say, but could not form the words.

Lisette laughed harshly.

'Oh Louis, if only you could see your face! It was my uncle, of course, who else? He took me into his bed first when I was just nine years old. And then, when I grew, he didn't want me any more. He had his new little girl, and I couldn't bear it. I'd thought I hated him, hated what he did to me, but when she took my place . . . oh, I minded so much! I couldn't stay and see her take my place! So I chose you.' She laughed again, this time a giggle of childlike delight. 'And it worked! It made him jealous, just as I knew it would. He wanted me again, even if only for a little while.'

'Dear God, Lisette! Are you saying your uncle molested and raped you . . . ?'

Her mouth hardened to a tight little line; the tears sparkled again on her lashes.

'At least he was kind and gentle with me! At least he loved me! He told me so! *You* . . . you hurt me. *You* hate me. And I hate you! But I have the perfect way of making you pay, don't I? What will they say, all your friends and business associates, when I tell them the truth? That Antoinette is not your child at all, but the product of incest?'

Louis was dazed with the shock of her terrible revelations. They were almost beyond belief – and yet, at the same time, all too believable. They explained so many of the puzzles that were Lisette – her precociousness at the time he had met and fallen in love with her, her desperate dependence on male admiration, her belief that her sexuality could buy her whatever she wanted, her rejection of Antoinette, her mood swings, her inability to settle into a normal life as a wife and mother. She had been damaged physically and emotionally, and, he was beginning to believe, mentally, too, for at this moment she appeared quite unhinged. Love, hate, dependence, all were hopelessly confused within her until there was no longer any logic in anything she thought, or said, or felt.

'Lisette – for God's sake think of Antoinette!' he said harshly. 'You cannot reveal this terrible truth. It would blight her for ever.'

Lisette shrugged. 'She's damned anyway. And why should I care about her? She doesn't care about me.'

'Because you have never been a mother to her.'

'And now she will know why! Now she'll understand!'

'Lisette – she is just a child! She must be protected!'

'No one ever protected *me* when he came to my bed. And no one protected me tonight when you forced yourself on me and hurt me!'

There was no reasoning with her, Louis realized. Always unpredictable, always volatile, she had now crossed the borderline into madness – and he was to blame. But that was no longer his chief concern.

Whether Antoinette was his child or not, he loved her. She was an innocent victim in all this. He could not, would not, let this selfish damaged woman blight yet another young life. Somewhere, somehow, the evil that had been spawned by a lecherous old Frenchman must be stopped.

Louis could think of only one solution.

Six

Louis was, I knew, greatly disturbed by my account of what had happened that afternoon between Antoinette and John, the gamekeeper's lad, and he went directly to her room to speak to her about it. As I freshened up and changed for dinner I heard raised voices coming from her room, and when we all met in the dining room she glared at me, resentment that was not far removed from hatred burning in her foxy green eyes.

I wished with all my heart that I had not had to tell tales on her, I would have much preferred to be in a position to win her confidence, but I did not regret it. The incident was far too serious for me to keep it to myself. It was only right that Louis should be aware of her behaviour so that he could take steps to ensure it did not happen again – though what those steps would be, I could not imagine. A girl as wilful and scheming as Antoinette would almost certainly find ways to do as she pleased, and short of locking her in her room and barring her windows, I could not see how Louis would be able to restrain her – in the long run, at any rate.

I was glad, however, that I had made no mention of the fact that she had been prying amongst my belongings. For one thing I had no proof of it, for another it was, I felt, something between her and me, and since she had flatly denied any such thing I would be forced to leave it there. Hopefully her curiosity was now satisfied and there would be no repeat excursions to the room that provided me with the only privacy I could expect whilst forced to live here at Belvedere.

Louis, too, was in a black mood, surly and silent, but now,

instead of disliking him for it as I had before, I felt a certain sympathy. Bad enough that Antoinette was rebellious, disobedient and frankly uncontrollable, but from the despair I had seen on his face and the comments he had made, more to himself than to me, I did not need to be clairvoyant to guess it was the repetition of a pattern. Had he not said on previous occasions that Antoinette was too much like her mother for her own good? I had not known where the comparison lay, now I could scarcely avoid knowing. Lisette had, in some degree or other, been a faithless wife. But there still remained the mystery of what her end had been.

I thought again of Louis' curt dismissal of her – *I do not have a wife* – of Antoinette's assertion that she had died of a fever, and of Bevan's curious remark that only Louis knew the truth of what had happened to her. Lisette was an enigma which should not concern me, and yet she did, for although she was long since gone, and I had not seen any portrait or likeness of her displayed anywhere, yet her shadow remained, long and dark, over everyone in this strange household, and simply thinking of her made me uncomfortable in a way I could not understand.

Gavin did not appear for the meal; after the quarrel I had overheard this morning, he had decided to stay away from Louis, I assumed, and I could not help but be glad he was not here. Although I had previously found some light relief in his company, his attention this morning had made me uncomfortable, and certainly there was enough tension around the table without the added strain of the bad feeling that existed between the brothers.

We had finished our main course of poached chicken and been served a delicious junket, when we were interrupted by Polly.

'I am very sorry, Sir, but there are some gentlemen here to see you. I told them you were at dinner, but they said their business was urgent.'

To my surprise, Louis pushed back his chair and rose without asking if his visitors had given a name.

'Show them into the study, please, Polly,' he said, and to me: 'Will you excuse me, Flora? I may be some time.'

'Oh, Papa and his business!' Antoinette said pettishly when the door had closed after him. 'He thinks of nothing else!'

'That's not true, I'm sure,' I said. 'But business is important to him. It has to be.'

'Well, at least he won't be here to glower at me for the rest of the evening!' she returned. 'He's in a dreadful mood, thanks to you. I don't know why you had to come here, interfering.'

Quite suddenly I decided I had had enough of her rudeness and aggression.

'I do not want to be here any more than you want me to be,' I said tersely. 'But since neither of us can do anything to change that, don't you think we should make the best of things? And as regards your father's mood, that is your doing, not mine.'

She tossed her head. 'You didn't have to tell him.'

'I certainly did!' I told her. 'If you think about it, I'm sure you will realize I had no choice. And if you are as grown-up as you like to think, you will learn to accept responsibility for the results of your actions, and not seek to try to lay the blame on others.'

Antoinette pouted, and I thought she was going to argue. Then she sat back, looking at me narrowly. 'Haven't you ever done something you shouldn't?'

I laughed. 'Well, of course I have! Plenty of times.'

'I can't imagine it. You are such a goody-goody.'

'I assure you I am not,' I said. 'And if it seems that way it is because I am trying to come to terms with my father's death, and a very unwelcome situation. Why –' my hands went to my throat, feeling the knubble of pearls beneath the collar of my gown – 'I am doing something I shouldn't this very minute. I am wearing jewellery when I am in mourning.'

Antoinette stared at me in amazement. 'What's the point of wearing jewellery if it doesn't show? My mama used to wear beautiful jewellery. It will be mine when I am sixteen, and I shall never hide it away. Not even if I were in mourning, which I never will be, since I have no one to mourn.'

'That is a terrible thing to say!' I said, shocked. 'And I don't believe for one moment that you mean it. Why, you would miss your father dreadfully, just as I miss mine.'

Antoinette sat back, considering.

'I suppose I missed Grandmama. Yes, I did. I remember crying a good deal when she died. She used to play with me . . .' Her eyes went far away. 'And she taught me to sew. And we'd go riding together in the carriage with a rug over our knees and she'd hold my hand – that was nice – and she'd point out the flowers and the trees and tell me their names. She'd come to my room when my nurse had put me to bed, and she'd sing to me sometimes . . .'

'After your mother died, you mean?' I asked, unable to contain my curiosity.

'Oh – and before. Mama never came. It was always Grandmama.' She was silent for a moment, lost in her memories, and something about her face, so knowing sometimes, so vulnerable now, tugged at the strings of my heart.

'I grew up without a mother, too,' I said. 'But I was lucky – I had her until I was nine years old and I have very happy memories.' I smiled faintly, picturing her in my mind's eye, her brown unpowdered hair coiled thickly, the sprigged muslin dress she wore for church on Sundays, the grey serge everyday gown that felt comfortingly warm against my cheek when I nestled on her lap. And smelling again the faint scent of lavender that clung to her, and which lingered in a room even when she had left it. 'She didn't own much jewellery,' I went on. 'There was no money to spare for such things. And she didn't have fine clothes. But she was very beautiful, all the same, and I loved her very much.'

Antoinette was looking at me intently, and there was something almost wistful in those narrowed green eyes.

'Who looked after you when she died? Did you have a grandmama too?'

'I had a granny, yes – Granny Livesay, whom I also loved very much. But she lived some way off, at Cockington. No, after my mother died, there was just my father and me.'

Tears filled my eyes suddenly; I turned my head away so that Antoinette should not see them, and the spell that had bound us together briefly was broken.

'And you had no nurse either?' she asked incredulously.

'No.'

'And no maid to wash your clothes and brush your hair?'

I shook my head.

'It must be very strange to be so poor,' she said. 'I wouldn't care for it.'

I brushed the tears out of my eyes with the back of my fingers.

'There are some things, Antoinette, that money cannot buy,' I said. 'Love and happiness chief among them.'

Her lips curled. 'Poor people always say that, don't they? I suppose one must allow them something. But I simply couldn't bear a life without pretty things – and servants to do the hard work.'

'Perhaps, then, Antoinette, you should learn to show a little gratitude for all you have, and take for granted,' I said tartly.

Her green eyes flashed. 'Gratitude to whom? To the servants? They are paid, aren't they? They have a roof over their heads and plenty to eat. Why, it's they who should be grateful to us!'

'To your father, perhaps, for working hard to provide you with all these things,' I suggested.

She tossed her head. 'Oh, I don't think I care to have this conversation. I am going to my room.'

'Where the window, I hope, will remain firmly closed,' I said.

She shot me a narrow look of dislike and stalked out of the room.

What a strange child she was! I thought, sipping the last of my dessert wine. Spoiled, thoroughly selfish, disrespectful, wilful. And at the same time lonely and rather pathetic. I did not know whether to feel sorry for her or to dislike her. And I wished with all my heart I could teach her the worth of the things she seemed to despise.

Perhaps there was some value, after all, in her friendship with John, the gamekeeper's lad. Not the dangerous liaisons in her room, of course; not the sexual experimentation I feared they might be indulging in. But John was of the class she looked down on so disdainfully, and yet she called him her best and only friend. She didn't dismiss him as if he were no more than a chattel. And she had seemed so wistful, too, when I had spoken of my happy childhood. Given time I might be able to find a way to influence her.

Given time! A small smile twisted my lips. I had no intention of remaining at Belvedere a moment longer than I had to. Though, for the moment, I could not for the life of me see how I could escape, any more than Antoinette could.

I was thinking of retiring myself when the drawing-room door opened and Louis came in.

'Ah, you are still here, Flora. Good.' His tone was purposeful.

'I would not sleep if I retired too early,' I said – and did not add that these days I had difficulty in sleeping in any case.

Louis crossed to the small drinks table, unstoppered the brandy decanter, and poured himself a good measure.

'I have a favour to ask of you, Flora,' he said, warming the glass between his hands.

I looked at him, surprised and questioning, and suddenly I experienced again that strange, unfamiliar twist deep inside me and the tightening of the breath in my throat. For a moment I could not tear my eyes from him; it was as if he was magnetizing me and the whole of my world was occupied by this tall, powerful man with the dark brooding looks. I lowered my gaze from his face, focussing on the hands that held the brandy glass, and that was every bit as bad, for there was something about those hands, strong and brown from riding in all weathers and often without gloves, that magnetized me too. So many gentlemen had hands that were soft and white, and I had always thought them unappealing and, frankly, unmasculine. My father's hands had been horny and leathered from hard work, and I had always considered them to be far more honest, comforting and reliable. But

Louis' hands . . . oh! The excitement twisted once again within me, so sharp that it almost made me squirm.

Somehow I regained control of myself. 'Yes?' I said faintly.

Louis sipped his brandy. 'I have to go to France tomorrow,' he said. 'It's a little unexpected, but trading can be. When an opportunity arises . . .'

'Your visitors came to tell you of it,' I said. 'Antoinette said you were occupied on business.'

'She is accustomed to my ways.' He smiled faintly. 'Where is Antoinette? Has she gone to bed?'

'She's gone to her room, certainly. As to whether she has retired, I do not know.'

He nodded, satisfied. 'Well, it is of no importance. Just so long as she is not about to burst in on us, for the favour I want to ask of you concerns her.'

My heart sank; I knew what he was going to say.

'I expect to be gone for about a week,' Louis went on, 'and I would be most grateful if you would keep watch over her whilst I am gone. What happened this afternoon has caused me great concern, and to be truthful, I would have preferred it if I could have arranged for her to stay with friends for a while so that she is well away from that wretched boy and his influence over her. I had been considering sending her to Bath or Bristol for the time being at least, and in the hope that with new experiences to fill her time and the company of other girls of her own age and class she might perhaps forget about John Frogwell. But this business opportunity has arisen sooner than I expected and there will be no time for me to make the necessary arrangements.'

His eyes levelled with mine. 'It's an imposition, I realize, Flora, but there is no one else I can ask, and I am most concerned for her welfare.'

'What about Gavin?' I suggested, unwilling to assume responsibility for such a wilful young woman.

Louis laughed shortly. 'Gavin, I am very much afraid, only encourages her. My brother sees no reason to control himself, let alone Antoinette.'

136

'Well,' I said. 'Certainly I will do what I can, but she has a mind of her own, and I think she regards me as an unwelcome interloper.'

'She knows she cannot twist you around her little finger,' Louis said. 'And she knows you will report back to me if she misbehaves. You proved that today. You are a strong personality, Flora, much stronger than the governesses she made short work of. I think she respects you more than you realize.'

I pulled a face. I did not think Antoinette respected me at all. I could scarcely refuse to even try to control her whilst Louis was in France, but the prospect was a daunting one.

'Will you at least tell her that you are vesting authority in me whilst you are away?' I requested.

Louis nodded. 'Of course. Provided she is still awake and I can speak to her tonight, since I shall be leaving very early in the morning. We sail on the dawn tide.'

My heart sank and I realized it was not just because I was reluctant to take responsibility for Antoinette without her father having explained the position to her. No, it was far more than that.

I would miss Louis. For reasons that had nothing at all to do with Antoinette, I did not want him to go.

In spite of the flutterings of attraction I had felt for him, the strength of my feelings now came as a shock to me. This went far deeper than the frisson of excitement evoked by the natural chemistry between a man and a woman. It was a twisting of my heart, not just my loins, an ache of longing so fierce it frightened me. And I was afraid, too, that what I was feeling must be written all over my face, and clearly obvious to Louis. Yet he seemed to notice nothing.

'I'll go and speak to her now,' he said. 'I won't be long. Will you wait?'

I nodded. I could not trust myself to speak.

He left the room and I crossed to sit in the little spindle-legged chair, my heart pounding. It was crazy, quite crazy, that I should feel this way about a man who had deprived me of my home without so much as a proper apology and brought me here against my will. A man who thought of nothing but business and making money, a man who could exile his brother simply because they did not get along, who seemed to have little interest in his daughter beyond disciplining her. Yet somehow, insidiously, I had developed feelings for him that I had never experienced for anyone else.

It must be, I thought, that the shock of my father's murder and my grief at his loss had left me vulnerable. I was grasping at straws, looking for something or someone to fill the empty place in my heart and distract me from my pain. It was a stupid infatuation, nothing more and nothing less, and it would go as quickly as it had come. It had to, for there could never be anything between Louis and me, and with the thinking part of me, I did not want there to be.

But it was not the thinking part of me that was instigating these powerful emotions. It was something dark and primal, something over which I had no control. That, I think, was what disturbed me most of all – to think that something like this could creep up on me so slyly and possess me so utterly with such suddenness.

My eye fell on the brandy decanter and suddenly I felt the need for something to calm my jangling nerves and steady the uneven beat of my heart. But it would not be proper to take a drink of Louis' brandy without asking, and I could never bring myself to do that – faith, it was not proper for a lady to drink brandy at all! But oh, I could do with that warming trickle down my throat and into my trembling stomach!

Louis' empty glass stood on the little drinks table where he had left it and I hovered, sorely tempted. There was no sound of footsteps on the stairs; he must have found Antoinette awake and be talking to her. It would be some time before he returned. Suppose I was to pour myself just a little, and drink it quickly – he would not be any the wiser – unless of course he smelled it on my breath. But since he had been drinking himself and we would not be in close proximity, the danger of that was not so great . . . was it?

I reached for the decanter, then stopped myself. If he *should* smell it and know I was drinking secretly, I would die of shame. Even if I ran up to my room and rinsed my mouth afterwards, the smell might still linger . . .

I stood uncertain, sorely tempted, yet afraid to give in to the longing that had become almost as overwhelming as my stupid, unreasonable longing for Louis himself.

'Flora.'

His voice from the doorway made me jump almost out of my skin, and hot guilty colour flooded my cheeks. I snatched my hand away from the brandy decanter as if it were a burning coal and spun round, hoping he had not noticed. But, of course, he had.

'Did you want a drink?' he asked, sounding surprised.

'No . . . I . . .' I was overcome with confusion.

'I'm sorry. I should have offered you one,' he said. 'I quite forgot that you come from an environment where such refreshment is readily available.' He sounded faintly amused and the colour flamed brighter in my cheeks.

'I didn't drink at home!' I protested. 'Well, not very often, anyway.'

'But you'd like one now. The prospect of being responsible for Antoinette is weighing heavily upon you. Oh, have a drink, chérie, if that's what you want. I don't mind.'

He crossed the room, took a fresh glass and poured some brandy into it, and also into his own glass – the one I had considered using. And as he did so I realized something else which shocked me almost as much as all the other realizations. Part of the temptation had been to drink from the glass that *he* had used, to put my lips where *his* had been . . .

'No, really . . .' I said faintly.

'Come on, I've poured it now.' He seemed quite oblivious to my confusion. 'Only if you really are not used to it, I think perhaps a little water . . .'

He lifted the small jug that stood on the tray and added some to my glass.

'I've spoken to Antoinette and told her that she is to answer to you in my absence. She took it very well – I think it's quite likely she will behave better for you than she does for me. If she does not, then she is well appraised that some of her privileges will be removed on my return. But somehow I don't think you will have too much trouble with her.'

He handed me my glass, and picked up his own.

'Perhaps you would feel less guilty about indulging if we had something to drink to,' he said wryly. 'The success of my trip to France, for instance.'

'Oh – yes . . .' The brandy fumes were already in my nostrils, pungent and uplifting. 'To your business trip to France.'

He raised his glass. 'Success – and a safe return for all of us.'

Though I did not think of it at the time, it seemed a strange way of wording the toast, and a strange tone of voice in which he said it.

I sipped the amber liquid and felt it run a trickle of warmth down my throat and into my stomach.

Oh, I should not like the taste, but I did! And I should not like what it did to me either. Strong drink could be very pleasant and even medicinal in some circumstances, but it could also make men quarrelsome as well as happy, and lead to the abandonment of values, and recklessness.

At that moment, I did not care. As the alcohol beat a warm path through my veins, my eyes met Louis' over the rim of the glass, and we smiled at one another.

And this time, when the sharp excitement twisted deep inside me, I did not wince, but welcomed it. Madness it might be, but at that moment, the feelings that were running riot in me made a welcome change from grief and loss and loneliness.

For tonight, at least, I would enjoy the diversion. And leave the bearing of the consequences until tomorrow.

Seven

W hen I rose next morning, Louis had already left – and I
was glad of it. With the liberating effects of the brandy
now worn off, I would have been mortified if I had been forced
to face him, anxious that in my abandoned state I had betrayed
the tumultuous emotions that had overwhelmed me, and
shamed that I had taken strong drink at all.

Antoinette seemed to be in good humour, as if she was glad
her father was to be away for a week or so, and I hoped that did
not mean she intended to try to take advantage of his absence. I
would spend as much time as I could with her, I decided. My
initiation into the mysteries of my new secretarial duties would
have to wait until Louis returned and I was relieved of my
responsibility for Antoinette.

As it so happened, there would have been little I could do in
that regard in any case, for Bevan sent a message to say he was
unwell again and remaining at home to nurse the cough that
plagued him. Clearly he had returned too soon, and made
himself ill again, and I could see why Louis felt the need of a
younger, fitter secretary. But as yet I did not have the experience to be of any use without considerable guidance, and
instead I suggested to Antoinette that since it was a fine bright
day we might take a walk so that she could show me something
of the grounds.

To my surprise, she agreed readily enough, and well
wrapped-up against the still-chilly wind, we set out. Clearly
she was proud of her home and its magnificent setting, and we
went much further than I had intended, circling the deer park
and even venturing into the woods beyond. My suspicions as to

her motives were aroused, however, when she pointed out to me the pheasant-breeding pens which would soon be full of strutting chicks, and I noticed, not far off, a dilapidated cottage with a thin trail of smoke spiralling from the chimney.

This must be the hovel where her friend John lived, I guessed, and instantly I was on the alert, fearing some kind of confrontation. But the door of the cottage was firmly closed, and of John or his dog there was no sign.

'I think it's time we went back,' I said.

She glanced at me, her foxy green eyes sharp. 'You are tired? You are not used to long walks, I suppose.'

'I am very used to long walks!' I returned. 'But it looks to me as if the path is becoming very muddy.'

'Oh, it's always muddy in the woods in winter,' Antoinette said airily. 'The ground doesn't get the chance to dry out under the trees.'

'All the more reason for staying in the park,' I said, and did not add that I had reasons of my own, which had nothing to do with the mud or even the risk of crossing paths with John, and everything to do with the little thrill I felt from being on Louis' land. Oh, the woods were his, too, I supposed, but they were wild and natural, they belonged more to the animals and the birds than to any man, whilst the park was tended on Louis' orders and kept to his design. It was foolish of me to feel so, I knew, yet I could not help it. It came from the singing excitement that filled my heart, an excitement not unlike that which begins when the first buds of spring burst on the trees and the sun is warm on the skin after the chill of a long winter. It was a measure of the insanity that had taken hold of me, but I could not care.

When we returned to the house we went in by the rear entrance so as not to tread mud from our boots all over the front hall.

'My, but you've roses in your cheeks!' Cook remarked. 'It's the first time I've seen them since you came here!'

She was stirring a cauldron and the aroma of good vegetable broth filled the kitchen, making me feel truly hungry for the first time in a long while.

'Fresh air works wonders,' I said. 'I hope it's not too long until luncheon!'

Antoinette and I went to our rooms to divest ourselves of our outerwear, and as I came back down the staircase, a small sound alerted me to the fact that someone was in the study. Had Bevan come in after all? If so, he would be wondering why I had not presented myself to assist him.

I crossed the hall, my slippered feet making no sound, and pushed open the door. Then I stopped, staring in surprise. Not Bevan, but Gavin, poring over some papers on the desk. When he saw me in the doorway, a startled look crossed his face.

'Flora! What are you doing here?'

'I thought perhaps Mr Bevan was better and had come in to work,' I said.

'Oh, that old fool is never going to be better!' Gavin said carelessly and rather cruelly. 'Only the Grim Reaper will put right what's wrong with him.'

As he spoke he was shuffling the papers on the desk into a hasty pile, almost as if he did not want me to see them, then he straightened, clutching them to his chest.

'You are not proposing to work now, are you?'

'Well, no . . .'

'Off you go then.'

It was so unlike Gavin's usual syrupy smooth charm, I was startled. He seemed eager to be rid of me, and for the life of me I could not understand why.

I turned, and it was then that I noticed that the bureau which I had found locked yesterday now stood open. Clearly the papers which Gavin was so anxious I should not see were the ones which were usually kept under lock and key.

'Shall I see you at luncheon?' I did not know why I said it, unless perhaps to give myself a moment longer to stare at the open bureau and wonder what was kept there that was so secret that Bevan had become agitated by the mere touch of my hand on the door, and Gavin hustled me out of the study as if I were a trespasser.

'I expect so, yes.' Again his tone was short.

I went to the parlour, puzzling over the incident. There had been something almost furtive about the way Gavin had scrabbled up the papers and dismissed me. Was it that he had not wanted me to see their contents – or that he had been taking advantage of Louis' and Mr Bevan's absence to pry himself into something he was not usually party to? I did not know why such an idea had come into my head, and I told myself I was making a mystery where none existed.

But my curiosity had been aroused all the same, and I thought I would very much like to see what it was that everyone else seemed so anxious I should not.

Gavin, when I next saw him at luncheon, seemed to have quite regained his usual breezy manner.

'I'm so glad you're here, Uncle Gavin,' Antoinette greeted him. 'I was very afraid yesterday that Papa had upset you.'

'Oh, he's always upsetting me, you know that,' Gavin said ruefully. 'But it would take more than a few harsh words to get rid of me!'

'I certainly hope so! I want you to have a look at Perdita for me. I thought she seemed a little lame, but Thompson insists there is nothing wrong with her.'

'Of course I'll look at her for you, sweeting.'

'And perhaps ride with me if there really is nothing the matter with her?'

Gavin raised an eyebrow. 'Faith, I am honoured! It's not often you ask your old uncle to ride with you.'

She dimpled at him. 'Oh, you're not old! You're much younger than Papa.'

'A couple of years only.'

'Well you *seem* much younger. And much more fun! And if you don't ride with me, I won't be able to go. Papa has forbidden me to go out alone.'

'Ah! Now I see it all. It's not like you to obey your father so readily, though.'

Antoinette gave me a sly look. 'I have to answer to Flora while Papa is away. And she is very strict, aren't you, Flora?'

I shook my head, smiling, and refusing to be drawn.

'Do you ride, Flora?' Gavin asked.

'I'm afraid not,' I admitted. 'Anywhere I needed to go, I went by trap. And riding can be expensive as well as time-consuming. Neither money nor time were plentiful at Tucker's Grave.'

'In that case, I think you should learn!' Gavin said. 'Why, I'd be happy to teach you myself.'

'Oh, I don't think so.' I couldn't help but wonder what Louis would say if he came home to find me trotting about the countryside on a horse belonging to him, and with his much-disliked brother for company.

'Well, you have only to say the word,' Gavin told me. Then his face became serious. 'If you could ride you could go back to visit your friends and even spend an hour or two in your old home, and no one the wiser,' he said. 'You must miss it all a great deal.'

'I do,' I agreed wistfully. 'But even if I could ride, I wouldn't be able to get into the inn. Louis has had it all boarded up.'

'But you must have a key.'

'No. There was only the one, and Louis has that. He is the rightful owner now, remember.'

Antoinette was becoming bored with this conversation. 'Uncle Gavin, can we ride this afternoon?' she begged. 'When you've checked out Perdita for me?'

He laughed. 'Don't you think I have any work to do?'

'No,' she said without hesitation. 'That's Papa's domain. You . . . I've never known you to choose work over pleasure. In fact, I don't think you do any work at all!'

Gavin's eyes flickered over my face and for a brief moment I saw an almost uncanny reflection of that look I had seen when I surprised him in the study. Then, just as quickly, it was gone, and Gavin was his laughing, confident self once more.

'Of course I never work if I can help it. Especially when your father is not here to drive me with a bull whip like some poor slave. Yes, Antoinette, if Perdita is not lame, we will ride this afternoon. And it is Flora's loss that she chooses not to come with us.'

*   *   *

145

It was almost certainly that conversation over luncheon which set me thinking again about Tucker's Grave and how much I missed it – and missed, too, all my old friends in Monksmoor, the nearby village. It would be so pleasant to see them again, and perhaps with Louis away this was my opportunity to do so, for I felt fairly certain he would not approve of me making any such visit, though for the life of me I did not know the reason why.

I would not be able to go into the inn, of course, since I had no key, but simply to be on familiar ground would be a comfort to me, and I thought, too, that I would very much like to visit my father's grave.

The next day dawned bright, cold and clear, and I suggested to Antoinette that we might take a drive in the carriage. To my surprise, she agreed readily enough, as if she were making an effort to make the best of our new situation.

The carriage was made ready and Cook prepared a picnic lunch for us in a wicker hamper – cold game pie and some pickles, and a stone flask of home-made elderberry wine. As we settled back, the carriage rug tucked snugly around our knees, I wondered if Antoinette might be remembering those drives with her Grandmama which she had spoken of, for there was a pensive expression on her sharp little face, and she said little.

As the countryside through which we travelled became more familiar it seemed to call to me, singing with the rattle of the wheels on the road and the sighing of the wind around the carriage, and the longing in me was a bitter-sweet ache. Yet somehow at the same time the sense of latent excitement that I had felt ever since I had realized my feelings for Louis was there too, and an edge of wonder that I could experience such a jumble of emotions, so sharply, so clearly, and see the old familiar sights through new eyes as if, like a newborn babe, I was seeing them for the first time.

At the top of the rise above the village I asked Thompson to stop for a moment, and Antoinette and I got down so as to have a better view. My stomach twisted with homesickness as I looked down on the little cluster of houses that was Monks-moor, the smoke curling up comfortingly from their chimneys, and the church with its square tower rising high above the churchyard trees as if to be the closer to God and heaven. I thought of how I had followed my father's coffin along the winding path to its great oak door, and felt again the great abyss of despair and grief opening up within me. But this morning, with the sun glinting on the roof slates so that they shone like polished pewter and the flag fluttering bravely from its pole on the very summit of the tower, I remembered other times – walking along that same path to morning service as a child, my mother and father one on each side of me, holding my hands as I skipped along with no thought of the tedious hour and a half ahead of me, simply happy in the company of the two people I loved most in the world. I remembered too a wedding when Agnes Grant, the butcher's daughter, had married a handsome young man from the next village. They had arranged for a large wagon to carry them and their guests out to Tucker's Grave when the ceremony was over so as to be able to celebrate in style, and even now I could see Agnes in her lovely new gown and flowers in her hair, squashed into that wagon between her fat old father and her new husband, laughing for joy.

The church might recently have been the setting for some of the darkest moments of my life, but that was not the whole story. It was the place my own mother and father had married, the place where I had been baptized. All life was encapsulated there, sorrow and joy, celebration and mourning, and the truth of it, striking me for the first time, uplifted me and seemed, in some way, almost to set me free.

'Can you see Tucker's Grave from here?' Antoinette's voice interrupted my reverie.

'Not really. You see where the road winds up again? It's just out of sight over the brow of the hill.'

Antoinette stood for a moment, shading her eyes and staring into the distance.

'What's that pile of stones in the middle of the fields?' she asked.

I followed her line of vision. Stark on the skyline were the crumbling remains of what had once been the stout walls of the abbey. I told her so.

'The abbey that is linked by underground tunnels to the inn?' Antoinette's usually bored tones had become animated – she was as fascinated by the romance of it as her father and uncle had been before her.

'Yes.'

'Did you never explore them?' she asked.

I laughed. 'Never.'

'Because you were afraid you might come upon the bones of the old monks who died trapped there?'

'Because of the spiders!' I told her with a shudder. 'I think we should be going on now, Antoinette, if we are to have time to do all the things I plan.'

We drove on, down over the hill and into Monksmoor village. At this time on a winter's day the main street was quite deserted, for the children were all at the dame school, the men at work in the fields, and the womenfolk busy at home with their daily chores. There was only old Toby Taylor, shuffling along leaning heavily on his stick. When he saw the carriage approaching he stopped and doffed his hat respectfully, much to my amusement. What would he think, I wondered, if he knew it was just Flora from Tucker's Grave Inn who was riding in such splendour!

'I should like to visit my father's grave and pay my respects,' I said to Antoinette, 'but I promise I won't be long.'

'Oh, I'll come with you,' she replied to my surprise. 'I like looking at old gravestones. And I might find some of my relatives buried here. My grandfather's family originated from this part of Devon, you know.'

I could not help but smile wryly. 'I do know, yes, Antoinette, since I am part of that family. And besides my father's grave, I can show you half a dozen more if you are interested – all relations your grandfather left behind when he made his money and moved away.'

'Oh of course!' she said, as if she had never before made

the connection. 'I suppose you and I are cousins in a sort of distant way.'

'It's the reason your father came to inherit my home,' I said. 'It's very unfair, I think, but there you are. It's the law of the land and will be until some enlightened politician sees fit to change it.'

'Because you are a woman,' Antoinette said.

'Yes.'

She was silent for a moment. Then she said: 'Does that mean then that if Papa were to die I'd lose my home too?'

I did not want to alarm her, but I could not be less than honest.

'I'm afraid it does. But I don't think you should worry your head about it. Nothing is going to happen to your father for a very long time. You'll be married with a home of your own long before then.'

I half expected Antoinette to retort, as she had once before, that she had no intention of marrying, but for the moment the question of inheritance was the only thing on her mind.

'Who would own Belvedere if something did happen to Papa?' she persisted.

'Well, your Uncle Gavin is your father's closest relative,' I said, cornered. And then, to lighten the tone: 'I suppose he'd own Tucker's Grave, too. *My* home.'

'He'd be a very rich man then,' she said thoughtfully. 'He'd like that.'

'But not the responsibility that goes with it, perhaps,' I said wryly. 'But nothing is going to happen to your father, Antoinette.'

'He goes to France.' Her face was very serious now. 'France is a very dangerous place at present, I've heard him say so. And there's the voyage too. Ships can be lost at sea.'

My heart seemed to stop beating at her words. She was quite right, of course. France *was* a dangerous place, and as for the crossing . . . I thought of all the ships that foundered, and quaked inwardly.

But Louis' captain would not attempt to make the crossing if the weather looked set to blow up a storm, I reassured myself. And the French revolutionaries, bloodthirsty as they were, would not have any interest in an English merchant.

'Stop this at once, Antoinette,' I said severely. 'You are frightening yourself, and me as well. Look – we're at the churchyard now. Are you coming in with me?'

The carriage had indeed drawn up at the lychgate. We climbed down and Antoinette wandered off, deciphering the inscriptions on the weathered old stones and tombs whilst I followed the path to the spot where my father lay.

The grave still looked new, and the headstone with my mother's name on it lay in the grass beside it. The earth had begun to settle now though and in a month or two it would be time to have the stone re-erected.

I would ask Louis if he would lend me enough money to have my father's name inscribed upon it by the stonemason, and perhaps have it cleaned of lichen before it was replaced, I decided. I did not like the idea of having to beg like a pauper but since I had no money of my own I had no choice if I was to accord my father the respect he deserved.

I fell to my knees beside the grave.

'Oh Father, I wish I could have brought you some flowers,' I whispered. 'But there are none to be had at this time of year. I'll come again in spring with daffodils and tulips. You'd like that, wouldn't you?'

You came, my dear. That's all that matters to me. His voice seemed to speak in my head, clear as if he had been right there beside me.

'Oh Father!' I pressed my fingers to my lips. 'At least you are with Mother now. But I do miss you, so very much.'

And the voice came again.

We are with you too. Always with you.

The wind stirred the branches of the trees that overhung the grave. I looked up. A pair of blackbirds had settled there briefly. They seemed to be watching me. And suddenly my spirit lightened and I felt my lips curve into a smile of wonder. For long moments I regarded them, motionless, and they regarded me. Then the wind stirred the branch again, they spread their wings and were gone, following one another across the churchyard in the sunshine.

I felt that my heart went with them.

'Flora! Flora, my dear, is it really you?'

So lost in thought was I that I had not noticed anyone approaching; now I looked up to see Alice Doughty on the path.

'Alice! Oh, how good it is to see you!' I got to my feet and ran to hug her. 'What are you doing here? You haven't . . . ?'

'Lost George?' Her lips twitched as she read my mind. 'Oh no. I know exactly where he is – at home, tending the forge. No, it's my turn for cleaning the church, and when I came out the door and saw you there, well, lawks, I couldn't believe my own eyes! Are you home again? Have you come back to us?'

'Only for the day, I'm afraid,' I told her. 'I've driven over with Antoinette – she's my father's cousin's daughter, and she is off somewhere seeking her long-lost relatives.'

'Oh mercy, is that your carriage at the lychgate? That grand affair with goodness knows how many guineas worth of horse-flesh between the shafts? My, you have come up in the world, Flora!'

'Oh, it's not mine,' I said hastily. 'It belongs to Louis.'

'Ah – him. I might have known.' Alice sniffed. 'Him as came to your father's funeral and took you away. Louis Fletcher, isn't it? Peter Fletcher's boy.'

I was surprised that Alice seemed to know so much about Louis. They had not seemed to be acquainted at the funeral. Alice laid a hand on my arm.

'So how have you been, my love? Homesick, I'll be bound. That's why you're here. Well, it's close on dinner time. Why don't you come home with me and have a bit to eat with me and George?'

'Oh, I couldn't impose,' I said regretfully. 'I did intend calling on you, of course, but it's not just me, it's Antoinette too. And we've a picnic lunch Cook packed for us, and she will be offended if we take it back uneaten.'

'And I shall be offended if you don't come and eat with us!' Alice returned smartly. 'I shall think you've got too grand for us, with your carriages and your picnic baskets! As for this Antoinette . . . well it will do her good to see something of the other side of life, if I know anything about it. If she's anything like the rest of her family, that is.'

I smiled. Alice was practically echoing my own thoughts. It would do Antoinette good to see that there were people in the world without the advantages of wealth who were still good and loving, happy, and content with their lot.

'Thank you, Alice,' I said. 'We'll accept your offer. The coachman can eat our picnic and take whatever is over home for his wife and family. Would you like to ride with us?'

And: 'Oh, I most certainly would!' Alice replied with relish.

We caused quite a stir arriving at the forge in the grand carriage. George came rushing out with the sweat from the furnace running down his face, thinking, no doubt, that he had some rich new customer, and Alice took great delight in climbing down to surprise him.

'Disappointed, George? Oh, you won't be! Not when you see who I've got here!'

George was indeed as pleased to see me as Alice had been.

'Flora, my dear! Well, well. Just let me go and get those irons out, and I'll be in to see you . . .'

'They're stopping for their dinner,' Alice said. 'And it'll be ready the minute I've got it on the plates, so mind you don't take too long about it.'

'As if!' George disappeared back into the forge and I followed Alice towards the cottage which adjoined it. But Antoinette, I could see, was fascinated by the fiery furnace glowing white hot in the dark interior of the forge and I could well understand that. It had fascinated me, too, as a child – a place that could have been a vision of hell, but was somehow more exciting than frightening.

'Do you shoe horses here?' she asked George, bold as if she had known him all her life.

'I do,' he told her. 'Amongst other things. You have the travelling farrier to attend to yours, I dare say.'

'Yes – but oh! This is wonderful!'

'I'm expecting the shire horses what pulls the brewer's dray in this afternoon,' he told her. 'And a little foal too. You can come in and watch if you like – if you can stop that long, that is.'

'Oh, we can, can't we, Flora?' Her face was alight.

I smiled. 'Of course we can,' I said.

Dinner with George and Alice was both comfortable and comforting. Alice was a good plain cook who dished up directly from the stove, something I imagined Antoinette had never experienced before. Her disbelieving expression as Alice banged spoonfuls of steak pudding on to the plates and set them unceremoniously in front of us was really quite amusing, but she refrained from caustic comment – afraid, perhaps, if she offended George she would not be taken to see the horses being shod – and she certainly seemed to enjoy the good wholesome fare.

When we had finished she went with George to the forge and I helped Alice clear the dishes and wash them in the big stone scullery sink.

'I'm glad I've got you by yourself,' Alice said, elbow deep in soapy water. 'There's things I want to say to you that can't be said in front of the maid. I've been worried to death about you, Flora, and that's a fact.'

'I'm well enough,' I assured her. 'Grieving and homesick, of course, but well enough.'

'I don't know . . . taking you off like that! You should have come to us. You know you'd have been welcome.'

'Of course, but I wouldn't have liked to impose,' I said. 'And I think Louis thought it wasn't safe for me to remain at Tucker's Grave after what happened.'

'Hmm.' Alice propped a dish on the cupboard that served as a drainer and turned to me. 'That's one of the things I wanted to talk to you about. There's been a lot of talk in the village as to who it could have been who did away with your poor father.'

I was silent, and she went on: 'Most of it comes from Jem Giddings, mind you, so how much attention can be paid to it I wouldn't like to say.' She sniffed loudly. 'You know what Jem Giddings is like.'

I nodded. Jem Giddings was little better than a vagrant who was too fond of strong drink – when he could get it – for his own good.

'He'd been to your place that night, so he says,' Alice went on.

Again I nodded. I seemed to remember seeing Jem amongst those in the bar when I had gone in to bid my father goodnight. 'I think he was, yes.'

'Well, he'd had a drop too much as usual, and fell in the hedge on his way home to sleep it off. But sometime during the night he was awakened by horses. Going hell for leather they were, he says.'

'The men who came to the inn.' My throat had gone dry. 'He saw them!'

'Not only that, he reckons he recognized one of the horses.' Alice had abandoned any pretence at washing the dishes. She wiped her hands on an old piece of cloth, drying them carefully. 'Now, it was a dark night, I know, but Jem says the moon had come out just then, and he saw a grey with a white flash on the muzzle and one white sock. He reckons he'd seen that horse before – and he'd know it anywhere. And whatever else you might say about him, Jem knows his horses.'

That much was true, I knew. Before he had fallen from grace, Jem had been a groom.

'So where did he think he'd seen it before?' I asked.

'Well, you know he covers a lot of ground on his travels. Has a bit of a round trip like, gone for months, then back again . . .' Alice paused, as if unwilling, now that the moment had come, to put into words what was on her mind. 'Well, he reckons he's seen that horse over Dartmouth way.'

'Dartmouth?' I repeated stupidly.

'That's right. And it's set folks wondering, what with the inn going to that Louis Fletcher, whether maybe *he* might have had something to do with it. To get his hands on Tucker's Grave, I mean.'

'Louis!' I shook my head vigorously. 'No! He'd never . . .'

'I'm not so sure about that,' Alice said. Her mouth was set. 'According to Jem there's rumours in those parts that he's killed before. Did away with his wife, so they say. Now, Flora, can you see why it is I've been so worried about you?'

Eight

T he dark little scullery seemed to close in around me, the heat from the range suddenly overpoweringly hot, the lingering smell of cooking sour in my stomach.

Louis a cold-blooded murderer twice over? No! I could not believe it!

'Alice,' I said, 'this is nothing but gossip and speculation, and all of it hinging on the word of a man who is drunk for most of his waking hours. Louis' wife is dead, yes, and has been for many years. But she died of a fever.'

Even as I said it, I seemed to hear Bevan's voice again. *Oh well, if that's what you've been told, it's not for me to tell you different.* And Louis' own: *I have no wife.* But I closed my ears to them, thrust away the sharp shiver of doubt they raised.

'As for Tucker's Grave, it's just a humble coaching inn, and Louis is a very wealthy man,' I went on. 'It couldn't possibly be worth his while to have my father murdered so as to gain possession of it. Why, it would be just a drop in the ocean to him – a month's profit would be less than he can make with business deals in a single day. In any case, he's had it boarded up.'

Alice's face screwed into an expression of bewilderment.

'What are you talking about – boarded up?' she asked.

'He had men sent over to do the job the very next day after I left,' I said. 'He wanted to make sure that it was not broken into by vandals.'

'Well, it certainly didn't look boarded up to me when we drove past there last week!' Alice said shortly. 'Deserted, maybe, but not boarded up.'

It was my turn to look bewildered. Why should Louis tell me the inn was boarded up if it was not true? Alice must be mistaken. The workmen had done their work so neatly it simply looked shuttered. Before I could say as much, however, the door opened and Antoinette came rushing in, bursting with excitement.

'Flora, you must come and see the foal! She's the prettiest thing! And the man who owns her says she'll soon be up for sale! I want Papa to buy her for me. Oh, come and see, please, so that you can help me to persuade him!'

'Antoinette, I know nothing about horses . . .'

And I have other things on my mind . . .

But Antoinette was not to be put off.

'Flora, you must! I insist!' She grabbed my sleeve, a gesture so unlike her I could scarcely believe it, and actually tugged me in the direction of the door.

I glanced back. Alice was watching us and the expression on her rosy face was one of deep concern. But the opportunity for confidences was gone. We would not be alone again today.

The foal was, indeed, every bit as pretty as Antoinette had said, a little bay who would doubtless grow into an elegant filly – even I, with no real interest in horseflesh, and my mind spinning around quite different matters, could see that.

'I have to have her!' Antoinette said. 'I'll die if I don't!'

'But you already have a horse,' I pointed out.

'Perdita, yes. But it would be such fun to have a little foal too! I could help break her – she'd be truly mine, as if she were my own baby. You will help me persuade Papa, won't you? He will buy her for me, won't he?'

Certainly Louis seemed to give Antoinette everything she asked for, in material terms, anyway. But it occurred to me suddenly – how much did I really know about Louis?

'I expect he will, yes.'

By the time George had finished the shoeing it was mid-afternoon and high time that we started back to Belvedere. But there was something else that I wanted to do, even if it meant we

157

did not arrive home until after dark. When we had bidden George and Alice goodbye – Alice clasped me tightly and bid me 'be careful, Flora' – I gave my instructions to Thompson.

'I'd like to make a short detour. Would you drive past Tucker's Grave Inn, please?'

He looked a little surprised. Though the inn had been on my original itinerary I suppose he thought that since we had been so long at the forge I would have decided it was now too late. But it was not for him to argue. Thompson had long been in the service of those whose word was law; the fact that I was a humble innkeeper's daughter of the same class as himself did not enter into it. I was now part of the Belvedere household, I had ordered the carriage and was in charge of the master's daughter, and my wishes were to be treated with respect.

'Can we visit the ruined abbey too?' Antoinette asked as the horses drew the carriage up the long hill out of the village of Monksmoor.

'I don't think there will be time,' I said. 'We'll come back another day, perhaps.'

She pouted, and I added: 'We very likely could have visited the abbey if you had not spent so long with the horses. You must realize that sometimes there are choices to be made in life.'

She was silent, sulking, and I thought again what a difficult girl she could be. She had enjoyed a day full of interest, yet the moment her wishes were thwarted she once more became pettish and miserable.

As the inn came in sight, my heart began to beat unevenly and the dryness increased in my throat. The carriage ground to a halt, and I climbed down, almost afraid, now I was here, to look on my old home.

When I did, my heart leaped again in my throat.

Alice had not been mistaken when she said she did not think Tucker's Grave had been boarded up. Though dark, deserted and forlorn, it looked otherwise exactly as it had when I had left it.

How long I stood there on the forecourt staring at my home, I do not know. My thoughts were whirling, yet a thick fog seemed to have clouded my brain so I could not get hold of any one of them to try to make sense of it. All I knew was that Louis had lied to me, for what reason I could not imagine.

And if he had lied to me about this, what else had he lied about? What secrets was he keeping from me?

'Miss Flora.' Thompson's voice, deferential yet firm, invaded my thoughts. 'If there's nothing else, I really think we should be making for home. It's best not to be out on these lonely roads after nightfall.'

'Yes. Yes, of course. We'll go now.'

I felt oddly vulnerable, suddenly, and conscious too that I was responsible not only for my own safety, but Antoinette's also. I climbed back up into the carriage, though my eyes still lingered on Tucker's Grave Inn as we drove away.

'It's quite small, isn't it?' Antoinette remarked disparagingly. 'A very ordinary-looking place really.'

Ordinary, yes. And yet Louis had wasted no time in coming to claim it as his inheritance, forcing me to leave it and then lying to me about having it boarded up.

Why would he do any of those things? All the questions that had puzzled me in the early days, and which I had put to the back of my mind, rose, clamouring once more like a flock of startled birds. He had no need of it for financial gain. He seemed in no hurry to put in a new landlord to run it. Yet he had refused to allow me to stay there. And he had lied to me about having it boarded up. That was the most vexing question of all.

But by no means the most disturbing one.

I thought again of all Alice had said. I had dismissed out of hand her suggestion that the men who had come in the middle of the night and shot my father might have some connection with Louis. The link was so tenuous, even if Jem Giddings had been a sober and reliable witness – which he was not. But I could no longer avoid making it.

Had Louis wanted Tucker's Grave for some reason of his own? Wanted it so badly that he had sent a pair of ruffians to despatch my father so that he could get his hands on it? I recoiled from the thought.

But they had not shot him outright, I reminded myself. There had been a heated exchange first. Could it be that they had come with some kind of proposal from Louis for illicit dealings and with orders to finish the argument by force if my father failed to agree? Which of course he would have done. My father would have no truck with anything that was not strictly honest and honourable; he was not that kind of man.

I had not thought Louis to be that kind of man either. Oh, it had crossed my mind he might be involved in a little free trade, and that the records concealed in the locked bureau in his study related to that. But something so serious that an innocent man should be murdered so that it could go on unhindered? No, not in a million years. It was beyond belief in the man I had come to know – and fallen in love with.

But then it seemed I did not know him at all. For if the other allegation Alice had made carried any truth, then he was already a murderer. The murderer of his wife.

I shivered, a chill similar to the one that had pervaded me in the days after my father's death creeping over my skin. I pulled the rug more closely around my knees and still gained no warmth from it. I felt nauseous too, and the rocking of the carriage exacerbated it.

Dear God, it was a nightmare, all of it. Just when I had thought that I had turned the corner towards a new life, just when spring had seemed to be waking from the cold depths of winter, I was plunged once again into dark confusion, despair – and fear. Was there no one in my new world that I could trust?

I pressed my fingers to my mouth, fighting back the nausea. And all the while the carriage took me further and further away from my old friends, and closer and closer to the dark secrets of Belvedere House.

When we arrived back, Gavin was there.

'I thought I'd lost the pair of you!' he said jokingly. 'Where in the world have you been?'

I was saved from answering by Antoinette, whose good humour returned at the chance to relive her adventures.

'Oh, we had lunch in a cottage and there was a forge where I watched a horse being shod, and I've seen the most darling foal that Papa absolutely has to buy for me, and we went to Tucker's Grave Inn and . . .'

Gavin glanced at me. 'You went to Tucker's Grave Inn? I thought you said Louis has the only key.'

'We didn't go inside,' I said. 'We only stopped on the forecourt for a few moments.'

'That must have been very upsetting for you, if it's been boarded up.' His narrowed eyes were watching me. Did he know, I wondered, that Louis had lied?

Again I was saved from having to reply by Antoinette's intervention.

'It's not boarded up,' she said. 'Just locked. I wish we could have gone in, though. I would have liked to explore the passages that lead to the abbey ruins. Not that I think Flora would have come with me. She's afraid of the spiders. *You* could take me, Uncle Gavin. You wanted to explore them, too, didn't you?'

Gavin laughed. 'When I was a boy.'

'Oh, say you will! You'd like to, I know.'

'Perhaps one day I will,' Gavin said. 'Provided you behave, yourself – and provided your Papa will let me have the key. But I don't suppose we should get very far. With the abbey end blocked up, the tunnels have no doubt collapsed over the years.'

And for the time being, that was that.

After we had eaten dinner and Flora had retired to her room, Gavin repaired to the parlour. Since Louis had been away, he had taken to remaining in the house instead of returning to the Lodge – taking advantage of Louis' absence, I surmised. I had made no objection for I was glad enough of the company and Gavin had not again overstepped the bounds of propriety as he had on the day Louis had brought me my pearl collar, but tonight I was in no mood for social intercourse. Rather I wanted answers to some of the questions that were bombarding me. I had no idea how much Gavin knew, given the bad feeling that existed between the brothers, but I had every intention of finding out.

I had been silent throughout the meal, for any attempt at normal conversation would have been beyond me, and I had been glad that Antoinette was so full of her day that she talked constantly to Gavin about it. But Gavin must have noticed my preoccupation, for when we were alone, and he had poured himself a large glass of Louis' good cognac, he said idly: 'You are very quiet tonight, Flora. Did going back to Tucker's Grave upset you?'

'Yes,' I said. 'Yes, it did.'

'Then I shall have to try to cheer you up, shall I not?' He threw himself down on the chaise beside me, stretching his long legs comfortably and sipping his brandy. 'Lightening dark moods is my speciality.'

'Not tonight, Gavin,' I said.

'Oh come! You'll ruin my good opinion of my own qualities!' He moved a little closer. I moved away. It was now or never.

'Have you ever seen a horse in these parts with a white flash on its muzzle and a white sock on the left hind leg?' I asked.

'I beg your pardon?' Gavin sounded bewildered, as well he might.

I took a deep breath. 'A horse like that was seen galloping away from Tucker's Grave on the night my father was murdered,' I said.

Gavin froze. I felt the sudden stillness in him, tangible as the bite of frost in the air on a sharp December night. Then: 'Why do you ask if I know such a horse?' he asked.

'The man who saw it is a vagrant,' I said. 'Over the months he travels far and wide through the countryside begging food and the price of a jug of ale, though his home, in so far as he has one, is our village, Monksmoor. According to what I heard today, he was sleeping off the effects of his liquor in the hedge not far from Tucker's Grave, saw two riders pass, and recognized one of the horses as one he has seen in the vicinity of Dartmouth. I wondered if it meant anything to you.'

For a long moment Gavin remained motionless. Then his breath came out on a short laugh.

'My dear Flora, have you any idea how many horses there are in the vicinity of Dartmouth?'

'Yes, of course. But this one is distinctive enough for Jem Giddings to have recognized it,' I persisted. 'Are you sure you don't remember having seen it?'

'Not that I recall. In any case, the man is a vagrant, you say, and a drunk to boot. Surely no faith can be placed in anything he might say?'

'That's true enough,' I agreed. 'But he's also a former groom, who knows his horses.'

'I'm sorry, but I can't help you,' Gavin said. 'If I should see a horse like the one you describe, I'll take note of who it belongs to, but I should think such a thing is very unlikely.'

I bit my lip. There was no arguing with what he said – why, it had been exactly my own reaction when Alice had told me of it. And yet . . . I couldn't avoid the disturbing certainty that what I had said had meant something to Gavin; that for all his protestations to the contrary he *had* recognized the description of the horse Jed claimed to have seen. And that could mean only one thing. He was denying any knowledge of it in order to protect Louis.

'Flora,' Gavin said, his voice gentle now, 'it's no wonder you are so upset if you have been reminded of the terrible thing that happened to your father. All this dwelling upon it will do you no good. Don't you think you should try to put it out of your mind?'

My hands balled to fists in the folds of my skirt.

'I saw my father lying dead on the floor of the bar in a pool of his own blood,' I said harshly. 'I can never put it out of my mind. And if there is the slightest chance that I can identify the men who did that to him and bring them to justice, then I shall take it.'

Gavin reached out and covered my hand with his.

'I can understand your feelings, Flora, but I really do believe that for your own good you should not pursue the matter.'

163

A chill whispered over my skin; there was something in the way he said it that made it something more than merely concern for my emotional well-being. Could it be that he was warning me – that he knew that if I discovered the identity of the horse and rider that I, too, would be in danger of my life?

I eased my hand away from the grip of his fingers. There were still more things that I needed to ask Gavin.

'What became of Louis' wife?' I asked.

'Lisette?' He sounded startled. 'That's quite a change of subject, Flora! I thought we were discussing your father's end.'

There was no way I could tell him of the connections that had been made for me that day, and how they were tormenting me.

'I thought you bid me forget about my father,' I hedged. 'And I can't help wondering . . . Antoinette told me that she died of a fever. But that isn't so, is it?'

I was watching his face closely, and I saw a strange expression flicker in his eyes. Something, I thought, confused, that might almost have been amusement.

'Lisette was quite a woman,' he said.

And all at once, I knew. Knew the reason behind the antagonism that existed between the brothers. There had been something between Gavin and Lisette. Something that had roused Louis to such jealousy and anger that even now he could not forgive nor forget. But it did not answer my question.

'Did she die of a fever?' I persisted.

Gavin sipped his brandy, looking at me narrowly. 'What makes you think she did not?'

'I don't know,' I lied. 'But I'm right, aren't I? That might be the story Antoinette has been told, but it's not the truth, is it?'

For a long moment he was silent; I waited, holding my breath. Then: 'No, Lisette did not die of a fever,' he said.

My heart gave a great painful leap. 'Then how?' I asked harshly.

Gavin shook his head. 'I cannot tell you, Flora.'

My hands clenched again, the nails biting crescents into my palms. 'Why not?'

'Because I do not know what happened to her. One day she was here – the next she was gone. That's all I know. I was living in Dartmouth, so I was not party to what went on prior to her disappearance.'

'She . . . disappeared?' I echoed.

Gavin took another sip of his brandy. 'There was a French nobleman staying here with us at the time – the Marquis de St Valla. She ran off with him, I imagine. Certainly she had been flirting with him outrageously, but I had thought nothing of it. Lisette flirted with every handsome man who came within a mile of her. It was her way – and it drove Louis insane with jealousy. I can only think that on this occasion it was a little more than a mere flirtation, and when Louis took her to task over it, she and the Marquis decided to elope together. Whatever. When I returned to Dartmouth that night, she and the Marquis were here, next morning they were gone. She went back to France with him, I expect.'

'Did you not ask Louis what had become of her?' I said.

Gavin laughed shortly. 'The mood my brother was in? No, I tell you when Louis has the black humour upon him, the wisest course of action is to avoid him as far as is humanly possible. Questioning him about Lisette would have been like setting a tinderbox to a keg of gunpowder. Especially if I were the one asking the questions.'

'She left Antoinette?' I said, disbelieving that any mother could do such a thing. 'She left Antoinette and never came back?'

Gavin shrugged. 'Lisette was never much of a mother,' he said. 'She wanted nothing to do with Antoinette from the time she was born. It would not have been out of character for her to have abandoned the child. No doubt she missed her life in high French society and saw her opportunity to return to it with the Marquis.'

I wanted to believe it. Oh, how I wanted to believe it! And yet . . . still I could not understand how a mother could leave in the dead of night with her lover and never so much as send to ask how her little daughter was faring. It seemed to me quite unnatural. I could not credit that any woman could be so heartless.

'And you never heard of her again?' I asked.

'I have never set eyes on her,' Gavin said. 'Louis may have done, I wouldn't know. He wouldn't tell me. And it would have to be kept from Antoinette. She was told her mother had died of the fever to save her from the truth. It would never have done for Lisette to flit in and out of her life like some butterfly.'

His hand closed over mine again. 'You are upsetting yourself, Flora, over all manner of things that shouldn't concern you. Forget about Lisette, she's not worth losing sleep over. She was the greatest mistake of Louis' life and he was well rid of her. But chérie . . .' His fingers stroked mine. 'You would do well to forget about Louis too.'

I felt the colour rising in my cheeks. 'What do you mean?'

'I've seen the way you look at him, and you are set on a path to heartache. Now me – I am much less trouble. Smile for me, chérie, and I will return your smile.'

I was aware, suddenly, of where this was leading – down a path I did not want to go. I pulled my hand away once more.

'Don't, Gavin, please. I like your company, yes, but that's all. Don't spoil it.'

He sighed, looking rueful but far from heartbroken. He would have been quite prepared to take liberties if I had allowed them, I felt sure, but he would have done the same with any personable young woman he found himself alone with. And perhaps with me there was the added inducement that he would be winning a small victory over his brother. For clearly Louis was still very much on his mind.

'Louis might have wished himself rid of Lisette,' he said, returning to our previous conversation as if the diversion had never occurred. 'But he has never been able to forget her. All these years, and she haunts him still like some wraith. All these years, and she torments him still.'

Why? Because she did not run away at all? Why does she haunt him? Because he killed her?

The question hovered on my lips, but I did not ask it.

I realized with a sick heart that I was afraid to hear the answer.

Nine

The days passed and still I did not know what to think. I tossed about like a boat on a stormy sea. At one time I would tell myself that it was exactly as Gavin had said – Lisette, faithless and flighty, had grown tired of life as a merchant's wife in isolated Devon and run off to her homeland with a noble lover. She had broken Louis' heart, and he had tried to pretend she had never existed, whilst being too deeply wounded to ever be able to forget. She had formed a liaison with Gavin, too, I felt sure, and if she had formed a liaison with Gavin, then it was more than possible that there had been other indiscretions and affairs too. Such a scandal could well have given rise to the rumours of which Alice had spoken – how much more fun to speculate that Louis had done away with her, and perhaps her lover too!

As for the horse Jem Giddings claimed to have recognized, that might well be nothing but a drunken dream.

And then I would remember Gavin's reaction when I had mentioned it, my momentary certainty that he, too, had recognized the horse from my description, and I would have to convince myself that that had all been *my* overheated imagination.

As well it might have been. I had been so anxious that night about the things Alice had told me and the indisputable fact that Louis had lied to me about the boarding-up of the Inn, I might, perhaps, have misinterpreted Gavin's response to my surprising assertion.

Looked at individually, each of the things that worried me could be explained away. But the lie about Tucker's Grave could not be explained. And it threw a different light over everything else.

I spent the days with Antoinette and the evenings with Gavin – who did not, mercifully, make any further advances towards me – and all the while I fretted, turning it all over and over in my mind. Yet still, for all my doubts and fears, my feelings for Louis were strong as ever. Different, perhaps, tinged now with anxiety, darker, and lacking the joy they had at first aroused in me. But just as potent, nevertheless. A longing in my heart, an ache in my soul, a shiver of excitement in my loins. And I could not understand it.

I recoiled from Gavin, who might be a philanderer and something of a ne'er do well, but at least was honest about it, and I was drawn inexorably to a man who had certainly lied to me and might well have killed not only his wife but also been complicit in the murder of my own dear father. It was a recipe for madness.

Louis returned just a week after he had left. He rode up the drive at about four in the afternoon, just as we were taking tea in the parlour – Antoinette, myself, and Gavin, who seemed to have been spending more and more time in the house.

When she heard his step in the hall and his voice speaking to one of the servants, she set down her plate with such haste that her cake rolled down on to the carpet, and rushed to greet him.

'Papa! Papa!'

He hugged her, his chin resting against her hair, and my heart pounded painfully, the feeling part of me wanting to be in his arms, the thinking part knowing that I had allowed myself into dangerous waters indeed.

'You're here again I see, Gavin,' he said at last when Antoinette released him.

Gavin seemed unabashed. 'Someone has to look after the ladies of the household whilst you are away. When did you get back?'

'On the morning tide,' Louis said.

'Faith – you've taken your time riding home then,' Gavin commented.

'I had business to attend to first.'

Louis looked tired, I thought, and a little drawn. But then, he was at the end of a voyage and a ride and he had been conducting business negotiations today into the bargain, so it was hardly surprising.

'So – the trip met with success then?' Gavin asked.

'To some extent. But I shall have to return soon to attempt to conclude what I have begun,' Louis said, and it occurred to me that he did not look like a man who has successfully achieved his objective.

He rang the bell, and when Polly appeared he instructed her: 'Bring another cup, please, Polly. After a week away from England, there is nothing I'd like more than a good dish of tea!'

Louis spent some time closeted in the study with Gavin and Bevan. When they emerged, Gavin left and Antoinette eagerly claimed Louis' attention. I was glad she was so pleased at his return, for it proved, I thought, that beneath that careless veneer she thought a great deal of her father.

'Have you behaved yourself in my absence, Miss?' Louis asked, and for all the sternness of his tone, his love for her shone through too.

'I have, yes! Ask Flora if you don't believe me!'

'I intend to. Has she behaved herself, Flora?'

I smiled. 'She has.'

'And how have you been occupying your time, if not with mischief?'

'Oh, walking and riding and . . . I had a special reason for being good, Papa. I thought if I was, you might reward me . . . There's a foal I want you to buy for me.'

She told him about the forge and the foal she had set her heart on, and as she did so, though he was smiling, a watchful look came over Louis' face.

'Where was this?' he asked.

'Oh, the village where Flora used to live.'

His eyes were on me, narrowed, accusatory almost. 'You went home?'

'I saw no harm in it,' I returned spiritedly.

'You went to Tucker's Grave?'

I held his gaze. 'Yes.'

I said no more than that. I did not want to discuss it in front of Antoinette and clearly neither did he. But we both knew the subject would be – must be – raised later.

'It's a very dull-looking place,' Antoinette said.

'Believe me, you wouldn't have thought it dull if the staging coach had been pulling up on the forecourt,' I said. 'The horses steaming, the coachman taking down the bags, the passengers climbing out all stiff from their journey . . .'

'I wouldn't have thought it dull if we could have explored the passages either!' Antoinette returned. And to her father, 'Uncle Gavin has said he'll take me there one day so I can do just that.'

Louis' face darkened. 'Uncle Gavin will do no such thing!' he thundered.

'But . . .'

'I have said no, Antoinette, and there's an end of it. Underground passages are no place for a young lady. Now, I am going to have a wash if the water is hot for me, and change my clothes. I've worn them for quite long enough.'

Without another word he left the room.

'I'll get around him, just wait and see if I don't,' Antoinette said.

I did not reply. I did not think that on this occasion Antoinette was going to get her way. It wasn't simply that Louis did not consider exploring underground passages a suitable pastime for a young lady. Rather, I felt sure, for some reason of his own he did not want either Antoinette or Gavin going to Tucker's Grave. And he was not best pleased that we had visited it today, either.

No further mention was made of the inn over dinner, but the subject was never far from my mind. It would be broached by

Louis the moment we were alone, I felt sure, for he must know I knew he had lied to me, and want to make at least some attempt to explain himself. And even if he did not raise the subject, I would, I promised myself.

'Time you were going to bed then, Miss,' Louis said to Antoinette at last.

'Oh Papa, do I have to? I'm not at all tired!'

'You need your beauty sleep.'

'Doesn't Flora need her beauty sleep too?' Antoinette asked slyly.

'Flora is quite beautiful enough.' His eyes rested on me for a moment, that look which could make my pulses race and my skin shiver with excitement, but at the moment, tense and anxious as I was, it had no effect on me.

'I'm sure she went to bed early too when she was thirteen years old,' Louis went on, 'and that is why she looks as she does today. When you are as old as Flora, you shall stay up as late as you want too. But for the present – bed, young lady.'

Reluctantly she wished me goodnight, kissed and hugged her father, and left, and Louis and I were alone.

For some reason, now that the moment of truth had arrived I wished I could delay it. If Louis could give me no good reason for his lie it would make it the more likely that there was some truth in all my other dreadful suspicions.

'So how was France?' I asked as the door closed after Antoinette.

'In a state of flux.' Louis' expression darkened at the mention of it. 'Things are very bad there, Flora. The guillotine does its ghastly work daily and still the prisons are full to overflowing with nobles and anyone else who dares oppose the so-called will of the people.'

'And is it?' I asked. 'The will of the people, I mean?'

'For the moment, yes, it certainly seems to be,' Louis said. 'They line the streets to watch the tumbrils which carry the condemned souls, and old women sit and knit as heads are severed from bodies. The streets run with blood, and they take delight in it, a delight that goes much further than triumph over the poverty and hopelessness that were their lot. It has become a bloodlust, Flora. A madness, when the humiliation of those they see as their oppressors is no longer enough. One day, I think, they may feel shame and regret for what they are doing. But not now. Not yet.'

The passion with which he spoke lent colour and life to his words; I could see all too clearly the scenes he was describing, painted in vivid crimsons and scarlets – the colour of blood, the colour of the fires of hell.

Horror overcame me, subduing all other emotions, that any human being, however downtrodden, could take such unholy delight in the suffering and death of another. And fear, too, for Louis, that he should even think of returning to a land where such terrible things went on; where, in his own words, the streets were running with blood.

'Why do you have to go there?' I asked passionately. 'How can you possibly conduct business discussions under such circumstances?'

'I have no choice.' He said it very softly, more to himself than to me.

'Oh surely that's not so! Your safety is more important than any business deal!'

'I do what I have to do.' He poured himself a large brandy, stood sipping it, staring into the fire, and I wondered what he was seeing there amongst the dancing flames. I thought that in comparison with the horrors that occurred daily in France my own problems were very unimportant. And yet to me they were the whole world.

I moved to sit in the little captain's chair, folding my hands in my skirt and staring fixedly as I wondered how best to broach the subject that had troubled me ever since my visit to Tucker's Grave.

The fire was burning low; Louis bent to toss another log on to it, and looked at me.

'You are very quiet, Flora.'

'Yes.' I drew a deep breath. 'Louis, there is something I must ask you. Why did you tell me that Tucker's Grave has been boarded up? You must know now that I saw for myself that it has not.'

He smiled slightly. 'I thought you would ask me that.'

'Naturally I am puzzled,' I said.

'I thought it unsafe for you to remain there.'

'So you said at the time you brought me here,' I persisted. 'It does not explain why you should lie to me about sending men to board it up.'

He moved impatiently. 'I thought, wrongly, it seems, that if you were under the impression the place was shuttered and barred you would be more likely to accept there was nothing for you there, and stay well away from the place.'

'But why? Why should you be so anxious I should not go there?' I was trembling; I fought to keep my voice even. 'And to be truthful, I do not really understand why you wanted me out at all. Oh, I know you say it is not safe for me to be there, but I can't help feeling there is more to it than that. I can't help feeling you have reasons of your own for all this, that have nothing whatever to do with my welfare. And I want to know what they are.'

Louis was silent for a moment; I held my breath. Then he crossed to the table where the brandy decanter stood, poured himself another good measure, and drank it in one hearty gulp.

'I cannot answer you, Flora, beyond saying that it is indeed your safety which is my primary concern. If you had remained at Tucker's Grave it is quite possible the same fate would have befallen you as befell your father. I could not take that risk.'

My head jerked up. 'Why should it? The men were not robbers – they took nothing. Their quarrel was with my father.'

'And perhaps would next have been with you.'

'Simply because I was there, you mean? Because I was in someone's way?'

'If you like.'

'But for what reason?'

'I can't tell you that, Flora. I must simply ask you to trust me.'

'Trust you!' I was beyond prudence now; I was ablaze with the certainty that Louis knew far more than he was telling about my father's murder. 'Why should I trust you? Your actions in all of this are suspect to say the least of it. And I have to tell you there is something more. One of the horses that galloped away from the inn that night was recognized as a horse from these parts. A vagrant named Jem Giddings saw it and said he has seen it before in the Dartmouth area. So you must see where such a suggestion leads me. Who benefited from my father's death? Why, you, Louis. Who came and removed me from my home against my will? You did. And who lied to try and ensure I did not return? Why – you again!'

'Flora!' Louis strode across the room, taking me by the arms and jerking me to my feet. 'What are you saying? That *I* was responsible for your father's murder?'

I met his gaze head on, not caring that I may have been placing myself in danger by challenging him. 'Were you?' I demanded. 'Did you have my father killed so as to get your hands on Tucker's Grave for reasons of your own?'

He thrust me away, releasing my arms so abruptly I almost fell.

'Of course not! How could you think such a thing? I may have many faults, Flora – indeed, I am sure I have – but I would never, never be a party to the murder of an innocent man. Before God, life is precious to me, even the life of the most hardened criminal. That you should believe me capable of instigating the murder of a good, brave, honest man such as your father . . . Pshaw!' He turned away with an oath, throwing back his head, then bowing it as if the weight of the world had suddenly descended upon him.

And in that moment I believed him. Perhaps because of his ardent denials, perhaps simply because I wanted to. I do not know. But, God help me, I believed him.

'Louis . . .' I could no longer keep the trembling out of my voice. I pressed my hands to my mouth, looking at his broad back, his bowed head, the dark pigtail against the stretched sinew of his neck making him look somehow intensely vulnerable, and loving him.

There was no denying it. I had just accused him of the most

unspeakable act I could imagine, and now I was overcome with love so fierce it seemed to set me on fire.

'Louis . . .' I touched his shoulder tentatively, as if such a little gesture could somehow make amends.

For a moment he remained motionless, then he turned. His face in the flickering lamplight was ravaged, the lines etched deeper than ever before.

'Flora.' He gripped my arms again urgently, but this time more gently. 'I swear to you I had nothing to do with your father's death. And I swear too that I do not know who the men were who shot him down. But if you are right and they do indeed come from Dartmouth, then I will find them and have them brought to justice.'

I nodded, unable to speak.

'You do believe me, don't you?' he said. 'For your own safety, you must believe me.'

It did not, at the time, strike me as a strange thing to say. I was too much at the mercy of the emotion that was washing through me in great drowning waves.

'Yes,' I whispered.

'And I would never do anything to bring harm to you, or to those you love. Especially not now . . .'

I was in his arms. Just how it happened I am not, to this day, entirely certain. But I was in his arms and it felt so right. His lips were against my hair, my head pressed to his broad chest. The warm male scent of him was in my nostrils, a glow spreading through every bit of my body, joy in my heart. I trembled again, not with fear or anger now, but with longing, a longing like nothing I had ever experienced before, though perhaps those little shivers of excitement his looks had evoked in me had been precursors of it.

Gently he lifted my chin, cupping it with one of his hands and looking down into my face, his eyes dark and fathomless, tender, and burning with a reflection of my own immeasurable longing. Then his lips were on mine, tasting of brandy and desire, gentle at first, questing, exploring, then harder, deeper. I clung to him and felt as if my very soul was being drawn from my body, and it was beautiful, so very beautiful, more perfect than I had ever imagined a kiss could be, and yet tantalizing with the prospect of more, much more, as yet undreamed of delight.

I moved my hands across that broad back, feeling the strong sinews beneath my fingers, pressed my hips shamelessly against his and felt again those shivers of ecstatic pleasure deep within me at the closeness of his body to mine, but stronger, even more insistent than before.

'I have wanted to do that for so long.' Louis' voice was hoarse with desire, his breath warm against my throat. 'From the moment I first set eyes on you, I think.'

'And I have wanted you to.' Artfulness was beyond me; I should not be allowing this, much less whispering encouragement, but I had never learned to be artful. I followed my heart and did as it bid me.

Oh, perhaps it was not quite true that I had wanted this from the first moment we had met, but certainly for a very long time. No man had ever stirred me as he stirred me, no man ever awakened such a singing response in every nerve ending so that nothing mattered in the whole wide world but being close to him.

He kissed me again, my nose, my cheek, my mouth, his insistent lips probing my unpractised ones so that they parted a little and his tongue touched mine. Breath caught in my throat and I gasped, a little gasp that was almost a sob, and he held me so firmly against him that we were more like one person than two.

And then, quite suddenly, I felt his body go rigid, felt him go away from me in spirit as well as in body. He released me, turning away abruptly, and I was left shocked, bereft, wanting.

'Louis . . . ?' I whispered, uncomprehending.

'I'm sorry, Flora.' His tone was harsh. 'I had no right.'

'But I wanted it too!' I whispered. 'You know I did! Don't say you are sorry, please, for I am not! Oh, I know maybe it's not proper, but I don't care about that! If we both wanted it, how can it be wrong?'

'It is wrong.'

'No! I won't let you say so! I know . . .'

'You know nothing,' he said harshly. 'And that is the way it must remain. I've told you that.'

Tears stung my eyes, tears of bewilderment and disappointment and hurt. I could scarcely believe that a moment ago this cold, hard man had held me so tenderly, kissed me so sweetly. He had become once again a stranger I did not know at all.

'I think it would be best,' he said, 'if you were to go to bed, Flora.'

'Sent off as if I were thirteen years old, like Antoinette!' I flared.

A strange look narrowed his eyes, a look almost like indecision crossing his face. Then: 'If that is the way you want to think of it, then yes,' he said cruelly. 'This is my house, and like her, you'll do what I say for the sake of your own good.'

There was somehow no reply I could make to that. Hurt, humiliated, bewildered, I gathered what I could of my dignity and left the room.

I scarcely saw Louis in the days that followed. He was out a good deal attending, presumably, to whatever business his French trip had thrown up.

Or perhaps he was avoiding me. Certainly when I was in his presence he was curt to the point of rudeness.

'Whatever is wrong with Papa?' Antoinette asked one morning. 'He is in a dreadful mood, and has been almost from the day he returned from France.'

'Perhaps his dealings there did not go well,' I suggested.

'He seemed in good humour at first. Why, he even agreed to come with me to look at that darling little foal. Now, whenever I mention it he snaps at me as if he were going to bite off my head!' She sighed in exasperation. 'If we don't go soon, someone else will buy her, and I'll never forgive Papa! Can't you speak to him, Flora?'

I pulled a rueful face. 'I think it is very unlikely he would take the slightest notice of me.'

Gavin was not much in evidence during those days, but when he was he must have noticed how downcast I was, for he gave me a look which said: 'What did I tell you?' and I remembered what he had said to me – that caring for Louis would bring me nothing but heartache. But still I could not understand Louis' sudden rejection of what had undoubtedly been between us. And all my old doubts resurfaced along with the pain that seared me each time he pointedly ignored me.

It was three or four days later, and I was helping Antoinette choose some silks for a new embroidery she was to begin, when Clara came in search of me.

'Miss Flora – you have a visitor. There's a young man downstairs to see you.'

'To see me?' I repeated, surprised.

'Yes. He gave his name as Ralph Tooze.' Clara's eyes were sharp on my face. 'He says he used to know you when you lived at Tucker's Grave.'

'Ralph has come here to see me?' I said.

'Walter made him wait outside,' Clara said primly. 'He wasn't sure if you would want to see him.'

'Of course I'll see him! Show him into the parlour, Clara.' I turned to Antoinette. 'Please excuse me, Antoinette. I won't be long.'

'Oh, take as long as you like!' She smiled at me slyly, knowingly. 'Just tell me – do you think I should use this pink for the roses – or the red?'

'The pink,' I said. 'And that green for the leaves, I think.'

But my mind was no longer on embroidery silks. I was wondering why Ralph had come to visit me.

By the time I had tidied my hair and gone downstairs, Clara had shown Ralph into the parlour. He stood there looking quite out of place amongst all the fine French furniture and artefacts, twisting his cap awkwardly between his hands.

Ralph was a big, fair-haired country boy with the brawn of a man and the fresh rosy complexion that comes from spending most of his time out of doors in all winds and weathers.

Once, before I had been put off by his puppy-like devotion to me, I had thought him rather handsome. Now, compared with Louis, he looked like nothing so much as an overgrown farmer's boy.

'Ralph!' I said, forcing a smile. 'What brings you here?'

'Flora,' he muttered, making no attempt to answer my question. He was clearly intimidated by his surroundings and I tried to put him at his ease.

'It's good to see you, but something of a surprise. Were you over this way for some reason?'

He gave a quick jerk of his head: no.

'What then?'

He looked around uncomfortably. 'Can't we go outside?'

'Whatever for?' I asked, puzzled. 'There's a very cold wind blowing. In fact I was just about to ask if you'd like a hot chocolate or a dish of tea.'

Ralph looked around again nervously. 'Alice Doughty said to be careful.'

'Alice! You've come from Alice?' I exclaimed.

'You went to see her the other day, didn't you?'

'Yes,' I agreed.

'You didn't come to see me . . .' He sounded aggrieved.

'There wasn't time,' I said. 'And in any case you know there's nothing between us, Ralph.'

'I still care about you though, Flora, we all do. And we're worried about you.'

A little shiver ran over my skin. This was no social call. Ralph had come from Alice and she had told him to be careful. And he was clearly anxious no one should overhear what he had to say to me.

'There's no one here but us, Ralph,' I said. 'Apart from the servants and Antoinette, who is upstairs in her own suite of rooms, we are quite alone.'

He nodded, twisting his cap between his hands again.

'Well go on then,' I urged him. 'Say whatever it is you have come to say.'

'There's lights at Tucker's Grave.'

'What?' Whatever I had expected, it was not this.

'I rode past the other night, and there was a light at the window. I thought you must be home and I tried the door, but it was all locked up. I knocked, but no one came. And the light went out.' He paused, chewing his lip. 'I tried to look in at the window, but with it being dark inside by then I couldn't see anything.'

'Ralph,' I said. 'Are you sure it wasn't just the reflection of the moon on the glass?'

He scowled. 'You think I don't know the difference between the moon and lamplight? Anyway, when I told Alice, she said she thought you ought to know. That given what you and she were talking about, it might be important.'

I pressed my hands to my temples. Important? Perhaps – but it made no sense.

'And there's something else,' Ralph went on. 'You remember old Jem Giddings? Well, he's dead.'

I almost smiled. 'That's hardly surprising. He's caught a fever, I should think, sleeping in cold wet ditches.'

'No.' Ralph's face was serious. 'He was in fine rude health only the day before. He fell, it seems, and cracked his skull open on a boulder. Dead drunk as usual, everyone says. But Alice . . . well, she wasn't so sure. She reckoned there might have been foul play. Now, I don't know why, but she was most anxious you should be told of it – and on the quiet, like. That's why I'm here, because she asked me. And now I've passed on the messages, Flora, I think I'd best be going.'

'Oh Ralph!' My head was spinning again, a great chasm opening up inside me, and I felt sick with sudden apprehension.

Ralph was moving to the door, easing his cap back on to his head, and suddenly I wished with all my heart that he would not go.

Country bumpkin he might be, as out of place here as a peasant in the court of a king, but at least I knew I was safe with him. In this uncertain world, Ralph was one person I knew with absolute certainty that I could trust.

But I could not ask him to stay. In this, as in everything else, I was on my own. Only I could decipher what this new information meant, only I could decide what must be done about it. The burden felt like a weight of lead upon my shoulders. I did not know if I could bear it.

Ten

How long I stood at the window after Ralph's horse was lost to sight I do not know, for all the awful implications of what he had told me were racing around in my fevered brain.

Ralph had seen lights at the windows of Tucker's Grave and they had been extinguished when he had knocked at the door. I could not escape the conclusion that my old home was being used for some clandestine purpose and Louis' assurances to me had been simply another attempt at deceiving me. Was it possible he had instigated the romantic encounter that had followed with the intention of diverting me? Had he taken advantage of the attraction he must know I felt for him for his own ends? His coldness towards me since then made it seem all too plausible.

Even more damning was the news that poor Jem Giddings was dead. Not of a fever, not even of drink – or not directly, anyway, but with his skull cracked open. Jem had seen and recognized the horse that had galloped away from Tucker's Grave on the night my father was shot. I had relayed that fact to Louis. And now Jem was dead.

Had he, and my father before him, threatened the security of some illicit operation such as smuggling or privateering? Was it such a profitable venture that those who stood to gain would go to any lengths, even murder, to ensure their business continued unhindered?

Somehow, I thought, I must learn the truth. I could no longer live with the uncertainty and the awful suspicions. And if Louis was indeed behind the death of both my father and Jem Giddings, then nothing would stop me from seeing him brought to justice, not even the treacherous feelings I still entertained for him. But how could I go about it? Louis himself would clearly never admit it and if I pressed him further I might be putting myself in real danger; and I would get nothing from either Gavin or Bevan. They had given me dark hints but nothing more. And in any case, I would need some proof. No magistrate or constable would act without it, especially when the man I would be accusing was as respected in the area as Louis.

It was then that I thought of the locked bureau in the study. Without doubt it contained something I was not supposed to see. If I could gain access, perhaps I would find the proof I needed. I cast my mind back to the day I had seen it open and Gavin poring over papers on Louis' desk. Could it be that a key was secreted somewhere in the office? I would go and search without delay, I decided.

Poor Bevan was still at home sick so the study was unoccupied. I went in, closing the door behind me in case Antoinette should come downstairs and see me there. Then, trying to control the uneven beating of my heart, I began to look around.

Everything was in apple-pie order, ledgers stacked away, letters and accounts in neat piles on the desk, quills in their stand, the inkpot covered. I sat down in the chair behind the desk and opened the drawers one by one, checking the contents with no success. Perhaps I was on a wild goose chase, I thought, and Louis, Gavin and Bevan all kept the bureau keys on their person. I closed the last drawer and checked behind the window drapes for hidden hooks, but there was none; I slid my hand along the underside of the furnishings, again without success.

I was on the point of abandoning my search when the wall clock struck the half hour, and a new idea occurred to me. The keys for winding clocks were often kept inside the casing – was it possible other keys might be put there too? Without much hope I tripped the catch and opened the carved wood door.

The clock key was there right enough, lying right on the outer ledge. Carefully I slid my hand around the cavity behind the pendulum, and my fingers encountered something cold and hard. A key, without a doubt, but too large, surely, for the pretty bureau . . .

I pulled it out – and breath caught in my throat. In my hand I was holding the key to Tucker's Grave Inn!

For a moment I stared at it as if I had discovered buried treasure, and indeed it seemed to me that I had, for I knew that I now had means of access to my old home within my grasp. But it was not what I was looking for. I felt about inside the cavity once more, and this time came upon another key, much smaller and fancier. Excitement leaped within me. What intuition or good fortune had pointed me in the direction of the clock case I did not know, but almost certainly this was the bureau key I had been seeking.

I replaced the inn key where I had found it and took the other over to the bureau. It fitted the lock perfectly and turned at once. My heart beat an uneven tattoo as I opened the bureau, then stared in surprise. I had expected the bureau to be packed with books and ledgers, but apart from one small journal and a sheaf of papers it was empty. The papers were, I thought, the ones Gavin had been leafing through, and the journal hardly looked big enough to record the illicit dealings of which I suspected Louis.

I took it out, opening it to the first pages. No figures, no accounts, simply a chronology of dates and times which might, I thought, relate to sailings, as some of the details appeared to relate to tides and weather conditions. Disappointment tugged at me. There was no concrete evidence here, or at least none I could make any sense of. On the point of replacing it, I flipped to the back of the book, and saw another couple of pages had been written upon in a sloping scribbled hand that was indecipherable in the dim light.

I took the book to the window, where the light was better, and found myself looking at a list of dates and names – French names, and each preceded by a title. Comte, Marquis, Marquise . . . On the opposite page, notes had been made to tally with each name, and I saw that 'Tucker's Grave' appeared at least half a dozen times, amongst the names of some of the great country houses of the district.

My heart came into my throat with a great leap; I could scarcely believe what I was looking at. I scurried back to the bureau and pulled out the sheaf of papers. Letters of thanks, all signed by French nobility, but written now from addresses in London, and all over England. Detailed maps of France, and a plan, drawn in pencil, which could only be of a prison compound – The Bastille. Lists of addresses, this time French-sounding . . .

My breath came out on a long sigh. I had learned Louis' secret.

He was not engaged in privateering or illicit trade. He was not a rogue and a vagabond as I had feared.

Louis was the Lynx.

As I stood there, shocked into immobility, trying to make sense of my discovery, I heard Louis' voice in the hall.

'Antoinette? Flora? Where are you?'

I took a quick step in the direction of the bureau with the guilty intention of returning the papers to their hiding place – too quick. I collided heavily with the corner of the desk, drawing attention to my presence, and the study door flew open.

'Flora!' Louis' eyes slid over me, standing there with the sheaf of papers in my hand, to the open bureau. 'What are you doing?'

'I . . .' I could not speak; the words simply would not come.

'You're prying!' His tone was sharp. 'Haven't you been told that bureau is not to be opened?'

He strode across the room, snatched the papers from my hands, and thrust them back into their hiding place.

'I'm sorry,' I said.

'How much have you seen?'

'Not much . . .' I still could not string more than two words together to save my life.

It was plain Louis did not believe me. His fury was evident.

'Why couldn't you leave well alone? I warned you. For your safety . . . for the safety of all of us . . . What possessed you?'

My chin came up. Suddenly I regained the use of my vocal cords.

'You shouldn't have lied to me, Louis. I knew you were lying and thought you were using Tucker's Grave for illicit purposes. I wanted to find the proof of it.'

'And instead you have come upon information that could endanger many lives. You fool, Flora.'

'Louis – I wouldn't – I'd never say anything! Do you really think . . . ?'

'At the present time any hint of involvement is dangerous,' Louis said shortly. 'Those who stand to gain from perfidy will stop at nothing to get information from you if they think you might be in possession of it. The fact that you would not, or could not, reveal what they wanted to know would certainly not save you. They would torture and kill for it, without a moment's hesitation.'

'You mean . . . as my father was killed?' I whispered.

He did not answer me.

'We have to talk about this. In private, and with urgency. But not if there is any danger of Antoinette overhearing. I don't want her knowing of it. I can protect her, at least. Where is she?'

'In her rooms,' I said, 'working on her embroidery.'

Louis frowned. 'That will not last for long, knowing Antoinette. Perhaps it would be best if we went into the garden, where there will be no danger of us being overheard.'

I nodded. 'I'll fetch a wrap.'

As I left him the shock of my discovery flooded over me afresh. It was almost beyond belief, and yet somehow there was a rightness about it, and I was glad, so glad.

Perhaps Louis had feigned interest in me, and kissed me, simply to steer me away from the truth, no matter what it was he was hiding. Perhaps he was in mortal danger every time he crossed the Channel, and, for all I knew, in this country, too, from those he had said would be only too ready to betray him. But he was not a common criminal as I had feared. He was not some low, despicable privateer.

The romantic figure who risked his life for the sake of noblemen he scarcely knew, who was hero-worshipped the length and breadth of England, and the man I loved were one and the same, and the knowledge filled me with fierce pride.

Already it was both a torment and a benediction.

Louis was waiting for me when I returned to the hallway; he wore a very serious expression but it was no longer angry. We went outside. The wind had dropped but there was still a bite in the air. For a moment we walked in silence, then Louis said: 'So you now know my secret.'

'Yes,' I said. 'You are the Lynx.'

'A romantic name.' There was a slight smile in his voice. 'Too romantic, I think, for such a grisly occupation. But a pseudonym had to be used for purposes of identification, and that is the one that was decided upon between the members of the organization.'

'It is a good name,' I said. 'It implies speed and daring.'

'Stealth, I think,' he said. 'The most important quality is stealth. But you can see now, Flora, why there were things I had to keep from you – secrecy is vital to such an operation. And also why I warned of danger.'

'Yes, of course,' I said. 'If it became known that you are using your business operations as a cover for smuggling aristocrats whose lives are at risk to the safety of England, you would never get out of France alive.'

'That is true enough!' He laughed wryly. 'But the danger is not only in France. It is here, too, at home – all around us. There are those who, for one reason or another, work for the French. They seek information for their own ends, and will stop at nothing to get it. To be involved in this business, Flora, in any way whatever, is to put one's life at risk. As the death of your own father proved.'

'My father worked for you?' I asked.

Louis nodded. 'He did. But then, I think you already knew that.'

'I knew that sometimes Tucker's Grave was used as a staging post for nobles who had escaped the Terror. And you are still using it, aren't you? That's the reason you took possession almost before my father was cold in his grave. The reason you wanted me out of the way.'

188

'The alternative would have been to take you into my confidence. I couldn't risk that, Flora.'

'And the reason lights were seen there a few nights ago,' I said.

Louis' eyes sharpened. 'Lights were seen? By whom?'

'An old friend of mine from Monksmoor. He thought it meant I was home and knocked on the door, then the lights were extinguished. He rode over this very morning to tell me about it, and that is the reason . . .'

'If lights were seen,' Louis interrupted me, his voice hard, 'then someone has been careless in the extreme. I shall have to deal with this, and urgently. If local people who know no better talk of it, and it reaches the wrong ears, then it could be disastrous.'

'There's talk already,' I said. 'And Ralph told me something else, too. Do you remember me mentioning Jem Giddings, the old vagrant who claimed to have recognized one of the fleeing horses on the night my father was shot? Well, he's dead. Found in a ditch with his skull cracked open. It might have been an accident, of course – he fell when drunk and broke his head on a boulder – but . . .'

'Equally it might not have been an accident.' Louis' tone was grim. 'The old man was telling anyone who would listen that he could identify that horse, and if it reached the ears of your father's assailant, or whoever had put him up to it . . .'

I bit my lip. I could hardly tell Louis that I had come to the same conclusion myself – and suspected that *he* might be the person responsible for Jem's death.

Louis was silent for a moment, deep in thought.

'This could well be a vital piece of information, Flora,' he said at last. 'If Jem's death was no accident, then it must mean there was truth in what he said. He claimed the horse came from the Dartmouth area, did he not?'

I nodded. 'Yes.'

'Which may well mean that whoever is working against me is closer to home than I thought.'

Again he was silent for a long moment.

'You think, then, that my father died because of his connection with the Brotherhood of the Lynx?' I said.

'Undoubtedly,' Louis agreed. 'What puzzles me is the exact
reason why. I can only think he was killed for some information
he would not give them.'

'Such as your identity, you mean?' I asked. 'Certainly I am
sure my father would have given his life to keep your secret.'

'I am sure he would, but he could not, in any case, have
revealed my identity, for he did not know it,' Louis said. 'As far
as possible we keep every link in the chain separate so that if
one falls it will not bring the whole house of cards tumbling
down. But my uncertainty as to what lay behind your father's
death is another reason I could not let you remain at Tucker's
Grave. If those men did not get what they wanted that night,
and I am confident they did not, then it was quite likely they
would have returned. If they were of the mind that your father
knew something that he was unprepared to tell, they might well
have believed that you were in the know, also. And God alone
knows what they would have done to you in an attempt to elicit
that information.'

A chill whispered over my skin. Though I had not realized it,
I could certainly have been in mortal danger.

'So you brought me here,' I said softly.

'It was all I could think of to do. If harm befell you because of
me, I could never forgive myself. Especially now. I care for you
too much. And God alone knows, I already live with a heavy-
enough conscience.'

'For the death of my father and poor old Jem, you mean?' I
asked, puzzled.

'More, Flora. Much more.' The silence hung between us.
Then he said: 'Tomorrow I return to France.'

My heart, which had soared when he spoke of caring for me,
dropped like a stone. Now that I knew the truth, the thought of
him going willingly into such a dangerous situation was almost
too much to bear.

'Why?' I whispered. 'Why do you do it?'

'Because maybe I can save lives.' He said it simply, yet with heartfelt emphasis. The lines of his face might have been carved in stone. 'And because it is my way of trying to assuage the guilty conscience I spoke of. To try to make amends.'

I frowned, puzzled. 'I don't understand.' He said nothing, and I laid my hand on his arm. 'Louis? What do you mean?'

'No action in our lives, Flora, is totally inconsequential,' Louis said. 'Each one is like a stone thrown into a pond and from it the ripples spread in ever-widening circles. We can never escape the consequences of our actions, and no matter how justified they may seem to us at the time, they may give us cause to torment ourselves with guilt for the rest of our lives.'

I was silent, waiting. There was nothing I could say.

'You know that my wife was a French noblewoman. It was not a happy marriage. She drove me to the borders of madness. But that does not excuse me for what I did. Now . . .'

He broke off, and suddenly the chill was whispering over my skin again, icy fingers clutching at my heart. Dear God, was Louis saying what I thought he was saying? Were the rumours of which I had been told true?

You killed her . . . The words were running around and around in my head but I could not bring myself to speak them.

'She . . . she didn't die of the fever?' I asked at last.

'No.'

I pressed my hand against my mouth.

'You understand now, Flora, why there can be nothing between us? The reason I had to put a stop to what was happening . . .' His expression was tortured. The agony of guilt, the regret, the longing for absolution, were there in his eyes, written in every one of the deeply etched lines on his face. And suddenly, whatever it was he had done, it did not matter to me at all, had no power to change my feelings. My love for him was too strong. If Louis had killed his wife, then she must have driven him beyond the bounds of reason.

'I don't care!' I cried passionately. 'I don't care about any-thing except you!'

His eyes narrowed. 'Flora, what are you saying?'

I was past caring about propriety. Set against the tumult of

191

my need for him, and the knowledge that I might lose him to a terrible death, propriety mattered not at all.

'All I want is to be with you. I love you, Louis.'

He threw his head back, the sinews of his throat standing out in sharp relief, staring up at the sky as if in prayer. Then his breath came out on a long sigh.

'Oh Flora, don't tempt me so! If I allowed such a thing, I would be no better than she!'

His words bewildered me. 'But . . . ?'

'Marriage vows are made before God,' he said harshly. 'They bind a man and a woman till death do them part. For better or for worse, Lisette is my wife.'

'But . . . she's dead,' I said stupidly. 'You said . . .'

Louis took my hand. He held it between his own, and those tortured eyes met mine.

'No, Flora, Lisette is not dead – at least, I pray she is not, for if I am too late . . .' He broke off, his jaw tightening. 'My wife is in France, where I sent her, and she is now at the mercy of the Revolutionaries. That is the reason I became the Lynx. To attempt to save her from the terrible fate to which I condemned her. The guilt I bear for that alone would be enough for me to risk all to attempt to avert the consequences of my action all those years ago. But I have yet another reason, even more pressing. There is someone else for whom I would gladly give my life if he can be brought out safely.' He paused. 'My son.'

Eleven

In that moment the world seemed to stop turning. A hush had fallen over the garden. No breeze stirred in the leaves, no birds fluttered in the bushes. And the stillness was in me too – my heart seemed not to beat, my lungs refused to draw breath. It was too much to take in all at once, this sudden revelation. Nothing was as it had seemed. And yet . . . and yet all the pieces were falling relentlessly into place. Louis' rejection of me. His dedication to the task he had set himself, the ruthlessness with which he pursued it.

From the time I had first heard of the Lynx and his fearless exploits, I had wondered why any man would return again and again to danger, no matter how worthy the cause, putting his own life at risk for the sake of others. Now I knew. He did it principally not for the arrogant, faceless aristocrats whose treatment of the poor had brought about their predicament. He did it for his wife, his conscience – and his own flesh and blood.

'You have a son in France?' I asked in a whisper.

Louis nodded. 'It's a long story, Flora, and not a pretty one, but I think I owe it to you. Just one thing I would ask of you – that you do not speak of it to anyone. Lives depend on the secrecy of this operation, my own included.'

'I would never breathe a word to a living soul,' I vowed.

'Not even Antoinette knows the truth so far,' he went on, 'though I think now I must enlighten her, for the new information I have in my possession will, I hope, mean that this time I shall find Lisette and my son and, God willing, bring them back safe to England. It would be a great shock to her if I did not pre-warn her of their existence.'

'But why have you not told her the truth before now?' I asked. 'Surely she had a right to know?'

Louis' features were set in granite. 'Lisette never cared for Antoinette,' he said harshly. 'For reasons I prefer not to discuss, she rejected Antoinette at birth and never relented. When she went back to France, she did not even ask to see the child to say goodbye, much less beg to take her. It seemed to me at the time it was in Antoinette's best interests to believe her mother to be dead, as she was, to all intents and purposes, to me. I can see now that I was wrong, but once such a lie is told, it is nigh on impossible to take it back. At the time I did what I thought was best to prevent Antoinette learning a truth which would have destroyed her.'

'Because your wife took your son with her, you mean,' I said. 'She chose him.'

'No, something far worse.' Louis bowed his head, hesitating as if he was considering explaining what it was that would have caused Antoinette such distress, and deciding against it. 'The boy was born after I returned her to France,' he went on at last. 'When she left, neither of us knew she was with child, and I learned only recently of his existence.'

'You mean she gave birth to your son and never told you of it?' I asked.

'That is so,' Louis agreed. 'It was, perhaps, her act of revenge because I had banished her, I don't know. Lisette is a law unto herself, and I do not think even she always understands why she does the things she does.'

He was silent for a moment, and I knew he was thinking of the turbulent past he had shared with his wife, and of things that I, for all that I loved him so, would never know. Then he sighed deeply, and continued.

'Lisette's family were aristocrats, living in their fine chateaux in the lap of luxury, and with connections to the court of King Louis. When the Terror began I knew, without doubt, that they would be taken by the mob and sentenced to death on the guillotine – and I made up my mind I must do what I could to save her. It was my doing, after all, that she was in France and in danger of her life. Together with some trusted friends I set up the first escape route and crossed the channel to try and find her. She and her close family had gone into hiding. But those from her circle that I was able to speak to told me of the boy. Pierre. My son. I knew then that I could never rest until I found him and brought him safe to England.'

'But . . .' I hesitated, then burst out: 'How can you be so sure that he is your son? If he was born after you sent her away, and if she was . . .'

'Unfaithful to me?' His lip curled into the parody of a smile. 'Yes, that is true enough. But Lisette made no secret of his parentage to her confidantes. The date of his birth fits exactly with . . . events before she went away. And everyone I spoke to who knows Pierre remarks upon the fact that he is, in appearance, growing to be very like me. There is no doubt whatever in my mind. I sired this child, at least. He is my son.'

I frowned, puzzled by his choice of words, and I wondered, too, if Louis' certainty might be misplaced, for does not every man wish for a son to carry on his heritage? But I did not dwell upon it. There were too many other questions to be answered.

'If your chief objective is to bring out Lisette and your son, why do you waste time rescuing others who mean nothing whatever to you?' I asked.

It sounded harsh, I knew that the moment the words had left my lips, and the quirk of Louis' eyebrow told me that he thought so too. But he answered me anyway.

'My network is in place and may as well be used. The poor souls I rescue value their lives too. And every one I am able to speak to is a link in the chain.' He smiled wryly. 'Besides, I could not help feeling that if I could do some good, God might look more favourably upon my prayers and lead me to Lisette and my son. And so it has proved.'

'You now know where they are?' I asked.

'I have the best information yet, from one who is the most likely to know Lisette's hiding place and tell me the truth.' His lips tightened. 'A person I would have preferred to have no truck with, and whose neck I would gladly wring myself. But enough of that. This information is the reason I must return to France tomorrow. It is imperative I find them before they move on again – or are taken by the Revolutionaries. There's no time to lose.'

'Oh Louis!' Dread filled me, ice-cold fingers clutching at my heart. 'I am so afraid for you.'

He reached out and touched my cheek. 'Don't be. I shall do my utmost to ensure I stay out of the clutches of those who would like to see me in the tumbril on my way to the guillotine along with the aristocracy they hate so much. And if I cannot . . . well, it is destiny. That is something, chérie, which it is impossible to cheat.'

I caught my lip between my teeth, biting on it hard to contain my emotion. There was nothing I could say, I knew, to dissuade him. Louis' course was set, and had been long before I had ever met him. He would not have been the man I loved if it had been any different. But oh, the fear for him! And oh, the pain of knowing that if he succeeded in this mission he had set himself, then when he returned once more to England he would bring with him his wife and child.

Whatever the outcome, whichever way the dice fell, I had lost him. The Revolution so far away across the sea had already cost me my own dear father. Now it would rob me of the only man I had ever loved in that special way that a woman can love a man.

'Louis . . .' I whispered. 'Do you love her?'

His eyes were far away. 'I did, once,' he answered. 'More than life itself.'

'And now?'

His eyes met mine. 'I think you know the answer to that, Flora.'

My heart was beating like a trapped bird. 'You love me. As I love you.'

'You know I do. But it cannot be.'

I reached out and took his hand. My love swept away all modesty, all propriety. It made me bold.

'I know that too, Louis. But can we not have just this one night?'

I felt him stiffen, withdraw.

'Please!' I whispered urgently. 'Tomorrow you sail for France. I pray that you will return safe, but it may not be. And if you do, and you bring Lisette and your son with you, then that too is an end for us. I know that. You are an honourable man, and I would not wish to impose upon you more guilt than you already bear. But if you love me, give me just this one night to remember. I swear that I will never ask for more.'

His eyes, dark and tortured, held mine, and in them I could see the inner battle that was tearing him apart. He wanted me, just as I wanted him, yet his chivalry and his fierce code of morality held him back as securely as if he had been manacled and chained.

'I cannot dishonour you, Flora,' he said, his voice low and gruff with emotion. 'You have already suffered enough because of me. If I should ruin you, what other man would want you?'

'That is of no importance to me,' I said urgently. 'I don't want any man but you, and I never shall. You would not dishonour me, quite the opposite. I shall think myself honoured that I have loved, and been loved by, the bravest and most gallant man in the whole of England.'

He laughed shortly. 'That is, I fear, far from the truth!'

'No, it is not,' I insisted. I caught his hand; he did not tear it away, though his eyes narrowed a fraction more. We were close, so close, and yet so far apart, and the few inches of air between us as charged as the air before a summer storm. I could feel every sinew of his body calling to mine, my nerve endings tingled, my skin shivered, my lips trembled.

I looked at him and knew that his self-control was such that unless the first move came from me it would not come at all. I reached up and kissed him, one hand still holding his, and in that kiss was all my longing and all my love. For a moment longer he stood like a statue. I whispered against his lips: 'Louis, oh Louis . . .' and I pressed the hand I held to my breast.

He groaned then, deep in his throat, and suddenly I was no longer the instigator, but the willing slave, and Louis the master. He swept me up into his arms as easily as if I were a child and carried me to the summer house. There he set me down while he took off his redingote and laid it on the bare board floor. He pulled me close once more and for a lovely timeless moment we clung together, kissing deeply, whilst anticipation sharpened all our senses to an unbearable height of ecstasy. Then, still clinging to one another, we sank to the floor.

I experienced just one fleeting moment's fear for what I was doing, then he was bunching up my skirts and petticoats; his hands and his hard body against the soft skin of my thighs sent new waves of desire rippling through me, and once again I cared for nothing but being with Louis, close as a man and a woman can be.

I had never heard that the first time is supposed to be painful for a young lady – I had no mother or close female relative to tell me such things, however delicately, so perhaps my lack of apprehension made it easy for me. There was just that one sharp knife-edge of pain that made me catch my breath, and then Louis was in me, moving easily and rhythmically in my wetness, and I was once again borne up on that rushing bore tide, higher and higher, faster and faster, until there was nothing in the world but our urgent need and our bodies moving in unison.

Quite suddenly Louis was still in me and I knew a brief stab of panic that even now, at the last moment, his resolve had returned, his control was greater than his desire for me. Then his hand slid between our bellies and his fingers found my mound, moving with the same compelling rhythm. I moaned as the undreamed-of sensations within me grew deeper and stronger yet, pressing myself into him, being swept ever upward until I thought I would die of the paroxysm of pleasure so intense it was almost pain. And then he was moving in me again, and united we reached the pinnacle of ecstasy, calling out each other's names.

It was over, but I could not let it go. I moved still against him as the aftershocks surprised me, one after the other, then weaker and more widely spaced until my satiated body relaxed, warm, luxuriously warm, luxuriously replete.

'Oh Flora,' he said, simply.

I tangled my fingers in his hair, I felt his cheek against mine, and the wetness between my legs. Gradually I became aware of the coldness of the bare boards surrounding the redingote island on which we lay, and could not care.

For this little hiatus in time, Louis had been mine. The joy warmed me, and gave the illusion of a heaven that could last beyond this day, this moment.

'Oh Flora,' he said again, and I pressed my fingers to his lips. I did not want him to say anything that might mar the magic of this moment.

Tomorrow he would sail for France. The likelihood was that never again would we be together this way. But I would have my memories, and I needed them to be untarnished by doubts or regrets.

They could sustain me then through all the long years that lay ahead.

The glow remained with me for the rest of that unreal day, for I refused to think for even a moment about the morrow, even though it hung like a dark shadow just beyond my conscious mind. These were moments to cherish; the touch of Louis' hand upon my wrist, light and lingering, as he filled my glass at dinner, the tone of his voice when he spoke my name, the tender looks we shared.

I felt sure it must be quite clear to everyone that I was different, that Louis and I were lovers, and I felt like a queen, but no one appeared to notice, not Antoinette, and not Gavin, who had joined us for our evening meal.

Antoinette was still a little preoccupied, and I guessed Louis had spoken to her some time during the afternoon, enlightening her as to the secrets he had kept from her for so long. But he had also asked Gavin to take her to see about buying the foal for her whilst he was away, and when she spoke it was of nothing but that. Horses, and her love for them, seemed to be Antoinette's way of coping with everything that she found upsetting or unsettling; when she turned her mind to them, the rest of the world faded to shadows. As for Gavin, he seemed a little tense, a little distant, rather than his usual breezy self, and I wondered if it might be that he was anxious because his brother was returning to France once again tomorrow. He must surely be aware of the real purpose behind the trips and be concerned for the dangers Louis faced. Though there was no love lost between them, they were still brothers and that must, in the last resort, mean more than any differences that had arisen as a result of his long-ago dalliance with Louis' wife.

Was he also involved in the Brotherhood of the Lynx? I wondered. When he visited France on business did he too risk his life to extricate nobles from their perilous predicament? Since I had seen him poring over the papers that were locked in the bureau it seemed likely that he did, and I resolved to ask Louis about it if the opportunity arose, for I thought that if there was someone with whom I could discuss my fears and anxieties for him whilst he was away it would make the waiting more bearable.

As the evening wore on, that shadow at the edges of my mind began to close in, deepening with the shadows in the corners of the room beyond the lamplight. I felt it growing closer and darker, prodding at me with fingers of dread, and the poignancy only made my love the sharper and stronger. I was on the edge of a precipice above a yawning chasm, clinging by my fingertips and savouring every sweet breath with heightened awareness.

Soon after dinner, visitors came, but I did not see them. Louis was closeted with them in his study for some long while, and I resented every moment he spent with them, though I knew they must be discussing important details which might, for all I knew, save his life.

Gavin did not join them; he remained in the parlour

with Antoinette and me, though I sensed he was listening when they emerged into the hallway and stood there for a few moments, talking. I listened too, but I could hear nothing of what they said, nothing but the rise and fall of voices, two cultured, the tones of gentlemen, one rougher, with a broad Devon burr.

Perhaps he was the captain of Louis' ship, I thought – or perhaps he was just another local man like my father who had been enlisted to provide a safe house. But that seemed unlikely. For one thing, Louis had told me he had never had direct contact with my father at Tucker's Grave in order to preserve the security of the line; for another no safe house would be needed, surely, for Lisette and Louis' son. They would come directly here, to Belvedere.

Sharp pain twisted in me and for a moment I wondered what I would do when they arrived. Louis had made it plain that I was not safe at Tucker's Grave, and would not be as long as the operations of the Brotherhood of the Lynx continued. But I did not think I could bear to remain here, in the same house as Lisette. It would be torture to see them together and know that she was his wife, sharing his name and his bed. And though he said he loved me now, was it not possible that when he was with her again the love for her he had once admitted to would be resurrected? *I loved her more than life* . . . How could feelings that strong ever die? Hurt and anger had made him send her away, but he must still care for her, or he would never have begun searching for her in the first place.

Perhaps, I thought, when Lisette and the boy were safe in England, Louis would disband the Brotherhood of the Lynx, for its chief purpose would have been served. Then, surely, there would be no reason for him to fear for my safety at Tucker's Grave. He might allow me to return there, and run it as my father had before the Terror, serving the ordinary folk who travelled on the stagecoaches and the handful of people from the village who used it as their local alehouse.

But I did not allow these thoughts to dominate me. I put

them out of my mind, determined to make the most of the little time that was left to Louis and me. And hoping, all the while, that when Antoinette had gone to bed and Gavin left for the Lodge, we could once more be together as we had been in the summer house.

I was not disappointed.

When we were at last alone, Louis came to sit beside me on the chaise and took me in his arms, kissing me hungrily.

'Oh Flora, do you know how I have been longing to do that?' he asked softly, his breath warm against my cheek. 'You are a breath of fresh spring air in this harsh cold world, a sweet memory indeed for a man to take with him into danger. I should not want you, but by God, I do. I wanted you, I think, from the first moment I saw you, all forlorn in your mourning bonnet beside your father's grave.'

'You had a strange way of showing it,' I said mischievously, for my elation in discovering that Louis felt as I did and my satisfaction in my new-found womanhood gave me the confidence to tease. 'I thought you most arrogant and unfeeling. Though very handsome,' I added.

'I expect I am arrogant,' Louis said. 'Yes, I am sure I am. But not unfeeling. And certainly not handsome.'

I smiled at him. 'Well, let's not quarrel about that. Time is too short.'

The shadow fell over us once more, the awful, pervasive knowledge that tonight was all that was left to us, all we could ever have.

'I wish with all my heart that things could be different,' Louis said.

'But they cannot.' Though I longed to beg him not to go, not to place his life in danger, and certainly not to bring his wife here to Belvedere, I knew I must not. Louis was an honourable man. He could not live with the guilt of knowing he had condemned Lisette to death on the guillotine. Not I nor anyone else could persuade him against the course on which he had set himself, and if I tried and was successful it would be a blot on any life we might share, corroding and eventually destroying our happiness and our love.

Even more important to him was the rescue of the son he had never seen, but who was, none the less, his own flesh and blood.

'I can scarcely believe Lisette kept the existence of your child from you all these years,' I said. 'How can you ever forgive her for that?'

Louis' eyes were very far away. 'It is not a question of forgiveness, though it is hard to think of all that I have missed in watching him grow up.'

'And all that he has missed in having you for a father.'

Louis grimaced. 'I cannot imagine what he has been told about me! That I am heartless, just as you said, I expect. If he is even aware that I am his father.'

'If Lisette told others, then she must surely have told him,' I reasoned.

'With Lisette, one can never be sure. There are many things about which she kept her own counsel.' The deep lines were there again in his face, dark shadows in the lamplight, and I knew he was thinking of things he would not speak of, not now, perhaps not ever. Then he shifted. 'Anyway, I know now, and if we are both spared and come home safe to Belvedere, then I shall do my best to make it up to them.'

If we are both spared . . . A chill ran over my skin.

'Where do you have to go?' I asked. 'Is it a hotbed of Revolutionaries?'

'All France is uncertain territory,' he replied. 'Don't ask me where I am going, Flora, for I cannot tell you. Oh,' his fingers tightened on mine, 'it's not that I don't trust you, but it's safer for you that you know nothing. As far as you are concerned, I have gone on business. Try to believe that, so that your anxiety does not give you away. For as we have already said, no one can be trusted but the members of the Brotherhood.'

'And I do not know their identities.'

'Exactly. That is how it must be. I don't want you placed in any more danger than you already are.'

That he should be concerned for my safety when I was on English soil and he was in a hotbed of revolution seemed ludicrous. And yet . . . I saw again my dear father lying dead in a pool of his own blood. He had never left English soil, yet he had died for the cause, and even Louis, the Lynx himself, could not explain the reason why.

'There's one other thing I want to ask you, Flora,' Louis said.

'Anything.'

'I want you to promise me that you will look after Antoinette.'

'You know I will! Why, we spent some very pleasant times together when last you were away . . .'

'Flora.' Louis' face was very serious. 'It is not the short term I speak of. Of course I know you will do your best to keep her out of mischief during my absence. But if I should not return . . . It is a great deal to ask, I know, but she likes and respects you more than any other woman. And you . . . I know you would instil in her the values that I would wish. She could not have a better pattern than you, Flora. I know you would guide her along the right paths and you are strong enough to stand up to those who might lead her astray.' He paused, then went on: 'I would like you to remain here at Belvedere and become her guardian.'

'But surely Gavin . . .' I broke off, frowning. This was not a subject I wanted even to consider, but now that Louis had raised it, there was no avoiding the truth. 'Should something happen to you – God forbid that it will – then wouldn't Gavin be master of Belvedere, and guardian to Antoinette?'

Louis' lips tightened. 'Master of Belvedere, certainly. But I don't think he would want the responsibility of Antoinette for very long. He would be happy enough to hand that over to you, I feel sure. And she needs the guidance of a woman in her life. You've seen for yourself how wildly she can behave – if I was no longer around I dread to think what would become of her. Please, Flora, set my mind at rest in this particular at least. Promise me you will not abandon Antoinette.'

What could I say? What could I do but agree? Louis' concern for Antoinette was clearly playing on his mind, an added burden he could well do without in the onerous times that lay ahead of him, and I could see how torn he must be regarding his responsibilities and the choice he had been forced to make – attempting to save the life of one of his children whilst risking the well-being and future care of the other.

'I promise,' I whispered. 'But you *will* come back safe, Louis. You will – I know it.'

'I hope so,' he said. 'Take care, chérie.'

He brushed my hair aside and kissed me on the forehead. All the love, all the despair that I was feeling welled up in me, and I raised my face to his.

'We have a few hours yet.'

'We have indeed. And we will not waste them,' Louis replied.

He took me to bed, the great master bed with a curved wooden roof supported by pillars and sheets of finest lawn. I had never seen his room before and I scarcely saw it now, shadowed as it was beyond the light circles cast by the lamps, and me with eyes for nothing but the man I loved.

He took me to bed and made wonderful love to me, tenderness shot through with bolts of pure unbridled passion, and I pretended to myself that this was how it would always be, nights of lying curled round his long hard body, my head against his shoulder, my lips tasting the faint salt of his skin, my body replete with his loving. I pretended, because to face the truth would be to sully the occasion, and the truth was more than I could bear. He loved me, again and again, and I fell asleep in his arms. But my dreams were troubled. My unconscious mind was busy with all the things my conscious mind chose to ignore. And when I woke, with the tears mingling with the morning sun on my cheeks, I was alone in that great bed, all alone. He was gone, and I had not even kissed him goodbye. The ache was a physical one, sharp as a knife in me, the sadness a weight on my chest, the fear for him a clamouring army of demons.

I sat up in that great empty bed that had so recently been my pleasure dome, closed my eyes and pressed my hands to my mouth.

It was over. One way or another, it was over. And though I knew that never again would he be mine, I prayed with every fibre of my being for Louis' safe return.

Twelve

I thought of him constantly in the days that followed, worrying, and wondering where he was, how he was faring. And remembering too the glory of those stolen hours we had shared.

Bevan returned to work, and I spent some time with him, learning more of the business and doing a few simple secretarial tasks. But concentration was difficult, and in any case my heart was not in it, for I knew that if Louis returned safely and installed his wife at Belvedere House, I could not bear to remain under the same roof. And if he did not . . .

I pushed the terrible thought from my mind, but knew all the same that if the worst happened and he did not return there would be no business to work at, for I could not see that Gavin would be capable of running it.

He came to the house often, as he seemed to when Louis was not there, almost, it seemed to me, as if he took some sly pleasure in taking advantage of his brother's absence. And it seemed to me too that he was paying a little more attention to me than of late.

Could it be that he had been aware of what there was between Louis and me that last day? Had it showed in our faces at dinner as I had thought it must? And did he now think that in Louis' absence I might turn my attentions to him?

Very conscious of his renewed interest, I did my utmost to avoid being alone with him whenever possible. But still he managed to lay a hand on my shoulder when I was working at the books on the pretext of overseeing what I was doing, or brush my hand with his as he passed me a glass of wine at a meal, and I felt his eyes on me too often, though when I did I was careful not to look up and meet his gaze.

I did not, of course, make any mention to him of Louis' mission. For one thing I did not want the extra intimacy such a conversation would imply; for another I had forgotten, in all that had happened in those last emotional hours, to ask Louis how much his brother knew of the real reason for his latest trip to France.

It worried me a little that I had not, for whilst I found it hard to believe that he could be unaware of Louis' double life as the Lynx, yet I could not forget the furtiveness of his manner the day I had found him poring over the secrets of the locked bureau. It seemed to me too that, given his low opinion of his brother, Louis was unlikely to trust him with the details of the organization. And I found myself wondering just why the bureau was kept locked. Only Gavin, Bevan and myself used the study; Bevan clearly knew all about the contents and though it was possible it had been secured to keep me from seeing the records stored there I could not help feeling it had been locked up long before I had come to Belvedere. That left only Gavin.

I told myself I was being fanciful and foolish, that such sensitive material would not be considered safe unless it was under lock and key, no matter that only the trusted few had access to the study. But I wished all the same that I had mentioned to Louis that I had seen Gavin with the papers spread out on the desk, and the omission pricked and worried at me like a piece of rose thorn buried deep in a finger.

Rather strangely, I thought, Antoinette never made mention of the things Louis had talked to her about before leaving, and I did not feel it was my place to raise the subject. It was as if, I thought, she was in denial. All that seemed to be on her mind was the foal her heart was set upon, and each time Gavin came to the house she asked when he would take her to see it.

Gavin, however, seemed in no hurry to make the trip; it was almost as if he were playing with her, enjoying his power in making her wait. Then, on the evening of the fourth day after

Louis' departure, he suddenly announced that he had been to Monksmoor to look at it that afternoon.

'Uncle Gavin!' Antoinette cried. 'Why did you not take me with you?'

He shrugged. 'I thought I'd have a look at it myself first. It could have had three bandy legs and be blind in one eye for all I knew.'

'Oh – as if!' She widened her eyes at him, then hung on his arm. 'So now you know it isn't like that at all, when are we going back to buy it?'

'It's coming up at the market at Twyford St Mary next week,' Gavin told her.

'Market?' Antoinette was horrified. 'Why did you not make a deal with the man who owns her there and then?'

'I tried, but he was insistent she went on the open market. He wants to be sure of getting a fair price for her,' Gavin explained.

'So why did you not offer him more than a fair price and have done with it?' Antoinette demanded. Her eyes were flashing emerald fire. 'Papa wouldn't mind – he can well afford it. Oh, Uncle Gavin, if I lose that foal now I shall never forgive you!'

'I'm sure we can still secure her for you. We'll go to the market early and make a day of it. You'll come with us, won't you, Flora? You might run into some of your old friends there. And perhaps we could make a detour to Tucker's Grave . . .'

'I don't think so,' I said stiffly, not liking the way he was looking at me.

'Oh you must come, Flora!' Antoinette cried. 'If you don't, Uncle Gavin will waste time drinking and yarning and I'll never get my foal! I don't know why Papa didn't ask *you* to make the purchase. You would never have allowed the owners to send her to market!'

'I don't know that I'd have had any more influence than your uncle,' I said. 'And in any case, ladies don't involve themselves in commerce.'

'But if she's sold before we get there . . . !' Antoinette was beside herself.

'If she's sold before we get there, then there will always be another one,' Gavin said, beginning to lose his patience.

Antoinette leaped to her feet. 'I don't want another one!' she cried. 'You know that! And I believe you're doing this on purpose! You don't intend for me to have her at all!'

'I'm sure that's not true,' I said, but Gavin looked merely amused, and I could not help wondering if there was some truth in what Antoinette said. Hadn't I already thought that Gavin was enjoying having the power to realize or dash her hopes?

'You are very mean!' she shot at him. 'Mean not to take me with you today, and mean not to buy the foal for me whilst you were there. I hate you!'

With that, she turned and ran from the room.

'Well,' Gavin said mildly. 'What a madam Antoinette can be.'

'You know her heart is set on that foal,' I said, flying to her defence.

'Well, she will just have to learn she cannot have everything she wants, won't she?' Gavin said carelessly. 'Some of us have lived with that indisputable fact for a very long time.'

I saw it then; saw clearly the jealousy Gavin felt because Louis had inherited everything he thought of as his.

'I know you and Louis have your differences,' I said, 'and I understand it is not easy for you, being the second son and entitled to nothing whilst everything passed directly to Louis. But please don't punish Antoinette for it. That is no more than petty spite, and beneath contempt.'

A slow smile crept across Gavin's handsome face. 'Gad, but you can be a spirited little thing, Flora! A rare treat for any man.'

'I shall certainly stand up for what I believe to be right,' I returned tartly. 'Antoinette has been promised that foal, and promises should be kept. You must do everything in your power to ensure she gets it.'

'So.' Gavin's eyes challenged me. 'Perhaps you would like to try to persuade me. I am sure, Flora, that you can be very persuasive indeed.'

I could scarcely believe what he was suggesting.

'I don't know what you mean!' I said sharply.

'Oh, I think you do!' His hand crept towards mine. 'A beautiful young lady cannot but be aware of all the weapons in her armoury, which can be powerful indeed.'

I snatched my hand away. 'How dare you!'

He laughed softly. 'Ah, the thrill of the chase! You know almost as well as Lisette how to lead a man on. Come now, we're quite alone. Let us make the most of it and I will show you I am a far better lover than my staid, would-be-respectable brother.'

I pushed my chair back and rose. This had gone quite far enough.

'I think, Gavin, that you have drunk too much wine and too much cognac,' I said coldly. 'Tomorrow you will regret this conversation – at least, I hope you will. Now I am going to my room.'

I turned for the door but he was there before me, blocking my way. There was a curious light in his eyes.

'A spirited little thing, as I said!' He caught me by the arms. 'But a knowing one, too, I think! Don't run away from me, Flora. Let me show you how I can pleasure you.'

He was close, too close, and pulling me closer yet. I could smell the brandy on his breath, and something else, the faintly feral taint of lust. I felt a moment's panic; Gavin, like Louis, was a big man, and far stronger than I. If he should force himself upon me I would be totally at his mercy.

Even as the thought crossed my mind his mouth came down on mine and his arm went about my waist, holding me against him. The taste of him, like the smell of his breath, revolted me, and as his tongue forced my lips apart I wrenched my head away so violently that I felt a cord in my neck twist painfully.

'Stop it!' I cried.

Startled, he released his hold on me a little, and I took advantage of the moment to bring my hand up and strike him full in the face. He took another step backward, his hand flying to his burning cheek, and again I felt a moment's fear that I had only inflamed his passion. Flight was impossible, physical resistance would be useless. I had only one weapon with which to fight him – and I used it.

'You forget yourself!' I spat at him with all the hauteur I could muster. 'How dare you treat me as if I were no better than a common strumpet!'

His lip curled. 'You do not say that to Louis, I'll wager.'

'What is between Louis and me is no concern of yours,' I declared. 'But he will not be pleased when he returns from France to learn of your indefensible behaviour.'

I had struck a raw nerve; I knew it at once from the look on his face. Then he turned away.

'*If* he comes back.'

The voicing of my own darkest fears sent a chill to the very core of me.

'Don't say such things!' I cried passionately. 'You are tempting the fates!'

Gavin laughed. 'Exactly.' He spun back to face me again. The marks of my fingers stood out on his cheek, startlingly clear. 'And if he does not come back, things will be very different, Flora. Belvedere will be mine, Tucker's Grave Inn will be mine – and you will be mine, too. You'd do well to remember that, and treat me with a little more respect.'

'Respect has to be earned, Gavin,' I told him. 'You might own all of Devon, for all I care. You will never own me.'

He took a step towards me. I feared for a moment that he was about to attempt to show me, in the only way he knew, who was master here. Then his hands fell to his sides and his mouth twisted into an unpleasant smile.

'We'll see, Flora. We'll see. When you have no roof over your head, no food in your belly, and not a single possession in the world, you'll sing a different tune, I'll wager. Until now, I have been the brother with nothing to offer. When it is I who hold your fate in my hands, you'll forget Louis soon enough – and a good thing for you, too. He couldn't satisfy his wife. What makes you think he'd keep you satisfied for long? But I somehow doubt you will have the chance to find out.' The smile left his mouth; he looked now like nothing so much as a sullen, pouting boy who has had a favourite toy snatched from him.

'You'll wish, Flora, that you had been more agreeable to me, just wait and see if you don't. For I will be master here, make no mistake of it, and I shall not forget tonight.'

'And neither, Gavin, shall I.'

I risked moving toward him, for his large frame still blocked my escape. 'Kindly move aside and let me pass.'

To my relief he did so. As I swept out of the room I heard the clink of decanter on glass, and felt a moment's satisfaction that Gavin was having to resort to liquor to find some relief for his pent-up feelings.

I went directly to Antoinette's rooms. Though more than anything I wanted to be alone until the trembling in my limbs eased, I was very afraid that she might have overheard something of what had passed, and even if she had not, I knew she was dreadfully upset at the prospect of losing the foal she so wanted. I tapped on her door, and when there was no reply, I pushed it open and went in.

'Antoinette!' I called. 'Antoinette – it's me, Flora.'

Still there was no reply. She would not yet be in bed, I felt sure, so I went through her drawing room to the bedroom, expecting to find her sitting at her dressing table, perhaps, brushing her hair, or looking at one of her books. The bedroom was empty.

'Antoinette!' I said again, foolishly, since it was quite clear she was not there.

And then I felt a cold draught, saw the drapes rippling, and realized the window was open. Wide open.

My heart leaped with alarm. Antoinette had gone out by the same way that John the gamekeeper's boy had come to visit her, presumably because she had thought she might be intercepted if she used the stairs and the door in the usual way. But that creeper had been badly weakened when it had given way under John's weight. Would it have supported her? Or was she now lying injured or even dead on the path beneath?

My anxious feet flew me to the window. I was almost afraid to look out for fear of what I might see. But to my immense relief the creeper appeared more or less intact, and I could see no bundle below the window.

My relief was short-lived, however. Where had Antoinette gone? Was it possible she had decided to ride over to Monksmoor in search of her foal? Oh surely not – at this time of night! But she was so obsessed by it, and so desperately afraid she would never see it again.

Anxiety knotted my stomach. She shouldn't be out alone in the dark at all, and certainly not on the lonely road to Monksmoor. There were all manner of dangers, and in any case, by the time she reached the village everyone would be in their beds and fast asleep – everyone but villains and drunks.

Well, wherever she had gone, this was not something I could deal with alone. Little as I wanted to face Gavin again so soon, I had to enlist his help.

I found him in the parlour, a glass of cognac in his hand.

'So – you've decided my offer is worth the taking after all, Flora?' he said in an amused drawl when he saw me in the doorway.

'Certainly not,' I returned shortly. 'I thought you should know your niece is not in her rooms, and I think she's escaped by way of the window.'

Whatever he had expected, it certainly was not this.

'Escaped by way of the window? What can you mean?'

'There's a creeper outside that I know for a fact is negotiable,' I said. 'Her friend the gamekeeper's boy was using it to visit her until her father and his own twisted ankle put a stop to it. Now I think she has gone out the same way so that we would not be aware she was missing, and it wouldn't surprise me if she hasn't gone off to Monksmoor in search of the foal she is so set upon.'

'The devil she has! At this time of night!'

'She's headstrong enough. I may be wrong, of course, but wherever she is, we have to find her, Gavin, before some serious harm befalls her.'

To give Gavin his due, he reacted with commendable speed, and if he had been a little drunk on Louis' brandy, he was instantly stone-cold sober.

'We'll see if her horse is in the stables,' he said. 'If she is gone, I'll ride after her. If not, we'll search closer to home.' He strode out.

'I'll fetch a wrap and be with you in a moment,' I said.

I ran upstairs to collect my wrap, and hurried out to the stables. As I crossed the yard I heard Gavin's raised voice coming from within and breathed a sigh of relief. He must have caught her in time.

My relief was short-lived, however, for suddenly the most terrible commotion broke out – the frenzied barking of a dog, Gavin shouting again, Antoinette screaming, the splinter of shattering wood, the frightened whinnying of the horses. I ran to the stable door, which stood ajar, then stopped short, horrified at the scene the moonlight illuminated for me.

Antoinette cowered, sobbing in a corner, whilst Gavin bent over what looked like a bundle against the broken-down door of one of the stalls. Before my very eyes he hauled the bundle to its feet, and in the fleeting moment before his fist cracked once more into the bloodied jaw, I saw that it was John, the gamekeeper's lad. The boy went down again, staggering backwards along the passage between the loose boxes before collapsing into a heap of straw, and Gavin followed, kicking viciously at the defenceless body.

'Gavin!' I cried, shocked by the violence of his attack. 'What are you doing? Stop!'

I grabbed his sleeve, and he shook me off as if I were no more than a troublesome fly, going once more for the boy who lay in the straw trying to cover his head with his arms.

'Little bastard! I'll teach you a lesson you won't forget! How dare you lay a finger on my niece?' Each phrase was punctuated by a fresh blow.

'Gavin, you'll kill him!' I screamed. 'Stop it at once! Do you hear? Stop it!'

'Keep out of this, Flora!' he shot at me. He dragged the boy

to his feet again and the expression on his face was pure
savagery as his fist shot into the already bloodied face, sending
the boy reeling back into the heavy wooden post which con-
nected two of the loose boxes. Again the boy's legs gave way
beneath him; as he sagged into a heap against the post, Gavin's
boot went into him with a soft, sickening thud.

'Antoinette – go for Thompson!' I cried. 'Quickly – go now!'

She did not move. She was, I think, frozen by shock and fear.
And in any case, it occurred to me that by the time she had
roused the coachman and brought him here it might well be too
late. I looked around wildly – and my eye fell on a pitchfork
lying against the wall and gleaming dully in the moonlight. I
grabbed it, pointing the prongs towards Gavin.

'Gavin – stop, or I'll . . .'

I do not know exactly what I was threatening; the pitchfork
was so heavy I could scarcely hold it horizontal, let alone drive
the prongs into Gavin, even if I could have brought myself to
do such a thing. And he could so easily have snatched it from
my grasp and either turned it on me or used it on the hapless
John. But by some miracle the simple sight of me there
brandishing the thing was enough to bring Gavin to his senses;
either that or the worst of his fury had spent itself without my
intervention. With a disdainful glance at me, he dragged John
to the stable door and threw him outside.

'Get out of here!' he grated. 'Get back to your hovel. And if I
ever catch you around here again, I swear I'll have you horse-
whipped from here to Plymouth!'

He turned, catching the terrified Antoinette by the arm and
jerking her forward so violently that she cried out in pain. 'As
for you, Miss – into the house. Now!'

For a moment she hesitated, still seemingly frozen by fear,
then, without another word, she fled.

'Put that thing down, Flora,' Gavin ordered me.

I lowered the pitchfork, unwilling to let it go even though the
worst of it seemed to be over.

'How could you, Gavin?' I demanded. 'How could you beat a
young boy senseless?'

'He's no business here, and deserved everything he got. He was trespassing to be with Antoinette. Do you think your precious Louis would have done any different?'

I could not answer that. Very likely, I thought, he would not. But I hoped he would have known when to stop, and I was certain he would have taken less sadistic pleasure in it.

My thoughts went to the boy, badly hurt no doubt, and thrown bodily out of the stable.

'He'll need attention,' I said tersely.

'He'll not get it from me.'

'You would prefer him to be found dead of his injuries and the cold in the woods tomorrow morning?' I demanded. 'If you won't tend him, Gavin, I will.'

I threw down the pitchfork and went outside. John was hunched against the stable wall, his dog whining at his feet.

'Are you much hurt?' I asked shortly, for although I was concerned for him, I was also angry with him, and with Antoinette.

He looked up at me groggily. 'What do you think?'

'I think you are fortunate that Mr Gavin did not horsewhip you as he threatened,' I said severely. 'You know very well that you have been warned to keep away from Miss Antoinette. You were taking advantage because you know her father is away.'

John spat blood into the dust. One of his teeth had been knocked out, I noticed.

'I only threw a few stones up at her window,' he said sullenly. 'She came down readily enough.'

What could I say? I had no doubt Antoinette was just as much to blame as he was.

'Can you walk?' I asked him. 'If you can, you'd better come into the kitchen and let me clean your wounds.'

He gaped at me in amazement, his slack mouth open, blood trickling down his chin.

'Come along,' I said. 'Lean on me.'

I put an arm out to help him and the dog growled menacingly.

'He'll have to stay outside,' I said. 'Cook wouldn't thank me for bringing a mangy cur into her kitchen.'

Braving the dog's low protest, I supported John into the kitchen.

'The gamekeeper's boy has met with an accident,' I explained to a startled Cook – I had no intention of telling her the truth of what had occurred.

She did not, of course, believe me, and she watched disapprovingly as I bathed John's cuts and fetched him a small snifter of Louis' brandy. By the time he had drunk it he was much recovered, and although every movement was clearly painful for him, he insisted he was fit to make his way home.

He left without thanks, but I wanted none. I only hoped that if Louis was in need of some assistance in a foreign land, someone would do the same for him. I watched John limp away across the stable yard, the dog at his heels, and went back into the house.

There was no sign of Gavin, but I suspected he was in the parlour. He might very well take advantage of Louis' absence to spend the night under the roof of Belvedere rather than returning to the lodge, I thought. I went to Antoinette's room and found her lying fully clothed upon her bed. I could see at a glance that she had been crying, but I was in no mood to let her behaviour go unchallenged.

'What were you thinking of, Antoinette?' I demanded.

She turned her face into her pillow, not answering.

'You cannot behave so,' I told her. 'If you do, you will certainly live to regret it. You might have played with John when you were small, but you are now a young lady, and he is not a suitable companion for you. But you know all this already. You would not have slipped out by way of the window, risking life and limb, if you had not been very well aware that you should not be going out at all. I won't have it, Antoinette. I am responsible for you in your father's absence and I mean to ensure you behave properly. Either you give me your word that you will not run away to meet John again, or I shall send for the carpenter and have your window secured.'

'He won't come back now,' Antoinette muttered into her

pillow. 'Not after what Uncle Gavin did to him. He won't risk another beating like that one.'

'Then perhaps your Uncle Gavin has achieved a measure of success where the rest of us have failed,' I said tartly.

She turned her head towards me and her eyes, reddened by crying, blazed green fire.

'I hate him!'

'For beating John? He was very angry, Antoinette. I don't know what he discovered you doing when he came to the stable – I don't want to know. But I can guess.'

'No you can't!' Antoinette retorted. 'We were talking about how I could buy my foal. And that's why I hate Uncle Gavin – because he has no intention of getting her for me, I know it. He'll ensure we are too late arriving at market – if he takes me at all. He's enjoying making me beg, enjoying me being disappointed. And I hate him. Hate him!'

'I thought you and your uncle got along very well,' I ventured.

Sometimes. When Papa is here he is really nice to me, and good fun too. But when Papa is away he changes. He can be horrid.'

That, I thought, was the crux of it. In Louis' presence he would undermine his authority and enjoy taunting Louis with his popularity. But when Louis was not here, he enjoyed wielding his power. I dreaded to think what would happen if Louis did not come back. This evening I had seen a very nasty side to Gavin, in more ways than one.

'I'll make a bargain with you, Antoinette,' I said. 'I will take you to the market myself very early in the morning to give us the best chance of being in time, and I will buy the foal for you. But you must promise me there will be no more excursions to meet John.'

'But you said ladies didn't deal with such things,' Antoinette pointed out.

'On this occasion I shall make an exception.'

'But you haven't any money . . .'

'I am sure your father's good name will secure us credit,' I said. 'But you have to promise me, Antoinette, no more escapades like tonight, even if we are for some reason unsuccessful in our efforts to buy the foal.'

'But . . .'

'Promise!' I said sternly. 'Otherwise I shall certainly leave it to your Uncle Gavin.'

'Oh, all right, I promise.'

She still looked sullen and tear-stained, but I knew she would never capitulate easily and I rather thought I had taken another step towards establishing some kind of rapport with the girl who, if things went badly, might yet become my charge.

I had given Louis my word that I would do my best by her. Helpless as I was in every other respect, I could at least ensure I did my best to keep that promise. Whatever happened, I would not let Louis down.

Thirteen

I n the event, Gavin came with us to market. I had asked Thompson to have the carriage ready early, and as soon as we had finished breakfast, we set off. But we had not gone far before Gavin caught us, riding his own horse, and galloped alongside, calling that he would see us in Twyford St Mary. Antoinette was delighted, and I must admit to being relieved. For all my good intentions I had been nervous about my ability to negotiate successfully for the foal.

It was a fine bright morning with a hint of spring in the air. All along the wayside new green leaf was peppering what had been bare brown branches. I thought of how my father had loved the spring and felt a deep sadness that this year he would not see it. But the edge had gone from my grief. One person can bear only so much emotion, and I was full to overflowing.

Though Twyford St Mary was some way from Monksmoor, I had been to the market there several times before, so the crowd that had gathered on the green came as no surprise to me. Travelling folk mingled with villagers, piebalds and Exmoor ponies rubbed fetlocks with fine thoroughbred horses, pedlars paraded their wares, a knife grinder honed sharp steel, a barrel organ churned out a merry tinkling melody. Antoinette, who had never seen such a gathering before, was high with excitement, though also touchingly anxious that we should find her foal before it was sold elsewhere.

As we wandered through the crowd looking for Gavin I was surprised and pleased to come face to face with George Doughty.

'Flora!' he exclaimed. 'What are you doing here?'

'We've come for the foal – the one I first saw in your smithy,' Antoinette told him.

'Is that so, Miss Antoinette?' He beamed at her. Clearly she had made a good impression on him with her enthusiasm on the day we had visited. 'Ah, you'll be pleased with her, I'm sure. She's a fine little animal, and no mistake.'

'We must make haste, I think, George,' I said. 'She'll find a buyer quickly if she's such a fetching thing. And we have to find Gavin, who is going to make the purchase for Antoinette.'

'Gavin Fletcher?' George frowned. 'Mr Louis' brother? You're with him?'

I nodded. 'Louis is away in France.'

'Hmm.' George's face spoke volumes. 'Well, I hope you'll find time to come and see us again soon, Flora. We've been so worried about you. Ralph gave you the messages about the inn all right, I understand.'

'He did.' I glanced anxiously at Antoinette, but all her attention was given to looking for Gavin, and at that very moment she bobbed excitedly.

'There he is! Uncle Gavin – over here!' She was waving to attract his attention.

'I must go, George,' I said.

'Well – take care, Flora.' And to Antoinette: 'I hope you get the foal, Miss.'

'We will. Come on, Flora!' She tugged at my sleeve, I bid George goodbye, we joined Gavin and went in search of the dealer who had been entrusted with the foal.

An hour later and the deal was successfully done.

'I'll take him home with me on a leading rein,' Gavin said, but Antoinette would have none of it. She did not want to let her precious acquisition out of her sight, and insisted she be tethered to the carriage as we had originally intended.

We were walking back across the green when suddenly one horse in particular caught my eye. I stopped short, my heart pounding so hard I thought it would burst.

Tethered with three or four others was a big grey, a magnificent beast that would, I am sure, have attracted my attention in any case if I had been a lover of horses. But it was not the size of the animal that arrested me, nor the way it pawed the ground impatiently. It was the distinctive markings. A great white flash on the muzzle, and a white sock.

Unless I was much mistaken, it perfectly fitted the description of the horse Jem Giddings had seen galloping away from Tucker's Grave on the night my father was murdered.

'Flora? Are you feeling unwell?' Gavin's voice seemed to come from a long way off.

My hand was at my throat; I could feel the blood pumping in my ears.

'That horse!' I whispered.

Gavin frowned. 'What do you mean? Which one? There are horses everywhere!'

'*That* one!' I pointed, then withdrew my hand as if I somehow knew that recognizing it might be dangerous. 'A horse was seen galloping away from Tucker's Grave on the night my father was shot, and the man who saw it met an untimely end also. That horse –' I jerked my chin in its direction – 'is just as poor Jem Giddings described it!'

'You are letting your imagination run away with you.' Gavin sounded impatient.

'Perhaps. But . . .' I could not tear my eyes away from the grey. 'If it is one and the same, then whoever owns it is one of the men responsible for my father's death!'

'The beast is clearly with a horse dealer,' Gavin said. 'You'd learn nothing from these people, Flora. They are mostly vagrants and vagabonds.'

There was no denying that. The man standing beside the grey was unkempt and dirty, a gypsy at best.

'But he must know where the horse came from!' My mind was chasing shadows as I spoke. 'Someone asked the dealer to sell him on – he must know who that was!'

'I think it unlikely.' Gavin spread an elegant hand to emphasize his point. 'Men like that ask few questions, for often enough questions are unwelcome. They know their horseflesh. If the beast is sound in wind and limb, that's good enough for them.'

'Are you saying that horse is stolen, then?' I asked.

'From the look of the vendor, it wouldn't surprise me.' Gavin shifted impatiently. 'But Flora, this is all speculation. You cannot even be certain that horse is the same one your old friend saw.'

'He was no friend of mine,' I corrected him. 'But he was very canny when it came to horses. And you have to agree, Gavin, those markings are very unusual. Heavens, it's not that common to see a grey at all! I am going to speak to that dealer. Will you wait for me?'

Gavin laid a hand on my arm and I instinctively recoiled. Since the night he had kissed me and looked for more, his touch was repugnant to me. Gavin, however, seemed unaware of my reaction.

'You must not do this, Flora!' His voice was low and urgent. 'If you are right and there was such a horse – if indeed that is the very same animal – then the likelihood is that he has been sent to market for a purpose. Your father's murderer heard the gossip and decided his best course of action was to get rid of the horse rather than have it linked to him. Didn't this Jem Giddings meet his end in suspicious circumstances? If he was killed because he could identify the horse that galloped away from Tucker's Grave, then the rider must be a desperate man. Desperate not to be linked to your father's death. Desperate enough to kill again. And if that is so, then you would be placing yourself in danger if you began asking questions. The next body found upon a lonely road could be yours!'

A chill whispered over my skin. Gavin was right in every respect, I felt sure. The owner of that horse might very well be desperate to avoid recognition. If he was working secretly against the Brotherhood of the Lynx it was likely vital to him that no shadow of suspicion fell upon him. And that he was dangerous, I had no doubt. He had already killed once, and perhaps twice. I did not think he would hesitate to kill again if he thought he was in danger of being unmasked. But I would risk anything to bring my father's killer to justice – and to learn who it was who threatened the safety of Louis and his comrades in the Brotherhood.

I raised my chin. 'I cannot let this opportunity slip away,' I said with determination. 'I have to try and see if there is any morsel of information I can learn.'

I made to go towards the dealer, and once again Gavin intercepted me.

'I am sorry, Flora, but I cannot let you do this. If you are determined the dealer should be questioned as to what he might know, then I should be the one to do it, for at least I am a man and capable of taking care of myself.'

I felt a stab of surprise at Gavin's unexpected chivalry, and also of guilt, that I had misjudged him. But his confidence in his ability to take care of himself was misplaced, I felt. My father had been no weakling, yet he had been gunned down without mercy.

'It's my fight,' I said stubbornly. 'I should be the one to take the chances.'

Gavin smiled briefly. 'As I have said before, a spirited little thing! No, Flora, I am afraid I must stand firm on this. Take Antoinette to the carriage and set out for home and safety. When you are well clear of this thronging crowd, any one of whom could be your father's murderer for all you know, then I will approach the dealer and make some enquiries. Don't argue, now, my mind is made up. Why, Louis would never forgive me if I allowed you to fall into any danger.'

He looked at me slyly as he said that, and I thought that without doubt he did indeed know there was something between Louis and me. But I could not worry my head about that now – and in any case, it was over.

'I'll likely catch up with you long before you reach Belvedere,' Gavin went on. 'If I do not I'll appraise you over supper of what I've been able to learn – though to be truthful, I am not hopeful of it being very much.'

'You'll do your best, I know,' I said. 'Thank you, Gavin.'

We headed back to where Thompson was waiting with the carriage, Antoinette leading the foal by the bridle, and I found myself fervently hoping we would not run into George again. Just now I did not want to be engaged in conversation, even by someone I loved as I loved him, and I did not want him to know about the horse either. If George had any inkling, he would no doubt be up to the green in a flash and asking the same questions Gavin had promised to ask, but without the same degree of tact. I could not bear the thought that some harm should befall George through my fault. But we did not see him.

We found Thompson yarning comfortably with some farmers. At Antoinette's insistence, he took a good look at the foal and pronounced her a sound buy before tying her up to the carriage.

'We'll have to go steady-like, not to frighten or overtire her,' he said. 'It's a good thing she's with us and not Mr Gavin, if you ask me. He'd make her go too fast for her dainty little legs, I wouldn't be surprised.'

'That's just what I thought,' Antoinette agreed. 'Uncle Gavin can be very careless.'

And also surprisingly chivalrous, I thought.

The track the carriage was parked on encircled the green, and rather than turn around, Thompson trotted around it. As we neared the place where the grey had been I leaned forward, peering amongst the constantly shifting crowds for another glimpse of it. But neither the horse nor the gypsy dealer were anywhere to be seen.

A little further on, however, I caught sight of Gavin talking to two men. Neither of them was the gypsy, but both were quite rough in appearance, and from what I could make out at this distance the conversation was animated and not altogether amicable.

Had Gavin established the identity of the horse's owner? Was he pursuing his enquiries – or could one of those ruffians be my father's murderer? Again my heart thudded uneasily, and I wondered if I should ask Thompson to stop and make sure Gavin was not in need of assistance. But I did not think Gavin would thank me for interfering, and in any case, I had Antoinette in my care. She should be protected from any unpleasantness or even danger at all costs. I peered back as the carriage pulled further away, and to my relief, saw Gavin moving off through the milling crowds.

I could scarcely wait to find out if he had been successful in learning anything of interest.

That afternoon, for the first time since Louis had left, Antoinette spoke to me about her mother and her brother. It was as if, now that the foal was hers, she could allow herself to think about other things.

'Do you think my brother likes horses?' she asked, quite conversationally, and for all the world as if he were no more than a visitor who had nothing to do with her at all.

'I expect he does,' I replied. 'Most boys do, don't they?'

'Mm.' She considered. 'How old is he? Eight? I hope he won't be too much of a horror. But the foal will soon be just the right size for him to ride. And if he doesn't know how, I shall rather enjoy teaching him.'

I was rather surprised by this, though perhaps, given how lonely Antoinette was, I should not have been. But to be so willing to share her beloved acquisition with a boy she had never even met was unlike the Antoinette I had come to know, and I was impressed by her generosity. A moment later, however, my illusions were shattered.

'She'll still be mine, of course,' she went on smugly. 'And if he falls off a few times perhaps he'll realize he is not so clever as he must undoubtedly think himself.'

'How much did your father tell you before he left?' I asked.

'Oh, just that my mother did not die at all, but went home to France. And that my brother went with her.' She sounded almost uninterested.

'It must have been a dreadful shock for you,' I said.

She shrugged. 'I suppose. I always suspected I hadn't been told the truth about Mama. After all, if she had died, why did Papa never take me to visit her grave? And why did he hate her name being mentioned?' Her mouth tightened and her green eyes suddenly grew very sharp. 'I've overheard things, too. When one is just a child, people think you don't hear, or understand. They talk as if you are not there. Grandmama and Papa used to say things that didn't make sense to me at the time, but later, when I was older, I drew my own conclusions.'

'Are you pleased to think your Mama may be coming back now?' I asked.

She shrugged again. 'I don't much mind one way or the other. I'm sure I won't like her, though. She was never very nice to me, and why should I like someone who chose to take my brother with her and leave me behind?'

The bitterness was there now in her voice and I realized she had not grasped the fact that at the time Lisette had returned to France no one had known she was carrying another child.

'I don't think that's quite the case, Antoinette,' I said. 'Your brother was born later, I understand.'

'When she was in France and my father in England, you mean?' Antoinette frowned. 'Then he can't be a proper brother at all. Only a half-brother, maybe.'

'I think not.' This conversation was taking a turn I did not like. It was far too intimate for comfort. And I found myself wondering too why Louis was so sure the boy was indeed his son. But since he was clearly convinced as to that fact, it was not for me to question his reasons. 'I think it is something you have to accept,' I said simply.

As suddenly as she had raised the subject she let it go.

'I'm going to see how the foal has settled in,' she said. 'I've time before changing for supper, haven't I?'

'I'm sure you have,' I said, relieved. 'Have you thought of a name for her yet?'

'Misty,' Antoinette replied promptly.

'Ah, that's a good name,' I agreed.

But it reminded me too of the grey horse. I hoped Gavin would not be too long returning, for the anxiety was gnawing again at the pit of my stomach. And I hoped that he would do so whilst Antoinette was still occupied with the foal so that I could question him freely as to what he had learned.

My hope was satisfied. Not long afterwards I saw Gavin come riding up the drive. He came into the house through the kitchen and I heard him snapping at Cook, and then at Walter. This was not a good sign. It was unlike Gavin to display ill humour. He was too fond of being popular with everyone.

I met him in the hallway, and he snapped at me too.

'Faith, you startled me, Flora! Do you have to creep about so?'

'I'm anxious to speak with you,' I said. 'Did you manage to learn anything about the ownership of the grey horse?'

'Can't a man at least get his redingote off before you begin nagging him?' he grumbled. 'And don't you have the good sense to wait until we are out of earshot of the servants before you start on your questions?'

'There's no one to hear!' I replied defensively, thinking he sounded more like Louis in the days when I had first come to Belvedere than his usual self. I knew now, of course, the reason for Louis' caution. Could it be that Gavin now knew something he considered to be dangerous?

He strode into the parlour and I followed.

'Since you are clearly bursting with impatience, I will put you out of your misery,' he said shortly. 'I'm none the wiser, I'm afraid, about how that horse came to be at market.'

'The dealer had left?' I said. 'I could not see him when we passed by.'

'No, I caught up with him, but as I thought, he was slippery as an eel.' Gavin was pouring himself a brandy – it was a little early to be beginning on the liquor, I thought, but of course I said nothing. 'He agreed that the horse came from this neck of the woods, but claimed he did not know the man he had bought him from.'

'Couldn't you get a description?' I asked, disappointed. 'You might have recognized him from it. After all, you've lived in Dartmouth all your life. You must know most of the local people.'

'I told you, he would say nothing. It was all: "Sorry, sir, I couldn't say, sir" and I didn't deem it wise to press him. As a matter of fact, I don't consider it was wise to ask questions at all. If the horse is the one owned by the man who murdered your father, and word gets back that we are on the point of discovering his identity, it might well be enough to precipitate some act of violence.' He sipped his brandy; his eyes met mine. 'Consider what happened to Jem Giddings.'

'But if we knew who was responsible, then we could set the law on him.' I hesitated, wondering if I dared broach the subject of the connection between my father and the Brotherhood of the Lynx, and deciding I must. 'It's more than just simply bringing my father's murderer to justice,' I said. 'I don't know how much you know about what Louis does, Gavin, but I think my father died because of his involvement. Someone, for some reason, is working for Louis' downfall. If we knew who it was, it could save Louis' life.'

Gavin's eyes narrowed. 'I had not realized you knew so much, Flora. Did your father acquaint you with the details of what he did?'

'No, he told me nothing. All I know, I know from Louis himself.'

'Louis has told you?' He sounded surprised.

'Yes.'

'Well, well! You are closer to him than I had realized.' He laughed softly. 'He's a fool, my brother. He risks his neck for no reason but chivalry. Well, you might as well know I have no intention of doing the same. My life is too precious to me. He'll be caught one of these days, make no mistake about it. Whether we discover the perpetrator of your father's murder or not.'

'But surely for his sake we can at least try to learn who is working against him?' I said desperately. 'Surely at least you owe him that much, Gavin! He is your brother, after all.'

Gavin was silent for a moment, deep in thought. Then: 'I have to go out again, Flora,' he said.

Hope flared in me. Had I touched a nerve, made him realize there might be something we could do to keep Louis safe?

'The gypsy *did* give you a clue as to the identity of the owner of the grey?' I whispered. 'Are you going to follow it up, Gavin?'

He finished the brandy in one gulp and strode to the door.

'You ask too many questions, Flora,' was all he said.

Gavin did not return in time for supper. Somehow I made conversation with Antoinette, but it was not easy when my mind was running in circles and my nerves were stretched to breaking point. He had still not returned when Antoinette retired to her room, and I did the same.

I undressed and brushed my hair, thinking of Louis, and thinking, too, of Gavin, both putting their lives at risk because of the rising of a desperate people in a foreign land. I climbed into bed and pulled the covers up to my chin, for with the coming of darkness the warmth of the day had gone as if it had never been and there was a sharp chill in the air once more. But I could not sleep. I lay staring into the darkness, listening for the sound of Gavin's horse's hooves on the drive, and wondering how Louis was faring in France.

I think at last I must have dozed, exhaustion getting the better of me, for though I thought I was still awake and aware of every creak as the house settled around me, I did not hear the approaching hooves. It was the loud knocking at the door that shocked me into full wakefulness, like the reprise of a bad dream, and instantly I was all a-tremble, remembering with every fibre of my being the knocking in the night that had led to my father's death.

I lay for a moment frozen with fear. Had they come again, those men with guns in their hands and murder on their minds, but this time to Belvedere, to dispose of others who threatened their evil business? Was Gavin home yet? Would he answer the knocking? And if I crept downstairs, would I find him lying in a pool of blood as I had found my father?

All these thoughts raced through my mind in less time than it takes to tell, and the knocking came again, urgent, demanding.

Nothing in the house stirred. Gavin could not be home, I

realized, or if he was, he had gone to the lodge. And the servants were unlikely to be roused. Their quarters were tucked away in the attics at the rear of the house. If I did nothing, then perhaps whoever it was would simply go away.

And then another thought occurred to me. Supposing it was a messenger with word from Louis! Supposing something terrible had happened to him! I knew then that I could not ignore the knocking. Whatever the danger, I had to know who it was who came to Belvedere at this hour.

I pushed aside the covers and got out of bed, reaching for my wrap. The window of my room was almost immediately above the great front door; there was no need for me to go downstairs to find out who it was on the other side.

I crossed the floor on trembling legs and threw the casement wide. A carriage was drawn up on the forecourt, and steam from the horses' flanks rose like fine mist into the cold night air. But I could see no coachman, and whoever was at the door was hidden from my view by the overhanging parapet. Even as I peered out, the knocking came again.

'Who's there?' I called; my voice, shrill with fear, sounded loud in the still night.

The figure of a man stepped out of the hidden doorway and into my line of vision, peering up at the window. My first impression was that he was a gentleman, booted and wigged, and wearing a tricorn hat.

'Is that Flora?' His voice was low and urgent.

I gathered my wrap around me. 'Who is it? How do you know my name?'

'I come from Louis. For God's sake open the door!'

My heart came thudding into my throat. I had been right! Or so it seemed. But how could I be sure? Just because the visitor looked like a gentleman did not necessarily mean he was not also the enemy. This could yet be a trap.

'I shall not come down until I know who you are and what you want!' I called back. 'If you really are from Louis, you must know I cannot take that risk.'

'It's Dartington!' he called back, and his upper-crust vowels and something in his demeanour suddenly struck a chord with me.

'Sir Jeremy Dartington?' I was incredulous that a member of the aristocracy should be here on the doorstep in the middle of the night, yet mindful that the Brotherhood of the Lynx very likely comprised aristocrats, and by necessity worked under cover of darkness.

'Yes. I'm a friend of Louis'. Now, will you come down and open the door?'

'For what reason?' I still needed to be sure. 'Have you a message from Louis? If so, you can tell me what it is from where you are. There's no one to overhear.'

'More than a message. I have someone here who needs to be inside, out of the cold night air.'

'But who?'

The carriage door opened, the slight figure of a boy climbed down and stood on the driveway beneath my window, rubbing sleep out of bleary eyes.

'Louis' son!' Sir Jeremy called back. 'Pierre Fletcher! He's eight years old, cold and exhausted. Now will you come down and open this damned door?'

Fourteen

My feet flew me down the stairs. With trembling hands I fumbled with the heavy bolts and threw the door open. The boy was on the doorstep now with Sir Jeremy, the man's arms round his shoulders. Shadowed there with the moonlight behind him he looked very vulnerable – and very frightened. A thousand questions were bombarding me, but for the moment I asked none of them. All that mattered was getting this child – Louis' child – into the warmth and safety of the house.

'Bring him through to the kitchen,' I said. 'The fire will be dead in the parlour, but the range will still be alight.'

I closed the door, bolted it once more, and led the way along the hall. The range was indeed still glowing. I poked it to life so that the flames flared up, hot and bright, and lit a lamp. Then, unable to contain my anxiety a moment longer, I turned to Sir Jeremy.

'Where is Louis? Why is he not here?'

'He's still in France. We'll talk about it later.' He pulled out a chair and motioned the boy to sit. 'Is there something to eat?' he asked. 'God knows when Pierre last had a meal. It's been a long and arduous journey. But you're safe now, lad, in your father's house as I promised, and Flora will look after you, I'm sure.'

'Of course I will! There'll be bread and cheese and maybe some cold meat . . .' Even as I spoke I was opening the larder door, fetching the plate with the leftovers of the lamb roast, covered now with a weighted muslin, a loaf of bread from the crock, and a dish of butter. 'I'll make a hot drink, too. You look frozen, Pierre.'

He said nothing, looking at me with suspicion, and I wondered just how much of what I was saying he understood.

234

'Do you speak English?' I asked.

'Of course I do!' His tone was scornful, full of resentment, and I was reminded sharply of Antoinette. Those suspicious eyes were like hers, too, green and slanting, and like her he was slightly built. But for the rest of him . . . if I had wondered if Louis was naive to take on trust that Pierre was his son, my doubts disappeared in a moment. The set of his head, the shape of his nose and mouth – oh, he was Louis' son, all right.

'Would you like some warm milk?' I asked him.

'I don't drink milk. I'm eight years old!' The same disdain. Oh, there were going to be spats between him and Antoinette, and no mistake!

'Chocolate then,' I suggested.

He said nothing and I set some milk to warm on the range, cut a hunk of bread and a few slices of meat, and set them in front of him. At once he began to eat ravenously.

'Will your hospitality extend to me also?' Sir Jeremy asked with a slight apologetic smile. 'I've had little to eat today either.'

'Of course . . . forgive me . . .' I cut more bread and meat and piled it on a plate for him. 'Would you like a drink too?'

'I certainly would – but perhaps something a little stronger than hot chocolate,' he said wryly.

'Ale?' I suggested. 'Cognac?'

'Both, I think. The ale to quench my thirst and the cognac to warm my stomach. It's a cold night to be on the water.'

'You sailed with Pierre?' I asked, fetching the jug of ale.

'I did. We met at a little cove on the north coast of France, did we not, Pierre?'

'And Louis . . . ?' Try as I might, I could not stop myself from asking about Louis.

'I met with him briefly, yes. He handed Pierre into my custody and asked that I bring him to Belvedere. To you. But as I already said, we'll talk later.' His tone was decisive, his eyes met mine briefly and flicked meaningfully to Pierre.

My heart lurched as I took his meaning. He did not want to discuss Louis or his plans in front of the boy. Pierre, however, had other ideas.

'He's gone back for Mama,' he said, his mouth full of roast lamb.

My heart lurched again. Louis was not yet out of danger then.

'Were you not together?' All very well for Sir Jeremy to say he would talk to me later; I was too avid for news to wait.

'Mama is staying with friends,' Pierre said. 'I have not seen her for a long time.'

He said it as if it was quite a usual occurrence. So Lisette was no better a mother to him than she had been to Antoinette, I thought. Unless . . . Could it be that she had been taken by the Revolutionaries, and he had been told she was with friends so as not to frighten him? If so, then Louis' mission would be more difficult and dangerous yet. There were ways, I supposed, that prisoners could be helped to escape the overcrowded gaols, daring raids were not unheard of, and some guards were not above accepting bribes. But the risks to anyone attempting such a feat were high indeed.

But if Lisette *had* been taken, then surely the rest of the household, and even Pierre, would have been taken too? Age was no barrier to the zeal of the Revolutionaries; a hated aristocrat was a hated aristocrat, no matter how young he might be.

Sir Jeremy's voice cut into my racing thoughts. 'Pierre, remember what I told you!' His tone was a warning one. 'You must not mention your Mama's whereabouts to anyone!'

The boy looked up and I saw both guilt and the fear with which he must have lived for many months in those sharp green eyes.

'But we are in England now! And you said Flora was a friend!'

'That is so. But you must trust no one, not even here in England. To speak loosely is to place lives at risk. The life of your Mama and those who seek to help her. Do you understand?'

'Yes,' he whispered. 'I'm sorry.'

'Well, no harm has been done this time,' Sir Jeremy said more gently. 'Flora is one of us. At least, her father was.' His eyes met mine. 'Your father was a brave man, Flora. You should be proud of him.'

'Indeed I am,' I said. 'And of course I would do or say nothing which might endanger Louis or any of the Brotherhood. I pray nightly for his safe return, and success with his mission.'

For a little while he and Pierre ate in silence and I noticed that the boy's eyes were beginning to droop. He must be exhausted, I thought; now the warmth of the kitchen, the hot chocolate and a full stomach were conspiring to take him to the borders of sleep.

'I'll go and see if the bed is made up in the guest room,' I said.

I lit a candle and went upstairs, through the silent sleeping house, a feeling of unreality settling on me though I went through the motions as if this were an ordinary day and the boy downstairs simply an ordinary visitor.

I had thought Louis would have left instructions for the room to be made ready since it had been his intention and fervent hope that his son would need it, but perhaps he had been wary of alerting the staff, for though the counterpane was neatly pulled up, there were no sheets beneath it, and I did not know where any could be found, for housekeeping played no part in my life at Belvedere.

Perhaps for tonight the best thing would be for me to let Pierre have my own bed, I thought, and I would sleep downstairs on the chaise. But if the little boy slept late in the morning, as well he might after his arduous journey, it would be most inconvenient, for I would be unable to wash, or brush my hair, or have access to clean clothing. A better option might be for him to sleep in Louis' room. His bed would certainly be made up and ready for his return, and I felt sure he would have no objection to his son using it.

I made my way along the corridor to the master suite where I had lain and loved with Louis on the night before his departure. The memory of it was poignantly sharp as I turned the handle and opened the door, a warmth as my heart and my body remembered the delights we had shared, a sadness from know-ing we would never again be together that way. Then I stopped short, holding the candle aloft, and staring in shocked disbelief.

The room was full of Gavin's things, his cloak thrown casually down on a chair, a book and his writing materials on the desk, a pair of boots discarded in the middle of the floor. The more I looked, the more of Gavin's possessions I could see.

I experienced a flash of outrage, and marched through to the bedroom. Just as I had thought, Gavin's nightshirt lay spread out ready and waiting for him on the bed. I had suspected he might be playing at being master in Louis' absence, but this . . . !

The outrage swelled until I thought it would choke me. Gavin had moved himself lock, stock and barrel into Louis' rooms! It would have been bad enough if they had been friends, but considering the bad feeling between them and Louis' insistence that Gavin should not live under his roof, but in the house in Dartmouth and the lodge, there was something deeply sinister about what he was doing. It was almost as if he were staking a claim. Almost as if he believed Louis would not be coming back. For if he did, and found Gavin here, or even suspected what he had done, there would be hell to pay.

Clearly I could not put Pierre in Louis' room. Though Gavin had not returned, and it might well be that he was staying the night elsewhere, there was always the chance that he might yet come home. To have him blundering into the room where Pierre was sleeping would give the boy a terrible fright, and heaven only knew how Gavin would respond to finding him in the bed he had appropriated as his own. No, there was nothing for it but to return to my original plan and let Pierre use my room.

In the event, when I returned to the kitchen, I found that Pierre had fallen asleep at the table, his head on his arms, and when I appraised Sir Jeremy of my suggestion, he would not hear of it.

'Pierre will be perfectly fine on the chaise,' he said. 'He's smaller than you and you need a night's rest in your own bed to be fresh to deal with the situation the morrow. Show me the way and I'll carry him through.'

I led the way to the parlour and Pierre barely stirred as Sir Jeremy set him down on the chaise. I fetched a rug and tucked it around him, my heart filling with tenderness as I did so. Just so might Louis have looked at his age, this boy who was his son and who might, for all we knew, already be an orphan.

'I assume you are one of the members of the Brotherhood of the Lynx,' I said when Sir Jeremy and I had returned to the kitchen.

'I have that honour,' he confirmed with a self-deprecating smile. 'I play but a small part compared with Louis, but I like to think I can be of some assistance to him in the mission he has undertaken. It is my task, sometimes, to escort the refugees to a place of safety, and that is what I was assigned to on this occasion.'

'But Louis, you say, is still in France.'

'Attempting to rescue Lisette, yes. He found the boy at an address he had learned from . . . his contact . . . staying with a family who have, it seems, enough friends in the new order to keep him safe at least for a while. But as Pierre said, his mother had gone elsewhere.'

'Why did she not take him with her?' I demanded.

'I cannot say. Doubtless she had her reasons. And doubtless they involved some gentleman,' he said tersely.

'Then why has Louis gone looking for her?'

'Because that is what he believes he must do. It can only be a matter of time before she is arrested, wherever she is,' Sir Jeremy stated. 'The family is much hated by the Revolutionaries. There's no doubt they'll catch up with her before long.'

My patience with a woman who could betray her husband and abandon both her children was at an end.

'It's no more than she deserves,' I said shortly. 'Why should Louis risk his life for such a faithless creature?'

'She is the mother of his children,' Sir Jeremy said. 'Louis is a man of honour. He believes he owes her a debt of care. If she prefers to stay with her paramour, whoever he might be, well, then at least Louis will have done what he could. But I doubt she will do that. Lisette will choose to save her own skin rather than remain at any man's side, if I know anything of her.'

239

'Did you know her then?' I asked. 'When she was living here at Belvedere?'

He nodded. 'Oh yes, I knew her.'

'And what was she like?' I could not keep myself from asking.

'Very beautiful. Very spoiled. And –' he hesitated – 'there was a darkness about her. I don't know what it was, but there was a darkness that somehow was a part of the attraction she held for every man who came within her orbit. She did not make Louis happy, that I do know, and she won't make him happy now. But Louis ceased to expect to be happy a long time ago. Duty is his reason for living. It has been so for many years. Until perhaps . . .'

His eyes scanned my face thoughtfully, as if he knew my secrets, and I felt the colour rising in my cheeks.

'How long do you think it will take him to reach Lisette?' I asked, anxious to cover my loss of composure as well as to learn what I could. He shook his head.

'Two or three days to find her, the same perhaps to get her back to where the ship will be waiting. If they are lucky and escape capture, that is. Who knows?'

'The ship *will* be waiting?' I asked anxiously.

'It will return tomorrow, with a fresh cargo of wool which, at this moment, no doubt, men are labouring hard to load. Then it will hide out, waiting for Louis. Pray God he reaches it safely, but I truly believe this must be his last venture into such dangerous territory. Each time, he attracts a little more attention. Sooner or later, suspicion is bound to attach itself to him, and when it does . . .' He shook his head. 'His life will not be worth a sou.'

I shivered.

'Let us not dwell on that, however,' Sir Jeremy continued. 'When Louis delivered Pierre into my care, he bid me bring him to you. He was confident that you would take care of him until such time as, God willing, he is able to do so himself. I would willingly have offered him shelter at my own home, but Louis was adamant that he wanted him to come directly to Belvedere, so that he may begin to put down roots.'

'Yes, I can understand that,' I said.

'I do apologize however for having had to wake you, and no doubt frighten you half to death,' Sir Jeremy said. 'The fact of the matter is, however, that until this last mission is successfully completed, stealth and secrecy are vital.'

I suppressed a sudden almost hysterical urge to laugh aloud, for the absurdity of the situation dawned on me suddenly.

'But how am I supposed to keep Pierre a secret? A boy who has suddenly arrived from nowhere in the middle of the night? A *French* boy?'

Sir Jeremy spread his hands helplessly. 'The servants will know, of course, but *all* they will know is that he is here. And servants are trained not to ask questions. Their livelihoods depend on discretion, and in any case they are not of a class likely to have connections with those who would betray the Brotherhood to the French.'

I thought of the men who had come to Tucker's Grave. They had not belonged to the class Sir Jeremy clearly thought would have the necessary connections to be a danger. But they had murdered my father all the same.

'What must be kept secret is my involvement in all this,' Sir Jeremy went on. 'And most important of all, no one must learn of Louis' likely whereabouts whilst he is in France. His life depends on it.'

I nodded. 'No one will learn anything from me.'

He moved to the door. 'Louis said you could be trusted, and now that I have met you I share his confidence. I know you will look after Pierre until Louis is here to do so himself. And I know you will protect Louis' secrets with your life if necessary.'

'That is in no doubt,' I vowed.

When he had left I bolted the door after him and looked in again on Pierre. He was still sleeping soundly as a baby. There was no more I could do that night. But I was unwilling to return to my room. If Pierre should wake and find himself in a strange place he would be frightened. I should be there to comfort him. And I would not, in any case, sleep any more that night.

I went upstairs, fetched another blanket, and settled myself in the big wing chair in the parlour where I would know at once if Pierre stirred. I left the lamp burning and sat watching him as he slept, and wondered at how events had turned my simple, pleasant, ordinary life upside down.

I had lost my father and my home, I had found such a love as I had never dreamed of, and lost that too. Now, all that mattered was the welfare of the little boy Louis had risked his life to rescue from the Terror. And that Louis himself should come safe home.

I was wrong to think I would not sleep. After a while my thoughts became muddled and fuzzy, my eyelids drooped, and utter weariness overcame me. I slept, though it was an uneasy slumber, punctuated by wild and disturbing dreams, and when the grey light of dawn crept in at the window I came slowly back to full wakefulness, all too aware of the stiffness in my neck and in my limbs, and the unpleasant furring of my tongue.

Pierre was still fast asleep – I need not have been concerned that he would wake during the night.

I think I must have dozed a little again, for the click of the door opening made me start violently. It was Clara, come to light the fire. She must have been as startled to find the parlour occupied as I was by her sudden appearance, for she stood in the doorway clutching the basket of logs to her chest as if her life depended upon it, her mouth agape.

'Oh, Miss Flora!'

Now that the staff were up and about, they would have to be told something, I realized.

'Leave that for a moment, Clara,' I said quietly, so as not to disturb Pierre. 'Come to the kitchen. I need to talk to you and the others.'

She set down the logs, staring all the while at the small figure on the chaise, then did as I bid.

In the kitchen I gathered the staff together, and told them as much as they needed to know.

'We have a visitor – though perhaps visitor is not quite the right word, since he will be living here from now on. He is eight years old, and he has come from France, where he was in great danger.' I paused, knowing what I said next was bound to come as something of a shock to them. 'His name is Pierre, and he is Mr Louis' son.'

Their eyes were wide, but for a moment none of them spoke. Then Cook said: '*Her* son, you mean. Miss Lisette's.' She did not trouble to disguise the scorn in her voice. So she had known Lisette, and had little time for her, I guessed.

'And Mr Louis',' I said firmly. 'Pierre has had a terrible time, I understand, and I expect you all to treat him with kindness and respect. Do you understand?'

They nodded, saying not another word. They knew their place, of course – though I was sure they would begin to chatter and speculate the moment my back was turned.

'I don't want this mentioned outside of the house,' I went on. 'When Mr Louis comes home he will no doubt introduce Pierre into society, and there will be no more need for discretion. But for the moment it is to remain within these four walls. If it becomes common knowledge in the district I shall know that it came from one of you, and whoever is responsible will be dismissed with no reference.'

I did not like speaking to them in such a manner; my own roots were too close to theirs for me to be comfortable issuing orders, let alone threats of dismissal. And I knew too that what I had said was not strictly true; there were bound to be others who would learn of Pierre's presence at Belvedere and perhaps talk about it. But with Louis in such a perilous position, I had to do my best.

'When Pierre wakes, I'm sure he'd like a cup of hot chocolate,' I went on. 'And I'd rather like one myself. Could you make it for me, please, Cook? And one for Miss Antoinette, too.'

When the chocolates were ready, I carried them up to Antoinette's room. I found her awake and already dressed.

'Flora – what are you doing here? I was just going out to see Misty!'

I set the cup down on her little table. 'Drink this first. And I'll have mine with you. I have something to tell you, Antoinette.'

'What?' She looked alarmed suddenly. 'It's not Papa, is it?'

It crossed my mind to wonder if she knew more than I thought of Louis' expeditions to France, and had done all along.

'No,' I said. 'Well, not directly. It's about your brother, Pierre. He's here.'

To her credit, Antoinette took the news well. I had been afraid that for all that she had seemingly prepared herself, the reality might be different. But she reacted with excitement and impatience to meet the sibling of whose existence she had known nothing until a few days ago.

She went down to the parlour and sat with the still sleeping Pierre whilst I freshened up and changed my gown, which was creased to little better than a rag. When he woke a little later, she took him to breakfast, and though I felt awkward and strained with the little boy, brother and sister struck up an easy rapport as, I suppose, only the young can do. I was more than happy to let them go off to the stables together, where Antoinette could not wait to introduce Misty to her new-found brother, for I was both weary and anxious, my nerves stretched to breaking point.

I did not see Gavin come riding up the drive, or I would have attempted to intercept him. The first I knew that he had returned home was when he came storming into the guest room where I was attempting to make things welcoming for a young boy who had lost his home as I had lost mine.

'What in the name of all that's holy is going on?' he demanded. His usually genial expression had been replaced by one of utter fury, his handsome features almost ugly with the rage that was possessing him. 'I found Antoinette in the stables with a strange boy she says you told her is her brother! What game are you playing, Flora?'

'No game,' I said steadily. 'Pierre is indeed her brother – Louis' and Lisette's son. He arrived very late last night, sent to safety by Louis.'

'Louis' and Lisette's son?' Gavin brought his fist down hard on the dressing chest. 'I don't believe it! If Louis and Lisette have a son, how is it I have never heard of it?'

I was startled – and puzzled. 'Louis did not tell you?'

'Indeed he did not! He has never so much as made mention of this boy.'

I was, I admit it, a little surprised, since he had acquainted Antoinette with the facts, and I could not think why he should not have told Gavin also. And I was surprised Antoinette herself had said nothing about it to Gavin. Her father must have expressly told her not to, I assumed, for she had talked of it to me quite freely.

'I believe he only recently learned of Pierre's existence,' I said, trying to assuage Gavin's obvious fury. It had no effect.

'How dare he bring the little bastard here!' Gavin struck the dressing chest again with such force that all the china pots jumped and clanked.

'He is not a bastard,' I said. 'He is Louis' son.'

'Who is set to inherit what is rightfully mine, if it is indeed true!' Gavin stormed. 'Faith, I never bargained for that!'

I knew then why he was so angry. He had believed that if Louis predeceased him, Belvedere and the whole of the Fletcher estate would be his. Now an eight-year-old boy stood between him and his aspirations. Louis' son. Louis' heir.

'I won't allow it!' Gavin's voice was lower now, but vibrant with passion. 'I will not allow a snivel-nosed boy to rob me of my inheritance!'

'How can you be so uncharitable as to concern yourself with nothing but material gain when the child is so much in need of all our support?' I asked coldly. 'Surely his welfare is what is important now. As for the matter of inheritance, the law is the law, so you might as well accept it with good grace.'

'Never! I'll find a way to make sure that brat does not make mock of all my plans, have no fear on that score!'

He turned on his heel and strode from the room.

The encounter with Gavin not only shocked me, it made me deeply uneasy. Beneath that genial exterior, his passions ran deep, I knew, and when he had beaten John, the gamekeeper's boy, so mercilessly, I had witnessed a streak of violence that came close to sadism besides. I took some comfort in reiterating to myself what I had said to Gavin – the law was the law, and however disappointed he might be, nothing could change that. But the unpleasant situation was just another reason for me to pray that Louis would soon return safely. He would take care of everything, and if he deemed it best he would no doubt ban Gavin from the house entirely.

To my surprise, however, Gavin seemed to overcome his filthy humour and his resentment quite quickly. In no time at all, he appeared to be making every effort to befriend Pierre, spending a good deal of time with him and Antoinette. The little boy was every bit as enchanted with Misty, the foal, as she was, and was an accomplished rider, so he was quite capable of handling one of the horses that was big enough to bear his weight, which Misty was not, and the three of them went out often for a canter on the moors.

On the one hand, I was glad of it, for I was so preoccupied with my concern for Louis that I felt incapable of holding a conversation, let alone entertaining a young boy, and the excursions were good for him, I felt, helping him to feel at home, and to take his mind off his recent experiences and his worries for his mother's safety. But my disquiet remained, all the same, for I did not entirely trust Gavin, though I told myself that the threats he had made had been born of his rage and disappointment at learning the inheritance had slipped from his grasp. And I did not feel it was my place to interfere, either, with Gavin's efforts to establish a relationship. He was, after all, the boy's uncle, and Pierre himself seemed glad of the male company, and attached himself like a limpet to Gavin.

Two or three days passed, and with each one I grew more anxious for news. Surely by now Louis would have had time to trace Lisette? Surely any day now he would be taking her to where his ship awaited? I counted off the hours and tried to put from my mind the ever-present dread that he might fall into the hands of the Revolutionaries. But my fears refused to be dismissed, however hard I tried, and more than once I woke, bathed in perspiration, from the most terrible nightmares when I saw Louis in a fetid prison cell, Louis in a tumbril, Louis with his neck on the guillotine.

On the evening of the fourth day I heard a horse on the drive. I was alone in the parlour – Antoinette and Pierre had retired to her rooms to play a game of draughts – and Gavin, who had eaten supper with us, had gone out, I knew not where.

I ran to the window, drawing aside the drapes and peering out, but the night was black, and I could see nothing – the horse had gone around the house to the stable block I thought. My heart was beating in my chest like a trapped bird. Could it be Louis? Oh please, dear sweet Jesus, let it be Louis!

I could wait no longer to find out. I hurried out through the back entrance, avoiding the kitchen, where I knew Cook and the maids would still be clearing away the supper things.

It was a cold night with a sharp blustery wind, and I had not waited to fetch a wrap, but I scarcely noticed the chill as my slippered feet flew me across the yard. A horse was tethered outside the stable, but of its rider there was no sign.

For the first time it occurred to me that I was taking a risk coming out alone into the darkness. But I could not go tamely back inside until I had learned who it was who had come galloping up the drive. I did go a little more cautiously and quietly though, every sense alert.

Voices were coming from within the stable and I recognized one as Gavin's. Nothing strange about that, of course – either he had ridden out and returned with a friend, or he had been in the stables all the time.

No, it was the other voice that turned my blood to ice and made me shiver though the cold of the night had not. A voice that transported me back to the night my father had been murdered.

If I had been asked whether I would know again the voice I had heard when I crept down the stairs, I would have replied that I would not. I had heard it for a few brief moments only; rough, with a local accent. Yet now, quite suddenly, I was in no doubt whatever.

The voice coming from inside the stables belonged to one of the men who had brought death to my father that terrible night. And he was here, now, with Gavin.

Fifteen

For a moment I was frozen with utter horror. One of my father's killers was here, within a few feet of me. Worse, he was talking with Gavin, as he had talked with my father. Was history about to repeat itself? Was Gavin about to meet the same awful death? I leaned against the cold stone of the stable wall to steady myself, for my legs had turned weak beneath me, and a sickness was rising in my stomach. Then Gavin spoke again, and I realized that this was no argument such as I had overheard before, but some kind of business meeting.

'You understand me?' Gavin's tone was authoritative. 'You know what you have to do?'

'Oh, I understand you all right.' It was the man from Tucker's Grave speaking. 'But what you're asking this time is different – and a sight more dangerous. You'll have to pay a great deal more for our help this time.'

I froze, listening.

'I've always been more than generous,' I heard Gavin say. 'You earn more from me than you'd get in a year working on the land – if you can find any landowner willing to employ you, that is. And you have no scruples about killing. You have the blood of the landlord of Tucker's Grave on your hands.'

So – I had been right! This was indeed the man who had been responsible for my father's death. But Gavin had known who he was all along – worse, the murderer had been in his pay!

A wave of faintness threatened me; I hung on to the wall, determined to learn the truth behind all this, and heard the man reply sullenly: 'That were different. We had no choice. The fool wouldn't listen to reason – tried to take a gun to us. Should we have stood there and let him shoot us? Any man would have done what we done that night. But this – this would be in cold blood. Oh, you'll have to pay a great deal more than you're offering for that, Mr Gavin, sir.'

'You would do well,' Gavin said silkily, 'to remember that I saved your skin less than a week ago when you were careless enough to take your horse to public market. I thought, when I let you know the beast had been recognized, that you would have had the sense to get rid of him much further afield, not to a dealer who frequents the local fairs. And talking of killing, did you not dispose of the vagrant who first recognized the horse? That was nicely done, I grant you, and accepted as an accident. But it was still murder, and we both know it. Two killings at the very least that can be laid at your door. If you turn your back on me now, Tench, I can't promise you I shall not go to the constable and tell him what I know.'

'Don't you threaten me!' the man, Tench, growled furiously. 'I'm not a one to take threats lightly.'

'And I am not one to be thwarted, Tench,' Gavin returned tersely. 'You know damned well that without my patronage your wife and children will go hungry – starve to death next winter, as like as not, if they don't die of the cold first. All right, I'll up my offer – double it, if that's what it takes. And there'll be a decent new cottage for you when I inherit.'

The man, Tench, snorted loudly. 'And when will that be, I'd like to know? Mr Louis looks in rude good health to me.'

'You think so?' Gavin's voice was cold and hard. 'Mr Louis is in France, on what will prove to be the last of his reckless expeditions. At last I am in possession of the information I required as regards his movements – no thanks to you. I have succeeded, Tench, where you failed, and this time the Revolutionaries will catch up with him in the most incriminating of circumstances. He will be caught, as the saying goes, red-handed. I think you may take my word for it, Mr Louis will not be returning.'

I clapped my hand to my mouth, rigid with shock and horror as the full, inescapable truth dawned on me.

It was Gavin, his own brother, who had secretly worked against Louis all along. Gavin who had seen an opportunity to get his hands on the only thing that mattered to him in all the world – the inheritance. Gavin who had sought the means to betray him. My father had indeed died because he worked for the Brotherhood of the Lynx and his life had been snuffed out because he had either remained stubbornly silent, or refused to do whatever it was Gavin's accomplices had asked him to do. For a while Gavin had been thwarted. Now, from what he had just said, it seemed he had learned enough to set the Revolutionaries on to Louis. But how? How . . . ?

And then, in a flash, I knew. I had thought it was strange that Gavin should behave in such a friendly fashion towards Pierre, given his furious reaction when the little boy had first arrived. Now, I knew the reason. He had befriended him and gained his confidence in order to elicit the one fact that could set the Revolutionaries on to Louis' tail – the whereabouts of his mother, Lisette. If they knew that, they could watch and wait, set a trap. And into it would walk the man they wanted so desperately, the man who had made fools of them over and over again by smuggling out their prisoners from under their very noses. The Lynx himself.

Tench's rough voice cut into my racing thoughts.

'You're a cool one, Mr Gavin, sir, and a hard one! I never before met a man who'd pay for the death of his own flesh and blood. But I can't afford to quibble over who I deal with. Pay me double your offer and guarantee me a good cottage before the end of the year . . . I'll do what you ask. Seeing as what you stand to inherit, and what you're asking me to do, it's cheap at the price. A child's a child . . . even if he is a French bastard . . .'

My eyes widened in horror. Pierre! Oh no – it couldn't be *Pierre* whose death Gavin was soliciting! But, shocked as I was, I could not deny the evidence of my own ears. Not only had Gavin betrayed Louis, now he was plotting to see that Pierre, who stood between him and his inheritance, should perish also.

'It seems you're squeamish, Tench,' Gavin was saying. 'You'd kill a full-grown man but not a brat, would you? I'm not sure I can trust you to do the job. Methinks I'd be better off doing it myself. Now I come to think of it, I've every opportunity for making it look like an accident. Who would suspect the boy's kindly uncle was the cause of his death? And I'd save myself a good deal of money into the bargain.'

'D'you want me to do the job or not?' Tench asked impatiently.

There was something that might almost have been a smile in Gavin's voice.

'Whichever of us gets to him first, Tench. Whichever of us gets to him first.'

Somehow I prised myself away from the wall. Somehow I forced my trembling legs to carry me back across the stable yard and into the house. Up the stairs to my room I ran; there I closed the door and stood with my back pressed against it and my hands pressed to my mouth. And all the while the terrible conversation I had overheard played and replayed itself in my mind. I could scarcely believe it, and yet it all made perfect sense, like pieces of a puzzle falling into place. And the key was Gavin and his insane desire to be master of Belvedere. His ambition had driven him to betray his own brother, and now, faced with an heir who stood to inherit all he desired, he was preparing to do away with him too.

He would do it, I had no doubt. He was ruthless, he was, perhaps, half mad. And only I could prevent him from carrying out his ghastly plan. There was nothing I could do to save Louis – my heart contracted as I thought of the terrible, mortal danger he was in – but somehow I had to find a way to save his son.

But how – how? How could I protect Pierre from Gavin's murderous intent? From what I had overheard, he was as ready to take the boy's life himself as to leave the dark deed to the man, Tench. That meant that Pierre would be in danger even here, at Belvedere. I had to get him out of Gavin's reach, and quickly. I had to take him to a place of safety.

The only haven I could think of was my old home, now under lock and key.

I would take Pierre to Tucker's Grave and pray that Gavin would not think of looking for us there.

I had to move quickly and stealthily, I knew. But how to do it? I could not ride, and I dared not ask Thompson, the coachman, to drive us, for I did not trust him not to inform Gavin of where we had gone. In any case, Thompson would most likely be in his bed by now – men such as he, who had to be up with the lark, retired early, especially during the winter months when darkness fell early. There was only one person in this house to whom I could turn for the help I undoubtedly needed – Antoinette. She was easy with horses, and for all her faults, she could keep a secret when it mattered. That much had been proved by the fact that she had not told Gavin of Pierre's existence. Yes, I could trust Antoinette.

But even given that she could harness the horses and drive the carriage, my problems did not end there. A carriage at Tucker's Grave, and horses stabled there when the place was locked up and supposedly empty would immediately betray our presence. I was in need of other assistance too, someone who would take care of the carriage and horses once they had deposited us there.

At once I thought of George. His loyalty to me was beyond doubt. He would know of a place to hide the carriage and he could house the horses in his own stables, just two more amongst so many.

My mind made up, I went straight to Antoinette's rooms. If I was to spirit Pierre away under cover of darkness, there was no time to lose.

I found Antoinette and Pierre still engrossed in their game of draughts. They were surprised and, I think, none too pleased to see me. Already they were forming a tight-knit unit, the ties of their blood breaching the barriers of their separate upbringing, their anxiety for their parents forming a common bond.

'You haven't come to tell us it's time for bed, I hope!'

Antoinette said tetchily. 'This game is at a critical stage. I am just about to beat Pierre soundly.'

'I think not! You don't concentrate, Antoinette. Your mind wanders, and . . . See!' Pierre took three of Antoinette's pieces in a swift swoop, grinning in triumph.

'You have to listen to me,' I said. 'What I have to say is far more important than any game.'

The seriousness of my tone arrested them; two pairs of green eyes fastened on me, puzzled, and even a little alarmed.

'You are in great danger, Pierre,' I said, and went on to tell them as much as was necessary of what I had overheard.

'I knew it!' Antoinette exclaimed when I had finished. 'I knew Uncle Gavin was up to no good! Oh, he's charming when he wants to be, and fun to be with, but . . .' Her lips tightened. 'I thought it was strange he was being so nice to you, Pierre. He was so angry when I first told him you were my brother! And he doesn't like boys much usually. He's nice to me because I am a girl, and no threat to him.'

Her perception and her cool reaction surprised me. I had underestimated Antoinette, I realized.

'I want to get Pierre away from Belvedere tonight,' I said, drawing the subject back to its most important elements. 'And I need you to help me, Antoinette.'

I went on to explain my plan, but to my dismay Antoinette shook her head.

'I'd never be able to handle the coach, Flora, and we'd never get away without someone hearing. Imagine the racket those great wheels would make on the gravel in the quiet of the night! We should almost certainly disturb Uncle Gavin, and he would catch up with us on horseback in no time at all.'

She was right, of course. And if Gavin caught up it would be disastrous for all of us.

'We shall have to take horses,' Antoinette said matter-of-factly. 'That way we can cut through the park under cover of the trees and avoid the drive altogether.'

'But I can't ride!' I exclaimed, horrified.

'Of course you can!' Antoinette said in the same matter-of-fact tone. 'You can take Betty – she's as gentle as a lamb. Anyone can ride her. It will slow us down, I admit, but if we do no more than trot, all you have to do is sit there. She's like a comfortable chair.'

'Oh – I don't know . . .' I hesitated.

'It's our only chance,' Antoinette said decisively. 'If you want to get to Tucker's Grave tonight, you've no other choice.'

Once again, I knew that she was right. But I quailed just the same at the prospect. If only I had taken up Gavin's offer of riding lessons!

'Very well,' I agreed reluctantly. 'But I shall give you the key to the inn, Antoinette, and if I should fall and injure myself, you are to go on without me.'

'You won't fall off,' she said confidently.

'But if I should . . . You must promise.'

'Oh very well, I promise! I didn't know you had a key though,' she added.

'No, but I know where it is. Get together what you need and can carry. Wait until the house has been quiet for an hour, then we'll meet in the kitchen. Are you both agreed?'

They nodded. Pierre looked frightened, but Antoinette's green eyes were sharp with something like excitement.

Soon after I had returned to my room I heard Gavin come upstairs and go to Louis' suite. Hatred burned within me. If he had betrayed his brother, it was small wonder he felt so confident in sleeping in his bed, already assuming the trappings of the position he aspired to.

I waited a few minutes, then crept downstairs. To my alert and straining ears, every little creak of a board sounded loud as a gunshot in the quiet house, and each time I froze, terrified in case I alerted Gavin. But I reached the study undiscovered and slipped inside.

I had not dared to bring a candle with me, but the night was not so dark that I could not see well enough to make my way across to the casement clock, open the door, and slide my fingers inside. At once they encountered the thick key to Tucker's Grave and I heaved a sigh of relief. I had been very afraid Louis might have changed its hiding place and so unwittingly foiled my plan to save his son before it had even begun. I slipped the key into the pocket of my skirts and felt inside the clock again. I had some idea of taking the book and documents with me, both to keep them out of Gavin's way, and also in the hope they might provide me with information as to whom I could turn to for help, but search as I might, I could not find the key to the bureau. It was not there.

And perhaps that was just as well, I thought, for though taking them for safe keeping was all very well if I could achieve that aim, should things go wrong, I could be delivering them straight into Gavin's hands. As for help – I would have to rely on George for that. He would, perhaps, at my behest, go to Sir Jeremy when – if! – he returned from France. Sir Jeremy would know what to do.

I crept back upstairs, got my few things together, wrapped myself in the warmest cloak I possessed, and settled down to wait out what remained of the allotted hour.

Then and only then did I allow myself to think of Louis. With all my heart I prayed that he had escaped the Revolutionaries, but I had little hope of it. If Gavin had passed on details of his intended destination they would be waiting for him, the Lynx himself, a prize indeed. A great despair filled me, and though I was beyond tears they gathered just the same deep within me, a leaden lump that I thought would be with me to the end of my days.

A clock chimed the hour; almost time to go. Somehow, I steeled myself to be strong. Whatever it cost me, I *would* thwart Gavin's evil plans. Whatever it cost me, I would save Louis' son. It was all I could do now.

When I crept down once more to the kitchen, Antoinette and Pierre were there before me, waiting with scarcely contained impatience. I gave the key to Antoinette, for though I could hardly bear to let it out of my hands again, I was convinced that was the best course of action. Then we all three crept out by the rear door and to the stables. Pierre saddled a horse for himself whilst Antoinette tacked up Perdita and Betty, the plump old mare she had selected for me to ride. Then she gave me a few hasty instructions, hoisted me up into the saddle, and placed the reins in my hands.

'Hold them like this. And remember to keep your heels down. You do not need to do anything else. Betty will follow where we lead.'

After the initial terror, when, as Antoinette hoisted me up, I felt certain I would slide straight out of the saddle on the opposite side, I felt surprisingly safe. Betty's back was broad – she did indeed feel like a comfortable chair. And even when she began to walk out of the stable yard and across the park, I felt myself moving with her. Only once did I almost lose my seat, when I risked looking around to make certain we had got away unobserved, and then, by grabbing her solid neck and tightening the grip of my knees, I was able to regain my balance. It was not a very ladylike way to ride, but necessity is a hard taskmaster. I clung on, and even felt a strange little surge of exhilaration.

It was short-lived. When we were clear of the park and the trees, and fairly certain we were not being followed, Antoinette urged Perdita to a trot and, just as she had promised, Betty followed suit. Oh, the discomfort of it as I bumped up and down on the hard saddle! Oh, the sheer terror that at any moment all three horses might break into a canter! And sure enough, when we reached open moorland they did, though I learned to my surprise it was actually easier and smoother. But mindful of my pathetic inexperience, Antoinette did not allow the horses to gallop, and whenever the going was rough she took them back to that bone-shaking trot.

It was, just the same, a nightmare of a journey that I thought would never end, and by the time we reached Monksmoor village and George's forge, and Antoinette helped me down out of the saddle, my legs were trembling so violently they almost gave way beneath me, and my buttocks were so sore that every step was agony.

The forge was, of course, in darkness, and I knew George and

Alice would be in their beds. But I also knew that Alice was a light sleeper. A few handfuls of gravel tossed at their bedroom window and she was there, peering out, her expression almost comical, so startled did she look.

'Flora?' She threw the window wide. 'Flora – is that you?'

'Yes,' I called back softly. 'I need your help.'

They came down at once, both of them, Alice as sharp as a little bird, George so bleary he scarcely knew what was happening. But by the time I had explained he was fully awake and ready for action as I had known he would be.

'Lawks, I knew there was something terrible going on!' Alice said. 'It's even worse than I thought!'

'You'll help us then?' I asked.

'You know we will! But you can't go to the inn this time of night! You'll stay here with us.'

I had been prepared for this.

'We can't bring danger to your door,' I said firmly. 'And so long as no one knows we are at Tucker's Grave, we'll be safer there. Word would travel like wildfire if it became known we were here with you. All I ask is that George should ride with us to the inn, then bring the horses back here and conceal them amongst his own. We'll see no one at this time of night, and we can hide out there until you can get word of our plight to Sir Jeremy.'

'Perhaps it's for the best,' George said slowly.

Whilst he went to his room to get dressed, Alice prepared a parcel of food – cold meats, cheese and a loaf of bread – and made us a hot drink, for we were all three chilled to the bone. Then George saddled up his own horse and hoisted me painfully back on to Betty.

'I never thought to see you on horseback, Flora,' he mused.

'And I hope never to be again!' I replied, wincing at my sore nether regions and aching muscles.

We did indeed see no one on the short ride out to Tucker's Grave. When it came into view, sparse and square on the dark skyline, my heart lurched. However terrible the circumstances, I was home. We all dismounted, and Antoinette handed me the key I had entrusted to her.

'Will I come in with you?' George asked.

I shook my head. 'The sooner you get these horses under cover, the safer we shall be. Dawn will soon be breaking, and it's vital you are not seen.'

'Very well.' He gathered the reins of the three tired mounts together. 'Take care, Flora. I'll come back by night tomorrow to bring you fresh supplies.'

'Bless you, George.' All I wanted now was to get inside my old home and close the door against the world.

George waited until I had turned the key in the lock and pushed open the heavy door. Then, with another soft farewell, he was off, the hoofbeats of the four horses quickly fading into the night.

'Oh thank God!' I closed and locked the door behind us. 'It will be cold, and the beds may be damp, but at least we can get some rest . . .'

My voice tailed away as I said it. To this day I do not know what sixth sense warned me. Some unfamiliar scent, maybe, or the fact that the chill did not strike me as it should have done. I froze, every nerve ending suddenly alert.

And then I heard it. Unmistakably the tread of a footfall on the stairs. I looked up and saw a figure silhouetted against the casement, and my heart seemed to cease beating.

Someone was here, in Tucker's Grave Inn.

We were not alone.

Sixteen

T he figure on the stairs might almost have been a ghost, so
ethereal did he look in the flickering light of the candle he
carried. But I knew he was no ghost. For all the stories
associated with Tucker's Grave, I had never encountered an
apparition from the spirit world, and I was not encountering
one now. This man was flesh and blood, though there was little
enough of him – thin, frail and grey, from his wispy powdered
wig to his silk breeches. In that first startled moment shock
robbed me of my senses, then I grabbed at Pierre's cloak,
meaning to push him behind me, for my first coherent thought
was for his safety.

Pierre, however, wriggled from my grasp and took a step
towards the foot of the stairs, staring up as if transfixed. And
the apparition spoke.

'Pierre?'

'Uncle Armand! What are you doing here?' He spoke in
French, but there was no mistaking what he said. Even I, with
my limited grasp of the language, understood it, though the
man's rapid reply was beyond my comprehension.

Somehow I found my voice. 'Who are you?' I demanded.

'I am Armand du Bois,' he replied in English. 'I am Pierre's
great uncle, the uncle of his mother, Lisette. May I ask you the
same question? Who are you, that you come here in the middle
of the night – and bring Pierre with you?'

We repaired to the kitchen, where the shuttered windows and
the absence of anything but the wild moors beyond made it safe
to light a lamp.

By its light I could see how unkempt he was, his fine clothes rumpled and stained, the powdered wig, which had no doubt once been the finest money could buy, hanging in ragged strands and furred up in places so that it resembled the spines of a porcupine. His face was thin and sharp, the cheeks hollowed, his eyes small and hard. Instinctively I disliked him, this man who was secretly occupying my home and who must be a fugitive from the Revolution.

'Did Louis bring you here?' I asked, though I believe I already knew the answer, for I was remembering the lost day that had elapsed between the time his boat had reached harbour and the time he had reached Belvedere on the last occasion he had come home from France.

'Incarcerated me here, more like.' There was bitterness in the reedy tones. 'I suppose I should be grateful to escape France with my life, but I could have wished for better treatment. The cells of the Bastille cannot be much worse than this.'

I bristled. 'At least you will not be taken from here in a tumbril,' I said spiritedly. 'At least you will not meet your end on the guillotine.'

He laughed slightly, a dry cackle with no humour in it.

'That's true, I suppose. Though I wouldn't be surprised if Louis had his own plans for me when I've served my purpose.'

'What do you mean by that?' I demanded.

'Louis has no love for me. Quite the reverse. I could almost believe he saved me for the express purpose of taking revenge on me . . .'

'That is not what I meant,' I said. 'What is your purpose, as you call it?'

'Why, to give Louis the information he was seeking, of course. As to where he might find Lisette and Pierre. He would not have risked his life for me, I assure you, if he had not needed me to discover their whereabouts. And in that, at least, it seems I have been of some use. Pierre is here. Where is your mother, Pierre?'

'Still in France,' I said, answering for him. 'Louis has gone back for her. She had gone, I understand, to stay with friends.'

'Ah!' A smile cracked the thin face. 'Still the same Lisette! And this, I suppose –' his eyes, narrowed and speculative, went to Antoinette – 'is her daughter.'

Antoinette drew herself up with a hauteur beyond her years. 'I am Antoinette, yes. But I still do not understand who *you* are.'

'I already told you who I am. You may call me Uncle, though . . .'

'He *is* Mama's uncle,' Pierre interjected. 'We went to see him sometimes at the Chateau du Bois.' He did not, however, say it with much fondness, nor did he seem as pleased to see a relative from his native land as I would have expected.

'So it was you who told Louis where to find Pierre,' I said.

'Exactly. I assumed Lisette was with him, but . . .' He spread his hands, bony and beringed. The nails had grown unpleasantly long, and there was grime beneath them.

'How long have you been here?' I asked.

'Oh, a week, two weeks – I've lost count,' he said, confirming my earlier thought that Louis must have brought him on his last trip from France. 'It's a miserable existence, I assure you. Apart from Louis and some ruffian who comes to bring me food and water, I have seen no one.'

Instantly I was alert. 'Someone brings you food and water?' I repeated, anxious suddenly that Tucker's Grave was not quite the safe hiding place I had believed it would be.

'Well of course they do!' the old Frenchman said irritably. 'How else could I survive? It's bad enough being cold and in the dark most of the time without starving or dying of thirst as well. Why, I've already been chastised for lighting a lamp that showed at the window, and I only dare light a fire when darkness falls for fear the smoke will be seen by someone passing by on the road.'

So – here was the explanation for the light Ralph had seen. But I was puzzled as to the reason Armand was prepared to remain here in such conditions.

'I'm surprised you haven't left by now,' I said.

'And where would I go? Oh, I suppose I could try to seek out

261

one of my compatriots who has escaped to England, and throw myself on their mercy. But I have nothing – nothing! The Revolutionaries were on my heels when Louis found me, and I fled with nothing but the clothes on my back.'

If he had been a more likeable man, I might have felt sympathy for him then. As it was, I felt nothing.

'You cannot stay here for ever,' I said bluntly.

'Mon dieu! I hope not!' he replied. 'No, Louis has promised to make me an allowance and find a home for me when he returns. Until then he wants me here in case he is in need of information as to other connections for Lisette, though it seems what I was able to tell him already was sufficient.'

'But why here?' I asked. 'Why did he not bring you to Belvedere, where you could at least have lived in some comfort?'

'For one thing, he wanted me where no one but his own trusted companions could ask me questions. For another . . .' He sniffed, a haughty expression of distaste which in a less cultured man would likely have been a snort. 'Louis would not have me under his roof. He blames me for all manner of things. And he would not have me near Antoinette.' A thin smile twisted his lips as he looked at her again with those same narrowed eyes. 'I can understand him there. She is a very pretty girl, and so like her mother at that age. I may be an old man, but . . .'

Though at the time I knew nothing of Lisette's story, yet I recoiled in disgust at the lechery I read all too plainly in his face.

'I think it is high time these two young people tried to sleep,' I said stiffly. 'And since this is the warmest room in the house, I shall settle them here, in the kitchen.'

'I have had a fire in the bedroom I am using too,' he said. And with the first hint of humanity he had shown since I had laid eyes on him, he went on: 'The children may use my bed. I can sleep on the sofa here.'

On the point of refusing, I relented. Both Antoinette and Pierre looked quite exhausted. They would come to no harm from this unpleasant old man so long as I was with them.

'Thank you,' I said. 'And I shall sleep with them.'

'As you like. It would be good to have company, though, after my solitary confinement.' His eyes moved over me, but there was none of the lechery in them that I had glimpsed when he had looked at Antoinette. I was, I suspected, already too old for his debauched tastes. 'You, I presume, are Louis' paramour.'

'No,' I lied, more for the benefit of Antoinette and Pierre than for my own. 'I am a friend. And this inn, as a matter of fact, was my home.'

Then, with as much dignity as I could muster under the circumstances, I ushered Antoinette and Pierre towards the stairs.

The Marquis du Bois had taken over the room that had been my father's, and the bed, though not as clean as I would have liked, was at least aired from his sleeping in it. We lay down, all three of us, fully dressed, and before long the children's exhaustion overcame them and they were dead to the world. Sleep did not come so easily to me; I lay, tossed about on a sea of emotions, tormented by anxiety and the racing of my thoughts. At last, however, I too fell into an uneasy slumber.

When I awoke it was morning. Soon, I thought, Gavin would be up and about and realize that we were missing. What would he do? He would be furious, that much was certain, but would he be able to hazard a guess as to where to look for us? I prayed he would not. He believed, as far as I was aware, that Tucker's Grave was locked and barred, and he did not know that I knew where the key was hidden. But supposing *he* knew where it was – and found it missing?

Well, it was no use fretting about that now. We were here, and here we must stay, for the present at least, as much prisoners as Lisette's detestable old uncle.

When I rose from the bed, I disturbed the children; they were stiff, bleary and bad-tempered, tired, already, of their adventure.

'How long do we have to stay here?' Antoinette complained as she tried to tug the tangles out of her hair with her fingers.

'I don't know . . .' I began, and Pierre interrupted me.

'Until Papa comes home, bringing Mama with him . . .' He turned to me, his eyes suddenly dark with anxiety. 'He will find her, won't he? He will bring her to England?'

My heart missed a beat. 'God willing.' It was all I could think of to say.

We spent a miserable morning, chilled to the marrow because I refused to allow a fire, afraid the smoking chimney would give away our presence, and hungry, for not knowing how long it would be before we got fresh provisions, I rationed out the bread, cheese and meat that Alice had given us quite stringently. No wonder the Marquis was so ill-tempered if he had endured these conditions for more than a week! Even being under my father's roof was no comfort to me now; somehow Tucker's Grave no longer felt like my home.

It was approaching noon when I heard a horse's hooves outside. I ran to the window, but could see nothing through the tight slats of the shutters.

'That will be the man with my supplies,' Armand said as a knock came at the door.

I frowned. 'He comes to the front of the inn? Within sight of the road – and in daylight too?'

'Generally he comes to the back door, but who else could it be?' Armand was already shooting back the bolts, his thin hands fumbling with the heavy metal.

'Wait! I must know who is there!' I cried desperately, but Armand ignored me, reaching for the upper bolt.

Hoping against hope that I was allowing my imagination to run away with me, I retreated to the kitchen just as the door swung open and I heard Armand's surprised tones.

'Oh – it's someone new today. Are you . . . ?'

'Out of my way, you buffoon!' It was unmistakably Gavin's voice.

My heart came thudding into my mouth. Somehow he had found us and we were caught like rats in a trap! The rear door was as securely locked and bolted as the front door should have been, I did not know what had become of the key in the weeks since Louis had taken me away so unceremoniously, and the windows were shuttered. There was no escape. Except . . .

'Quickly! It's Gavin! He's here!' Even as I spoke, my voice no more than an urgent whisper, I was pulling aside the rug, uncovering the trapdoor that led down into the secret passages. As I lifted it, the smell of damp earth and stale air rushed up to meet me, and the access yawned below, much deeper than I remembered it. There had been, at one time, some kind of ladder to assist descent, but it had long since gone, rotted away by time and the elements.

'In you go!' I instructed Pierre and Antoinette. 'Just drop! Quickly now!'

Antoinette's eyes were bright once more with excited anticipation; had she not begged to be allowed to explore the secret passage? She wriggled into the aperture, holding steady for just a moment by her fingertips, then letting go and disappearing with a soft thud into the blackness below. Pierre, however, hung back, white with fear.

'No! I cannot! J'ai peur . . . !'

'You must!' I ordered. Gavin was in the inn now; I could hear him blundering about in the bar. 'Your life depends upon it!'

'I cannot!'

I caught him by the shoulders and, finding a strength I did not know I possessed, lifted him bodily, squirming and struggling, and deposited him into the abyss. As he landed I heard his muffled cry of pain and winced, but more from fear that Gavin should hear than for any injury I might inadvertently have caused him.

On the point of following, another thought struck me. I ran to the wall cabinet, grabbed my father's gun, and slammed the door shut once more. With a warning shout to Pierre and Antoinette, I tossed the gun into the access hole. Then I grabbed the silk rope from the window drapes, twisted it through the eyelet catch on the trapdoor, and launched myself into the passage, jerking the trapdoor shut after me. The rug, of course, would no longer be covering the entrance, but there was nothing I could do about that. At least *we* were out of sight – and not a moment too soon!

Footsteps sounded loud on the boards above our heads, and Gavin's voice filtered through the cracks in the trapdoor, no longer the pleasant tones he generally affected, but a low, unpleasant snarl.

'Where are they? They came here, I'm certain of it!'

'Why should you think they are here?' Armand asked, and I was only grateful he had chosen not to betray us immediately.

'The ground is soft at this time of year – it was child's play to follow the horses' tracks through the woods!' Gavin replied scornfully. 'Once they reached the road, granted I could follow them no more. But where else would Flora go but home?'

'I'm alone, you can see,' Armand said.

'You're hiding them, you old fool. I know it!'

The footsteps started towards the door and I almost dared breathe again. Then I heard Gavin's exclamation, and the steps changed direction.

'They are here – and there's proof of it! That's Antoinette's cloak!'

I almost gasped aloud in horror. Antoinette's cloak had been lying on a chair, and in my haste, I had not thought to remove it!

'Are they hiding in the bedrooms? I'll find them, have no fear!' Another exclamation. 'Faith, I know where they'll be! The underground passages! And that's the entrance to them, if I'm not mistaken!'

He must have seen the misplaced rug, I realized.

'Get back!' I hissed to Antoinette and Pierre. Antoinette did so, and as I followed her, a long feathery cobweb brushed my cheek and I had to bite back a scream. But Pierre remained where he was, crouched at my feet.

'I can't!' he sobbed. 'My ankle . . .'

Gavin's fingers were scrabbling at the trapdoor; light flooded in and I saw his head and shoulders silhouetted against it as he knelt on the floor, peering down.

'Ah!' He grunted with satisfaction. 'I was right! So – you

thought to hide from me, did you? Well, since you like it so much, you can stay there whilst I deal with our friend the Marquis. In fact –' he laughed softly – 'leaving you there is an easy answer to my problems, is it not? Did you not tell me, Flora, the passage is blocked up and has been for years? That this is now the only way in – or out? Did you not tell me how the monks died there, like rats in a trap? Well, you can do the same, my friends, and there'll be no evidence to lay at my door. What if there are three more skeletons in the depths? It could well be another hundred years before they are discovered, and by then Belvedere will have been mine and my heirs' for generations!'

'Uncle Gavin – it's me!' Antoinette cried, appalled. 'You can't do this! I thought you were my friend!'

'No daughter of Louis' can be a friend of mine!' Gavin snarled. He was mad, I thought, quite mad!

'You won't get away with this!' Antoinette persisted. 'When Papa gets back from France he'll come looking for us!'

Gavin laughed, the same mad laugh. 'Your Papa will not be coming back, chérie. Pierre kindly informed me of his mother's whereabouts and I have been able to alert the Revolutionaries. They'll set a trap and take him. Oh, no one will come looking for you, Antoinette!'

'Pierre! How could you!' Antoinette cried.

'I didn't!' Pierre protested. 'Papa had told me it was a secret – so when he asked, I lied!'

'What?' Gavin roared, and in spite of our plight and the terrible danger we were in, joy and relief burst in my veins. There was hope for Louis yet, then! Then my alarm returned in a rush when he grated: 'Little bastard! I'll beat it out of you, and then toss you back to starve or die of suffocation!'

'Would it not be easier,' the dry tones of the Marquis interjected, 'if you and I were to have a little chat? Pierre's knowledge of his mother's friends is limited – you know Lisette never likes her children around when she is on her assignations. But I know all her friends and acquaintances, anyone she is likely to have taken refuge with. I could, I am sure, be of considerable help to you.'

'And why should you tell me the truth any more than the boy?' Gavin demanded. 'She's your niece, after all.'

The old man cackled thinly. 'I have no doubt you can be very persuasive, Gavin, in your own way – and I am averse to pain. I am safe now – why should I risk that for such an ungrateful wench? Leave the boy where he is and talk to me. I'll tell you whatever you want to know and not cause you the trouble you'd have eliciting it from Pierre, who seems, for all her neglect, to remain touchingly loyal to his mother.'

My heart was in my mouth. I could only hope that the Marquis intended to mislead Gavin further. Or that Louis was already on his way back to England and any betrayal would come too late. For the moment, however, he had saved Pierre from the cruel beating Gavin would have undoubtedly inflicted in an effort to gain the information he so desperately wanted.

'Very well,' Gavin said, 'we'll talk first.' His silhouette appeared once more in the aperture above our heads. 'As for the three of you, you can stay where you are until I need you. I must say I hope I will not. Armand will be co-operative, I think, and I shall leave immediately to pass on details of Louis' whereabouts to the French. So . . .' He laughed unpleasantly. 'I think I should say goodbye to you all. We shall not meet again in this life.'

The trapdoor slammed so that once more we were in total blackness, and a scraping sound on the floorboards indicated that Gavin was dragging some heavy piece of furniture – the old sea chest, perhaps? to cover it. There was no way, I knew, that we could open the hatch with that weighting it down, even if we could climb up to it. Undoubtedly we were trapped, all three of us, just as Gavin had said. For had not the passage been blocked off at its other end?

'Oh Flora!' Antoinette sounded terrified now. 'We're going to die, aren't we? He's going to leave us here to die, just as the monks did, in this horrible place!'

Somehow I controlled my rising panic. 'It may be possible to get out at the other end of the tunnel,' I said.

268

'But . . . you told me that was blocked by all the stones from the ruined abbey . . .'

'And so it's supposed to have been. But local children have always been fascinated with the place. They may have gone there even if they were forbidden and dug a way through . . .'

Even as I said it, I knew it was a slim chance, but it was our only hope. 'Come on, it's only half a mile or so. We'll make our way there and see.'

I had, of course, forgotten the injury Pierre had sustained when I threw him into the passage.

'I can't!' he whimpered. 'My leg – it hurts! I can't move it!'

'Try!' I urged him.

'I can't! I can't!'

'Then you must remain here,' I said, 'and Antoinette, you stay with him. I will go alone and if I can find a way of escape I'll run for help.'

As I took my first uncertain step, my toe stubbed into something, and I suddenly remembered the blunderbuss I had thrown into the tunnel. Oh, how could I have forgotten it! I could so easily have discharged it into Gavin's face when he had leaned over to taunt us! And I'd have done it, too! I cursed myself for having been panicked into not thinking clearly, picked up the gun, and turned to Antoinette.

'Take this. If Gavin opens the hatch again, point it at him and pull the trigger.'

She shrank back. 'I couldn't! I've never fired a gun in my life!'

'Nor have I,' I told her, 'but it's easy enough, I am sure. Our lives may depend on it.'

'Oh very well, I'll try.' She took the gun from me and I started to inch my way along the narrow tunnel into the pitch darkness. The rough walls scraped my fingernails as I felt my way, the earth through the thin soles of my slippers was damp and cold as the grave. An image rose, unbidden, in my mind, of my father's coffin being lowered into that same clammy earth and I sobbed in fear and despair. But somehow the thought of my father gave me courage. It was as if in that moment he was with me, his presence urging me on. Spiders' webs flapped at my face, and soon my hands were sticky with them, but I pressed on, inching my way through the blackness, the fetid smell of damp entering me with each shaking breath and gathering like a sickness in my stomach.

On and on I went; never had a mere half-mile seemed so far. Once I ran into a fall of stone covered with earth and thought I could go no further. But I scrambled on to it, wriggling on my belly until the tunnel opened out once more. After a while it seemed to climb a little, a steady, gradual incline. Hope flared briefly within me, and then, to my utter despair, I reached a barrier comprised of larger stones and rubble, and knew this was different to the other one I had manoeuvred around. This, I could tell from the texture of it, was not rocks that had fallen from the walls of the tunnel, but huge chunks of masonry. I was under the ruined abbey, and it had indeed collapsed into my only way of escape. Tiny chinks of light shone through, confirming that I had indeed reached the end of the tunnel.

With my scraped and bleeding fingers I began to tear at the slabs, but though I dislodged a minor avalanche of rubble, the dust from which rasped in my nose and throat, making me cough, there was no way I could move the stones that lay between me and freedom.

So near – and yet so far! To be able to see those chinks of light, know that fresh air and sunlight were just a few feet above my head, and not to be able to reach it, was the most exquisite torture. I hauled and hauled at the blocks, aware that if I succeeded in moving one that was supporting others I could bring down sufficient to crush or trap me, yet struggling still with a desperation that devoured me. But try as I might, I could no more move those slabs than I could have moved the chest that Gavin had placed over the trapdoor from underneath.

And then, to my utter disbelief, I heard what sounded like someone moving about in the ruins above my head. I could not think who could be here, miles from anywhere, unless it was a vagrant who had taken shelter or a child from the village, playing in the ruins.

I straightened up, holding on to the rubble, hope flaring.

'Help!' I shouted as loudly as I could, for my throat was dry with dust and with terror. 'Down here! Help, please!'

The sounds ceased, as if whoever was there was listening, and I called out again. But after a moment I heard the crunch of footfalls once again, not coming closer, but going away at a run.

A sob broke in my throat. Someone had been there and now they had gone. If they had heard me at all they had likely thought they were hearing the spirit voice of some long-dead monk who haunted the ruins of his former abbey. There might be a chance that if whoever had been there spoke of hearing cries for help someone would come to investigate. But somehow I did not think anyone would. The vagrant or child who reported them would be dismissed as a superstitious fool.

There was nothing for it but for me to return the way I had come and admit defeat. Perhaps if I brought Antoinette to help me we might yet be able to shift those stones, but I had little hope that two women would have much more success than one.

I found Antoinette and Pierre where I had left them, Pierre sobbing softly from the pain of his leg, which I feared might be broken, Antoinette holding my father's blunderbuss with steely determination.

'Did you find a way?' she asked.

'It's blocked, just as the stories tell,' I said wretchedly, and ashamed almost of my failure. 'Half the abbey has fallen into the tunnel, I should think. Boulders as big as travelling chests. I couldn't move them.'

'Oh.' Antoinette's voice wobbled, then rose hysterically. 'What are we going to do?'

With an effort I kept my own rising panic under control for the sake of the children.

'I don't know . . . Have you heard anything of what is going on up there?'

'No.' Antoinette, too, appeared to be fighting to control her panic. 'It's all been quiet. I think they must have gone to another room . . .'

She broke off. Quiet it might have been, but now, suddenly,

there were footsteps above our heads and the sound of the chest being dragged back from the tunnel entrance. Antoinette grasped at my arm as the trapdoor opened and Gavin's voice reached us.

'I'm sure you'd like to know, my friends, that Armand has been most co-operative. I now know the whereabouts of the French harbour where Louis' ship waits for him. If they have yet failed to catch him, they'll intercept him there, I have no doubt.'

My heart missed a beat. So Armand had, in the end, betrayed Louis.

'And now,' Gavin continued, 'I am going to send the old man to join you in the tunnel. He's not well, he seems to be having some sort of seizure, but I dare not leave him here. Puny and sick as he is, he might manage to remove the chest and help you to escape or at the very least raise the alarm. And I can't risk Pierre living to inherit what I've worked so hard to gain. So you might as well all die together.'

The footsteps went away and a moment later the sound of something being dragged across the floor above reached our ears. It sounded like nothing so much as a sack of grain, but I knew it was not. Armand must have been taken ill and be unable to walk unaided; Gavin was hauling him bodily to share our underground prison.

'Get back, both of you!' I hissed at Antoinette and Pierre, and grabbed my father's gun from her unprotesting hands.

With the trapdoor open, this was the chance I had prayed for! But supposing Gavin never came close to the tunnel entrance? Supposing he simply threw Armand in as I had thrown Pierre? Why, I might even shoot Armand by mistake, for I would be half blinded when the light from above came flooding in . . .

Somehow I had to ensure that I was able to make the most of this one opportunity to save us all.

'Gavin, can I speak to you one last time?' I called. 'There's something I have to tell you concerning Louis . . . something you do not know. If you do not listen to what I have to say, you will never be master of Belvedere!'

I held my breath, the heavy gun pointed upwards, steadied against my chest. And my ruse worked.

'What then . . . ?' Gavin's face appeared in the open trap.

I pulled the trigger, almost at point-blank range. The reflex of the shot barrelled into my shoulder, sending me crashing back against the tunnel wall; blood and gore sprayed all three of us. But I could feel nothing but overwhelming relief.

Gavin was, without doubt, dead.

It was over.

Seventeen

Except, of course, that it was not. Gavin might be beyond harming us, but we were still trapped. In vain I called to the old Marquis, thinking that if he fetched us some sheets from the beds and made them into a rope we should be able to clamber up. But my cries elicited no response. Clearly he was either unconscious or dead from the shock of what Gavin had done to him. We would have to help ourselves.

'I'm going to try to hoist you out, Antoinette,' I said. My voice, like the rest of me, was trembling, but my head was surprisingly clear. 'You must fetch some blankets to cover Pierre and then run for help. Try not to look at Gavin. He won't be a pretty sight.'

'I'm glad of that!' she returned spiritedly. 'And I hope he burns in hell!'

'Don't say such things,' I begged her. 'He was mad, I think. Now look, if I cup my hands, put your foot in them and I'll try to lift you . . .'

Though Antoinette was a slight little thing, she was still a great deal heavier than she looked, and it took several attempts before I managed to hoist her high enough for her to get a grip on the boards surrounding the trapdoor. Then I got a hand underneath her, shoving with all my might whilst she scrambled, and at last, in a flurry of dusty petticoats, she wriggled out on to the kitchen floor.

'Oh Flora . . .' I could hear the panic in her voice again as her eyes met the scene there, for though I had warned her, I believe she had still almost believed she was living in some adventure

274

story. 'Flora, it's terrible! And Uncle Armand . . . he's not moving either! I think he's dead!'

'Just get the blankets and then run for help as fast as your legs will carry you,' I instructed.

To my relief, she pulled herself together and did as I had bid.

All Gavin's talk of how the Revolutionaries would catch up with Louis was clearly playing on Pierre's mind.

'Papa will be safe, won't he?' he whispered to me as I tucked the blankets Antoinette had fetched around him. 'I didn't tell Gavin where Mama really was, truly I didn't.'

'You were very wise,' I said. 'But then, I expect you learned to trust no one after the Terror came.'

He was silent, and I realized for the first time how little he had talked about his experiences. Perhaps when this was all over I would try to encourage him to do so. For now, however, I thought that what he was most in need of was comfort.

'Gavin is dead now, so anything the Marquis told him won't help them to arrest your father,' I said. 'Soon, God willing, he will be home, and bringing your Mama with him.'

We settled down to wait for help to arrive, clinging together for warmth. It would take Antoinette some long while to reach the village on foot, I knew. But to my surprise in a very short time there were sounds of life from above our heads, doors banging, voices calling, and George and several other Monksmoor men came bursting into the kitchen, a panting Antoinette close behind.

'They were already on their way,' she gasped. 'Someone had seen Gavin heading for the inn and when George heard of it he organized a posse . . .'

'Flora! Oh my Lord, this is a pretty pickle . . . But you're safe. We'll have you out of there in no time . . .' Never had I been so glad to hear George's steady, homespun tones.

I had quite forgotten my father's old ladder, kept in one of the outhouses and used for making necessary repairs to the inn, but George had not. He fetched it and I was able to scramble up, then two of the men went down for Pierre. As they gently raised him I steeled myself to look around the kitchen. Gavin was a hideous sight; my stomach turned to see him lying there, and I fetched a tablecloth to cover him with before Pierre was brought up from the passage. One of the village men was examining the old Marquis for signs of life; he shook his head, pronouncing him dead, and I found another cloth to cover him too.

When Pierre was gently lifted up into the kitchen we were relieved to discover his leg did not appear to be broken. It was, in all likelihood, merely a bad sprain.

And then the shock and horror of all that had happened came washing over me in a torrent. My legs turned to jelly, my whole body was trembling, I felt quite faint.

'Oh George, I shot a man!' I whispered. 'God help me, I killed him!'

And George merely nodded and put an arm round my shoulders.

'Good for you, Flora. And now you look like you could do with a drop of your father's brandy.'

They took charge of everything then, my good friends from Monksmoor. One man had already ridden for the constable, and George assured me that he would see the bodies were removed for decent burial. 'Though whether Mr Gavin can be laid to rest in hallowed ground, I've got my doubts. I think it's outside the village for him,' he said.

'Like Tucker.'

'Aye, like Tucker. The inn will be renamed Fletcher's Grave, if you ask me.' Kind and honest and good as he was, George never stopped to give a lot of thought to what he said.

At last the necessary formalities were completed. George wanted to take us to his home, where Alice would look after us, but I declined his offer. I felt it was only right for Antoinette and Pierre to be at Belvedere. And it was there, too, that we would receive the first news of Louis. George said he would drive us in his trap, so that was decided upon.

This time, as I closed the door behind us and turned the key in the lock, I felt no regret at leaving. Too many terrible things had happened here. It no longer felt like my home.

As the trap pulled away, I did not even look back.

I kept as busy as I could. One of the first things I did on returning to Belvedere was to clear all evidence of Gavin's occupation from Louis' room. I could not bear to think of them there, defiling Louis' private space and the place where we had shared our brief, wonderful loving. I asked Walter to package them up and have them distributed amongst the poor and needy. The lodge, however, I left untouched. It would be for Louis to deal with that when he came home. And if he did not . . . I pushed the terrible thought aside.

Two days later, the constable came to Belvedere and told me that two men, believed to have been working for Gavin, had been arrested. I was glad that my father's murderers would be brought to justice, but it was of little consolation to me. My father was dead; seeing the two ruffians swinging on a gibbet at the crossroads would not bring him back. I had lost my taste for revenge when I pulled the trigger and despatched Gavin, I realized. He had been the instigator and the men who had worked for him, though bad, cruel men, had no doubt justified what they did as a way of improving the lot of their struggling families. Now nothing mattered except that there should be no more death, no more grieving, for I had had my fill of it; I could take no more.

But somehow, for the sake of Antoinette and Pierre, I had to remain strong. Nerves stretched to breaking point, I strove to maintain some sense of normality at Belvedere. But each day stretched longer than the one before, days when I woke with a sense of hope, and felt it die and drain from me as the hours passed. I could no longer run eagerly to the window when I thought I heard hooves upon the drive, for the disappointment at discovering it was not Louis was more than I could bear, yet I would pause in whatever I was doing, ears straining for the sound of his beloved voice, hands clasped in silent prayer.

Would I know, I wondered, if something terrible had occurred? Would not Sir Jeremy bring word? But if the ship had been discovered and all the crew taken, there would be no one to carry the news home. We would learn it eventually, I supposed, for the French would be so cock-a-hoop at capturing the Lynx they would be unable to resist spreading word of their success. And would I, in any case, not know in my heart? The love I felt for Louis was so strong I could scarcely believe he could leave this world and me not know it. But my torment was so great, my hopes and fears such a tempestuous sea, that I could no longer hold on to any one of them, no longer trust my own intuition.

The fifth day dawned bright and clear with a smell of spring in the air, and the early sun was warm through the windows of the morning room. When we had finished breakfast, Antoinette and Pierre went, as they so often did, to ride. I no longer worried that she might meet up with John; she had Pierre now for company and I thought that even if she did see the gamekeeper's boy, she could not get up to mischief with her half-brother there, an unwitting chaperone. I was glad, too, of a few hours when I did not have to keep up the pretence at normality, for the strain of it was becoming unbearable.

I went to Louis' room. Now that I had disposed of Gavin's things it was once more the room where we had lain and loved and I felt close to him there. I ran my fingers over the silver-backed brushes on his dressing stand, I opened the cupboards and buried my face in his clothes, to which the faint smell of him still clung. It was of some small comfort, but it was also exquisite pain, and tears ached in my throat and pressed behind my tight-closed eyelids.

The rattle of wheels on the drive sounded above the roaring in my ears; my heart seemed to cease beating. I stood taut, the fine lawn of one of his shirts bunched between my hands, then, cautiously, I went to the window and looked out.

It was the same coach that had brought Pierre, and Sir Jeremy was climbing down. My heart gave another painful jolt. There was news! Oh, dear God, there was news. But why was Sir Jeremy here? Where was Louis? I caught my lip between my teeth, all my terror for him flooding over me.

And then I saw him. I gasped; joy burst in me like the sparking of kindling before the tinderbox. He was here! Climbing awkwardly from the carriage with Sir Jeremy's help. I did not stop to register that he must have been wounded, gave no thought as to whether or not Lisette was with him. Nothing mattered but that he was alive, and he was here.

My feet flew me down the stairs. Nothing on earth could have stopped me. I rushed past a startled Walter and threw open the door.

'Louis! Oh – Louis!'

I forgot all propriety and ran to him like the eager lover I was. Then I stopped, awkward suddenly. There was something different about him. A stiffness, a greyness. His face was gaunt with pain, both physical and emotional, the lines deeper than ever I had seen them. There was a stoop to his shoulders. My strong, upright Louis had become an old man who made no move towards me.

'Oh Louis, you're safe!' I whispered.

His mouth tightened, the lines bit deeper.

'But I could not save her,' he said. 'Lisette is dead.'

And to my eternal shame, I could feel nothing but relief.

We went into the house, Sir Jeremy assisting Louis for, as I later discovered, he had taken a gunshot wound to the right knee in a run-in with the Revolutionaries. We went into the house, where although it was not much past ten in the morning, Sir Jeremy poured cognacs for Louis and for himself, and they proceeded to tell me what had occurred.

Louis had found Lisette, but en route back to the harbour where the ship awaited them the Revolutionaries had caught up with them. There had been a gunfight, in which Louis had been wounded. And Lisette had been shot dead. They told me all this in the baldest terms, with no unnecessary detail, and all the while Louis' eyes were bleak as a winter landscape where no sun shines.

'Where is Pierre?' he asked at length. 'I have to break the terrible news to him.'

'Out riding with Antoinette,' I said, glad to have this little reprieve. 'But there are things I must tell you, too, Louis. Terrible things have happened here too.'

'I know,' he said. Word had, it seemed, reached Dartmouth, as I should have known it would, and Louis and Sir Jeremy already knew what had occurred at Tucker's Grave on the day that Gavin and Armand died. 'I am so sorry, Flora, for putting you into such danger. I never for one moment thought that my own brother . . . I knew he was a rascal. I never realized it was he who was working against me, and that he would go to such lengths to see me dead – and Pierre too.' His face was dark with this added pain.

'It was his jealousy,' I said. 'He wanted what was yours.'

'Flora . . .' He made the smallest move towards me; withdrew again. 'It is your doing that Antoinette and Pierre are safe. For that I can never thank you enough. I was not here to protect them. You were.'

'What else would I do?' I asked simply. 'I gave you my word.'

'Yes. You are strong and true, as your father was . . .'

My throat closed; I suddenly felt very alone, very apprehensive for the future. Louis was a widower; there was no longer anything to keep us apart. Yet he spoke to me as if I were a stranger.

I had lost him. When he had been home for a week and still kept me at arm's length, I knew I had lost him.

Pierre had taken the news of his mother's death far better than I could ever have thought; there had been little love between them, I realized. Lisette had been almost as distant with him as she had been with Antoinette; she had played so little part in his life that her passing left no great void. But Louis . . . Oh, the effect it had had on Louis! He had gone within himself to a place that no one could reach. He did, to his credit, make some effort with the children, but beyond that, as soon as he was fit enough, he buried himself in his work.

It hurt me to see him so, for I knew he was a soul in torment. And it hurt me for myself too, for I knew now that whatever my illusions, there could never have been anything between us. It was Lisette he had loved, Lisette he had lost. How could I have thought differently for even a moment? Had he not been prepared to sacrifice his life for her, even though she had been unfaithful to him with his own brother? Had not he loved her still, even when he had not seen her for nine long years? Now he had found her, only to lose her again, and that, together with the final betrayal by his brother, had broken him. The ghosts of Lisette and Gavin were there between us and they would not be denied.

At first I remained at Belvedere because I felt that Louis was not yet strong enough to give the children the support they needed so much after the trauma of their experiences, nor even to give proper thought to their care and well-being. And perhaps because I still hoped, deep in my heart, that when his grief dulled a little he might yet turn to me. I swallowed my pride and hid my pain. But after a while I came to realize there was no longer a place for me here. Somehow I must put all that had happened behind me and carve out a new life for myself.

With a heart as heavy as lead, I packed my few belongings together and sought an audience with Louis. I found him in his study, poring over the ledgers with Mr Bevan.

'Can I speak with you?' I asked.

He glanced up, and his voice, when he spoke, had all the impatience that had characterized him when first we met.

'Can't it wait? The business has been sorely neglected these last weeks.'

'No,' I said, 'it cannot.'

'Very well. We'll go to the parlour.'

He limped ahead of me. Though his leg was healing, I thought it unlikely he would ever walk without a limp again.

'Well?' he said when the door was shut behind us. 'Is it one of the children? Antoinette up to her old tricks, perhaps? Or Pierre . . . ? Is he not settling in? I thought he had accepted his mother's death too readily . . .'

'It is not the children,' I said. 'They are both very resilient. No, it's me. It is time I moved on, Louis.'

He looked at me blankly.

'I was wondering,' I said, 'what plans you have for Tucker's Grave. I thought perhaps that now the Brotherhood of the Lynx is no more, and you no longer need the inn as a safe house, you would consider allowing me to go back to run it.'

He frowned. 'You want to go back there, after all that has happened? The place where your father died for our cause, and where you shot a man dead?'

A shiver ran through me; the horror was still there, just beneath the surface. I bit it back.

'Yes,' I said. 'I have to learn to put that behind me. And unless I seek employment somewhere, as a lady's maid, perhaps, I have nowhere else to go.'

He looked bemused. 'But why do you have to go anywhere? I thought Belvedere was your home now, and the children need you.'

I swallowed hard. No mention that *he* needed me.

'Certainly I have remained this long for their sake,' I said, 'but they will get used to being without me. They will have to. For, to be frank, after what happened between us before you went away, I think it would be for the best.'

Again he stared at me blankly, almost as if he had forgotten.

'I always knew there could be no future for us,' I went on. 'I accepted that. And I promised to look after Antoinette if you did not return. But now you are safe home it is time I left you with your family and your memories.'

'Flora!' His voice was anguished. 'Not you too!'

'Louis.' I was trying very hard to hold on to my dignity. 'This surely can come as no surprise to you. You have barely spoken to me since your return, and I think I must be something of an embarrassment to you. I know you must be regretting what occurred between us . . .'

'Regret!' Louis exploded. 'Oh Flora, I have many regrets, but that is not one of them!'

'But . . .'

He was across the room in a flash, taking me by the arms. 'Oh, I have been a monster since I returned home, I know it. I have blamed myself a million times over for Lisette's fate. I cannot get it out of my head that I failed her.'

'Louis, you did more to try and save her than any man could reasonably be expected to do,' I said. 'I know why you did it. I know you love her still, and I don't blame you for that. She is, after all, the mother of your children.'

'The mother of my son, yes, whom she kept secret from me for all of his life . . .'

'And your daughter,' I reminded him.

His mouth hardened. 'Not my natural daughter, Flora, though I love her as my own. But that is another story, one that I will acquaint you with one day, if I can bring myself to own the truth. Oh, it's not *love* that I feel for Lisette, or have done for many years. It's guilt and my failure that has been tearing me apart. I could not come to you, chérie. I had to lick my wounds alone, and if that has hurt you, then I am sorry. But don't talk of leaving, I beg you . . .'

I was trembling, tears blurred my eyes. Through them I saw his anguished face, the face I would gladly have died for.

'I love you, Flora,' he said softly, the words torn from the heart he had learned to harden. 'I love you so much.'

It was all I needed to hear. Without another word, we were in one another's arms. Perhaps there would still be times when the darkness gathered, but the worst of it was over. We had come through the fires, and we had each other. Nothing else in the world mattered.

There is a new landlord now in Tucker's Grave, and sometimes, when I drive past with the three little ones that Louis and I were blessed with, I tell them that it was once my home. But I make no mention of the secret passages that lie beneath. I try my best to forget they exist.

The story I am always happy and proud to tell them is of the bravery of their father, and how he saved not only their half-brother, Pierre, but many other beleaguered French nobles who would otherwise have died in the Terror. And their faces shine, and their eyes are wide, for his reputation has never been forgotten.

My dear husband – their beloved father – who was once The Lynx.